4/14

Brotherhood of Fear

ALSO BY PAUL GROSSMAN

The Sleepwalkers
Children of Wrath

Brotherhood of Fear

⚡⚡

Paul Grossman

A WILLI KRAUS NOVEL

ST. MARTIN'S PRESS ❧ NEW YORK

BROTHERHOOD OF FEAR. Copyright © 2014 by Paul Grossman. All rights reserved. Printed in the United States of America. For information, address St. Martin's Press, 175 Fifth Avenue, New York, N.Y. 10010.

www.stmartins.com

Library of Congress Cataloging-in-Publication Data

Grossman, Paul.
    Brotherhood of fear : a Willi Kraus novel / Paul Grossman.
        pages cm
    ISBN 978-1-250-01159-6 (hardcover)
    ISBN 978-1-4668-4091-1 (e-book)
    1. Detectives—France—Paris—Fiction.   2. Murder—Investigation—Fiction.
3. Paris (France)—Social conditions—20th century—Fiction.   I. Title.
    PS3607.R675B86 2014
    813'.6—dc23

                                                    2013031354

St. Martin's Press books may be purchased for educational, business, or promotional use. For information on bulk purchases, please contact Macmillan Corporate and Premium Sales Department at 1-800-221-7945, extension 5442, or write specialmarkets@macmillan.com.

First Edition: February 2014

10 9 8 7 6 5 4 3 2 1

Book One

TROMPE L'OEIL

(Trick of the Eye)

One

JUNE 1933

Rain slashed the taxi as it pulled in front of Maxim's. The doorman waiting there looked like a hit man, Willi thought. Or perhaps it was only shadows. Perhaps that crooked smile as he helped them from the cab didn't really conceal a merciless cutthroat. In the right light, half this town looked ready to knife you. Under the wildly flapping awning Willi clutched his two young sons by the shoulders, wanting them near. As the white glove ushered them past, Willi got a whiff of the muskiest cologne he was certain he'd ever smelled around Paris, an almost overbearing scent.

Inside the art nouveau temple Bette Gottman inhaled as if entering nirvana. "They haven't changed a thing." Her eyes roamed the soft-lit paradise of colored glass. "It's like coming home."

Her husband, Max, taking off his trench coat, didn't miss the irony. "Something like that. I'm just grateful we all made it."

From what they knew of those still in Germany of course, he was right. Refugees though they were, they were the lucky ones. If only Willi didn't feel as if he were one of the walking wounded.

It had been six weeks since he'd fled Berlin, slipped across the border with barely his life. But the euphoria of freedom and family reunion had faded to dark uncertainty. The trauma of his violent uprooting refused to fade. Though he tried to conceal it, from his sons especially, he felt something vital, irreplaceable had drained from his being.

The rest of them had been in Paris six months already and had had more time to adjust, as Ava'd pointed out. "You'll revive," she'd promised. But Willi was less certain. He felt too much had been cut away—his past, all he'd worked so hard to achieve, all his dreams for the future. Glad though he was to recapture even a hint of the old world tonight, he understood it was only that—a semblance. They were stateless exiles around this table at Maxim's, with no prospects of returning home.

Across from him Max Gottman, the family patriarch, normally so levelheaded, was growing irritable by his inability to differentiate between *Sole Albert* and *Timbale de soles Joinville*. His wife Bette, certain *timbale* was some sort of mold, didn't want him sick again and insisted he bypass it despite the waiter's assurances the mold was not an organism but a baking dish. Willi couldn't stifle the impression that although they'd slipped past the Nazis with their wealth mostly intact, his in-laws, with only a slightly better grip, were hanging on by their fingertips too. Should they apply for citizenship in France or try their luck in Amsterdam? Should Max rebuild Gottman Lingerie? He was fifty-five. There was opportunity in South Africa, they'd heard, but whom did they know there? For all the money, their bewilderment and isolation went unmitigated.

"I remember the night Leopold II dined here with the Maharaja of Kapurthala." Bette's older sister Hedda gazed about through opera glasses. Having married a Frenchman and been in Paris since before the war, she functioned now as a sort of oblivious hostess, as if the German side of the family had arrived on some prolonged holiday. "Or was it the Aga Khan? How much more elegant everything was back then. It's gotten rather tawdry, I must say."

Willi stared at the menu, unable to keep the beaux arts lettering from appearing to drip toward his lap. From the moment the Nazis took over in Germany he felt as if he were having a nightmare from which he couldn't awaken. Now, dispossessed, lost and adrift, it seemed he'd surfaced in one of those bizarre surrealist paintings so popular in Paris these days: everything in a familiar world misplaced or melting.

How wrong he'd been about so much. The republic. The Germans. The triumph of justice. Until his family photos came crashing to the pavement along with the rest of his belongings—courtesy of the brownshirts—he would never have believed a gang of criminals could become the law. And that he, his country's most famous detective, would have to flee like a thief in the night. In Germany, a mere flash of his badge had been enough to command respect. Now he had nothing. Not even a driver's license.

Off the death list thankfully, he was anything but free, burdened instead with all he'd lugged along from Berlin: the grief and despair, the fear and outrage. Images that wouldn't quit haunting him. Three years at the Western Front hadn't seemed as bad as three months under Hitler. And yet, how he missed the flashing lights along the Ku-damm. The rattle of the S-Bahn. The frantic whirl of Potsdamer Platz. His heart burned to go back home, though his head knew there was no home to go to.

"I'll have *Coeur de filet de Charolais Renaissance,*" he heard himself trying to sound alive. "And for the boys, *Crêpes veuve joyeuse, s'il vous plaît.*"

He'd arrived without papers, passport, money. His French luckily was decent enough, although there was no mistaking his accent. And even luckier, he had a well-to-do ex-father-in-law. The day he'd shown up at their apartment in the swank sixteenth arrondissement, after many hugs and kisses from his sons and his sister-in-law, Ava, and her mother, Bette, he was pulled aside by Max. "If it hadn't been for you, we'd be paupers now, Willi. So don't be afraid to ask for what you need. And stay with us as long as you want. There's plenty of room."

The first ten days he'd had no choice. He was too deeply in shock to make any decisions. He'd spent half the day in bed. The boys loved having him around. Sometimes Stefan would climb under the blankets with him. But the strain of putting on a smile for everybody was too much. He was up to his neck in despair and not a good enough actor to fake it. As deeply as he loathed having to abandon his sons again, he had to find his own place, he knew, at least for now. They had a better life with his in-laws than anything he could offer.

"I understand, Willi." Max nodded. "You're a proud man. My wife and daughter think too proud perhaps. But I admire you."

The kids had other feelings. "Why can't we live with you?" Stefan, the younger, whined unashamedly. Erich, the older, had kept his eyes down.

Willi explained as best he could. Before he could take care of them, he had to be able to take care of himself. Establish his legal status. Earn a living. He didn't mention regain his sense of worth or trust in humankind. They'd lived apart in Berlin since Mom died he said, so they'd have to stick it out a bit longer. They were comfortable at Grandpa's, weren't they? Aunt Ava was like a mom . . . even nicer sometimes, right? They were doing well at school. Making friends.

"It's all I want," he reassured them, taking Erich's chin and making him look up. "For us to be a family again."

This wish alone got him out of bed each morning because rebuilding his life felt otherwise impossible; he didn't even want to try. He feared the boys were too young to understand how badly injured he was having been thrown out of his homeland, and that the longer they stayed apart, the harder it would be to bring them together. So he mustered whatever strength he had and put a first foot forward.

Clothes. He'd arrived with only what he was wearing, and a useless Berlin police badge in his pocket. Ava insisted he had to look good in Paris, French not German, so she dragged him to the finest shops, arguing with him always to get more. Then she helped him hunt down a furnished room. He was fine with the first one they saw, near the Porte Saint-Denis.

"A five-flight walk-up?" She'd frowned unhappily. "And so small. Willi, you don't have to sink this low. You heard what Dad said."

But low was exactly how Willi felt, and the dark apartment over-looking one of the ancient gates of Paris was as good a place as any to crawl into. Accepting only what he needed from Max to pay the first month's rent, he moved in with two full suitcases and flopped onto the mattress to try to figure out what the hell to do next.

Stranger in a strange land.

Like all refugees he was required to register with the police, fill out endless forms regarding finances, work history, political activity. In ten to fifteen weeks if all went well, he'd receive a short-term work permit, at which point he could apply for the Right of Domicile. Unlike Germany, France based her citizenship on residency not race. The land of *liberté, égalité, and fraternité* had room for all who wanted to come—so long as there was a labor shortage. To tide him over until he could legally work, officials suggested he try HEAL, the Hebraic Emergency Assistance League.

Established by his Parisian coreligionists alarmed at the sudden influx of what had been Europe's most assimilated Jews, the league offered not only financial assistance but much needed job referrals to refugees of Nazi Germany. The thought of having to make use of such a charity made Willi want to jump in the Seine but he couldn't just sit around waiting for official permits.

"I'll check and see if there's anything in your field." He was interviewed by a redheaded fellow with sympathetic brown eyes, Levy. "Unfortunately you'd never be hired by Paris police unless you were a citizen. Tragic I realize, considering your credentials. But if you're desperate for something right away . . ." Levy's voice lowered. Making it clear this was off-the-record, he'd slipped Willi an address.

It proved a ramshackle building in immigrant Belleville, a Jewish-owned firm that specialized in the manufacture of ladies' fur-trimmed garments. They took Willi on as a "finisher," no questions asked, and taught him the job in fifteen minutes: sewing glass eyeballs onto snouts that dangled from fox collars. All day, vacant gazes stared up at him. How similar they were to those he met each morning in the mirror. By the end of the first week it felt as if he'd been born with a needle and thread in his fingers. By the end of the third, it seemed he'd die with them too. He was used to being out in the field, meeting new people, doing different things every day. Working in an airless, gloomy workshop full of depressed refugees felt like a fate worse than death, live entombment.

Then ressurection, or so it seemed: a call from Levy at HEAL. A private investigator with an office near the Place de la République could use an extra hand, he said in a tone indicating what a stroke of *mazel* this was. Willi should see the man Friday, ten.

Right on time this morning he'd knocked at a door on the fourth floor of a building on boulevard Voltaire. Henri Gripois looked like a walrus on a crash diet, pants, face, mustache, everything drooping. His tiny office smelled of mustard. A framed license was on one wall, until a battered filing cabinet and old wooden desk, a small pile of papers and a framed photo of his wife on it, her features surprisingly fine. He was terribly happy to see Willi, he proclaimed, because he'd taken on more work than he could handle. Of course, he understood Willi was far too qualified for the job. Monsieur was a famous detective. Nevertheless, if he was willing to stoop a bit . . .

Willi wasn't even sure he wanted to be a detective anymore. He sure as hell didn't want to be buried alive in a factory the rest of his life sewing eyeballs onto fox snouts. But the conviction that used to drive him so hard each day, that everyone deserved justice in life, was in tatters.

This assignment, as Gripois explained it, shrugging his sunken shoulders, was not terribly glamorous. It was downright pedestrian after all Monsieur had done in Germany. It simply involved following a young man enrolled at the polytechnic institute, he said, taking out a photograph of Phillipe Junot, a typical-looking student if slightly pudgy faced: round tortoiseshell glasses, stringy hair, pink, heart-shaped lips that gave him a little cupidlike expression. His parents wanted to be certain he was doing what he ought to, not caught up in any distractions plaguing so many French students these days, politics and the like. Hardly cloak-and-dagger, the private eye chuckled ruefully.

And damned depressing, Willi'd thought. He'd risen to the top of his field in Berlin, had a staff of detectives working under him, cracked some of the most heinous cases on record there. Now, here he was being offered a junior detective job following some schoolkid.

But according to Gripois, this family was well-placed and, if things went well, had friends in high positions who could be useful in expediting immigration, not only for him but his family. Willi took it. Whatever was necessary to enable them to stay, he would do.

Now, however, far from the mustard-smelling office, surrounded by his family and the opulence of Maxim's restaurant, he was starting to feel foolish. What kind of parents had their son followed? And what kind of detective agency did this Gripois run?

"Could that be who I think it is?" Aunt Hedda fixed her glasses like a skilled bird-watcher. "What a sighting!"

Willi looked across the aisle, spotting the pair of glamorous patrons at a nearby table, a handsome man in an apricot necktie chatting with a long-legged woman in a backless cocktail dress. The bright-colored necktie should have looked ridiculous, Willi thought. It would have in Berlin. But this man wore it with real savoir faire.

"Adrienne and André Duval." Hedda's glasses plunged triumphantly. "Even better looking than in *Paris-Soir*." She seemed compelled to take another peek.

After a pause to camouflage her excitement Bette Gottman asked who they were.

"Something to do with municipal bonds," Hedda chirped through a mouthful of caviar. "Anyone able to scrape together a dime puts it with Duval." She pecked at her fingertips. "It's a positive mania!" Her eyes glittered at the deliciousness of it all.

Max made clear he knew all about the man: "A phenomenon for years. Jewish fellow."

"Very handsome," Bette added. "Isn't he?"

Willi focused in on a gilded mirror to his left offering a full profile of the chap. Sparkling chandelier light seemed to cast a halo around him. From the alligator shoes to the emerald pinkie ring he looked quite the bon vivant. Thick waves of copper hair danced above a large nose and friendly gray eyes. His expansive gestures—smiles and hand motions, tosses of the head—would have been distasteful in Germany, signs of a need to impress. This Duval though seemed quite content in his skin. Willi found himself envying him.

How assured he was. And affectionate with his wife. He hardly left her fingers alone long enough to let her eat. It was rather touching, Willi thought. Until in the mirror he caught sight of Ava, her sparkling eyes dark with criticism. *What plumage these French manage to display,* she seemed to be thinking. *Everything to excess.*

A shiver of bewilderment tore at his heart. The breach between them only seemed to widen, and he still wasn't sure why. In the terrible times after Vicki's death her younger sister was the closest he could get to the warmth of his cherished wife. When she took charge of Erich and Stefan, they all grew so near. Willi wanted to believe that they were destined to fall in love themselves and form a new little family.

After the Nazis seized power, though, he no longer felt like the same man. The faith he'd had in himself, in his perceptions and choices, even his own feelings, had been trampled. He had no idea anymore if what he'd felt those last months in Berlin was real or merely his trying to hold on to a world that was being torn away. No idea if he could provide for himself anymore, much less for anyone else. No confidence. So he withdrew. Every effort by Ava to bridge the gap only pushed him further away.

Sometimes he thought to just make a clean break. Let 1933 be Year Zero. Everything from here on in, new. But then he'd wonder, what about the boys? What would be best for them? And everything got hazy.

He glanced across the table. Stefan, nearly nine, napkin tucked eagerly into his collar, was narrating some epic to his grandfather about his day at school. Erich, eleven, was leafing through the wine list. For a moment he looked up, but as soon as he saw Willi, he turned back to the wine. He could be moody Willi knew—especially if the subject of Berlin came up. Erich had worried when he left he'd never see his home again, and Willi had chided him, saying it was only for a while. Now the boy seemed angry at him. For what? For not telling the truth about the Nazis? Or for not moving in with them when he'd arrived in Paris, taking his own room? Or maybe it was grief still for his dead mother. Three years wasn't long. You never got over that sort of thing, did you? Then again, Willi thought, maybe Erich wasn't even angry. Maybe Willi was projecting his own loss and despair onto his child.

"I think it's time for a toast." Ava finally brought up the occasion, throwing back a wave of chestnut hair. She looked lovely tonight, Willi observed. Her fine features and intelligent gaze glistened in the crystalline light, smart, regal eyes on the world. If only he could love her the way he had her sister. It would make life so much easier. The whole package so neatly wrapped. The kids fitting right inside.

"To my wonderful parents, Max and Bette Gottman." All the champagne glasses rose. "On the occasion of their thirty-third anniversary." Ava's voice cracked with sudden emotion. As she looked around at them, her mother, father, Aunt Hedda, all began to tear up, the glasses in their hands trembling. When Ava's eyes met Willi's, he felt a little shock. An almost palpable glint of understanding seemed to reach across the table to him.

"Words can't convey how much I love you all. Mom, Dad, may the rest of your years together bring the happiness you deserve."

The glasses came together and clinked.

"That we all deserve!" Max insisted, then took a sip. "Come, give a kiss." He leaned to Bette.

Tears were falling from everyone's eyes now, even Willi's, because it was beautiful to see Max and Bette kiss, and because they all missed Vicki so much.

And Berlin.

"I thought we were supposed to be happy," Stefan observed. "Why is everybody crying?"

"Never mind, darling." His grandmother hugged him. "Adults can be such big babies."

Across the aisle Willi noticed the maître d' leaning over and whispering something to the man in the apricot necktie. The guy's eyebrows rose, and as he looked up for an instant, his merry gaze collided with Willi's, offering a flicker of what seemed real happiness.

———

In the men's room before they left, Willi got a surprise when the same apricot necktie addressed him at the urinal. "Do pardon me. You're Willi Kraus, the famous Berlin detective."

"Yes," Willi said, wondering if the guy expected him to shake hands while peeing. Such odd behavior, as so many things here were. Not that it felt bad to be recognized. It used to happen all the time in Berlin, but this was a first in France. Except Orsini. Which didn't exactly count.

Two days after he'd registered for asylum he'd received a summons commanding him to room 602, Palace of Justice. He'd sweated bullets all night knowing that this was where the Paris police were headquartered. But was it a good summons or a bad? The next day he was amazed to discover room 602 was the commissioner of police.

Victoir Orsini was one of the most powerful men in Paris, his office a kingly suite overlooking Notre Dame. Behind a massive Louis XIV desk he sat surrounded by medieval tapestries depicting characters from the Old Testament, including, Willi noticed, one of the great Jewish queen Esther, radiantly beaming at her coronation. A porcelain clock on the desk chimed as Willi took a seat, its painted figurines commencing a waltz.

A short, barrel-chested man with a great hooked nose, the police commissioner was famous for his three-inch elevator shoes. "Herr Inspektor-Detektiv!" Willi'd been touched by the use of his former title, although he couldn't exactly tell if it was a putdown. "Don't think we're unaware of you. We're all terribly concerned about events across the border. More exiles arrive each day. Of course our economy's not impervious to the worldwide crisis so it might not be possible for all to stay—but *you* are exactly the kind of refugee we like! A man whose talents could be very useful."

Orsini had smiled in a way that made Willi feel he was about to be offered some plum position with La Crim, the criminal police. But a man with a tripod camera arrived instead and, in a blast of phosphorescence, took their photo together. It appeared in several late-edition newspapers that day with captions such as TOP GERMAN DETECTIVE FLEEING NAZIS EMBRACED BY ORSINI. Embraced, or manipulated? Willi wondered, furious when he saw it. Here he'd been trying to keep a low profile, and because of this egomaniac everyone in Paris knew he was here, including the Gestapo.

"You're far too good a man to waste." The commissioner had patted Willi's back, guiding him to the door. "Don't worry; you'll be hearing from us soon enough."

But that had been weeks ago, and Willi had a growing suspicion the interview was only a publicity stunt. Nothing got him more upset than being taken advantage of, and in darker moments he thought he might expect as much. As a schoolboy he'd been inculcated with all kinds of racial slurs against their neighbors across the Rhine, that French were liars, braggarts, hypocrites. As an educated adult he'd rejected such cultural stereotypes. Now though, living here and at their mercy . . . he wasn't so sure.

"I'm a huge fan." The man in the apricot necktie remained next to him at the urinal. "I've read everything about you in French. I'm a hopeless addict of crime magazines. It drives my wife insane. Everyone knows Berlin's Kripo is the best in Europe, except for Scotland Yard. Here it's all rather different; the police aren't exactly up-and-up." The man zipped his pants and joined Willi at the sink. "Might I invite you for a drink sometime?" His face gleamed with boyish anticipation. "You've no idea the thrill it would be to hear about your exploits."

Willi wasn't the type to enjoy being fawned over, but his parched ego stirred at this dose of nourishment. Besides, he told himself, accepting a towel from the chamber attendant, he wouldn't mind gleaning what insight he could about the French police. And he couldn't quite figure out why—he had a strangely fraternal feeling toward this fellow.

"Why not. Let's have a drink."

"*Très bon!*" The financier stuck out a hand. "My name's André Duval."

Two

Established during the reign of Bonaparte, École Polytechnique was the most elite of all the *grandes écoles,* traditional training grounds of France's future leaders. Of the ten thousand annual applicants less than four hundred were accepted. One had been Phillipe Junot, twenty-one, according to the sketchy biography Gripois had supplied. Willi leaned against a tree as the cupid-faced kid lumbered across the street and disappeared through the university gates. It was better than facing fox snouts all day. But this assignment was odd, to say the least.

Atop how degrading it felt to be reduced to trailing a student, after a few days of it, this case was making no sense. Three mornings in a row now Junot had emerged from the building where he lived by nine, trudged the two blocks to classes, and stayed all day. From across the street Willi had observed a pinched, slightly strained expression on his otherwise placid face. Polytechnique was one of the most competitive academies in Europe, the pressure extreme.

Each night when the kid reemerged through the main gate he walked alone to a small bistro down the block, had a light supper while studying the whole time, and then went home. Alone. His bedroom light remained on until two. As far as Willi could tell, he didn't socialize, period. So what the hell were his parents so concerned about?

In addition, although Gripois claimed the family was "well-placed," nothing Willi saw corroborated that. The building the student lived in was shabby. His clothes cheap. Posture lousy. The more Willi watched, the less he could buy the elite-background stuff, or even that he was slumming it. Most of these students came from the upper classes he knew, but a handful had to be on scholarship, no? Perhaps Junot was one. So why would Gripois say otherwise? And who was paying Willi's wage?

Willi had gone up to his new boss's mustard-smelling office again yesterday. "Don't hesitate to make minor purchases you might need for camouflage: newspapers, food, clothing, et cetera." Gripois had been fairly liberal tossing about francs but stingy as hell with facts. Mere grunts greeted Willi's inquiries about Junot's field of study or the political activities he might supposedly be involved in. Or even if Willi could have the kid's class schedule so he didn't have to wait outside all day. The detective's sunken face remained strangely non-cognizant. Now, leaned against the tree staring at the arriving students, Willi wished he could just walk away from this whole crappy assignment, whatever it really was. Visions of statelessness and poverty though hung like warning signs before his eyes, and since he had no intention of taking charity from his in-laws, he stood there. Too proud perhaps.

It was chilly for June. Damp. His hands were in his pockets. The fashionable clothes Ava had convinced him to get were incongruous here. Double-breasted suits might look great on Avenue Foch but in the Latin Quarter they stood out. He needed something far more casual. He wished he knew the kid's schedule; he could go buy something now. But he didn't. Deep in his pocket his hand wrapped around the sole souvenir of the life he'd once had: his Berlin police badge. If only he could get one in Paris. The very firmness of its leatherbound shape lent him power though, and a sudden thought sparked in his brain. Why not? People everywhere responded to badges, didn't they? It was better than just standing here.

Stepping across the street, he passed for the first time through the gates of the famed academy. The halls were filled with serious faces, dark-circled eyes, expressions of misery. Everyone was too preoccupied to know where the registrar's office was. Willi found it on his own. *"Bon jour, monsieur."* He took off his hat, smiling at the sallow-faced fellow behind the counter. "I was wondering if you might help." The man stiffened, his neck withdrawing as if at a stench. Willi chilled. He knew what it was: the damned German accent.

Once again he found himself entangled in circumstances of impossible irony. Although he was German born and bred, in Germany he was forever an *ein Ausländer,* a foreigner. Jew. In France he was a Jew too but, even worse, un *Boche,* a German—the ancestral enemy. True, fifteen years ago his reconnaissance had brought artillery shells crashing down on French troops. And he had fought hand to hand in the kaiser's uniform against more than one Frenchman—perhaps this one, or his son. Yet here he was seeking sanctuary among those he'd fought with because those he'd fought for had turned murderous against him. There was no shortage of hatred here for Germans. No nation had suffered more than France in the Great War. Her scars ran to the marrow. Willi's accent was impossible to miss.

The clerk simply stood there.

Willi'd voiced this concern to Gripois before he'd taken the job. His boss simply advised him not to speak. "Just follow the kid and report back." The droopy mustache had puffed slightly. "If anyone asks, tell them you're Swiss."

Instead, Willi slid his badge across the counter to the clerk. "I'd like to find the class schedule of a student," he pronounced with great care, hoping propriety might overcome prejudice. "It's in regard to something stolen from him last summer, in Berlin."

"I see." The clerk gazed at the badge, not wanting to touch it. "I've heard of German efficiency. Amazing. You'll have to fill out a request form of course and wait until I take my break. What's his name?"

Determined to uphold the honor to French *in*efficiency it seemed, the fellow did come back with what Willi wanted, forty-five minutes later.

"Merci, merci!"

Phillipe-Jacques Junot was finishing his third year, majoring in math. Most of the week he spent in seminars or working on research for two professors, Drs. Dominique and Frédéric Pasquier, either siblings or a husband-and-wife team Willi surmised. He was in school every day but Sunday. It all seemed to confirm what Willi had observed: Junot was pretty much of a bore. Back in the moist spring air outside, Willi memorized the schedule, then tore it up just to be safe. Crossing rue Descartes, he took off in search of a men's store.

There was time not only to buy a more appropriate outfit but to ride the metro home, lunch, read the paper, and return with an hour to spare. Why couldn't Gripois have simply given him the information?

Six p.m. his eyes were on the big gate outside the Polytechnique. Now at least, in a short-brimmed cap, leather jacket, and black trousers, he blended in. A steady stream of students began exiting the four o'clock lecture on differential equations. Willi scanned the faces carefully, confident if nothing else of his eyesight. Junot must sit up front, Willi figured, because he was always one of the last out. Willi sprang to attention finally, lifting hands from pockets. Here he came.

Junot wore his collar without a necktie as usual, stringy brown hair half over his round glasses, pink, angelic lips pressed together. Making his way down the sidewalk, he moved his heavy bookbag aside for a mother with two children. In the few days Willi had trailed him, he'd come to rather like the kid. He was obviously intelligent. Hardworking. Thoughtful. Last night he'd surprised Willi by taking after a poodle that had gotten away from an old man, waving off a grateful reward as if anxious just to get back to work. One fault, possibly, Willi thought as he watched the lad trudge with only books for company—might be gambling. Twice Willi had found newspapers at Junot's bistro table opened to the racing pages, the words *daily double* encircled in pen.

Not surprisingly Junot took his usual place on the sidewalk outside Les Pipos, cracking open a large, mud-colored text. Fortunately a bench by a bus stop almost directly across the street offered an unlit vantage point Willi found expedient, a sort of front-row mezzanine. The show tonight though was strictly routine. From the waiter's nod he could tell Junot had ordered the usual soup with bread and wine, after which he hunched over his book monklike, pausing only to take notes or shovel spoonfuls. It was difficult not to yawn. Only this time, the story was about to take a new twist.

A shapely, young brunette with short, wavy hair had entered the bistro and appeared to be heading directly for Junot's table. She sure knew how to dress, Willi saw, and like so many French girls her age she all but radiated sensuality. When Junot spotted her, he jumped up and threw his arms around her, kissing her passionately.

This job, Willi thought, feeling his pulse accelerate, just got a lot more interesting.

From his dark vantage point he watched the two share a bottle of wine, their torsos leaning nearer as the bottle emptied. After a while he saw her shoe had slipped off and she was rubbing his shin with her toe. It made Willi shift on the bench, embarrassed by the stirring in his own trousers. The mademoiselle was *très sexy*. When Junot paid and they finally left, it was arm in arm. The kid's parents had been right about one thing, Willi considered, rising to follow across the street: their cupid-lipped son turns out no mere bookworm.

The two swerved down the sidewalk, pretending to be tipsier than they were, laughing with childish glee. Junot, who'd seemed so ungainly before, exhibited a masculine grace invigorating to witness. When they disappeared into his building, Willi stood on the sidewalk, stabbed by an almost shocking sense of abandonment. He found his eyes actually casting about for some means of peering into Junot's second-floor window, telling himself they might be spies or drug dealers or God knew what, but really because he didn't want to be left out here alone.

It took an hour before she reemerged, running a hand through her wavy hair. Willi was still across the street, shuffling foot to foot to keep from falling asleep.

"Vivi!" Junot whispered out the window, waving.

She turned up to him, startled.

"*Bonne nuit!*" She blew a kiss, adjusting the strap on her shoes.

"*Bonne nuit!*" Junot's face broke into an adoring smile.

She hadn't gotten halfway down the block before a bearded man stepped out of the shadows, a brute of a fellow in a black beret who grabbed her arm. Ready to approach in her defense, Willi held back when he saw the guy launch into what looked like a lecture, wagging a finger in this Vivi's face. Might it be someone she knew he wondered, a relative? Relieved, he watched her break free and storm indignantly down the sidewalk. For a second he feared the beret might go after her, but the fellow hurried the opposite way. Willi took a deep breath, glad it ended peacefully. The last thing he needed was to get mixed up in defending her.

The next day he was surprised to see Junot among the first out of his classes. He was hoping the kid had plans to again see the girl, Vivi. All day Willi could hardly keep her sexy figure from slinking around in his brain, naked. But instead of toward Les Pipos bistro, Junot went the other way. Willi took after him, disappointed.

If you had to trail somebody, the Latin Quarter had its advantages. The streets were filled with plenty of atypical-looking people, so it wasn't hard to remain inconspicuous. On the other hand, as one of the oldest sections of Paris it was a warren of medieval streets a cinch to get lost in if you didn't know your way, which Willi didn't. So when Junot made a right down an alley he'd never taken before, Willi's shoulders tensed. What was this creature of habit doing?

On a zigzag course between buildings of the Sorbonne, Willi had to stick uncomfortably near, his hands growing clammy. If he lost the trail here, he knew, that'd be it. He hadn't a clue which direction they were even walking. Eventually they emerged onto rue des Écoles, which he recognized, then the boulevard Saint-Michel, where Junot turned toward the river. Perhaps he'd come to browse the many used-book stores or art stalls along this famous Left Bank avenue. But the kid kept walking. Past the bookstores, the art stalls, the bistros.

Willi drew his cap lower, sticking at least four people behind. It was overcast. A mist had settled in, dampness tickling his face. He could see the great boulevard ahead blurring into an impressionist painting, the balconies and mansard roofs fading gray. Paris had a beauty Berlin could only dream about in its most drunken reverie, a timelessness and romance. But it had none of Berlin's drive, its frantic forward hustle. Except perhaps to get home from work, nobody ever seemed in a hurry. What then was Junot's rush tonight? Was he late for an appointment?

At the Place Saint-Michel Willi thought the kid might be joining a small political demonstration. Was this what his parents feared? Twenty or so people stood in front of the baroque fountain holding placards decrying last month's Nazi book burnings. Tens of thousands of "degenerate" volumes had been set aflame. WHERE THEY HAVE BURNED BOOKS, one of the placards read, THEY WILL END IN BURNING HUMAN BEINGS—HEINRICH HEINE. Willi averted his eyes. There was no time to think about the tragedy of his homeland. Junot had descended to the metro.

Following someone underground was tricky, and in Paris the trains were narrow, crowded, the people aggressive. Willi knew he had to stick with him; the kid was leaving his turf. It might be important. Relieved, he spotted Junot heading down the steps to the northbound Line 4. The platform was nearly overflowing. When the train arrived, there was barely room to squeeze on. Willi managed to get in the same car but not through the same door, just able to make out the kid's face. He hadn't gotten a good look at him today. Now he could see Junot's expression was tense, something clearly bothering him.

At Gare de l'Est he exited. What was this kid planning? Willi hoped not an out-of-town excursion. He had a date with his own kids tomorrow, an outing at the Bois de Boulogne, and no intention of missing it. When they got upstairs, he was glad to spot the student leaving the station. Just a few minutes walk from Willi's own apartment, this neighborhood was far less crowded, lonely almost, the first-floor shops of Haussmann-era apartment blocks already shuttered. Footsteps echoed like snare drums off the pavements. He had to keep a full block behind and hug the doorways in case Junot turned.

After some minutes a briny stench filled the air. They had reached Canal Saint-Martin. It was quiet except for some barges sputtering along the water. The kid suddenly stopped, turning. Willi fell back against the wall. Had he been spotted? Junot though seemed only to have reached his destination. He used a knocker and disappeared into a door.

Willi approached from the far side. The building, 234 quai de Valmy, was dilapidated, its shutters ready to fall off. Even odder, no lights were on, the whole place dark. He felt his nostrils sting and moved upwind. Paris may have been beautiful, but everywhere you went stank of piss. Burying his hands in his pockets, he allowed himself a sigh. There was nothing to do but wait.

Leaning against the rail, he glanced over the embankment. All kinds of crap were floating by. A broken barrel. A chair. He half expected a dead body. Whatever Junot was doing in there, Willi hoped it didn't take long.

It did. Over two hours. When Junot came out, he was in a rush, hurrying down the sidewalk. Willi wished he could see the kid's face. In the darkness, though, all was shadow. He hoped they were heading home, but Junot's night wasn't over. Boarding the metro again at Gare de l'Est he switched directions to the Place Bastille. Willi had never been to this part of town but knew its reputation. Just north of where the notorious prison once stood now sprawled one of the seediest districts in Paris. Small hotels promising *confort moderne* . . . every brick coated in grime. Red-lipped women nodding from doorways. Pimps and toughs on every corner. What was this kid up to? He seemed to know exactly where he was going.

Seeing him enter the narrowest, seediest street, where the music was loudest, the crowds thickest, Willi waited a moment then followed into the rue de Lappe. Sidewalks barely wide enough to navigate were lined with bars and bordellos and dance halls one after the next: the Maiden Aunt, the Soiled Shirt, the Bowl of Fruit. Grinding melodies of java music, Paris's homegrown accordion waltz, swaggered from every door. Swarthy sailors and hard-faced laborers spun around with women in fishnet stockings and too much makeup.

Keeping a safe distance Willi watched Junot go into several of these dives and come quickly out again. What was he looking for?

Or for whom? Perhaps he was running some kind of errand. At the Soiled Shirt, observing through a window, Willi spied the kid whispering to a bald bartender. Did he pass him something? Willi couldn't tell. What had gotten into this hardworking math student?

After some minutes when Junot didn't come out of a place called the Red Room, Willi peeked in the door. He didn't dare get trapped where he might be noticed, but this place seemed big enough, dark, crowded. He slipped inside. There was barely air, just cheap perfume and cigarette smoke. Eventually his eyes adjusted. People were crammed about tables or at the bar, everyone talking, laughing. How drunk and jolly they all seemed, not a care in the world. Willi'd forgotten people still let themselves get like this. All the girls wore long skirts and suspenders and had locks of hair on their foreheads oiled in big curls. The guys all wore caps pulled far to the backs of their heads. Not a necktie in sight. Willi was glad at least not to have one on.

One one side of the room an accordion and drum duo produced a very French, romantic, slightly vulgar music. Over the dance floor a mirrored ball showered flecks of light on couples moving in a crowded circle, up and down, herky-jerky, like figures on a carousel.

Taking a fast look around, he didn't see Junot. The walls bore signs warning DEFEND AGAINST SYPHILIS! or WATCH YOUR HAND-BAGS! The imitation-leather banquettes were nailed to the floor—probably so as not to be turned into weapons during fights. What kind of wealthy kid would come to a dump like this? No bows or curtsys accompanied invitations to dance here. Just a stare, a nod, a *psst!* When a new song started it was *Psst! Psst!* Like an insect mating call. But there was something beautiful about it, Willi saw. Watching the couples out there, revolving around each other in their own little universes, his heart began to ache. He felt so alone.

Then he spotted Junot. Whatever the kid been doing all evening running place to place, he seemed finally to have found happiness in the arms of his sexy girlfriend. Willi was jealous. Vivi's bright eyes flashed with excitement as she and Phillipe spun around the dance floor, her dark waves of hair pulled beneath a thin beret, a silky, red scarf flying from her neck. She was radiant, more sensual than ever, throwing her head back to expose her white throat as they danced.

She and Junot were turning in one direction then in reverse, clasping each other. With one arm she held the back of his head; the other touched his heart. Junot pressed her close from behind. Their faces came only inches apart. Their noses almost touching. Willi filled with hunger so sharp it hurt.

He fell back against the wall. After they'd buried Vicki, he'd suppressed his needs for so long. Now he was craving intimacy. Sex. But not the kind you got in hotels around here. The kind you had with someone you loved and wanted to make happy. Someone you were so grateful each morning to wake up next to. For eleven years he'd shared such joy with Vicki. Could he ever find it again?

Three

"A *hotel*?" She squinted skeptically.

Ava was next to him on a bench at Bois de Boulogne the next day, Paris's great park, watching the boys feed swans. As a matter of conversation Willi'd mentioned he'd been invited tonight for *apértif* with André Duval, the big bonds man, at his home. Ava's reaction was annoying as hell, more judgmental than her mother's. "They live in a hotel?" She kept insisting on using French, saying people looked askance when they spoke German.

Willi's head was aching from French all day, and he returned to their native tongue. "What's the difference where he lives if he can afford it?"

"It just doesn't sound like brilliant finances, that's all," she returned *en français*. "For such a brilliant financer. And the Lutetia of all places. It's so ostentatious."

Willi tried not to show his anger. If Ava was such a financial wizard, why didn't she make some of Duval's millions? Where did her family fortune come from? Underwear! He held his tongue for the kids' sake.

To make matters worse, trying to cheer themselves up at a park café, they wound up next to the Hollanders of all people, neighbors of the Gottmans' from Berlin. Big as Paris was, with tens of thousands of German Jews taking refuge here, it wasn't all that shocking to run into someone from home. The Hollanders had gotten out just days ago and were obviously still traumatized. Without the least consideration of the boys' sensitivities they launched into a harrowing tale of the national *Judenboykott* last April.

"Nine a.m. *pünktlich* two brownshirts descend on the shop with paint cans." Frau Hollander wrung her hands as if seeing them again. "Sloshing the word JEW in huge letters across the window, painting faces with giant noses." Willi wanted to stop her. Didn't she realize both his children were victims of Nazi hatred too, uprooted from their homes, uncertain about tomorrow? "In half an hour a whole truckload arrives shouting, 'Jewish vermin need extermination!' I was never so terrified." The kids' shocked expressions didn't stop her. Frau Hollander's need to recount overwhelmed all else. "The whole day anyone who approached our door was abused, even women. We didn't make a single sale."

"After that, the decrees began," her husband put in. "Anyone with a single Jewish grandparent is now non-Aryan and no longer allowed to hold civil service jobs. Forbidden from being doctors in state-run institutions." Willi finally ordered Stefan and Erich to go look at the ice creams up front so they didn't have to endure this. "They're trying to strangle us out, Willi, as they said they would." Herr Hollander didn't miss a beat. "We thought Max was crazy to liquidate, but now we see he was right. We were happy to escape with the clothes on our backs."

Sometimes Willi didn't think Paris was far enough.

Facing the Square Boucicaut and Le Bon Marché department store, the Hôtel Lutetia was indeed one of the premier addresses on the Rive Gauche, the Left Bank. Part-time home to luminaries such as

Josephine Baker and James Joyce, its sculpted, undulating façade from 1910 was a forerunner of the soon to blossom Arts Décoratifs et Industriels Modernes movement: The top-floor rotunda suite where the Duvals lived was a world of polished marquetry, recessed lighting, and lavish furnishings.

"Ah, Detective . . ." Duval arrived in a smoking jacket and Turkish slippers. "What an honor!" He offered a white smile.

He was forty probably, Willi figured. Polished to a shine, yet anything but stuck-up. Willi felt bathed in radiance as they shook hands; the financier focused on him as if this were one of the great moments of his life.

"It's like when I met Houdini. He's Jewish too you know. The kind of Jew I admire. Tough. Like you! Fearless. You don't believe I've read all about you? Come."

He took Willi by the arm and led him to a rose-paneled study, pointing out bookcases full of mystery novels, then yanking out a massive leatherbound volume containing, he claimed, every issue ever printed of France's most popular crime magazine, *Detective*.

"You"—he opened it—"are on multiple covers. Here . . . the Neukoln Tenement Murders and here . . . the Prenzlauerberg White-Slave Ring. And here . . . three issues on the Child-Eater case! You'll sign them for me, won't you?" Duval pulled each from its binder. "My son and I are mystery hounds. I know it's kind of childish, but I don't think there's anything wrong with grown-ups keeping their childish aspects, do you?" He offered Willi a pen.

"Not at all." Willi thought of his own sons, feeling remiss for not having a hobby with them. Perhaps he'd become too grown-up.

As he signed, Willi gave quick scans of the many photographs above Duval's desk of him with famous people. The Duke of Windsor. Greta Garbo. Prime Minister Daladier. And the commissioner of Paris police, Victoir Orsini, with whom he was pictured shaking hands. Duval and Willi had that in common.

"Merci!" Duval returned each signed copy delicately to its holder. "Claude will be so happy. I understand you have a son his age too, yes?"

Willi wondered if that had been in *Detective* magazine.

"They must meet sometime."

"Yes. I'm sure Erich would like that."

Duval led Willi to the living room, commenting on the lavish décor. "A fellow named de Brunhoff designed it all." Duval sparkled with enthusiasm. The expressiveness of his face, his open manner, Willi thought, seemed a bit un-Parisian. French overall in his experience were rather reserved. But, Duval was Jewish, Willi reminded himself, taking in the angular Semitic features. Did that account for their fraternal feeling?

"He's one of the top Parisian designers, working now on the interior of an ocean liner meant to rival your German *Bremen*."

"Not mine," Willi said a little too sharply. "Anymore."

"No, of course not." Duval cast an understanding glance.

"Although I did board her once, on the Child-Eater case."

"Ah, yes, when you were chasing that scientist from the health department. Very clever."

It was dusk, the perfect hour for *apéritifs* alfresco. A Moroccan valet in a red fez brought them pastis with grenadine. Beyond the terrace the Left Bank glittered in purple twilight. Ensconced in deck chairs, like passengers on a cruise, Duval pumped Willi for details about his cases, revealing real knowledge about them, asking how the Prenzlauerberg Ring operated with such impunity or why the Berlin Missing Persons bureau failed to notice so many women vanishing while sleepwalking. The one thing Willi really wanted to talk about, though, what he came here for most fundamentally, his host seemed to avoid.

"Our police?" Duval shrugged when Willi pressed him. "They're all right. We have good and bad units. La Crim's pretty decent. Nothing like your Kripo of course. And no one like you."

Willi wasn't fishing for compliments. What he wanted was a bit of hope. In his heart he still harbored the fantasy that somehow his reputation would enable him to overleap the system, and that he might land a real job with the Paris police. A far-fetched notion he understood, given his immigration status. But here, even more than in Berlin, he knew, the rules of games could be bent. And connections meant more than protocol.

"I take it from your photo you know Police Commissioner Orsini."

"Oh, yes." Duval smiled. "He's more famous in Paris than the Louvre. Quite a chap. Founded the largest charity in France, you know. A good thing too now with unemployment spiraling. Not like Germany but the situation's worsening, believe me. The French have got to wake up."

Willi sighed. Duval didn't want to discuss the Paris police, clearly.

"I'm sorry." Duval read Willi's eyes. "I keep mentioning Germany as if you still lived there. It must be awful for you . . . having to leave everything behind and start anew in a strange country. I can't even imagine. You mustn't let yourself get too down about it, though. A dictatorship like that can't last long."

"I'm not so certain."

Duval's head cocked. His eyes tightened with concern. Willi was surprised when Duval leaned across the table and reached an arm toward him. "Don't give up because of those bastards." He squeezed Willi's shoulder. "The world can be so splendid."

For the first time since he'd lost his best friend, Fritz, Willi wondered if he hadn't found someone who could read him.

"I've got an idea." Duval rubbed his jaw. "This Wednesday I'm running up to the coast. Come along. It's only two hours, the way I drive. I'd love the company. And if you've never seen the Norman countryside, well. Trust me . . ."

He swore if Willi just relaxed a single day, he'd see the world a little differently.

"You're going to Normandy with him?" Ava made no effort to mask her dismay when he called to say he had to change plans with the kids. "Willi, for God's sakes you know how much I respect you. Generally speaking your character judgement's exemplary. You married my sister after all. But this guy? Come on. He's all flash and no substance."

"I'm not marrying him, Ava. Just driving to the coast."

Duval let loose in his open-topped, black-and-yellow Bugatti the next morning as if seeing the flag go down at Le Mans. Thin leather gloves with no knuckles smacked the gearshift to take corners, and again to accelerate on the straightaways, swerving to avoid horse carts and old ladies. Willi held on for dear life. Crossing the serpentine Seine what seemed several dozen times, the countryside gradually grew magnificent as promised: narrow roads lined with towering poplars, long, straight, shining canals, little stone villages nestled in meadows.

Behind dark glasses, hair flying, Duval let loose rollicking monologues on how as a boy he'd been trained as a classical violinist and hated every minute, how he'd spotted Adrienne for the first time in the lobby of the Paris Opera, fallen instantly, hopelessly in love, loved her even more now, a dozen years later. How his company, Confiance Royale, had exceeded even his wildest expectations and earned him riches he'd never imagined. Now, he was working on the most ambitious plan of all, a scheme that could lift the whole of continental Europe from its economic quagmire: the Pan-Europa Bond. Its concept, which he outlined in some detail, sounded on the grandish side to Willi—but who was he to judge? Duval was the financial expert. Besides, what did Willi care? Poplars flying, wind in his face, the powerful throb of the Bugatti motor had lulled him into torpor. It was such a relief, after all he'd been through, just to relax and feel in good hands.

The business they'd driven up for turned out to be on a picturesque farm maybe ten miles south of Deauville, one of the main horse-breeding regions of France. André had a thoroughbred in the Grand Prix this summer and needed to confer with his trainer.

"I'll tell you a secret," he said as they pulled into a dusty yard and climbed from the car. "I'd give it all up in five minutes to live out here." He nodded at the long, white stables and half-timbered house, the sparkling tree-filled hills in the distance. "Adrienne needs the city, though. Her stores. Friends. You sacrifice for those you love, eh? Can't have it all. That, I learned long ago. At least, not all at once!" He laughed, throwing an arm around Willi.

When they reached the farmhouse, he patted Willi's back, asking if Willi'd mind waiting outside so he could speak alone with Deschevaux, his trainer. "It's only shoptalk, nothing interesting. Take a look round the stables," he suggested. "The horses are magnificent."

Wandering past stalls of robust young thoroughbreds, Willi couldn't help feeling badly about his sons again, growing up without him. Just marry Ava he told himself, watching a stallion lovingly groomed. Forget the differences. Forge a new family—before it's too late. The breach with her though seemed impossible to mend. And sadly, all he could think of when he saw a pretty mare shake her glistening coat was Phillipe Junot's new girlfriend. Vivi.

An hour later they were in Deauville, France's famous seaside resort, home of poker, polo, and Chanel. It was lined with neo-Norman villas and sprawling luxury hotels, the best boutiques, the swankiest eateries. André headed straight for the casino. Sun and sand were one thing, he said as the valet took the car. But for relaxation, nothing beat roulette.

Men in satin bow ties and women in low-cut evening dresses crowded around the tables. Willi cast a glance at André as the small, white ball he was playing bounced down the wheel. His eyes focused hopefully but fearlessly. With André it was all a game—despite the fifty thousand he had on it.

"Eighteen, red. Three, odd and manqué," the croupier called, to a chorus of soft moans. André's was one of the few smiles. He'd come in handsomely on an outside bet. Third time in a row. The croupier swept the chips his way as people applauded. They all knew who André was and appeared to view him with admiration, even awe.

"Place your bets." The next round was called.

Willi wondered how far this would go. André seemed just warming up. He surprised everyone though by pulling out. "Fewer things in life are more certain," he whispered to Willi as he scooped up his winnings, "than that the longer you play, the more you lose. The only decent odds are at the track."

They dined on the Promenade des Planches overlooking the wide, white beach with its famous rows of striped tents, the gray-green English Channel beyond. Sunshine, soft breeze, delicious food and wine—it was impossible not to relax. A lot more relaxed than Willi'd felt in a long time, the pain and fear and frustrations of his exile feeling like memories of long ago. When Duval asked if the beautiful woman he'd seen Willi with at Maxim's had been his wife, Willi found himself uncharacteristically candid about Vicki, her sister, Ava, and his confused feelings toward her. Duval proved surprisingly comforting.

"These are complicated matters." He took Willi in without the least judgment but a real glow of compassion in his eyes. "You're in a difficult frame of mind. Take time. You'll know what to do in the long run."

On the car ride back Willi got so relaxed he fell asleep. Duval shook him awake only when they were already in town. "I trust you had an enjoyable day."

"Highly medicinal, as promised." Willi stretched. "Thank you, very much."

"And now . . . do you see the world a little differently?"

Willi squinted out the window. "Too dark to tell."

They laughed.

When the Bugatti pulled in front of Willi's run-down building, André turned the motor off.

"We haven't been acquainted long but I know you well enough to tell you're a proud man, Willi." Duval's gaze suggested a deep understanding. "I've avoided asking about your career, how you're managing here in Paris. There are many ways I could help, but I doubt you'd accept." He reached into his pocket. "So let me just offer this." He opened a gold case. "My personal card." He handed Willi one. "I have many friends. They know this comes from only one place. It can open doors that may otherwise remain closed, help when you might not expect. Don't be afraid to use it."

Willi smiled awkwardly. Favors for him were hard to accept, even from someone he liked. He put the card in his wallet. "Thanks again. Not many people take time to understand my plight. It means a great deal to me that you do." He opened the Bugatti door. "Let's figure out a way for our sons to meet soon, huh?"

"Oh, definitely!" Duval's gray eyes lit. "And by the way." He reached to stop Willi. "I meant to ask." A finger went to his lip. "The gentleman you were with at Maxim's—he was Max Gottman of Gottman Lingerie, right?"

Willi felt his stomach tighten. How would André know that? And why would he care? "Yes. That was him." He recalled the maître d' whispering in André's ear.

"Dear God. I hope he got his assets out. Those Nazi bastards are tightening the screws more each day around Jewish money."

Four

With each long, creaky flight to his apartment Willi's chest pounded harder with misgiving. He didn't want to believe it. Not this time. He wanted Duval to be all that he seemed. A bit ostentatious, okay. A bit of a narcissist. A splendid fellow though, brimming with joie de vivre. His warmth, humor, his gusto, today had been a real balm, and Willi didn't want to learn he'd just been burned again. On the other hand, how old the story was. Old as the earth, really: newcomers, uprooted, unfamiliar with the territory, the easiest of all targets, a cinch to fleece. Is that what it had all been? Apéritifs at the Lutetia. This drive through Normandy. All the talk about Willi's detective genius, just Duval's fancy dance to get at Max Gottman's money? Talk about your ulterior motives! Your bald-faced hypocrisy! Reaching the fifth floor he fumbled for the key. Your two-faced, premeditated manipulation. Damn these French!

Then again, he thought, kicking open the door, maybe that wasn't really how it was. Maybe he was overreacting. After all, Gottman Lingerie was a huge company. Max's exile to Paris must have been reported in the business press. Everything got reported here. Maybe Duval really was asking out of pure curiosity. How could Willi be certain? In this strange new land so near and yet so far from Germany, it was almost impossible for him to feel confident with his perceptions of people. So many signals were different. Smiles, laughs, handshakes, didn't mean the same. He'd been so proficient once at discerning motives.

Barely had he kicked off his shoes when the phone rang.

"Hope I'm not disturbing." It was Max Gottman himself. "I've been trying you all day, Willi. It's just that, when Ava told me you'd made a personal acquaintance with André Duval, well, I couldn't believe my ears. How did it happen? Never mind! When can you introduce me? Have you any idea how hard it is to meet that man? People stab each other for a chance to invest with Confiance Royale. Everyone in France wants in."

Willi got up. He poured himself a glass of calvados he'd just brought back from Normandy, feeling the soothing heat down his gut. Well, there it was: the stamp of approval. If anyone should know about Duval, it ought to be Max Gottman. Great, then. What a relief. He poured himself another shot. Everything's all right. Just a little nervous overreaction, again. He promised to set up a meeting as soon as possible between the two.

The next morning he was still so relaxed he turned off the alarm in his sleep and missed Junot's walk to the École. He couldn't believe it. He hadn't done that in years. Feeling slightly dazed and out of sorts there was nothing to do but fritter away the rest of the day on errands then take the Métro down to the Latin Quarter.

At six o'clock though, when the rest of the students poured from of lecture hall, Junot was not among them. Willi stood across from the front gate growing increasingly concerned. The kid was always so regular. Had something happened the one damned day he'd overslept? Up and down the block he kept strolling, hoping for a sight, maybe at Les Pipos. But eventually the crowds thinned and he began to feel conspicuous out here so long. He considered: perhaps 234 quai de Valmy.

Along the lonely Canal Saint-Martin he planted his feet in the briny night. Plenty of traffic went in and out of that dark, dilapidated building. But no Junot. What the hell was inside that place, anyway? He intended to find out, one of these days. Checking his watch, he saw it was after ten. Home was only a couple of blocks away. Should he call it a night and try tomorrow, or give it one more shot?

Rue de Lappe was crowded as ever, its narrow, canyonlike sidewalks flooded with rouged-up girls and thick-armed men laughing and hanging on to each other. Willi squeezed into the Red Room, straining for a sight of Junot, worried by now something might really have happened to the kid. He'd be to blame in a way, wouldn't he? It had been on his watch. Through the darkness and cigarette smoke though, and the hurdy-gurdy of java music, his vigilance paid off. Out there perspiring on the dance floor were Vivi and Junot.

A sigh of relief escaped Willi's chest. He was getting soft, he told himself, standing back against the wall. Perhaps this job wasn't for him anymore. A detective was never supposed to care about the people he trailed. Yet he was glad as hell that—

He squinted, staring hard at the dancing couple. Something wasn't right. He could tell by their postures. Junot was holding her too near, as if he was trying to protect her, not dance. Willi inched forward for a better view, until they passed just feet away, then he saw: Vivi had a huge black eye. Junot was livid about it. No matter how hard she tried to explain something, he squeezed her nearer, unwilling to listen. At last, helpless and resigned, she let her head fall on his shoulder.

The next morning a message had been left under Willi's door. His boss, Gripois, wanted to see him at his office for a full report, 7:00 p.m. Willi decided he would tell him everything except about Vivi's black eye. He was getting protective of those two kids, which wasn't necessarily a good thing.

When Junot emerged from his building on his way to class, Willi's concern only magnified. The kid's hair looked like tangled wiring. Hurrying aggressively down the street, ignoring the beggar he always had coins for, he surprised Willi by jumping onto a bus.

Clearly he wasn't going to his early seminar. Willi had to make a dash across the street not to lose him.

Before boarding Parisian buses you were supposed to take a numbered slip to ensure adaquate seating. Willi hadn't time to get one and the conductor gave him hell. "Are you mad running like that?" Willi pretended not to understand French. "Where're you from, Jew? Poland?" The guy sold him a ticket so Willi refrained from a choice response, but only barely.

Junot had taken a seat up front, his head against the window. Willi waited on the outside platform, opening and closing his fists in his pockets.

Where you from, Jew? Everywhere he went it was the same.

Crossing Pont Saint-Michel onto the Île de la Cité, Junot along with many others got off near the Palace of Justice. Allowing several people between them, Willi followed. Just as he was about to reach the sidewalk though, the kid turned around, trying to get back on board, and they wound up facing each other, practically nose to nose. Willi's heart jumped. Junot was better looking up close, his skin smoother, more freckled, his eyes much brighter than Willi had realized. His expression, however, brimmed with resentment. As he pushed by slightly, Willi craned his neck to watch, grimacing as if annoyed. What was he supposed to do now, follow back on board? It would hardly look inconspicuous. Junot, though, was only after a book he'd left on the seat, the same orangey, mud-colored text Willi had seen him studying before. After he grabbed it and jumped back off, Willi slowed on the sidewalk and let him pass.

Putting the book in a canvas bag slung over his shoulder, Junot went toward the river then turned along the quai de l'Horloge along the embankment, approaching the *bouquinistes,* the booksellers who plied their trade from long, green display boxes. Perhaps he was going to sell the thing, Willi considered. But it didn't look that way.

From across the street he didn't hear but saw the kid yelling at one of the seated *bouquinistes.* When Willi noticed the guy's black beard and matching beret, Willi's stomach tightened. That was the one who'd accosted Vivi outside Junot's building. Had he been the one who'd blackened her eye? Clearly Junot thought so. He looked ready to fight. The bookseller though was twice Junot's size.

He kept waving Junot off, didn't want a scene, people watching. But Junot wouldn't let up.

The bell on the clock tower overhead suddenly chimed, making Willi swallow. The *bouquiniste*'s bullish face was turning red. Junot was going to get pummeled if he didn't back off. A burst of the sunlight illuminated the student's emphatic expression. Beneath the anger it bore a humiliation that pained Willi's heart. He knew the feeling all too well, as if you'd been beaten to within an inch of your life then scorned for having done it to yourself. As the *bouquiniste* rose to his feet though, Junot, dwarfed, grasped that he stood no chance. With one final, vulgar gesture he stormed off, the book dealer pretending not to care. From across the street though Willi saw that once the student was halfway down the block, the bearded *bouquiniste* hurriedly made use of a nearby phone booth.

Junot fortunately got back on a bus. Willi'd feared he might do something stupid, such as take a flying leap into the Seine. What would Willi do if he saw the boy climb the embankment barrier? His job was to shadow not interfere, but no way in hell would he let the kid dive. He'd have run across traffic and grabbed him. Then what? What would he have said? How would he have convinced him whatever was wrong couldn't be worth his life?

The kid exited the bus at the university and disappeared into its gates. Willi went one stop farther, then got off, bought a newspaper, and sat for lunch at the same bistro Junot frequented, Les Pipos. The food, he'd discovered, wasn't at all bad, and the sidewalk tables were a fine place to relax while the kid was at school. Halfway through his meal he looked up, surprised to see Vivi across the street exiting the post office. She was wearing dark glasses covering the black eye, and a tight-fitting, blue cotton dress. He put the newspaper back in front of him, peering to one side. Was she coming here? He couldn't tell. She'd stopped and was reading something whose striped envelope revealed it had come via local *pneumatique*. Her fluttering dress seemed to sing about the delights of her body. He was amazed at the arousal he felt. Watching her put the letter in her purse, he thought he saw an unhappy look. Then she disappeared around the corner.

That evening, the nearest thing Paris had to a Roman bacchanal, the Bal des Quat'z'Arts, was in progress near the École des Beaux-Arts, and the whole Latin Quarter sizzled with students parading toward the fun. Gangs of young men in togas and laurel wreaths pranced about topless girls painted silver and gold, everyone pouring wine down each other's throat. Outside the Polytechnique Willi was so absorbed by the spectacle he realized too late he'd missed the appointment with Gripois. How insanely unprofessional. Twice in two days he'd missed the time, as if he were single-handedly trying to destroy the myth of German punctuality. He'd have to check in with his boss tomorrow. Hopefully there'd be no repercussions.

The atmosphere grew ever more riotous: students on horseback or hobbling down the street on tall wooden stilts festooned with streamers. One girl had a goat on a leash. Suddenly a flood tide came pouring out the gates of the Polytechnique. Willi snapped to attention. He hoped the class on analytic geometry had soothed Junot's nerves. In a study of Dionysian lunacy though, down the crowded sidewalk came five scantily clad girls chained together and driven by an Egyptian overseer pretending to whip them. Students coagulated in a cheering, street-blocking mass. Willi had to stand on tiptoe not to miss Junot. Wasn't that Vivi by the gate too, still in her sunglasses?

A phalanx of spear-carrying Gauls penetrated the mayhem followed by what looked like Aztec priests. In the midst of it all, trying to push through, Willi saw the stringy brown hair and round tortoiseshell glasses he'd been searching for. Not only wasn't he in costume, Junot looked distinctly disinterested in the festivities. He was clearly thrilled though to see Vivi, as if she'd shown up unexpectedly. He picked her up and swung her side to side, kissing her like a soldier back from war. Taking her under the arm, he forged a path through the crowds.

Willi followed on the opposite sidewalk. In between, a black Citroën was trying to inch forward too, finding it almost impossible without blasting its horn. Costumed students filled the street. Vivi looked like a blind woman in her dark glasses clinging to Junot as if afraid to lose him. That shiner she had could take a long time to heal, Willi knew. Wherever they were off to, the black Citroën had turned the same direction.

At rue Cardinal Lemoine when the Citroën made the same left, a shrill whistle sounded in Willi's head. Could it be following? He thought of the *bouquiniste* this morning and that phone call as soon as Junot left. Straining for a look in the car, he made out two men in colored fedoras, one blue, one green. Neither had a beard. A second later the mental alarm died off. In front of the entrance to the metro, Vivi had taken off her sunglasses and was kissing Junot passionately. When she finished, she turned and ran off through the crowd while Junot descended into the station. Suddenly the alarm went back on. The man in the green fedora had flung himself from the passanger's side of the car and was taking the metro steps two at a time.

The detective in Willi wished he had a gun, but the refugee in him warned him to play cool, that he was a foreigner, that even the slightest trouble could mean deportation. He plunged into the underground station anyway, adrenaline pumping, wondering which staircase Junot had taken. Direction Gare d'Austerlitz, or St. Cloud? He spotted the green fedora first, halfway down the Saint-Cloud platform. Practically behind Junot. A powerful urge seized Willi to cup his hands and shout to the kid, *Phillipe, watch your back!* But even if he had, the train had already rattled in.

He managed to elbow his way on just before the doors closed, a full car behind the student and the man in the green fedora. As they pulled from the station, the uniformly bored expressions of his fellow passengers made him wonder what the hell he was doing. Did he just overreact again, misinterpret the facts? Wasn't it more likely the guy in the fedora had nothing to do with Junot, that he was just some fellow picked up in front of the Polytechnique and dropped at the same station? Willi put a hand on his forehead as if to take his temperature. His nerves were affecting his thinking. Dutybound though, as soon as the train pulled into the next station, he squeezed into the car ahead.

Junot was on the far side, hanging on to a pole, stringy hair over his glasses, pink, heart-shaped lips stretched into a smile. What was he thinking, Willi wondered, about Vivi? Did he love her? The green fedora was leaned against the nearby exit, back toward Willi reading a newspaper. He looked muscular, bullish. For a second Willi caught of whiff of pungent cologne he'd smelled before in Paris. Who would wear such a heavy herbal scent? Was it coming from that guy? Junot certainly didn't seem to notice it. He'd lifted his head, lost in thoughts, his pale cheeks flushed with crimson. Was he off to that place on the canal again? Willi wondered.

As the train pulled into Odéon, he saw the kid snap from his reverie and move toward the exit. Willi kept an eye on the fedora. Was he going to follow? It didn't appear so. Folding his newspaper, he stepped aside allowing those exiting to pass. The station was thronged, people pressing on before everyone who wanted had gotten off, among them a cluster of students dressed as Babylonians on their way to the bacchanal. Junot was forced to squeeze around them, past the man in the green fedora, facing him a second before stepping to the platform. Just as the doors closed, Willi exited one door back, watching the fedora stay put, the paper unfold, the large, broad shoulders fade as the train pulled out. What a relief to be wrong this time.

A student dressed as Pan skipped by barefoot, playing a flute. Willi felt the pressure lift from his heart until he spotted Junot trailing the crowd toward the exit. The kid was staggering badly. A wine-colored stain was spreading across the left of his suit, the baggy trousers buckling. When his tortoiseshell glasses suddenly tumbled to the floor, Willi ran to him, catching the kid just as he collapsed, stunned how soaked in blood he was.

It was gushing in spurts from under his shirt. Willi slipped down, cradling him, feeling for the wound. It didn't take his experienced fingers long to find it right between the ribs. What was shocking was how small it was, a toothpick prick it seemed, straight to the heart. Willi tried to staunch it with his handkerchief, casting a desperate look around. "Someone call an ambulance!"

A woman screamed when she saw the pool of blood widening on the floor. People thronged around.

Junot's face was opalescent. His green eyes grasped for attention. All the pink flushed from his lips as he seemed to summon every ounce of will he still had. Willi leaned all the way down to him. Why did this have to happen?

Willi heard a rattling whisper: "Vivi."

So the boy did love her. Did he want Willi to deliver a message? He had no idea where the girl lived. "You'll be okay, kid, don't worry. Help's already on the way." He took comfort at least the boy's mind was on something as lovely as Vivi. But what about his parents; what would they think? Whom would they hold responsible? How would he feel in their place? Clutching Junot's face, he hoped to God the medics had been called, even while he knew it would make no difference. The boy's cupid lips, going purple now, were trying to add something.

"Vivi," they repeated, eyes clinging to Willi, craving comprehension. *"Il est elle."* It's her. Junot gurgled, vomiting blood. His eyes rolled back. And with a little shiver, Willi saw he was cradling a corpse.

The crowd gasped collectively. People broke into tears. Somewhere in the distance police whistles echoed.

Willi was so shocked he couldn't move, felt he might never move again. He'd seen more than his share of death over the years, from Flanders fields to the back alleys of Berlin, but no one had ever expired in his arms like this, looking into his eyes. Choked with anguish, he cast his gaze around, certain to encounter the sympathetic expression of some fellow traveler. But no. Only cold skepticism greeted him, eye to eye as he'd suddenly come with the harsh face of French law.

"Monsieur! Hands in the air! Rise to your feet!"

Five

The cell door slammed, the iron rails throwing black shadows across his face. Icy fingers seemed to grip his throat. Willi had been in plenty of jails but never behind the bars. It was a whole new, horrifying perspective. He tried to take comfort that they were only holding him for questioning, that it would all be done in hours, but the scornful shriek of the turning lock and the jailer's fading steps undermined his certainty.

Sinking to the metal cot in his coarse, striped uniform, his street clothes too bloody to wear, he chastised himself for plunging so recklessly without thought of consequence. At least by providence he'd forgotten his Berlin police badge this morning. They'd confiscated all his belongings and it would not have helped to have that on him. If only he knew about the judicial system here. Images of hard labor writhed through his brain. Dreyfus had been innocent too. How long had it taken him to prove it? How did the process work? What were his rights in the land of human rights? There was only one certainty: he was alone in a cell, and nobody knew where he was.

Over and over he relived the moment Junot's eyes had rolled into his head. That final breath rattling through him. If only he'd followed his instinct and shouted a warning to the kid to watch his back. But it wasn't his back that got it, he recollected darkly. When Junot had slipped past the man in the green fedora, that's when it happened—when they'd faced each other. So swiftly Junot hadn't even grasped what had happened and continued walking as if nothing were wrong. Whoever this assassin was, Willi comprehended, the guy was some kind of artist.

Falling back into the dank mattress, a leaden heaviness overcame him, reminding him too much of last year's pneumonia. For several days he really thought he'd had it. Ava had come to the rescue then. Who would come now? How he ached to see his boys, have their shoulders tucked beneath his arms, hear their goofy laughter. Surely the police couldn't believe he'd murdered Junot. Why would he have tried to help him? It might not matter though. He was an alien. A Jew. What chance would he stand if someone found him a convenient scapegoat? In Germany he'd have been able to speak to a lawyer by now—at least the Germany he remembered. How long were they allowed to hold him here? Whom would he call if they gave him a chance to phone? The one who got him into this mess: Gripois.

But they never came. Never let anyone speak to him. Behind bars in a foreign country, no embassy. No nation of any kind to back him. Staring at the ceiling with its cobwebs and filth, he might as well have been awaiting a firing squad. Sometimes he felt drenched in Junot's blood all over again, and horrified shivers chilled his veins. He wanted to cry aloud in outrage, but everything was jammed inside, until finally his brain overloaded and deep, dreamless sleep dragged him under.

"Monsieur." He jumped awake, amazed he hadn't heard the cell door open. Standing over him were two baton-wielding guards. From the small, barred window beyond their shoulders he could see it was already morning. Every muscle ached as he pulled himself to follow as commanded.

Up flights of stairs, down mazes of hallways, he grew cognizant of just how deeply he'd been swallowed into the belly of this beast. Once in, he wondered, was there an exit? Sallow-faced clerks lumbered past pushing carts piled high with files, disappearing into offices shaking with typewriters. More than one glanced coldly at his prison uniform, sending waves of humiliation through him. A quick peek out a window offered a view of the silvery Seine. This had to be the famous 36 quai des Orfèvres he realized, home of the Police Judiciaire. A sign above a set of doors seemed to confirm it: BRIGADE CRIMINELLE.

Paris had one of the largest police forces in Europe. Some of its resources, such as its well-known criminal archives, were the envy of the Berlin Presidium, although working here Willi knew was not. With something like eight hundred inspectors under one roof, promotions were notoriously slow. Newcomers spent years in administrative drudgery before moving to the prestige brigades, such as the unit they now entered: Special Investigations Squad 1.

Third door left they turned into the office of one Inspector Jules Clouitier. He was waiting behind a desk stacked high with files and photographs, magnifying glass in hand. His lengthy face took Willi in with the curious gaze of a ferret. Over his shoulders a large wall map outlined all twenty arrondissements of Paris, a black arrow pointing at their location dead in the center: first arrondissement, Île de la Cité. Just a few blocks north, Willi saw, was the corner where Junot had exploded at the *bouquiniste* yesterday. Ought he tell Inspector Clouitier about that? How should he play this hand? He'd never been great at gambling. A bead of sweat dropped down his temple.

"Monsieur Kraus." Clouitier put down the magnifying glass. "Have a seat."

The most logical thing of course was to lie. Portray himself as some random passerby who happened to see a young man fall and rushed to help. Clouitier however did not look stupid. It wouldn't be hard to uncover the facts, and then there'd be real suspicion. Tugging at his innards was a strong instinct to confess the truth. Tell the inspector everything: how he'd been trailing the kid, 234 quai de Valmy, the *bouquiniste*. The Citroën and the man in the green fedora. Give Gripois's address to confirm the whole damn story. But there was one little problem with that. A big one actually.

Sweat dripped from his armpits. The job for Gripois was off-the-books. Working without papers, he recollected from the documents he'd signed upon entering France, was grounds for immediate deportation—back to the country of origin.

"You should have told us you were a friend of Monsieur Duval's." The inspector pursed his lips, his lengthy fingers now waving the personal name card he'd found in Willi's wallet. "It would have spared you an undignified night." The inspector put the card back and returned the wallet to Willi. "My sincerest regrets." He indicated a coatrack where Willi's clothing hung cleaned and pressed. "And that you had to be such an unfortunate witness to such a terrible crime." The inspector leaned back in his squeaky chair. Touching fingertips together, he regarded Willi with a distant fascination. "The young man was a student at our national school of engineering. A tragedy on all accounts. Is there any light at all you might be able to shed on who might have done this to him?" His head cocked slightly.

Willi felt his stomach tighten as the sharp eyes bore into him. It took all he had not to rub his burning palms against his legs. How many times had he been in Clouitier's chair, interrogating someone, and, from a cheek twitch or the way his hands folded, knew he was lying. Yet how difficult it was to control such impulses. Especially when you really *were* trying to conceal something. After all, he'd been an eyewitness to a murder, observed multiple incidents leading up to it. Withholding what he knew made him accessory to the crime. But picturing Erich's and Stefan's faces waiting for him to come home, he lifted his chin.

"I wish I could, Inspector." Willi opened his palms. "I just happened to be walking toward the exit when I saw the lad stagger. I did what any decent man would have and tried to help." He felt something like a small rodent trying to claw from his throat. "How awful it must be"—he forced it down as subtly as he could—"for the boy's parents."

Clouitier's lips tightened. "Yes." His heavy eyelids fluttered. "Poor, simple factory workers. The kid was the light of their lives, apparently."

Willi walked as fast as he could from 36 quai des Orfèvres. Why had the inspector let him off so easily? Not a single question, who he was or were he'd been going yesterday on the metro. Was Duval's name that powerful to offer such immunity? Had they phoned him? Or did Clouitier simply have too much on his desk to worry about someone so obviously not a suspect? It was too close a call. He didn't even want to imagine the reception he'd get back in the new Third Reich.

Hands in pockets he was walking too rapidly for a man who didn't know where he was going. He needed to slow down. Think. But he couldn't. He wanted to fly, he felt so happy to have escaped that place. The day was radiant, trees sparkling. His street clothes felt like the finest garments from Savile Row. He never wanted to be in a prison uniform again! But he couldn't shed a nagging suspicion that maybe now, instead of poor Junot, he might be the one under observation.

He looked over his shoulder. Nothing. Only a couple kissing on a bench.

Why had Gripois lied to him, claimed Junot was rich? What kind of sham agency did that guy run? At least he knew where he was going. Place de la République. God how he hated being played. Plotting the most expedient route, he turned on boulevard du Palais and saw the old clock tower he'd stood beneath yesterday watching Junot. Was it only twenty-four hours ago? What did that *bouquiniste* have to do with all this? He pictured the phone call after Junot had stormed off.

Reaching the embankment, he saw the bearded figure next to his book stall, chatting with a middle-aged woman. Willi watched him write something down, then accept an envelope from her, offering just a nod in return. What was this fellow's game? How did he feel about Junot's murder? Grief? Guilt? Willi wanted to know.

One step from the curb though, he heard the prison door slam again and smelled the stench and saw the cobwebs—and froze. Exposing himself meant risking all that, he knew. He needed to use logic, not emotion. Be strategic. Compelling his feet to the far side of the street he forced them across the Pont au Change. At least confronting Gripois he had no qualms about. Even though he was the one who'd missed that meeting the other night.

From the center of the bridge he saw the long, low *bateaux mouches* fighting the currents, tourists rushing back and forth taking pictures. He thought about what police pathologists might have learned about Junot's wound. Had they figured out what kind of knife could have made such a slender puncture and caused such massive bleeding in a single thrust?

The square at Châtelet seemed like a song about Paris in springtime, tulips swaying in the sunshine, children feeding pigeons. At the top of the metro entrance looking down, Willi was stunned by his powerful aversion. He could still feel Junot in his arms, smell his blood, hear the gurgling throat. The idea of going down there again to such a tight, enclosed space made his knees want to implode. Gripped by a soft but definite wave of nausea, he decided just to walk.

Along the way he regained his equilibrium and stopped for some nourishment. It had been a long night. At a café terrace watching people pass, he wondered what the hell he was going to do now, without a job. Go back to the coat factory? He wasn't fool enough to take another assignment from Gripois. Poor Vivi, he thought, breaking apart a croissant. How would she react about Junot? She'd already gotten slugged once this week.

Gripois's office proved a real hike. Not knowing Paris, Willi turned the wrong way and had to backtrack. He hated getting lost. What kind of excuse would his employer make for the lies he'd dished out, telling him Junot's family was "well-placed" when in fact they were factory workers? Cruelly promising they might be able to help procure Right of Domicile papers for him and his family. Gripois would probably say something idiotic, such as it was for Willi's own good, to protect him from something best not known. He couldn't wait to see the look on that droopy walrus face when he walked through the door.

At Gripois's building though, Willi was the one registering surprise. The private eye's nameplate was no longer there. He could see the outline of where it had been removed from the door.

The concierge pretended never to have heard of him. "Grip-who? No one by that name ever here."

"But I was up there, more than once. Suite 4A."

"You calling me a liar, *boche*?"

Willi swallowed. "I'm Swiss."

"Get lost." Her eyes flared. "Before I call the cops."

Six

The ceiling fan barely spun. Lying on his back in bed, Willi watched it, sweating. A sudden burst of summer had shot the temperature into the eighties. It might as well have been a fever though, as low as he'd been laid. Junot's murder and Gripois's disappearance had drained the last of his trust. He was so sick of double-dealing. Of blood. Never knowing what tomorrow would bring. He needed something stable to count on. A job. A relationship.

If only Jules Clouitier would hire him, Willi fantasized. He'd find Junot's murderer all right. Surely the inspector had learned by now Willi was one of Germany's top detectives. Or maybe not. Maybe Police Judiciaire was so overburdened they didn't have time to put together such obvious two-and-twos. Willi even thought of going back to tell them but didn't dare, not when it might end in a train journey back to Berlin. Clouitier probably had no authority to hire detectives anway.

Willi stared at the rotating blades. The wisest thing would be a retraining program as the people at the Hebraic Assistance League had recommended. His old pal Mathias Goldberg, designer of Berlin's most sophisticated neon billboards, was training to be an auto mechanic. Willi ought to do something like that too, he knew. Only he wasn't going to. He pulled himself from bed. He was going to find out who the hell Gripois really was.

On the fifth floor of a crowded street in the Marais district, Paris's century-old Jewish quarter, the people at HEAL were gathered around a radio. The Nazis, Willi learned, had just outlawed all political parties but their own, turning the Third Reich into an official dictatorship. A new wave of refugees was expected soon in Paris and had to be prepared for.

"At least the German Jews are cultured," one of the secretaries commented. "Can you imagine a wave from Poland? France would toss us all out."

Willi walked to the office of the man who'd connected him with Gripois, finding the door open and seeing Levy behind his desk, working. Across from him in the visitor's chair a fellow in a bow tie was flirting with a slim, well-groomed female who was leafing through a filing cabinet. Willi was more than a little surprised to recognize her.

"But, my dear, your French is absolutely flawless. As is your complexion."

"That's very kind. Are these the files you're looking for, Mr.—"

Willi cleared his throat.

Ava's eyes widened when she saw him. "Willi."

She looked beautiful he thought, her skin indeed bright and lively, her well-defined features brimming with intelligence. How vividy he recalled a night in Berlin they'd discovered each other with similar surprise. What a different world then.

She came up and kissed his cheek. "What are you doing here?" Her scent was soft and familiar.

"I could ask the same." As much as he was confused about her, he felt so close to her still.

"I'm volunteering now. Figured they could use me, since I can't get a real job."

Levy stretched a hand. "*Bon jour,* Inspector. I gather you and Mme. Gottman are acquainted."

"She's my sister-in-law."

"*Quel charmant.*" The man in the bow tie quickly interjected himself into the conversation. He had a long nose and easy grin that seemed to have too many teeth. "I'm Levy's *brother*-in-law, Nathanson. We're all *mishpoch* then, aren't we!" He used the Yiddish term for "extended family" which Willi found distasteful. Too familiar, too fast. Plus, there was something supercilious about the guy, as if he were looking down that long nose at the world. Too Parisian.

"Unfortunately I've got to run." He started gathering a briefcase. "Off to another municipal news conference. Apparently the murder rate is climbing faster than unemployment. Those idiots at the Police Judiciaire can't even solve what they've got."

Ava looked at Willi ruefully. "Pity they can't use my brother-in-law."

Nathanson paused to take him in. "Ah, yes, the famous detective. Well, who knows, maybe once you're naturalized . . . *if* you'd really want to work for *them*." His toothy grin flared. "We should get together, the three us—for an aperitif."

Quel charmant, Willi was thinking. One big, happy family.

The guy really topped it by kissing Ava's hand as if he'd never seen such beauty. "Mademoiselle . . . until I am lucky enough to behold you again."

As much as she tried not to show it, Ava was lappng it up.

Willi's jaw clenched.

"My wife's brother," Levy explained after he'd left. "A bit flashy but an ace reporter. And your sister-in-law here, well . . . she's already made herself indispensable." He looked at Willi as if he ought to be proud. "Tell me, what can I do for you, Inspector?"

Willi wondered if he ought to ask his indispensable sister-in-law to leave but decided not to. Let her know, he thought.

"You can tell me about that man you sent me to work for, Levy—this Gripois. Who was he really? What did he want with me?"

"I don't get you." Levy frowned. "What do you mean *really*?"

Ava put down a file. "Are you all right, Willi? You don't look—"

"I'm fine. I just want to know the truth. Who was Gripois?"

"You met him. You know who he is. A detective with a private—"

"No, he's not. It was all a front."

"Why do you say that?"

"Because I was the only detective working for him. And then two days ago"—Willi snapped his fingers—"vanished. The whole office with him, like it never existed."

Levy went white. "Without paying you?"

Actually, this morning a messenger had arrived at Willi's door with an envelope, no return address. Inside, six lavender, French thousand-franc bills. No note, nothing else. If it was an apology, Willi had no idea. Only that it didn't change things. "He paid me, but gave me false information, sent me on a fool's errand, then disappeared." Willi skipped the murder part.

Ava's dark eyes flared. "You mean you're working illegally? As a detective?"

Willi eluded her. They'd been through all this already . . . his need to always feel powerful . . . the children he ought to be thinking about first. She was right, but he ignored her, continuing to Levy, "The whole thing was a big setup; I want to know who and why."

"I can show you his request form." Levy pushed from his chair and went to the files. "I took it myself over the phone." He rummaged around. "Here." He came up with a page.

Willi looked it over. "Did he ask for me specifically?" The document seemed innocuous enough.

"By name?" Levy thought it over. "No, of course not. How could he even know you were registered here? He merely asked if we might have someone with a police background, *detective* I believe was the word he used. Now that I consider it, of course, it does seem odd. Why call here, of all places? There aren't many Jewish detectives. And a refugee from Nazi Germany—"

"There's only one," Ava put forth, her chest rising with emotion.

"Is there anybody else you give the names of people who register here?" Willi put the page down.

"Absolutely not." Levy's brown eyes flared, but then turned a shade embarrassed. "I mean, other than Sûreté Générale of course. That's completely standard. The national police always require us to submit names."

Willi left the offices of HEAL if not recovered, at least on his feet again. Thinking. The Sûreté Générale though, he considered, pressing for the elevator. What to make of that? If the national police were behind it, why him of all people? He stepped into the cage. And why not just come out with it, why the setup? If he was supposed to be a fall guy, he pondered the whole squeaky ride down, how come they let him off the hook? Was he being dangled out here as some kind of bait? Who might the sharks be? When the cage door opened in the lobby, he paused to take a breath, his hands hot and clammy. He hadn't felt this ill at ease since he'd gotten out of Germany.

Back home he pulled out the gold-embossed name card still tucked in his wallet. Had it really been his sole ticket out of jail, he wondered, dialing the private line printed on it. Or might Inspector Clouitier have spoken to André Duval?

"Ah, friend." The financier instantly recognized his voice. "I was hoping to hear from you. Where have you been?"

It would have been nice to tell him the truth: witnessing a murder, locked behind bars. But Willi came up with some nonsense about looking for work, and although he was hardly in the mood for small talk, he forced himself to beat around the bush before getting to the point. "Say, André, has anyone made any . . . inquiries about me?"

"To me? Absolutely not. I'd have told you right away. Why, did something happen? What's wrong?"

"Fa-ther," an irritated voice whined in the background. "It's getting late."

"For God's sake, Claude." Duval put his hand over the receiver, his anger penetrating anyway. "Can't you see I'm on the phone?" He came back to Willi with a sigh. "These boys."

Willi understood. How he wished he could unburden himself to André. The isolation was so painful. But experience made him keep his hand tight to his chest. You never knew who was over your shoulder. "Just for immigration purposes," he offered as a plausible explanation. "I gave you as a reference."

"Ah, well, don't worry about that. I'll have nothing but exaltation for them. By the way, Friday night—Adrienne and I are having a small dinner party. Very casual. Just a few folks. Say you'll come, won't you?"

Early the next day Willi intended to take the metro to attend the funeral of Phillipe Junot. It was being held in a working-class neighborhood far on the eastern edge of the city. But he couldn't get himself into the station. It was ridiculous. For something like twenty minutes he stood atop the stairs trying to coax himself down, breathing slowly to calm his heart, fighting to expel memories. But even one or two steps and the first hint of that heavy underground air brought back the horror: the gurgling, the gasps, the stench of blood. Cold waves of nausea seized him, and he wound up having to go by taxi so as not to be late.

The funeral wasn't in a church but a workmen's hall, Junot's parents evidently of the revolutionary left. Many in the audience wore hammer-and-sickle pins or carried *L'Humanité*, the Communist newspaper. No one looked like a student from the Polytechnique. Had Junot really not made any friends his three years there? Willi was hoping to see Vivi, but she didn't come either.

The ceremony was short and progressive. Several poems were read about the burdens borne by the laboring classes. An elegy was played on flute. One testamonial was given by an anonymous intellectual who seemed genuinely grieved. His wife had to hold his hand the whole time he spoke. He extolled Junot as a brilliant mathematician who'd gained admission to the École Polytechnique on a rare national scholarship and yet was stricken down in the blossom of youth by a random act of violence—the future of France darkened.

Random? Willi wondered. Is that what the police had told them?

"Thank you for coming." The bleary-eyed mother shook Willi's hand on a reception line afterward. Her son looked frighteningly like her. Same pink cupid lips. Willi wanted to ask her so many things, but didn't dare. Not without a badge. When he looked into her eyes though, her grief reached him, and he was back again cradling the boy in the metro, bathed in blood. A desperate need to escape seized him, and he mumbled condolences, staggering from the hall.

Depleted and uneasy, he bolstered himself nonetheless to have his kids over for dinner that night. For weeks now he'd been promising to invite them to his furnished room and make them Wiener schnitzel the way their mother used to, but it was so hard for him to muster the energy. Stefan was happy enough, chattering away about his friends, his piano lessons, the Gottmans' dogs. But Erich was all complaints. Willi's room was too small. Too hot. It had no radio. It wasn't exactly clean. Worst of all, Erich didn't like the schnitzel Willi had worked so hard to prepare. The recipe came from Bette Gottman herself. He'd made certain to flatten the veal with a good, hard pounding and not forget the paprika. But Erich announced it wasn't anywhere near as good as Mom's used to be, and later when Max arrived to take the boys home, Willi's older son was out the door without so much as a hug. Willi was mortified. He had to get over the shock of exile, he told himself, before it destroyed what was left of his family.

He didn't know what to expect when he arrived at the Hôtel Lutetia Friday night. The place was so grand it was hard to imagine a casual dinner. He half anticipated hundreds of people, an orchestra, and dancing. Instead, the few faces he did encounter surprised him even more.

"Ah, Willi." Duval was in the white foyer wearing a white suit and tie. "Come, join us! We're having a celebration. It wouldn't have been the same without you."

In the sunken living room, in addition to Duval's wife and son, Willi saw his own sons and his in-laws Max and Bette Gottman. "I don't get it. What's going on?"

"You'll find out soon enough." Max came out and hugged him.

Everyone was there except Ava.

"No, no, she has a prior engagement." Bette kissed Willi's cheek when he came in to greet them.

"Let's go to the family room." Adrienne Duval pointed the way. She was gracious, fair-haired, rather more understated than Bette, but at every turn, Willi noticed, she managed to get in a glance at a mirror.

A mood of familial accord prevailed. Adrienne showed Bette around the apartment. Claude showed Erich and Stefan his room.

Erich, who'd been so sour the previous night, proved exuberant. "Look, Dad." He came running out with a framed photo of Duval's thoroughbred. "Some beauty, huh? Claude says we're invited to see him run at Longchamp next weekend—if you allow."

"You could come too!" Stefan made sure to clarify.

"Really? Me too? That sounds perfectly fun. Let's do it!"

Both sons cheered and hugged him.

No one was in a better mood than Max. "Quite a shack, these penthouse suites."

"You may be able to afford one soon." Duval threw a quick glance at him.

After cocktails they all sat for dinner in the small dining room. It was cozy, with a view of the Eiffel Tower.

"This gefilte fish is out of this world." Bette Gottman rolled her eyes as she tasted.

"It's from a little place on the rue Cadet," Adrienne boasted. "I'll take you there sometime. I'm not Jewish myself, but over the years I've learned."

Gefilte fish. Chicken soup. What's going on? Willi wondered.

Between the soup and the main course it all grew clear. At the head of the table Duval hushed everyone down. "None of us here is religious," he acknowledged, his gray eyes flickering warmly. "But at times like these—with anti-Semitism on the rise from Berlin to Moscow, we have to remember one thing: we're all family. And when trouble strikes, families come together. Help each other out."

"What he's trying to say," Max interrupted, slightly red faced from the wine, "is that we've gathered here tonight to celebrate the future. Instead of reopening Gottman Lingerie I've invested the bulk of my principal in bonds with Monsiuer Duval's company, his very highest yielders I might add."

Adrienne and Bette, to whom this clearly was not news, applauded. The kids joined in for fun. Willi realized from the various looks that he was expected to applaud the announcement too.

"Max told me he wants his grandsons to have the biggest nest egg possible," Duval injected toward Willi with a smile. "He loves those boys very much, Willi."

"Yes, I know he does."

"Well, with the kind of money they'll have someday," André elaborated, "they'll be able to do anything, go anywhere, never have to worry about leaving and starting anew if necessary."

"There's no better investment in Europe." Max seemed impatient for Willi to grasp this. "In the whole world, perhaps. Why, in ten years that principal is going to—"

"Never mind the details, dear." Bette Gottman refocused things. "The point is, now our futures are secure."

"And very much entwined." Duval poured more wine, looking at Willi.

"I see." Willi nodded, finally feeling the general exuberance beginning to get to his head. He didn't know the first thing about high finance, but he hadn't seen smiles this big on his family in a long time. Perhaps there was hope for all of them, if, as André said, they stuck together. "Then let's drink to our futures," Willi proposed.

Everyone raised glasses toward André and Max, who draped their arms around each other's shoulders.

"To our futures!" they all toasted.

Seven

Despite his renewed hopes of a better tomorrow, some underground wellspring seemed to keep feeding Willi's uncertainty. He grew ever more anxious to unravel the invisible net he felt still hung around him, waiting to pull him in. Who had set him up, and why? Who was Gripois working for? More than once he tried to convince himself he was growing paranoid, that his sense of foreboding had more to do with the Nazi terror he'd lived through than anything that had happened in France. But Gripois was no figure of imagination. Nor was Phillipe Junot. Someone had definitely played Willi, hard. With funds enough to survive the summer he decided to revert to what he knew best and get to the bottom of this.

He was itching to pay a visit to the book stalls along the Seine embankment. That *bouquiniste* clearly knew something. If he'd really informed on Junot though, Willi thought things through, it meant he had contacts with assassins that could get away with murder in the middle of a crowded subway car. No thanks. He might be miserable but he wasn't suicidal. Without careful planning, confronting the *bouquiniste* was far too risky. But the Canal Saint-Martin, he considered. Nothing was stopping him from finding out what went on at 234 quai de Valmy.

It was considerably less picturesque by daylight than in fog. The factories and residences that lined the canal looked as if they hadn't been painted in a century; 234 quai de Valmy, only two stories tall and leaning alarming to one side, looked as if it had never been painted. It appeared condemned, or least abandoned, though Willi knew it couldn't be. He'd seen Junot enter and leave multiple times. Seen other people come and go too. All men, now that he thought about it. Could it be a brothel? It hardly seemed possible. That place?

Instinct from his days behind enemy lines made him wary of approaching without ample reconnaissance. Out here by the canal, however, he was too conspicuous. Nobody else was around. Next door though, a brasserie had a pair of tables outside. Unfortunately the better one was occupied. The table he took proved less than optimal, the view obscured by hanging plants, but he settled in anyway, thrilled to discover Berliner Kindl on the menu. My God, how long had it been?

The first sip exerted such power he could almost see and hear and smell his home again, a terrace café on Tauentzien Strasse, the air so fresh, the lindens rustling, streetcars rushing by. If only he could go back for an hour! Opening his eyes though, he could hardly help but notice the bizarre-looking woman at the other table, tilted against the wall like a shipwreck.

Corpulent, in her upper sixties, as much lipstick around her mouth as on it, she was clearly a derelict from better days. Her once-elegant clothing, haute couture generations ago, was disintegrating off her frame now, satin hat, silk stockings, velvet shoes, fraying to pieces. An overabundance of necklaces, broaches, bracelets, and gaudy rings on every finger made her look like some kind of moth-eaten mannequin from a flea market. Alone with a tall glass of green spirits in her fist, her sharp, dark eyes, he saw, were fixed directly at him.

"*Bonjour.*" She straightened herself with a shrewd smile, as if it were obvious fate had delivered him to her. "Madame Bijou at your service. Palm reader extraordinaire. You look as if you could use some spiritual guidance."

He had to keep from laughing. "No thanks."

"Bosh." Her ring-laden fingers reeled him in. "It'll only cost ten francs."

Her table, he saw, had the unobstructed view next door. And her unremitting gaze indicated she was not giving up anytime soon; she viewed those ten francs as hers. In intelligence gathering only one thing mattered more than camouflage, he knew, and that was vantage point. So it'd cost him a few. He sighed, rising.

"Wise move, my man." She inhaled serenely.

Despite her obvious entropy, something about this ancient dame was weirdly inspiring, he thought. Perhaps her very survival.

"You're a good-looking fellow." As he sat across from her, she raised an eyebrow. It was completely painted on. Not a single hair. "Too bad I'm not thirty years younger." She vanquished the rest of her drink. "But after all"—she banged her chest, necklaces jangling—"what does age matter?" Her laughter turned into a coughing fit. "Character's all that counts. François!" She snapped fingers at the waiter. *Encore, s'il vous plaît.*

While she rolled a cigarette, humming, Willi noticed the door at 234 had opened; a middle-aged man emerged. Looking both ways, he tugged up his zipper then hurried down the block. Might it actually be a brothel? Such a dump? Perhaps, as in many Parisian buildings, a courtyard inside led to something else in the rear.

The waiter arrived with a second glass of green liquid, over which he rested a slotted spoon topped by a sugar cube. So that's what it was, Willi realized, absinthe. The green fairy. Seducer of the belle époque. In the 1890s half the avant-garde artists, painters, writers, and musicians were stoned out of their minds on it. Intrigued, he watched the water from a carafe drip onto the sugar, which slowly melted, turning the jade-colored liquid a cloudy white. Madame Bijou nodded with gratitude, and after a few reverential sips, her mummified face began to reincarnate. Lighting her cigarette she turned to Willi, eyes ablaze, demanding a truthful accounting. "Left- or right-handed?"

Left, he confessed what few people knew. As a schoolboy he'd been compelled to use only his right hand and used it still today to write. But when searching the ground for evidence, feeling his way down a dark corridor, or picking through a minefield in war, nature took over, and it was always the left that guided him.

"Good. Your right then, please."

Wrinkled, tobacco-stained fingers gripped his hand, making the back of his neck shrink.

"*Oui, oui.*" She squinted, pinching, prodding, tilting his palm. "You have many challenges in life, monsieur. Many triumphs too. But you live with great joie de vivre. And that is *très bon*. Even if sometimes the bitter seems to out-taste the sweet—never mind." She paused to imbibe her absinthe. "This head line shows a refined capacity to see more than one point of view." Her lips smacked. "Probably you excel at what you do. Am I right?" She didn't wait for an answer. "Persistence is your forte. You never give up—nor must you ever!" Groping for her cigarette, she took a puff, letting the smoke curl from her nostrils. "But this"—she traced a nail down his palm—"is fascinating." Smoke obscured her altogether.

Willi used the opportunity to flash a glance at two dowdy housewives who'd appeared down the street. Surprisingly they'd stopped next door at 234 and were using the iron knocker. After a moment, someone appeared, a man holding a newspaper. The women spoke something, then went in. So much for his bordello theory. But what had they said? A secret password? Was it a religious cult?

"*Mon Dieu!*" Madame Bijou's visage reappeared, her ringed fingers clutching her bosom. "This heart line, it's beautiful." Evidently she was deeply moved for rivulets of mascara began dripping under her eyes. "Your capacity for love is quite extraordinary." She squeezed his hand. "Observe this curve between the middle and index fingers. What a sex drive you have, eh? But look here where it straightens out. It shows you also have too much feeling for unhappy people. Monsieur!" Her old, cracked lips trembled as if she saw something terrible. "You must be careful who you fall in love with. Please. You cannot save the whole world."

As he let the knocker drop, Willi held his breath. Madame Bijou had stuffed his ten-franc note down her cleavage before falling asleep over a third absinthe, but offered no advice about getting into

234 quai de Valmy. Footsteps approached and he still had no idea what to say. The door creaked, slowly opening. The guy stood there holding his newspaper.

"My, uh, brother-in-law sent me." Willi swallowed, feeling idiotic.

The man looked annoyed enough to punch him. "Who the fuck cares? What are you in for?"

Willi's mind flailed about trying to seize on something to respond with. Seeing the newspaper in the guy's hand was *La République,* he recalled the same paper Junot had left more than once at the bistro, open to the racing pages, and flung out the phrase Junot had circled in pen: "Daily double." The guy shook his head as if Willi were an idiot, but stepped aside.

Willi hurried down a dingy hallway and into a courtyard, which, as he'd speculated, opened to a larger building in the rear, noise pulsating from its basement. Applause. Jeers. Through another door and down a flight of steps, then he paused, taking in the spectacle. A huge room crowded with people was lined with chalkboards posting listings not only from Paris but London, Palm Beach, Hong Kong, Bombay, with gate times, odds, winning numbers. Every few feet a radio blasted another race to nervous listeners, a boxing match, a soccer game, wireless operators jotting down figures. Hopeful faces darted from board to board, hunting for bargains, crowding counters to put down cash. A group of men broke into cheering while others shook fists, cursing. Evidently, 234 quai de Valmy was a bookies' department store.

The best preparation was useless without luck. The only certain thing, Willi told himself as he walked the quai de l'Horloge, was doing nothing. After spying on the *bouquiniste* half a day, it had grown abundantly clear that the guy was selling more than antique books. Customers kept coming up and handing him cash for slips of paper. He was obviously running numbers. Willi's first hunch had been right: Junot had had a gambling problem. What this guy's connection was, why he'd confronted Vivi late that night, and why Junot had come to argue with him the last day of his life, Willi hoped to learn. But he dare not risk exposing his identity. Or getting the cops involved. That at all costs had to be avoided. How sad it had come to this: the famous Inspektor, scared as a common pickpocket of the police.

He knew he had to camouflage himself, and as disguise was often an ingredient in information gathering, he was practiced enough in its arts. During the war, to pass within range of French observation posts his reconnaissance unit more than once had to dress as farm girls. This time as he sauntered down the Seine embankment on a crowded Saturday, dark glasses, shabby clothes, several days' beard growth, plus the cane he used lent the image of a disabled war veteran, which he capped off with a dusty beret pinned with an *Insigne des blessés militaires*, the famous red star for battle wounds—all acquired at the Clingnancourt market, secondhand. It was preposterous, the former German reconnaissance captain, Iron Cross winner for bravery behind French lines, posing as a French war veteran. But all that really troubled him was the damned accent. It was like a cross to bear. As he approached the green display box where the bearded *bouquiniste* sat, he could only hope luck was with him.

The guy was singing softly to himself in a language Willi didn't recognize, his coal-black eyes glistening as he gently swayed back and forth. Perhaps he'd prove sympathetic, Willi thought, offer assistance and help find Junot's murderer. But probably not. He recollected the phone call and the black Citroën at the gates of the Polytechnique. The bookseller's reaction though, whatever it was, had to reveal *something*. Which was better than nothing. Willi couldn't just sit around waiting to be manipulated again.

"*Bonjour,*" he spoke softly, deeping his voice.

The *bouquiniste* returned the greeting with a cautious but amenable gaze. He was not much older than Willi, rugged faced with a swarthy complexion. His large, dark eyes appeared wary as if by nature.

"I am looking for this man." Willi gave the wariness cause to amplify, handing him a newspaper clipping.

The bouquiniste's gaze narrowed as he saw the picture of Phillipe Junot. Though he tried to mask it, Willi could hear the irritation in his voice. "Why do you show this to me?"

"I'm looking for him, that's all." Willi kept his voice low. "Someone told me he saw him around here."

"Well, I never have." The man practically flung the photo back at Willi. "Now get lost."

Relieved the guy hadn't reacted to his accent, Willi figured it might be because he had an accent of his own, something slightly Italian or Spanish, but not quite either. He was hot-tempered too; Willi saw the meaty fists closing at his sides. Swallowing, he realized he was pressing his luck. "That's funny. Because I have it on good word you and he were having a rather vociferous confrontation one morning."

The guy's swarthy face whitened. He shifted in his seat. "Who the fuck are you? A cop?"

If only Willi was. Without a badge though he knew he was powerless to get any further with this guy. He saw no option but to go for broke, glean whatever he could.

"The very same morning in fact Junot was killed."

The *bouquiniste* rose and stared at Willi, shifting foot to foot. Willi hadn't neglected the possibility the man might get physical. He was considerably bulkier and no doubt could throw a mean punch. But before he'd ever get one in, Willi knew, he'd have him over the embankment wall and swimming in the Seine. As much as he'd tried to preconceive the range of responses though, from violence through confession, Willi could never have imagined how the *bouquiniste* did react.

Flustered to the point of rage, wanting to pummel Willi but stifling himself and not sure what else to do, in what seemed a single motion he turned, yanked his bookstall closed, hurled a padlock over it, and stampeded down the nearby steps. Amazed, Willi peered over the ledge after him. All the way below he saw the guy take a flying leap onto a boat along the river's edge, a cabin cruiser maybe fifteen feet long with a shiny red wheelhouse. Spotting Willi, rage flamed across the *bouquiniste*'s face. He used both arms to give an Italian *Fuck you!* and then cast off, gunning the motor and sending a ferocious spray as he bolted upstream. Before the boat vanished under the Pont au Change, the sun illuminated the name on the stern. *Achille Baptiste.*

On the outskirts of the city the most famous of all French race-tracks, the Hippodrome de Longchamp, was awash with banners announcing POULE D'ESSAI DES POULAINS, the silver cup for three-year olds. They couldn't have gotten a better day. Climbing from the upholstered interior of Duval's limousine, a Hispano-Suiza, one of the world's most luxurious cars, Willi and his boys along with the Duvals—André, Adrienne, and their son Claude—emerged into brilliant sunshine, a royal-blue sky. Before them, crowds were streaming up the walkways toward the great white grandstands, excitement fluttering in the air.

"Of course training's critical." Duval was putting on sunglasses, reminding the chauffeur to retrieve them at four. "But Chanson was born under a lucky star." He spoke with such enthusiasm Willi found it hard not to catch a bit of the fever himself. "Son of a gun's taken every race this year." Duval held up the fingers. "Eight! Never seen such a colt. If he grabs it today, we could have one of the greats on our hands." He slapped Willi's shoulder, laughing.

"Bragging jinxes it," flaxen-haired Claude reminded, delighted to have caught his father breaching one of his own aphorisms. André pretended to box him. His wife grimaced in faux reproach. "For God's sake, André, don't take it out on him." She glanced over her face in a compact mirror. "You have to practice what you preach."

She was archly charming but unashamedly vain. In the car she'd checked her mirror three or four times.

"Father." Claude continued to box André. "I told Erich and Stefan we could get them souvenir booklets and have the jockey sign. Inspector Kraus signed our magazines."

André put his hands up in surrender. "Why that's very thoughtful of you, Claude. Of course we can. I'm sure the jockey will be happy to oblige."

"Can we place a bet?" Willi felt a tugging at his sleeve. Thinking it was Erich, he got a shock to see the younger Stefan. How trim and defined his face had gotten, all the baby fat gone. Vicki would hardly recognize him. He'd only been six when she died. Now nearing nine. How would she have felt about the boys betting? He doubted her sister would be thrilled. Ava'd probably think it was some kind of negative precedent. She hadn't been very pleasant today when he picked the kids up.

"Honestly, between you and Dad I don't know who's fallen more under their spell. Imagine investing with him like that." Her gaze fixed from the window down to the Duvals' limousine. Tossing a wave of hair from her face, she'd cast her brown gaze coolly at Willi. For whatever reasons, she'd taken up against André, which was too bad he thought. She could have come along to the races. The boys would have loved it. Goodness knew there was room in the car.

"You can place a bet, but only a small one," he told Stefan. What the hell. Ava would find out and he'd have to justify his decision. What in life *wasn't* a gamble? He was only teaching the kids.

Willi watched the Duvals start up the walkway arm in arm, André in a blue, wide-shouldered jacket, his copper hair glinting in the sun, his wife in a slender suit and white gloves. It wasn't their stylishness though that emanated magnetism, Willi saw. It was their devotion. There was nothing pretentious about it. The two were crazy for each other. People kept coming up to take pictures. André was a celebrity. He symbolized more than just prosperity, but fortitude in the face of calamity, native intelligence, savoir faire. Willi had once had a similar public presence himself in Berlin. He didn't think it was one of the things he missed. But every so often . . .

Approaching the main entrance, he kept a firm eye on the kids. Thousands of people were here. Before them opened the vast, green racecourse framed by distant hills. At one end a giant board showed the minutes to post time, horses running, turf condition—*bon* today. The whole place pulsed with activity. Making his way to the betting stands, Willi placed a few francs down for each of his sons, while André went to the next window and put up his money. Willi could see a wad of bills in his hand but couldn't tell the amount.

Farther along at the concession stand they were disappointed to hear the souvenir booklets had all sold out. Not a single one left. When Claude turned with a hurt, pleading look, Willi saw anger flash through André's eyes and was somewhat surprised by what transpired next.

Duval leaned across the counter to the man there. "I promised him we could get those booklets signed by my jockey. Are you going to make me look like a liar in front of my son and his friends? "

"*Your* jockey?"

"That's right. I own Chanson d'Amour."

The fellow withered under André's gaze. Willi was not unfamiliar with the financier's powers of persuasion but had never witnessed them employed to such effect.

"I guess I can try to come up with a few more."

"Do that, won't you."

The man was back in what seemed under a minute, handing André half a dozen of the glossy booklets, gratis. André knew how to get what he wanted. And he didn't like appearing inadequate in the eyes of his son.

What father did?

The boys got the souvenirs signed at the *rond de présentation*, the parade ground where the grooms or "lads" were walking the horses for a last view before the run. André's jockey let them pet the champ, Chanson d'Amour—a magnificent creature with a white diamond on his nose and long, powerful legs. His rival Tempest, across the ring, was not quite as striking but had statistics just as solid. According to André, the two were shaping up as the main contenders for France's big race at the end of the summer, Le Grand Prix de Deauville.

"Thoroughbreds are touchy but their speed's supreme," Willi heard Claude explaining to his sons. Willi was glad to see the kids getting along, even if Claude was a bit show-offy—which, considering all he had in life, it'd be hard for him not to be, Willi supposed. He'd gotten his parents' amicability though. He was charming. "What will you do with all your winnings on Chanson?" he asked Erich and Stefan. "I'll tell my dad to let you invest with him!"

"Your sons are lovely." Adrienne let her eyes fall on Willi. "So well behaved. Your wife must have been a wonderful mother. I'm sure it's difficult for them without her."

Willi swallowed. "Yes, well, her sister has assumed that role to the best of her ability." He loosened his tie, the day suddenly warming. "The results I'd say are as good as can be expected."

Adrienne pulled off her gloves. "That woman you were with at Maxim's? Very beautiful." She dropped them in her purse. "And if you'll pardon me saying—very much in love with you." She snapped the clasp shut and grinned.

"Adrienne." André turned to her, irritated. "You mustn't. Willi told me something about it, and it's complicated."

Her brown eyes filled with remorse. "Oh, I don't mean anything by it. You know that, Willi, don't you?" She checked the expression on his face. "And as for complications, well . . ." She blew air from the side of her mouth. "I had a complicated romance in my youth; it was awful. When I met André, it was all so easy. Love shouldn't be complicated. I know many women who'd be delighted to meet you."

"Very kind." Willi smiled. "There may come a time I'll take you up on it. Right now, as long as we're being honest, I'm not really open to a new involvement. I only arrived in France a few months ago. I need to feel the earth a little more solidly beneath my feet."

"Of course you do." She touched his hand warmly. "It's very manly of you to admit. I'm certain you're not at all the type to have trouble finding females."

In fact he was—though not in the sense Adrienne Duval meant.

Night after night, trying to fall asleep, he kept picturing Junot's girlfriend, Vivi, that black eye of hers. He'd gone to Les Pipos and sat for hours hoping to see her sexy figure appear. Even asked the waitstaff about her. They knew whom he meant, but she hadn't been around the last few weeks, nor had they any idea how to find her. Willi didn't know her last name, had no clue where she lived. With over 2 million people in Paris there wasn't much he could do. Luck again. That's all it would be.

The competitors were saddling up, jockeys in their colorful uniforms taking their mounts, parading the horses one last time around the ring.

"Come on!" André hurried them to the VIP area with just minutes to post. Willi thought he detected an edge of anxiety in André's voice. If so, it would be the first time Willi had heard it.

They had reserved spots along the rail, almost at the finish line. Leaning up against it, sunshine ignited the distant hills.

"And they're off!"

A dozen horses hurtled from the gate. Willi's ears filled with cheering, the ground rumbling. Far down the track they could see Chanson d'Amour leap into the lead, Tempest right behind, the two horses pulling ahead, leaving the pack. It was only a sixteen-thousand-meter sprint so the animals grew larger by the second, the shuddering beneath their feet more violent.

"Go!" André was shouting so fiercely it set off a strange anxiety pounding through Willi's veins. In Deauville when he'd put a small fortune down on the roulette table, Duval had been so cool. This time he was really sweating it, invested in victory far beyond mere sport, Willi saw. How much had André put down? Was he the kind of man who could bet everything on a horse?

"*Chanson still with a slight lead as they come to the top of the stretch,*" the announcer's voice echoed from the loudspeakers. "*Tempest right behind. And now it's neck and neck as they thunder past the halfway . . . neither giving way. Chanson dropping a nose as they reach the final furlong. What a dramatic confrontation! Chanson d'Amour battling it out with Tempest. They hooked up at the start and they're going at it to the bitter end. And it's Tempest who forges to the front now as they come to the final sixteenth! Chanson d'Amour coming back at him! Tempest takes a bad step—only feet from the wire. Chanson d'Amour comes up and snatches it, victory in the final stride!*"

Photographers crouched behind their tripods, phosphorescent bulbs exploding. Poses with André and his jockey. Deschevaux, the trainer. The Duvals embracing their champion colt, draped now in horseshoes of flowers. And then André and François Coty, the famous perfumer. André and Pierre Taittinger, of the champagne dynasty. André and rising star of French cinema, Jean Gabin. Among the well-wishers Willi shouldn't have been but was slightly surprised to see was Victoir Orsini, commissioner of the Paris police. It was almost impossible to miss that shiny head with its prominent eagle beak, the insouciant swagger, the platform shoes boosting his stature. His fat, rather homely wife, Mirabelle, was on his arm with a bouquet of orchids pinned to her bosom. "Magnificent, Duval," Orsini offered congratulations. "You've got quite a steed there."

Strangely though, after kissing Adrienne on each cheek the commissioner gamely rejected pleas to pose with André for photographers. "No, no, I've got to get back to the city for a charity event." Willi found it odd considering all the major papers that were there, and what a publicity hog Orsini was. He hadn't forgotten the commissioner's manipulating that picture with him at the Palace of Justice. You *are exactly kind of refugee we like! A man whose talents could be very useful.* Orsini came out looking like roses. A real humanitarian. But Willi hadn't heard from him since.

When Orsini swaggered past, Willi cast his eyes down catching a glimpse of the made-to-order elevator shoes with their three-inch heels. What a surprise when the shoes stopped in front of him. "Inspektor-Detektiv." Willi looked up to find Orsini smiling at him. "I had no idea Duval counted you among his inner circle. How fascinating. But of course, you're all the same people! You must be thrilled today. By the way, don't think I have forgotten you. Oh, no, not at all."

Orsini walked off wagging a finger at Willi, his wife smiling demurely.

Eight

The July sun baked Willi's little top-floor room. Heaving the window as far as it went, he realized there wasn't a drop of air in the courtyard, only a small, gray dog down there chasing its tail. It reminded him of the schnauzer he'd had as a boy, and he dropped into a chair depressed. The Nazis had just denaturalized tens of thousands of resident Jews born in Poland and were talking about making marriage between Jews and Aryans illegal. More and more it looked as if he would never get to go home again. That he would have to make a new home here.

He looked around the room. It was a mess. He remembered Erich's comment about the dust and forced himself off the chair to get a broom.

Yanking aside the bed, he began sweeping, thinking of his parents. He'd probably never get to place a stone on their graves again. How proud his mother had been of those plots they'd gotten at the fancy Jewish cemetery in Weissensee, among the scientists and philosophers and business magnates. Could she have imagined a day the fatherland would reject them? Willi pushed the bed back, grabbing a handkerchief from his pocket and mopping his face. No sooner than she could have imagined her brilliant son cleaning his own room, an exile abroad.

Wie ein Hund mit einem Knochen, she used to say when he wouldn't give up trying to find something out. "Like a dog with a bone—you don't let go." Persistence, he believed the quality was called. Obsession, some might argue. Okay. It was a character trait that had served him well. But one that was keeping him awake too many nights now. Getting him up too early.

He went to the icebox and popped open a bottle of beer. If he didn't find out soon who'd set him up and why, it might be too late. He was basically a fly in a web, waiting for the spider. You don't bother with a fake detective agency, a bogus story, and thousands of francs—he swigged thirstily—without something big behind it all.

A month had passed since Junot's murder and he'd basically gotten nowhere unraveling it. What had that poor kid done to deserve such a fate? His dying face wouldn't quit haunting Willi. Several times he'd gone back to the embankment by the quai de l'Horloge, only to find a different *bouquiniste* working the book stand. He didn't dare approach the guy. The *Achille Baptiste* was no longer docked below. Which just about said it all, Willi figured. In one way or another, the original *bouquiniste* was guilty as hell. Or felt like it, anyway.

Numerous times he'd gone back to the rue de Lappe too, wandered the sidewalks late at night past the seedy hotels and raunchy dance halls, the hoodlums and the hookers, scanning for Vivi. But nothing. She was like a dream he sometimes wasn't sure he'd really even had.

He'd had equally little luck trying to locate that damned Gripois, if that's what the guy's name even was. If the son of a bitch really did work for Sûreté Générale, he might be locatable, Willi had figured. He'd gone to every library and archive that had anything on the national security service, but couldn't find a single reference to an employee named Gripois. Of course, the guy might have been just a contract player or received information from a mole inside. But the Sûreté Générale was hardly the only one aware of his presence here, Willi realized. The Police Judiciaire certainly knew a former Inspektor-Detektiv of the Berlin police had taken up residence; he'd registered with them upon arriving. And he'd been announced to the whole of Paris when his picture had appeared in the papers with Orsini. So Gripois might work for anyone. For all Willi knew Gripois could be an agent of the Third Reich. He'd heard more than one horror tale of émigré Jews kidnapped back to Germany, forced to sign papers handing over all their money. Max Gottman was a ripe enough plum for blackmail.

Willi swept with increasing vigor, sweat hanging on his eyelids, blurring his vision.

There was no way he could find any of these people except through sheer luck. Or . . . if he had a badge. Then his questions would have to be answered. At least he might establish some leads instead of groping around in the dark. The idea kept coming back to him of asking André for help. He was always offering it. But how far was he willing to go?

The top-floor room was really starting to bake now, the ceiling fan useless. He forced himself to keep sweeping, pushing aside the dresser with a grunt, recalling the face of Commissioner Orsini back at the racetrack. *But of course, you're all the same people!* Willi couldn't shake the feeling that something not merely anti-Semitic but ominous was in his tone: *Don't think I've forgotten you.* Might Gripois actually be an agent of the Police Judiciaire? Willi's motion grew almost violent. If so—he heaved the dresser back—then he really was just a fly in a web. A pawn at least in a deadly game. He wiped his face.

As he shoved aside the little couch, a long, brown envelope slid to the floor, the one Gripois's payment had been delivered in, those lovely lavender thousand-note bills. Bending to throw it away, he caught sight of a slip of paper wedged inside he hadn't before noticed. He pulled it out. A receipt. It was blank, except at top where the company name was printed: Flèche.

The address was easy enough to find. Right in the phone book under "Mèssenger Services." A nondescript block not ten minutes from where he lived, above a bicycle-repair shop. He waited across the street until ten, closing hour. Three men came out in shirtsleeves and headed in different directions, two by motorbike, one by bicycle. One of the motorbikes turned and came almost directly in front of him. Willi threw himself into the shadows until it passed. Upstairs, the office light remained on. A large window was open, a man up there mopping. Looking both ways, Willi crossed the street, relieved to find the stairwell open. The steps creaked too loudly as he headed up. At the top was an office with a big, red arrow painted across the door—Flèche. Taking a breath, he knocked.

"Hold on!" He heard a mop against a pail. The door opened and the janitor stood there, obviously expecting one of the men who'd just left. His face went blank when he saw Willi.

"Can you let me in for five minutes?" Willi sometimes found blunt truth to be the most disarming. "I won't touch a thing. I just need to find the receipt from a delivery that came through a few weeks ago. It means a lot to me—and for you, fifty francs." The man's eyes flashed on the bill waving in front of him. Cash, Willi also found, worked wonders. His heart was pounding like an alarm bell though. Just don't call the police, eh; he was picturing that train ride back to Germany. Their gazes interlocked.

"Five minutes." The guy stepped back, snatching the bill. "Touch anything and I'll break your arm."

Willi smiled, not wanting to mention he could cripple the guy in the time it took to take a step toward him. He spotted the file cabinet.

"The way these politicians are taking things," the janitor groused, kicking the door shut, "you can't have enough stuffed in your mattress." He picked up his mop and threw some water down.

Willi pulled the first drawer open and began fingering the labeled files for the date the money had come to him. June 19.

"Idiots." The man slopped the mop around. "Ruining everything."

June 7. June 12.

"As if they're not lining their own pockets. You can bet their wives are in silk nighties, while ours can't afford a . . ."

There it was. Willi pulled the file.

"One of these days." The janitor vindictively wrung the mop. "This place is just going to . . ."

And there was the receipt.

"The whole republic, right down the toilet. Pffsht!"

One envelope delivered to 23 rue du Faubourg Saint-Denis.

"Then maybe somebody with a spine will take over."

But the sender's name was completely blank. How could that be? Below that though, what was this? . . . an address. He felt a rush of heat through his face. Rue des Saussaies. Number 11. So it was them. He recognized it right away.

The Paris headquarters of Sûreté Générale.

From the terrace atop the Hôtel Lutetia the July sun seemed a distant tribulation. Beneath the shade of a striped umbrella Paris looked like a postcard: the green of the Square Boucicaut, the gold of Saint-Louis des Invalides, the rusty sweep of the Eiffel Tower. Willi observed it all, sipping a cocktail, trying hard to swallow his pride along with it. He'd come to beg a favor from André Duval. A big one. And broaching the subject was hell.

First off, the phone wouldn't stop. It was Saturday but Duval seemed to be keeping office hours, repeatedly having to retreat to his study for minutes at a time. In between he barely let Willi get a word in. Willi had never seen him quite this talkative.

At first he was still in raptures over his victory at Longchamp, the extraordinary possibilities it opened. The press, he said, wouldn't quit hounding him. Then, on the terrace settled in with drinks, he launched into an emotive rant about the economy. France, he claimed, had not been of this earth these last few years but on some distant planet, as if the worldwide crisis had been light-years away. Because the French put little stock in the stock market and placed their confidence in gold—his eyebrows rose at what he clearly felt was some absurd conjunction of circumstance—their wealth had not diminished, at first. Low birthrates kept the labor pool shallow so there was none of the mass unemployment plaguing everywhere else. The banks remained solid, the franc firm, the balance of payments positive, thanks to luxury goods—perfumes, wines, the tourist industry.

"But how long can such a state last?" he asked, holding open his hands. "If everyone around you is in ruin, who is going to buy your champagne and fragrances? Who is going to honeymoon in your capital? And now"—he smacked a newspaper, eyes ablaze with ridicule—"they're shocked to discover the sand beneath their feet is washing away. Fools." He flicked his hand derisively, the emerald on his pinkie flashing. "Higher walls, that's all the French know how to build. The solution isn't tariffs. What we need is economic integration. And I have a plan, Willi—a real plan!"

His sparkling gaze fell onto Willi thirsty for acknowledgment, a response, questions, applause. Willi's well, unfortunately, had run dry. He smiled vapidly, nodding in agreement. But Duval saw right through it, and for a second his handsome features looked as if he'd fallen from a cliff. Willi felt the urge to reach and save him, but the bonds man quickly regained his footing and graciously shrugged it off. "Never mind. It's a labyrinth of complication. Just keep your fingers crossed for me, won't you, Willi?"

The phone rang again.

Relieved not to have to endure the finer points of the Pan-Europa Bond, Willi nevertheless felt perilously close to a cliff edge himself. He knew very well it wasn't the interruptions or Duval's near-manic chatter making this so hard. He'd always detested asking favors. And what he'd come for today could land them both in jail. He had no idea how André would react.

They'd only known each other a short time, but they'd gotten rather close, he thought. After the initial suspicion André might be angling to get something from him, Willi had found real pleasure in André's acquaintance. He always felt revitalized around the guy—as if by an electric generator. And despite the many differences between them, oddly at ease. André obviously felt similarly. After all, he knew almost everyone in Paris, but here he was on a Saturday chatting with the detective from Berlin. How had Orsini put it? His "inner circle"? The last thing Willi wanted was to breach that link. But he'd come up with no other plan. The worst he could think of was doing nothing. If Sûreté Générale had him on a hook, he needed to free himself before he was reeled in for good and pickled.

When Duval returned, Willi just leaped.

André listened to him, tilting his chin back as if weighing each word. When he finally grasped what Willi wanted, though, a fissure seemed to split down his middle. Half of him, Willi could see, was in thrall with the idea, the intrigue and adventure it implied. The other, a little shocked perhaps. Uneasy at best. "That's quite a request." André put down his drink, interlocking fingers.

Willi's throat began to tighten. Had he just blundered badly? André was a huge figure in France; he had half the country eating out of his hand right now, plus he was cooking up his big deal to try to revive the economy. The press, he'd just made clear, was all over him.

"Identity papers . . . driver's license . . . even a passport I could comprehend."

And here Willi comes with a personal need that could undermine it all.

"But a police badge?" André's dark gaze searched Willi's face for a possible explanation. "I don't even want to imagine the trouble you could get into."

It's all right to say the trouble *you* could get into, Willi wanted to tell him, but didn't. André was shrewd enough to calculate the risks. He also knew Willi wouldn't ask unless it was crucial. Which it was, the irony bitter enough. One of Germany's top cops having to beg for a fake police badge in Paris. But he didn't see how he could go on without one. Especially now that he knew whom he was up against.

"I don't suppose you want to tell me why?" Duval's head cocked to one side.

He was itching to know, Willi could see. More than that, André was dying to join the hunt himself, to stick a pipe in his mouth and become a sleuth. Jump high fences and run alleyways in pursuit of his man. Why else would he have every copy of *Detective* magazine ever published, bound in leather? God, how Willi wished he could enumerate to André the powers a badge conferred and why he needed one. A to Z. The *bouquiniste* right through Vivi. There was nothing

Willi would wish more than a powerful man such as Duval pulling strings for him, keeping an eye out, guiding him through all that was so unfamiliar here. He didn't dare though. For everyone's sake, the less André knew the better.

"I can't, or I would. You know that, don't you?"

The sparkle in André's eyes dimmed. The two sides of him seemed to zip back together. Willi's stomach stiffened. He'd asked too much, he understood. Placed himself in too vulnerable a position, handed his friend an untenable choice. He regretted it. André did too.

"Whatever it is, Willi, you don't want to get mixed up in it. Your father-in-law is a rich man and going to get richer; you don't need this."

Why then, Willi wondered, when he comprehended the determination in Willi's face, did that grin slowly spread across André's lips?

Nine

Fortitude alone delivered Willi to the Place Beauvau. Paris was in the grips of a real heat wave. For days the temperature had soared past ninety, the July sun blazing. The sanest route would have been by metro of course. But yet again, as he descended the steps, the stench of blood had filtered through his nostrils turning his legs rubber, curdling his stomach. How long this neurotic aftershock would last he had no idea, only that it seemed not to diminish. He needed to conquer the bus routes, he knew, even though the maps looked like hieroglyphics. In the meantime there was nothing to do but hike the city.

It proved a monumental journey: Les Grands Boulevards past L'Opéra, La Madeleine, Le Palais de l'Élysée. Had he been sightseeing it would have been splendid. As it was, he stared at the gilded gates of the Ministère de l'Intérieur, feet baking, face dripping, eyes taking in the uniformed marines on either side, wondering how the hell he was going to do this. This morning he'd opted for bold action. Great. Too bad he'd never finalized a plan. He'd discovered another gray hair and that was it, simply plunged on impulse, unable to wait. Uncertainty was aging him. Now here he was half-dead on the sidewalk, still uncertain. But he commanded his miserable legs onward, turning the corner onto the rue des Saussaies.

It was a long, dark, narrow street. Halfway down it, his fingers reached for the reassurance of the talismans in his pockets, one a memento of the past, the other a gift from the present. Duval had surprised him the other day on the terrace at the Hôtel Lutetia. Beneath the cool shade of those giant umbrellas he'd agreed not only to procure a counterfeit badge for Willi, but in a gesture so typical of him, opened up in a way he never had before, taking Willi to heart.

"I'm a pretty good judge of character, you know." Duval's words rang through Willi's ears still as he tred the burning sidewalk. "I never met anyone I instinctively trusted more than you Willi—except of course Adrienne. Would it be all right if I shared a little secret? It'd do my heart good."

"Of course, André," Willi had said.

"My parents weren't poor but they weren't rich." André stared across the rooftops of Paris as if in a dream. "My father sold life insurance. My mother owned a dress shop. When I was twenty-one, I wanted to go into bonds. They thought I was crazy. They laughed at me. Called me *meshugge*. You know what that means, right? 'Crazy.' But that was all I ever wanted. Finance is my calling . . . like yours is detective work. Making money always fascinated me. I never viewed it as dirty or low, but an art form that could be used for good or evil. Look at the world today, Willi. People all across the globe—" He stopped himself, clenching his teeth. "Never mind. My dreams are always getting the best of me. The point is, in order to make money you need to *have* money. And I didn't have a centime. What I had were friends." He shrugged. "But that's what gregarious people like me do, eh? I'm sure I don't have to tell you that, Willi. We make friends."

Willi shared the view beyond the terrace, the whole of Paris seemingly veiled in a haze of gold.

"I met this man in Avignon. Ever been there? Fantastic place. An ancient walled town in Provence. Heavenly. Anyway, this guy had a jewelry shop there. He was Italian actually, from Genoa. Brilliant. Spoke like fourteen languages. He had the most extraordinary skill, like a master surgeon or pianist. This guy could take green glass, and I don't mean everyday crap but only the highest-quality Venetian crystal, and cut it so flawlessly even experts couldn't tell it wasn't emerald."

He'd stopped talking, eyes aglow.

"Being in law enforcement I suppose you might be able to sketch in some of the blanks."

Willi's heart had by then twisted miserably.

"In France we have something called *crédits municipaux*, a sort of combination pawnshop/municipal credit union. Every city has them. I went to the one right there in sunny Avignon and in my pocket took a small bag of emeralds. With the right combination of references and promises I was able to collateralize on them to finance a unique and extremely lucrative deal, whereby I sold municipal bonds issued by the crédits municipaux and pocketed a percentage. That's how I got my start. My company, Confiance Royale, was launched on a bag of counterfeit jewels."

He'd laughed, slapping Willi on the shoulder.

"I know what you must be thinking, Herr Inspektor-Detektiv: your father-in-law's investment . . . your sons' inheritance. But let me assure you that was lifetimes ago. I paid every cent of those emeralds back with interest, trust me. And in case you were wondering"—he'd waved his pinkie—"this one's genuine. From Ecuador, the world's finest. I've come a long way. I'm not proud of my youthful deception. And it's definitely *not* something I'd want people to hear about, you understand. In my game confidence is everything. You trusted me, so I trusted you. It's invaluable to me to be able to unburden such a thing after all these years. I've never told anyone. Not even Adrienne. It's like in those American westerns, eh?" He nudged Willi with a laugh. "Where they cut themselves and become blood brothers!"

Willi thanked him, deeply touched André was willing to stick out his neck for him. A badge gave him a fighting chance out here and restored a bit of his faith in humanity. In friendship. He only hoped he could return the favor someday. But as much as he understood why André needed to confess that original swindle, he really wished there'd been some other way they could have become blood brothers.

After all the monumental buildings, 11 rue des Saussaies was so unspectacular he almost walked by it. Only the sweaty-faced marine at the door reminded him to look above for the inscription, SÛRETÉ GÉNÉRALE. He reached into his pocket.

Three days after drinks with André it had arrived, a perfect forgery in tin and brass, thoughtfully encased in worn leather as if having seen good use. He could have kissed that beautiful swindler. *First Inspector Olivier Boucher, Paris Police Judiciaire.* Truly magnificent, Willi thought. If it wasn't good enough for others though—he clutched it tightly—there'd be hell to pay.

He decided to try for the top, say he was here to see Director Tondreau. He knew the guy's name, done his homework. What the hell. It always helped to seem important. If the guard checked, he'd have to play it by ear. Trust his instincts. Pray. But the guard didn't check. One look at the badge and he pulled the door right open for Willi, the talisman working its magic.

Willi wiped his forehead, blinking. Unspectacular as it looked from the street, inside, the building exuded a cool imperial power, portraits of the past directors hanging in gilt frames, thick red carpet leading up a flight of stairs. A gold-embossed sign indicated the directions to the various units: Executive, Foreign Affairs, Criminal Investigation. All eerily silent.

Luckily, he spotted a men's toilet and casually sauntered toward it, locking the stall as soon as he got inside. He took a deep breath, removing the fake Police Judiciaire badge, and felt behind the water tank. Just enough space. He shoved the leather case inside, making certain it wasn't visible, then stepped out and guzzled from the faucet as if it were his last drink. He washed his face and dried it, then straightened his tie in the mirror. Noticing the anxious look in his eyes, he took several long, slow breaths, then went back out, proceeding up the staircase.

His palms grew hot as he reached the second floor, his shoes sinking in red carpet, the quietness of the place chilling him. Which unit might that two-timing Gripois work in? he wondered. He didn't care about the risk anymore. The waiting was killing him anyway. One way or another he had to have his questions answered. Past an office with an open door, he peeked inside. Didn't anybody work in this place? A loud metallic click just behind his ear seemed to answer the question.

"Hands in the air." A pistol came to his head.

His heart clenched as he sullenly obeyed. He hadn't failed to anticipate this possibility, but it didn't make it any more pleasant. Rough hands rifled through his pockets, pulling everything out. Then a second, strangely familiar voice said, "Take him to my office, blindfolded."

A handkerchief tightened over Willi's eyes.

"Cuffs?" the guy with the gun asked.

"I don't think that'll be necessary, will it, Inspector Kraus?"

When the blindfold came off, Willi found himself seated in a book-filled office across from a man he definitely recognized, but only vaguely. His blood began to boil. That son of a bitch. He'd finally caught up with him. Fifty pounds heavier. Gripois. A real walrus now.

"Hello, Inspector." The alleged head of the detective agency smiled wanly. "Congratulations on having found me. It must have taken quite a bit. How exactly did you manage it?"

Now it was Willi's turn to smile wanly. "I'm a detective, remember."

"Yes! How could I forget? An excellent one, as you've once again demonstrated. I guess you must be rather riled with me, disappearing as I did." Gripois's thick neck twisted, jiggling his double chin. "I hope you didn't take it personally. It was purely professional. I made sure you got paid, didn't I?"

"Is that supposed to make me forget the whole setup?"

Worst of all, Willi thought, was the promise of those residency papers Gripois had hinted at to lure him into it. How about those to make up for things?

The phone rang and Gripois grabbed it, grunting several times before returning the receiver. "My boss, whom I believe you told the guard you had an appointment with, will be delighted to see you. Seems he's rather impressed with your performance too. Before we go up though, tell me, Kraus—how did you get in the building? That marine said you showed him a badge from the Police Judiciaire. But the only badge we just found on you was this." He held up Willi's old Berlin badge.

"Yes, well." Willi smiled. "They look quite similar—don't they? Don't blame your guard. He did his job. I'm pretty skilled at this, you know."

"That's never been in doubt." Gripois's cheeks puffed. "But you didn't recognize me at first, did you?" He chuckled. "Last time I was recovering from gallbladder surgery." He patted his big, fat belly. "Now I'm fit as a fiddle. Real name's Marsolet by the way. Come along."

Compared to police commissioner's antique-filled palace, the office of the director of the Sûreté Générale glistened starkly with national pride. Tricolor flags sprouted from silver holders on the large polished desk, portraits of the president and heads of the military stared from the walls. Tondreau was a chiseled-looking man with perfectly groomed salt-and-pepper hair who exuded the air of a country lawyer, unpretentious though wily enough. He offered Willi tea in a Limoges cup.

"Believe it or not we regretted it all very much. We never meant to deceive you, except about the boy being rich. It was a weak idea perhaps—but meant for your own protection. I'm sure you discovered Junot had a gambling habit, a rather nasty one. He got into trouble and was being forced to work off his debt. Our little office on Place de la République was to track the gang that coerced him. They operate in several cities. We were hoping you might be able to deepen our understanding of their Paris network. It was our assumption the kid was just a runner, delivering orders, making payoffs. We hadn't an inkling he was in danger, certainly not that he'd get murdered on your watch. Then, once you wound up in the hands of the Police Judiciaire, why . . . there was nothing we could do; we had to back off to protect our operations."

Willi stared at Tondreau with disbelief, that night of terror in jail coming back to him, the weeks of anxiety after, the sense of betrayal when Gripois had vanished. "Monsieur, pardon my ignorance, but you and the Police Judiciaire . . . you're on the same side, aren't you?"

Tondreau offered him a slender smile, along with a butter cookie. "Yes, of course." He bit into one himself, cupping his hand so he didn't drop anything. "On a theoretical level. Unfortunately, practically"—he glanced at Willi with evident meaning—"it doesn't always work that way. In this case we had to be exceedingly prudent." Tondreau's eye scanned his desktop as he chewed. "Because, you see, we have reason to believe some tentacles of this crime network might actually have penetrated"—he spotted several renegade crumbs and pressed his index finger down on them—"into the Police Judiciaire itself."

Willi felt a slight headache as he watched the director thrust them to his mouth and swallow.

"I'm sorry it turned out this way, Kraus, really." Tondreau smiled as he bit into another cookie. "You're clearly a man of great talent." He sipped his tea but kept his eyes trained on Willi. "However did you manage to track us down?"

Willi shrugged with a faux-hangdog look. "The phone book?"

Tondreau laughed. "A sense of humor too. Well, it's unfortunate we haven't funds to take you on. I'm sure you could teach these clowns a thing or two. But times are hard; I needn't tell you. Our budget's just been slashed again. Perhaps, if circumstances change . . ."

Willi looked at the dimpled chin, the salt-and-pepper hair, the slightly dancing eyes, and knew Director Tondreau of the national police wasn't exactly lying—just leaving out as much as he was saying. The gaps were in fact rather absurd. Such as, why had they chosen *him* for the job? Just because he was an out-of-work refugee, they figured they could get a good detective on the cheap? If so, why the cover story and the nice cash salary if their budget had been slashed? It didn't add up. But it no longer felt decisive to Willi because the worst of his fears had been alleviated. Sûreté Générale, he felt certain, was not out to get him. They didn't have him dangling from a hook as some kind of bait, certainly not for any foreign agents. They'd used him. Not illegitimately. Just clumsily.

Tondreau flicked the last of the crumbs from his fingers. "Before you go"—he wiped his thin lips clean with a napkin—"you might want this back." He slid Willi his wallet. "I couldn't help but notice you carry a personal name card from André Duval. Is he a friend of yours?"

"I haven't known him long, but, yes. I consider him one."

"I see. How interesting. Allow me to ask you one last thing, Inspector." Tondreau smiled vaguely. "You followed Phillipe Junot for us for ten days. Your first report portrayed him as near angelic, attending classes, kind to fellow students, to beggars on the street. The second mentioned the house along the quay d'Valmy, which was very helpful to us. Is there anything more, the slightest detail, that might come to mind you could share with us? It's a terribly important case, you see."

Really? Willi raised his eyebrows, stalling over a sip of tea. All the more reason *not* to share what he knew. Not about the *bouquiniste*. The Citroën. The man with the green fedora. The more cards up his sleeve, the better. Besides, the murder fell under the jurisdiction of the Police Judiciaire he knew, not the Sûreté. On the other hand he didn't want to seem to be holding back.

"There is one thing." He broke into a slow grin. "This girl." He noticed Tondreau's head cock. "One night after classes, Junot brought her back to his place."

Tondreau's eyebrows rose. "I see. Did you happen to find out anything more about her, a name or address?"

"I wish!"

"Why, was she pretty?"

"Are you kidding? She was beautiful. That kid was lucky—even if just for one night."

The director sat still a long moment considering. "Yes, well." Air shot from the side of his mouth. "All of us are lucky to find love, Inspector. Even if just for one night."

Assuring him that if anything further came to mind he would call at once, Willi pocketed the card with Tondreau's direct line. When the interview ended, chubby Inspector Marsolet, formerly the shrunken-walrus Gripois, was kind enough to escort him downstairs with instructions to make certain Willi exited "safely." Before leaving 11 rue des Saussaies though, Willi begged Marsolet's forgiveness and took a fast detour to the men's room, where he retrieved his Paris police badge from behind the toilet and tucked it in his pocket.

Ten

The next day Willi awoke to find a small, white envelope slipped beneath his apartment door. His heart pounded as he bent to pick it up. It was a message via pneumatic post. His hand shook as he opened it. Please, not deportation. He could see Gestapo agents awaiting his arrival in Berlin. But it wasn't deportation. It was a summons from 36 quai des Orfèvres, Criminal Division Police Judiciaire. He was to appear today at noon. Room 342. Why? Had he stumbled from the frying pan into the fire?

Sitting there trying to figure it out, razor wires of anxiety coiled around him. Perhaps they'd found out about the fake badge. If so though—he forced himself to think this through—it'd be police at the door, not a summons. Might it have to do with the commissioner? At the races Orsini had made it clear he hadn't forgotten Willi. Perhaps they wanted to bring him onto the Junot case after all. A small thrill seized him at the possibility. According to newspapers, there were still no leads on the murder. Perhaps they'd realized he could be of use. And how great that would be—a real badge, residency, security.

At twelve o'clock he arrived at the great gray building along the Seine, feeling a pain in his stomach. He could hardly forget the awful night in the dungeon here. The hall he was directed down started looking familiar. As soon as he entered room 342, he understood why.

Inspector Clouitier peered up from his desk full of files and photographs. "Ah, Kraus." He put aside his magnifying glass, politely enough but without a smile. "Back again I see. Such an interesting person you turned out to be. Sit, sit." He cocked his ferretlike face, interlocking his long, white fingers. "Had I been aware of your background, I'm sure I would have had quite a few more questions for you at our last meeting." One of the fingers waved at Willi reproachfully. "You should have been more honest, Inspector. I would have liked to know for example how you happened to be behind Junot at precisely the moment of his murder."

The razor wire of anxiety coiled around Willi once more. This was not a hiring session. Was he about to be charged? Clouitier's mouth twisted into an insidious smile, as if he saw right through Willi to the psychotic killer inside. No doubt the overworked inspector bore the brunt of all sorts of pressure to pin the blame on someone. A stateless Jew would be perfect. Willi could almost feel that cell door slamming again, leaving him in blackness.

"Maybe I went to his assistance," he spoke in his own defense, calmly but as firmly as possible, "precisely because I *am* a detective. I saw blood soaking through his suit, Inspector. I'm not unfamiliar with such things."

Did Clouitier know he'd been doing a job for Sûreté Générale? A job to help track a criminal ring that might have "tentacles" in the Police Judiciaire?

The ferret face had grown expressionless. "I suppose it might make sense in an inexplicable sort of way." Clouitier chewed on his inner mouth. "And goodness knows this world is rife with mystifying aspects. But I've summoned here you on a rather different matter." He straightened his spine and smiled again with what Willi felt was subtle menace. "One that has nothing to do with Phillipe

Junot. We're here to discuss a friend of yours, a good friend I believe."

Willi's heart skipped a beat.

It turned out Police Judiciaire had a job for him, all right. Starting at the bottom. All the way.

With a series of shrugs, sighs, and twisted lips Clouitier explained that rumors had been circulating of late regarding the soundness of the highly profitable bond business run by André Duval. Only rumors, nothing more—but they bore investigation. Willi was to help in this investigation. Naturally, he would be paid. Not as a full inspector, of course but—

"As a mole," Willi interrupted him, with the French word *mouche*, "fly," not as in "on the wall" but more like maggots on a dung heap—because that's what it was. You couldn't get much lower, especially for a top detective. And it didn't get much worse than spying on your friend. "Suppose I decline—"

From between Clouitier's teeth came a low tsk-tsk. "Herr Kraus"—he used the German pointedly—"you're far too smart. Think about it. What rights have you in this country? You have no rights anywhere as far as I know. Nor"—he frowned regretfully—"does anyone in your family. So." His bony fingers twisted back together. "Unless you're curious to witness firsthand the triumphs of the New Germany . . ."

"Perhaps the police could help allieviate that fear and gain a more enthusiastic employee"—Willi felt he had nothing to lose by trying—"if permanent-residence and work permits were thrown in as part of the bargain."

"Yes, that would be nice." Clouitier didn't smile. "Unfortunately it's out of the question. Far beyond my jurisdiction."

Willi felt his fists bunch, sensing this new net closing around. "Can you explain how I'm supposed to learn what goes on in Duval's company when I haven't the faintest concept of high finance? When, in fact, I can barely balance a checkbook?"

Clouitier's narrow nostrils flared. "It's my guess, Inspector, that Monsieur Duval, concerned as he is with the plight of refugees—particularly his own people—might have offered assistance to help you get on your feet here in France."

Willi felt his breath catch.

Cloutier leaned both arms on the desk and thrust his face toward Willi. "Ask him for a job."

My God. Willi shuddered. They had this all worked out. Orsini had to be behind it, that day at the racetrack when he realized Willi and André were friends.

"What kind of job? He knows all about my background in law enforcement."

"Don't worry, Inspector." Clouitier now smiled, a dark, hard gleam in his eyes. "He'll figure something out. The man is renowned for resourcefulness. All you need to do is—gather information. I understand you managed quite well behind our lines during the war." Clouitier raised an eyebrow and leaned all the way back in his squeaky chair. "I'm sure this will be a far less dangerous assignment."

The fourteenth of July was France's national holiday. It was also André Duval's birthday, and he was celebrating in style—a grand soirée in his rotunda apartment. Seventy-five select people, luminaries from across Europe, Willi somehow among them. Max and Bette Gottman were going too, and despite his protests about how far out of the way it was, they insisted on picking him up. Squeezed with them in the back of a taxi, he could barely breathe. The nearer they got to the Hôtel Lutetia, the more he felt like jumping from the car. The idea of having been reduced from an Inspektor-Detektiv to a police informant coiled his guts. A year ago he could never have imagined it. Now he knew he had to do whatever was necessary to protect his family. But what about his dignity?

Bedecked in jewelry, Bette Gottman was in a rare mood. Willi hadn't seen her so animated since they'd left Berlin. Despite the holiday firecrackers exploding practically underneath their tires, she chattered incessantly, flush with excitement.

"It's been so impossible connecting socially even through my sister. No one wants to mix with *refugees*. It's like a disease. People say Germans are frosty, but I find Parisians far worse, don't you? Even the Jews here." She didn't wait for an anwer. "Being asked to come tonight though"—her ringed fingers entwined with her neck-lace—"somehow I feel like we've finally arrived."

"We have," Max said, looking out the window.

"Wise guy." She straightened his collar.

"Personally"—Max paid the driver—"I'll feel we've arrived once we get our Right of Domicile papers."

"*Ach.*" Bette waved a hand as they climbed out, convinced their darkest days were behind. "After we're in with a crowd like this?"

In the elevator up, Willi loosened his tie, feeling as if he were strangling. It wasn't the tie though causing the sensation. He'd phoned André yesterday and asked for a job, trying to keep his voice from trembling. André had been surprisingly receptive, happy almost, and said he'd come up with something, not to worry. Willi loosened his tie even more. If his throat got any tighter, he'd need a tracheotomy.

"You look very handsome." Bette smiled, reaching over and tightening it again.

Willi hated formal wear to begin with. He especially hated that he'd had to go with Ava to buy this outfit.

"Would you take it in a bit at the waist?" She'd demonstrated at the shop she'd taken him to. She hadn't been invited tonight nor was she thrilled about Willi or her parents attending. But as long as they were, she'd said, they might as well look good. "Much sharper." She'd run an approving hand down Willi's spine.

As they approached the Duvals' apartment Max and Bette each took one of Willi's elbows. "Now, don't you run away," Bette quipped. Willi wondered if she could read his mind.

As they stepped into the sunken living room, Adrienne greeted them with kisses to each cheek. "Max, Bette . . ."

"Here he is." Bette passed Willi to her. "Signed, sealed, and delivered."

What did that mean?

"A million thanks." Adrienne winked conspiratorially. "I'll catch you in a few minutes." Her button nose crinkled as she seized Willi's arm. "Come. André asked me to take special care of you."

How regal she looked in a backless, silver gown, her neck sparkling with rubies. "This is far more than a party to him, you know."

She steered Willi through the crowd. "André considers this his grand salon, an annual gathering of illustrious minds to amuse as well as to refine. Or, as the Romans put it, *aut delectare aut prodesse est!*" She laughed. "You can't imagine the pains he takes on it. Anyway, who do you suppose is one of his *invités d'honneur* this year?" Her gaze bore into Willi's.

"Not me."

She shrugged ruefully. "I've instructions to bring you the moment you arrive."

Now he really felt like running away.

"I'm sorry, Willi. It's nothing really. Just a little speech where he tries to make everyone cry. I'm quite sure you've survived worse. Look, the prime minister—"

Édouard Daladier was pressing through the crowd *avec entourage* trying to get out. "Adrienne!" He kissed her cheeks. "I'm so sorry. I'd rather stay of course, but I've got to be at the damned grandstands for the fireworks."

"Go do your duty, but first you must meet Inspektor Kraus, formerly of Berlin Kriminal Polizei, an exile now here as all their best are."

"Yes, yes." Rushing past, Daladier pumped Willi's hand. "I do hope France welcomes you!"

It was hardly surprising André had been born today of all dates, Willi considered. Bastille Day. He'd said more than once he was more French than Cartier. His luxurious apartment tonight was indeed resplendent with some of the brightest gems in Paris. Cleared of furniture, the terrace doors thrown open to display the brilliant setting—la Rive Gauche—the polished floors and paneled walls embraced a collection of the capital's most glittering elite.

If, as some said, France was ruled by a plutocracy of two hundred families, half of them seemed here. Adrienne led Willi on a guided tour. To one side, the head of Michelin Tire. On the other the director of the Crédit Lyonnais. Straight ahead, the publisher of *Le Matin*. On all sides ministers of state, senators, members of the Assembly.

"Those of the right, those of the left." Adrienne swept Willi along on her arm. "André wants to prove even political opponents can be humane. In his salon, *liberté, égalité,* and *fraternité* exist only within old-regime etiquettes of *politesse, civilité,* and *honnêteté.*"

Honor, yes. Willi felt the word press like a steam iron against his throat.

They passed designer Elsa Schiapparelli, debating with the leader of the Parisian surrealists, André Breton. "It has nothing to do with *perspective,*" she was insisting rather vehemently. "The Ritz has *always* mixed finer cocktails than the Crillon."

"The age of conversation hasn't died in our home," Adrienne said drolly as she navigated farther.

Willi noticed a tall, rugged-faced man sitting straight-backed, being pushed around by a nurse. "Who's the fellow in the wheelchair?"

"The head of the largest veterans' association in France," she whispered. "Extremely rich, old guard. A monarchist or something, at any rate ultranationalist. We have nothing in common but he positively *adores* André. Wouldn't miss these parties for the world. "

The only one not here, Willi couldn't help but observe, was the commissioner of police. Why not? No one loved a star-studded party more than Victoir Orsini.

On the terrace they saw their host with his back turned, chatting to someone his wife whispered was the Baron de Rothschild, scion of the international banking dynasty, race-car driver, and one of the most successful wine growers on earth.

"Just what I like about you." The baron was slapping André's shoulder. "Always careful not to get blamed if things go wrong."

"I never advise people what to do with their money," André replied without the least hesitancy, "only help earn them more if they ask. Now, I've no more information, Phillipe." André was still unaware of his new guest's presence. "If you want to bet on Chanson, you know the odds as well as I."

"Don't be fooled, Baron," Adrienne put in, letting her husband know she and Willi had arrived. "André's dying to brag about his horse. He just doesn't want to jinx the race next month. He pretends not to be, but he's superstitious as a granny."

André had turned, his handsome face brightening, the gray eyes twinkling as he kissed his wife's hand. "Ah, my dear. Always revealing my little secrets." He pretended to bite off her fingers. "And Willi, finally!" He threw an arm around Willi's shoulder, causing him to wither inside. How mortified he was, having to betray André. He hoped his eyes didn't give away his shame. "At last we can get this evening under way."

Beyond the terrace Willi noticed the sky had descended into the deep violet of dusk. Firecrackers were exploding from the Louvre to Napoléon's Tomb.

"Friends—please." André rang a glass. Having come inside and taken position on a step to the dining room, he was waiting patiently, eyes sparkling, looking one by one around the crowd until his gaze had silenced even the senators and film directors. What a spellbinding air, Willi observed with a mixture of fascination and disquiet. André stood like a great biblical figure, almost impossible to look away from, some message ready to emanate.

"Now that our *invités d'honneur* have arrived, I'd like to thank you all for joining Adrienne and me tonight. Besides my birth of course this is the one day we celebrate our beloved republic, cradle of European liberty. To help remind us of just how precious that liberty is, now more than ever I've invited two very different men tonight who share one significant similarity: both were banished from their homes by dictators, and both have sought refuge with us here in France.

"The first"—André held his hand out toward the front of the apartment—"hardly needs introduction." The crowd parted to reveal an extraordinary-looking bespectacled figure with a bush of gray hair, matching mustache, and long, pointed goatee. Leon Trotsky, savior of the Russian Revolution, expelled from the Soviet Union by his archnemesis, Joseph Stalin, was standing over a glass of champagne next to Georges Simenon, the mystery writer. Willi had read that Trotsky had recently immigrated to France but thought he'd been relegated to the provinces. André apparently finagled a visit for him to Paris via André's connections with the prime minister.

Now the famous revolutionary acknowledged his applause with the triumphant serenity of a Nobel Prize winner.

"Our second guest perhaps needs a word or two."

Willi realized the speaker's hand had shifted, all eyes turning. It wasn't embarrassment he felt, but loneliness. If only he had someone at his side he felt closer to than Max and Bette Gottman.

"Germany's most celebrated detective, Willi Kraus, served his country since his seventeenth year, first as a soldier earning his nation's highest medal for bravery, then as an investigator with the criminal police, solving some of Berlin's most terrible crimes."

Willi swallowed down the lump in his throat. André was being so supportive it hurt. Like the older brother he'd always longed for.

"And yet with the ascendancy of Adolf Hitler this hero was turned into a criminal, forced to leave everything behind, cast into fear, uncertainty, isolation."

Bette dove for a handkerchief.

Willi bit his lip. Now he was faced with something almost as dreadul. One of the ugliest things he'd ever had to do. André's compassion only made it that much worse.

"Tonight we honor the disposessed." André placed a hand on Willi's shoulder. "Every day Paris fills with more. More scientists, more artists, more businessmen, driven to seek sanctuary from persecution and imprisonment. We celebrate the courage of our forefathers one hundred and forty-four years ago in toppling despotism and declaring the rights of man, but we dare not ignore the rise of tyranny across our borders. For millions, it has spelled the doom of freedom and the dawn of a new dark age."

If only André were exaggerating. Willi had to battle his memories. Brownshirts hauling people from apartment buildings. Rows of prisoners herded through the streets, hands in the air.

"There are those who feel that another war is now just a matter of time. I don't necessarily agree. The wall of mechanized fortresses nearing completion along our frontier is sure to offer us physical protection for many decades to come. On the other hand, as our esteemed guest Comrade Trotsky has pointed out, fascism is not the product of mass hysteria but a profound crisis eating at the soul of Europe. If that is true, my friends, then no walls could be thick enough, no walls high enough, no walls long enough, to defend our beloved republic from all that threatens her. It is a different defense we must devise. A new sort of fight we must mobilize for."

Willi shrank from the light blazing in the eyes before him. They burned with almost messianic passion.

"We must rouse ourselves to wage a conflict not against neighbors east or west, but against the common enemy of all—the Great Depression itself. To conquer financial catastophe and resurrect our world economy, because if we don't"—Willi felt so small next to André. The timbre of his voice, the confidence radiating from him, made you believe that if anyone could win such a war, he could— "God help Europe."

Almost the moment the speeches ended and the party resumed, the man in the wheelchair, of all people, the "ultranationalist" as Adrienne had called him, rolled over to greet Willi.

"Welcome to Paris." He reached and shook Willi's hand with painful firmness. Willi could see he was wearing a small pin on his lapel that read FRATERNITÉ D'HONNEUR. Brotherhood of Honor. "You and I were on opposite sides of the trenches. A German bullet crippled me at Verdun. But I want you to know, Inspector—I've boundless admiration for you. Those who keep law and order are the guardians of society."

"That's very kind of you." Part of Willi wanted to add that he'd been at many battles but never Verdun.

Fortunately a moment later someone else leaned in to talk over the noise of the party. "So tell me, what keeps you occupied while in exile, Inspector?" Willi looked up to see Trotsky with a drink in his hand. "I'm working on a history of the Russian Revolution."

Before Willi could reply an arm embraced him tightly around the shoulder. "Funny you should ask, Comrade." It was André.

Willi felt his cheeks burn.

If only he could confess what had happened at 36 quai des Orfèvres. André was such a powerful man, friends in the highest places. But who was more powerful, André or Police Judiciaire? Willi had no idea. It was odd Victoir Orsini wasn't here. Was it that he no longer wished to be associated with the Duvals—or did that have nothing to do with it? Why wouldn't he have his picture taken that day with André at the racetrack? Willi felt blind, dumb, his foreignness making it almost impossible to assess the cultural nuances. But at least, he consoled himself, he hadn't let the cat out of the bag to that weasel Clouitier about the emeralds. God, how he wished André had never told him that story.

"I believe I've found Willi quite an excellent new position," André declared proudly to Comrade Trotsky.

Willi sucked in his breath, not expecting it to come this fast. Maybe, he rationalized, he could balance on a tightrope awhile without hurting anyone—until he saw a way out.

"Yes, the owner of a small but influential newspaper happens to be looking for an ace reporter. An investigative reporter, naturally. Which is right up Willi's alley."

"Ahh!" Trotsky beamed as Willi tried to hide his shock. "Then that's another thing we have in common, Comrade Kraus!" Trotsky raised his glass just as fireworks started exploding around the Eiffel Tower, red, white, and blue igniting the Parisian sky. "Both of us, diggers for the truth!"

Book Two

CHÂTEAU DE CARTES

(House of Cards)

Eleven

JULY 1933

La Vérité—The Truth, as Willi grasped it—was a biweekly scandal sheet catering to the rich and powerful. Barely veiled political exposés and allegations of financial fraud were mingled with innuendos of love triangles and impending divorce. What Willi was doing at their cramped little offices in the Boulevard Poissonnière he only slowly ascertained. Henri Beliveau, publisher and managing editor, was offering an on-the-job orientation while tending to a forest of plants.

"I realize investigative reporting isn't exactly your line of work, Inspector." Beliveau balanced on a ladder while watering a pot of ivy, a short, rather comical figure, Willi thought, his head too small for his waxed mustache. It seemed to flap birdlike across his face. "When you think about it though"—he had to speak loudly over the din of ringing phones—"reporters and detectives aren't that different." He soared to his toes making sure the ivy was soaked. "Posing questions, getting answers." He maneuvered down, wiping his forehead. "That's all. You needn't worry about article writing or anything." He pounced on a violet, plucking dead leaves and crushing them. "We'll take care of all the technicalities. You just unearth the facts." He grimaced at his fingernails. "Sort of a plainclothes cop."

He'd almost succeeded in reassuing Willi until they were alone in his office. Then the tightrope Willi had been hoping to balance on—giving the police as much as possible without hurting André—seemed to fray underfoot. His first assignment, the editor explained, rummaging for something in his desk, was to get to the source of some ugly attacks on France's most successful bond house, Confiance Royale.

Willi's brains seemed to scramble. It was either a sickening coincidence or a sadistic setup. How many ways was he being played here? Unemployed for weeks, he was suddenly twice employed—first by the police to spy on André, then by André via this newspaper to spy on . . . whom? The whole crazy picture unfurled like a Picasso painting, everything refracted with bizarre polarity. Each of his new "bosses" had laid out the same task—from diametric angles: Clouitier wanting to know if these rumors, whatever they were, were true, André wanting to find out who was spreading them. It was beyond a balancing act. More like a slide down a sharpened razor. His armpits were getting damp.

Beliveau opened a manicure kit on his desk, examining its contents while laying out the situation. Three of the largest insurance companies in France—Compagnie d'Assurances Générale, La Paternel, and Lloyd de France, all of which were also the largest holders of Confiance Royale bonds—had each received anonymous letters last week strongly urging "abstention" from any further dealings with the company. The editor selected a curve-tipped digging rod from his manicure arsenal.

"In an industry founded on faith"—Beliveau began meticulously digging the dirt from beneath his nails—"it's all but a declaration of war." He puffed, rooting furiously. "Your job is to find out who fired the shots." He looked at Willi with a thin smile. "Why so glum? You're back on the job again, Inspector. No need even to show up here if you don't wish. Just get to the bottom of this, sooner than later."

It wasn't a tightrope but a minefield. A single misstep and . . .

"Monsieur Beliveau"—Willi reminded himself he'd been through minefields before—"tell me, what is *your* opinion on this matter?" He understood the editor would never be able to speak freely, but also that nonverbal reactions could say as much. He recalled the *bouquiniste*. "Do you think there might be merit to these warnings about Duval's company?"

Beliveau instantly stopped filing. "Monsieur Kraus." He expelled an aggrieved sigh. "I don't know how things are in Berlin, but Paris is not Aristotle's Athens." His black mustache fluttered. "There isn't a company in France that some charge or another couldn't be leveled against. Monsieur Duval is an honorable man, no?" He looked at Willi, making it clear he was well aware of their friendship.

"Let me ask you one last thing." Willi had a dim sensation of floating out to sea. Clinging to the side of Beliveau's desk, he tried to keep his chin up. "Do you invest your money with him?"

Beliveau threw his head back with a small, sardonic laugh. "Yes, of course, all my millions—and they just keep multiplying!"

"Worked out rather nicely I'd say," Clouitier looked pleased enough to hear about Willi's new job. He leaned back in his office chair at police headquarters drumming on the desktop. "*La Vérité*. I told you Monsieur Duval would figure something out. And you're to find out the source of these warnings? So you'll be poking your nose right in the thick of things. Very nice. Just make sure to report every week, eh, without fail. And, Kraus"—the chair let out a scream as Clouitier sat up—"don't try any funny stuff. We have other people on this case. It would be most ill-advised to hold anything back."

Willi was trapped, forced to betray the closest thing he had in France to family. Unless he wanted to face that hell ride back to Germany, all he could do now was proceed as ordered and hope—a dangerous road to go. There was only one logical place to start. With a clammy sensation he picked up the phone and set up an appointment for the following afternoon at four to visit Confiance Royale.

He was miserable the next day, leaving his apartment late, giving himself just half an hour to get there. It was pouring rain. His feet got soaked halfway to the corner as he dreamed of America or Canada, anyplace you didn't have to stab people in the back to survive. He'd mastered one or two bus routes by now and often took the #25 on boulevard de Bonne Nouvelle to run errands or pick up the boys, usually around this time. Today though, as he neared the stop along the boulevard, his feet refused to proceed. He couldn't believe his eyes. Through rain ahead, huddled under an umbrella, the beauty mark on her cheek seeming to beckon him, was Vivi. He felt the blood tingle in his veins. He'd looked for her everywhere and there she stood, practically in front of his building.

When the bus arrived, so many people were trying to get on he was afraid he wouldn't make it. As luck would have it though, he got the last seat. Vivi was six or seven people ahead facing him. She was wearing a trench coat turned up at the collar and a low-slung hat, her red lips pouting as she broke out her black journal and began scribbling. When she crossed her legs in their sheer rayon stockings, Willi was embarrassed to have to use his hat to cover his lap.

As they inched along in the rain, boulevard de Bonne Nouvelle changed into boulevard Poissonnière. He hoped a seat would open nearer to her but more people kept getting on. He had to strain to catch whatever glimpses he could. Finally, as boulevard Monmartre changed into boulevard Haussmann, he saw her rise and squeeze down the aisle. Almost exactly as she passed him, she glanced his way, and for an instant their eyes collided. Passion boiled through his veins.

Every inch of him wanted to get off and follow her, but checking his watch, he saw it was already four. Desperate, he twisted around trying to see out the window where she was going, catching her just as she entered the employee entrance to Galeries Lafayette.

Arriving late, he found himself pressing a buzzer at the ornate gates of what looked like a small palace, a bronze plaque to one side proclaiming CONFIANCE ROYALE. All he could think of was Vivi. Perhaps, if she really did work at Galeries Lafayette, he might be able to find her. It was only Paris's most massive department store.

The chief financial officer, one M. Hubert, greeted him in the lobby with a clumsy handshake. A surprisingly handsome man, he spoke in such a dreary monotone Willi wondered if the guy was trying to hypnotize him.

". . . a fully state-regulated, certified brokerage . . . duly approved, authorized . . . endorsed by state ministers as well as the Board of Finance." Hubert droned all the way up a long, winding staircase, his shoes squeaking a dull accompaniment. Reaching a blue-carpeted hallway filled with chandeliers and mirrors, he opened a set of carved doors and showed Willi the executive boardroom. "We have the highest rating of any independent bond house in France."

Willi hadn't come here without reading up on the matter, and there was little doubt about the company's success. What he found interesting was less its achievement than its trajectory. Confiance Royale had performed outstandingly from its inception in 1921, but not until 1929, when it put together a bond offering dividends at an irresistible 8 percent, did it explode into a national mania from which it had yet to emerge. Article after article touted Duval's financial wizardry at being able to keep afloat such propitious packages, year after year. Even in the throes of the Great Depression, the company's spring 1933 release—two hundred thousand bonds at five hundred francs each—sold out within half a day. From the docks of Marseille to the tables at Maxim's, everyone in France wanted in.

The offices reflected the extent and lavishness of Duval's achievement. Exquisitely inlaid parquet floors, the richest mahogany furnishings, departments not only for bond sales but land development, public works, a construction unit. The whole place emanated solidity and assurance.

"About these anonymous warnings . . ." Willi took out a pad and pen. How ironic, he was thinking, that for the first time in his life he truly hoped whatever he uncovered was useless to the police. "How does Confiance plan to respond?"

"There are always jealous people," M. Hubert replied with drowsy regret. "Our books are multiple-checked by our own as well as outside auditors." He forced his hands into a monklike clasp as they passed a secretarial pool, half a dozen well-groomed women putting on airs of great efficiency as they typed. "Naturally in private"—he lowered his voice—"we've taken great pains to reassure our investors."

André appeared down the hall, his waves of copper hair shining under the incandescent bulbs. Even at twenty paces he radiated energy. The idolizing look on the secretary he was addressing reflected his ability to make a person feel there was no one else he'd rather be talking to.

"Willi!" he called as soon as he saw him, striding down the hall. "Fantastic you could make it." He clasped both Willi's hands, his bright eyes sparkling. "How do you like this place? Amazing, huh? Used to be an aristocrat's town house. Come." The emerald on his pinkie beckoned. "I'll show you my hideaway."

Not Renaissance Revival but genuine Renaissance, André's office had floor-to-ceiling Flemish tapestries, mounted suits of armor, and an antique map of Europe beneath which he sat like Lorenzo de' Medici.

"You must be angry with me." The gray eyes lowered, the long lashes seeming to bow with penitence. "I'm sorry I didn't explain right away. For both our protections though, I thought it better you didn't work directly for me, you understand?" His gaze reached out hopefully, then darkened, the veneer of confidence suddenly stripping off. Fumbling for a cigarette, he let out an injured sigh. "Anyway, now that you know . . ." His fingers were unsteady as he tried to light up. Willi had never seen him so anxious, never seen him smoke. "I hope you can get to the bottom of this. It's like a knife in my side. I've no idea who could have done it, Willi." Dark moons hung under his eyes. "I've been wracking my brains trying to figure it out. Now of all times, when I'm this close to announcing the Pan-Europa Bond." His gaze fixed desperately on Willi through a haze of smoke.

Willi felt for him. His friend looked like a nervous wreck. Now that the tables were turned, Willi hoped he could be the one to offer a helping hand. He didn't mince words. "You need to be honest with me."

"Of course! Why else would I have brought you in?"

"Then tell me, André"—Willi stared into his friend's glistening eyes—"how many people out there would like to see you destroyed?"

"Destroyed?" André's eyes faded. "I can't even conceive it." He clasped his thumbs in his fists. "I mean, I'm aware people dislike me, Willi. Find me brash, overconfident." He shifted in his seat. "Plenty envy my achievements. Others dislike what I'm trying to achieve. But *hate* me, enough to try to destroy me?" He threw up both hands. Slowly, though, his movie-star face grew pinched by what Willi sensed was a painful memory. "There's ony one I'm aware of who might feel that strongly. Well . . . perhaps two."

Twelve

That night Willi went to the Gottmans' to see his sons for dinner.

"Hey, everybody," he said at the table, figuring there was no point delaying it, "you're looking at a man with a new career: *un journaliste d'investigation*. I landed a job today—at a newspaper of all places, *La Vérité*."

Max Gottman looked impressed. "How did you get that, without papers? That's a reputable journal."

"Yes, Willi, how?" Ava's face reddened. "As I recall, your written French is pretty terrible."

Willi sympathized with her indignation. He had no right to the job. She was the one with a degree in journalism and experience working for *Ulstein Press* in Berlin. "The emphasis I believe is more on investigative than reporter," he tried to mollify her.

"But how can you work without papers?" Bette Gottman twisted a napkin with her fingers. Willi's dark mood since his arrival in Paris had been evident to all. No one could deny a job would do him good. But they were refugees after all. "If you're caught with-out permits, I hear you're on a train back to Germany in hours—"

"The publisher's pretty well connected. He might be able to get me papers," Willi lied. "It's worth a try."

"I'd feel a lot better if you had them before you started," Ava insisted.

"Of course, but he can't just sit around forever." Max seemed to give his blessing. "A man like Willi's got to do something. Earn a living."

"Then it's great news, Willi." Ava attempted to sound as if she meant it.

"Thank you." He gulped down some wine.

After dinner he and the boys took the Gottmans' retrievers for a walk.

"Dad, how come you don't like Aunt Ava anymore?" Erich turned to him with arrowlike aim.

"Why would you say such a thing?" Willi was mortified. He thought he'd done a good job masking his feelings.

"Because you barely speak to her," the boy observed. "And when you do, you don't even look at her."

"You don't like Aunt Ava?" Stefan was trying to figure this out.

"Of course I do." Willi hated to undermine his son's perceptions, but he had no patience just then to explain his complex feelings. "I've just been distracted, that's all."

He'd given up the fantasy of being a perfect father.

Erich though would make one hell of a detective.

It was the last week of July, and the boys, like much of Paris, were preparing to flee on holiday, their grandparents having rented a cottage on the Norman coast.

"They still need a million things," Ava informed Willi as he kissed them good-night. "I'll have to take them shopping tomorrow."

"Then I'll come too," he casually suggested. "Why don't we meet at ten o'clock, say . . . Galeries Lafayette?"

She eyed him suspiciously knowing full well shopping was his least favorite activity, especially in giant department stores. But Galeries Lafayette, she agreed, was fine with her.

They met at the main entrance.

"And of course they'll need bathing suits," Ava said as they pushed through the swinging doors. "We didn't bring a single one from Germany."

Willi tried not to start looking immediately for Vivi, though he could hardly help it.

"Will it be the ocean or the sea we're near?" Stefan was jumping with excitement.

"Neither, dummy," Erich snapped at him.

"Hey!" Willi scolded more harshly than he'd have liked. "Just because he's smaller doesn't mean you can abuse him."

"It's not the ocean *or* the sea, all right? It's the English Channel," Erich repented.

The place was jammed, a labyrinth of people and display cases. The chances of finding anyone in such a maze were minuscule, Willi realized hopelessly. Perhaps he'd come back, use his badge, check the employee rolls. How many women could be named Vivi?

Even with ninety-six departments Ava knew the exact route to the children's section.

"Are you ready?" The boys stopped Willi, insisting he close his eyes when they reached the main hall. This grande dame of Parisian department stores was a pleasure he had managed to avoid all these years, even when he'd been in Paris with Vicki. But he'd heard enough about Galeries' famed glass cupola.

"Okay, look up!"

He opened his eyes and was instantly swept into a spectacle of architectural splendor. A dome that seemed to rival St. Peter's arched overhead in a celestial whirl of colored glass and wrought iron, a majestic brocade of iridescent oranges and peacock blues encircled by levels of scalloped balconies in an orgy of curves. He'd never seen anything like it. All perspective grew askew in an extraordinary optical illusion, his eyes unable to discern whether the dome was concave or convex, whether he was looking up or down, or even—the longer he stared—if the whole thing hadn't begun spinning like a giant kaleidoscope. Gradually he felt his body almost lifted off the ground, and his mind begin to tumble backward, back, back, until he was seeing not this dome but the giant dome of the Reichstag building that nightmarish night last February when the whole world seemed to collapse in shattering glass and flame.

"Come." Ava tapped him. "Children's wear's on two."

Trailing the others up the grand staircase, golden light poured through the opaque cupola, illuminating the vast hall below with its maze of counters and salesgirls hawking scarves, gloves, wallets, watches. A sudden flash accompanied what felt like a blow to the forehead. There she was . . . behind one of the counters.

"These ensemble suits are quite the rage," the saleslady upstairs announced beneath a sign proclaiming THE NEWEST VOGUE FOR LITTLE MEN. "They have their own belt and buckle and this very handsome harmonizing tie."

Willi couldn't concentrate. Could he excuse himself and go back down? What would he do, confront her? Use the badge and make her talk? He had it in his pocket. But with Ava and the kids here?

". . . ideal for active boys. Roomy, comfortable, extremely popular . . ."

He'd made use of André's gift more than once already. A few days after his penetration into the Sûreté Générale, he'd employed it to get into the Department of Vehicles Registration, inquiring about a little cabin cruiser called *Achille Baptiste*. He hadn't forgotten the murder of Phillipe Junot, nor the *bouquiniste*. The yacht he'd found out was berthed at the Port de l'Arsenal. Why couldn't he shake the feeling he knew the name Achille Baptiste too, from somewhere other than that boat?

More nerve-racking was when he'd used the badge to enter police headquarters itself. If anyone at 36 quai des Orfèvres got suspicious or checked the name First Inspector Olivier Boucher against the rosters, Willi knew, he was doomed. André's forgery though was apparently a gem, for Willi not only breezed into the building but easily gained access to the pathology report from Phillipe Junot's postmortem. The kid, Willi learned, had died of a single stab wound—no surprise. But the tiny size of the entering puncture—there was even a photo of it—made the nature of the weapon, according to the report, undeterminable. What kind of blade was so thin and skewerlike, yet so instantly deadly?

"Elastic waistbands are *très* up-to-the-minute. It keeps the shirt tucked in no matter how hard the youngster plays."

"Go behind the curtains and try these on," Ava instructed the boys. "Then come out and show us."

"I'm sure they'll love them." The saleswoman hovered. "Mothers love them too." She smiled at Ava. "They're so easy to launder."

"Thanks," Ava said with a slight crack in her voice. When the lady finally gave them space, Ava was still a moment before flashing a taunting glance Willi's way. "I've been meaning to ask, how's that job going for Monsieur Duval?"

"Duval?" He turned, startled. "I told you I work for a newspaper."

She snorted. She obviously hadn't relinquished her opposition to André, and it sent a familiar chill through him. She could be so obstinate.

"From what I hear, there's no difference."

"What's that supposed to mean?"

"It means"—she faced him with a small, blue vein popping in her neck—"that once upon a time the owner of a *La Vérité* was a big critic of your pal André. Then overnight"—she snapped her lovely fingers—"he made an about-face. Now he's one of Duval's biggest boosters. Isn't that strange, Willi?" Her chestnut eyes flamed.

Willi took a step back. "What are you implying Ava, that André bought him off? Who's your source?"

"Marc Nathanson." She raised an eyebrow, then dropped it with what seemed a tug of regret.

"Who the hell is Marc Nathanson?"

"You met him at the Hebraic Assistance League, Levy's brother-in-law.

Ah, yes, Willi remembered now: that creep who'd kissed Ava's hand. *Until I am lucky enough to behold you again.*

"He and I have been . . . spending time. I happened to mention your new position and he told me the whole story. I thought you ought to know."

"Yes, well, thank you. Would you excuse me? I really need to find a men's room." He turned and walked away from her.

Hurrying down the great sweeping staircase, he looked up at the glass dome and felt his whole world tilt off-kilter again. Just focus, he told himself, fighting to resist the hundred thoughts spinning through his brain. As he carefully scanned the direction he thought he'd seen her before, halfway down his kneecaps jammed. He clutched the iron rail. It was her all right, behind the perfume counter, spraying someone with Chanel No. 5. His heartbeat quickened. As soon as he could, he'd have to come back and follow her.

"But you've got it all wrong, Kraus!" Henri Beliveau gave a shrill, amused laugh. His mustache came to rest as he stroked the begonia on his desk. "The truth is quite opposite—it's terrible what we news-papermen must do to survive." He twisted a dying leaf. "We're all being driven mad by competition, desperate to transform some ob-scure incident into a national melodrama. The whole French press is addicted to scandalmongering. I think it's the fault of the mass dai-lies. They've completely withered the intellectual content of—"

"Monsieur Beliveau." Willi tried not to sound as irritated as he was, but now that he had two jobs, he felt he could afford a slightly less browbeaten posture. "Please get to the point."

"Pardon me. I'm French after all." The waxed extensions hovered. "I know how Germans love efficiency so I'll make an attempt at bluntness." Beliveau pushed aside the begonia. "When an influential newspaper such as *La Vérité* prepares to attack a person of high fi-nance, whether or not the charges have substance is of little conse-quence: it is *always* the newspaper that comes out on top, *comprenez?* Financiers know only too well it's better to settle before damages occur, because in the money business reputation is worth all. Usually this 'settlement' takes the form of an advertising contract. In my case—one that keeps this utterly profitless enterprise of mine from sinking into the sea, *comprenez?*" Beneath the black wax the tiny mouth twisted into a smirk of satisfaction. "So you see, Inspector, your source did in fact have it ass-backward."

Hourly, Paris emptied of inhabitants. Anyone who could was off. The richer, the farther. Where Claude Vermette was headed Willi had no idea—only that from across the rue de Charonne he could see the nervous, wiry fellow tying suitcases to the roof of an old Renault, repeatedly checking over his shoulder as if locusts were about to descend on Paris. The longer Willi watched, the more the man appeared in a borderline frenzy, his hair blowing crazily as he scurried back and forth lugging one valise out after another, tossing them atop his car and tying them on, keeping an eye all the while over his shoulder. Willi pulled his hat lower before crossing the street. This guy was on the run from more than just summer in the city.

"Monsieur Vermette—"

The man froze, turning his head from the car roof.

André had said only one person hated him enough to possibly want to launch a smear campaign—and this was him. André had sketched the picture that afternoon in his office, smoking cigarette after cigarette, so upset he couldn't even sit, just paced in his double-breasted suit and hand-sewn Italian shoes.

"A few years back when I was extremely flush, including I might add, from an extraordinary night at the roulette wheel, which I'll tell you about sometime"—André's fingers had set an antique globe spinning—"I allowed myself to indulge in yet another of my passions: the theater." Willi could barely see through the smoke, only that emerald on André's pinkie; it sparkled so. "A grand old place on the boulevard Bonne Nouvelle called the Queen." Willi recalled passing it on the way here. It didn't look so grand.

"I refurbished her with the intention of presenting unknown plays, discovering new talent." André's gleaming gray eyes sought acknowledgment. "Nurturing the next generation of artists, you know." He spun the globe again, round and round. "To run the place I hired an avant-garde playwright and director widely regarded as one of the best of his generation. Up and down this Claude Vermette assured me he would turn the Queen into the greatest theater in Paris. But some people's genius"—Duval stopped the globe—"is short-lived. Vermette's died painfully. Play after play.

"After two years I'd had enough. The Queen had become a heartache, so I sold her. They turned it into a burlesque house—which it still is today. Vermette never forgave me. He accused me of destroying his life. Ruining his reputation. Sullying the good name of French theater. Kept showing up, verbally attacking me in public, once at a wedding, another time in front of a restaurant, even challenged me to a duel. The man is really quite crazy, Willi. And it only got worse. Eventually I had no choice but to use strong-arm tactics on him. After that, I never saw him again, but he's the only one I can think of with irrational hatred enough to want to do something like this to me."

"What exactly do you mean, André, by 'strong-arm tactics'?"

André looked away a moment, then back at Willi earnestly. "Threats, that's all. Some very large men. Scared the shit out of him."

"How long ago was that?"

"Two, maybe two and a half years."

Willi took a breath, glad at least he'd gotten here before the playwright made his getaway.

"Who the fuck are you?" Vermette jumped from the luggage on his car roof, his posture indicating he was either ready to make a dash or pull a gun. Not a healthy-looking specimen, Willi saw: forty, maybe forty-five, prematurely gray, dressed in a suit years out-of-date, his fingers covered in orange nicotine stains. His tense brown eyes seemed unable to achieve a moment's peace. They quivered as if receiving a low-dose electric current.

"I'd like to ask a few questions."

"Oh no, no, no. I'm way too busy."

"Just a few."

"Get lost—"

"It's a subject you'll be interested in."

Vermette paused long enough to run the stained fingers through his frazzled hair.

"What are you, cop? A reporter?"

"Which would you prefer?"

"Screw you." Vermette turned and went inside.

Willi could have kicked himself for getting snide, but even the most seasoned pro fumbled now and then. It was this assignment.

He didn't want to be doing it. Didn't want to be spying on André. Or for him. Or whatever the fuck he was doing. Luckily he didn't lose the guy. Vermette reappeared a moment later not with a suitcase, but four fat pugs on leashes, wheezing and snorting like piglets.

"I'm a reporter," Willi tried again, watching him throw the squealing things into the backseat. "Doing a story on André Duval."

For a second, even the dogs seemed to hush.

The car door slammed. Vermette took a breath and turned to Willi, staring at him with dark, pulsing eyes. "I've got to get the hell out of here."

Sensing no possibility of cooperation, Willi opted for shock. "You still hate him, don't you, Vermette?" He observed the man's haggard face, his nervous body, the balling hands. He was bitter all right. And fearful. Not just of André. But of life. The compulsively twisting neck, the popping eyes, the crazy, frazzled hair, all seemed to mirror an unmistakable paranoia.

"Me, hate him?" He gave an exaggerated laugh. "Now why would I do that?" He reached for the driver's door.

Willi wasn't quite ready to play his police card yet, so he let him by. He'd taken the license number. It wouldn't be hard to track him.

"Besides how could anyone *hate* André Duval?" Vermette squeezed in behind the wheel, fishing for keys. "What an idea! A man who promises to help someone reach the pinnacle of self-expression, all the backing they'll ever need, all the support—then dumps them like a child's toy? Ha! A man whose every breath persuades of his trust, his confidence in someone's brilliance, then who gets in his limousine and pushes them in a cesspool—sending a goon squad after to rub in the shit!? Does that sound like someone hateful to you?"

Vermette found the keys. In the Renault's backseat the pugs were melting into a drooling mass. Vermette's stained fingers reached for the ignition. "If you really want to know"—the motor rumbled on—"ask Lulu." For a moment Willi feared this might be one of the dogs—but apparently not. "She'll tell you all about it." Vermette gripped the clutch so tightly his knuckles whitened. "She was the one he was going to make the world's greatest star."

He slammed the gear into place, then looked at Willi through the open window. "Now let me ask *you* something, mister." The dark eyes shimmied. "Didn't you ever wonder how a town the size of Avignon could offer bonds with such generous terms, when everywhere else interest rates were plummeting? Didn't you once ask yourself?" Small bits of foam oozed from the corners of Vermette's mouth as he released the hand brake.

Willi stepped aside to let him go.

The frazzled man threw up his hands, then turned the steering wheel with his orange fingers. As he drove off, Willi heard him singing the famous, old French children's song loudly as possible:

On the Bridge of Avignon—
We all dance there . . . we all dance there.

Thirteen

Paris was unearthly quiet that hot August day. Even the halls at 36 quai des Orfèvres echoed not with clerks or typewriters but with Willi's lonely footsteps. Inspector Clouitier, waiting just for him it seemed, sat behind a desk cleared of all files. Willi took the chair opposite trying not to look forlorn and began his report.

He started with Vermette.

"Not what you'd call a portrait of mental health. Nurtures a grudge the size of Siberia. Cast aspersions"—he had to battle what felt like a cat clawing inside his throat—"on the value of bonds issued by Confiance Royale, although I doubt his assessment would stand up to Ministry of Finance scrutiny. Listen, Inspector, what I'd really like to do is get my hands on the original letters sent to the insurance companies and see if they match. It could be we're looking for more than one person here. Unfortunately, since I'm not on the force—"

"I'll make sure you get them." Clouitier made a big display of writing himself a memo. "What about Lulu Jourdain?"

Jourdain? Willi's neck tensed. He hadn't said a word about her. Was he being spied on? Or did the inspector just associate the two—Vermette and Jourdain—from their old theatrical alliance?

"I used to be quite a fan," Cloutier acknowledged with a small, nostalgic sigh.

Willi had found Désireé, née Lulu, Jourdain under a hairdryer at a posh salon in the sixteenth arrondissement, practically around the corner from where the Gottmans lived. André himself had given Willi the address, or more precisely André's secretary, who called to say Mme. Crevecour—for that was her married name—could be found Fridays at 2:00 p.m. at Salon Sasha on the avenue Henri-Martin.

"*Bonjour,* Madame Crevecour?" He practically had to shout to get her attention. "I'm from *La Vérité.*"

"A who?" She frowned, motioning for him to lift the thing off her head.

She stared at Willi with large, overly attentive eyes, her hair screwed tightly in curlers. The stench of permanent-wave solution mixed with nail polish was dizzying. Plus the whole place, including the ceiling, was covered in a vine-print wallpaper that made Willi feel like a beetle in a jungle.

"*La Vérité.* I'd like to ask a few questions."

"Not another retrospective. I've nothing more to say!"

"The subject's André Duval, madame."

"Duval? What about him? And why are you bothering me here of all places? Can't a woman get a little peace anymore at her own salon?"

"I'm terribly sorry. I only need a few moments."

"Well, then you'll have to wait. I'm almost dry."

Almost proved another forty minutes.

Finally she transferred to a styling chair. "All right Mr.—"

"Boucher." Willi tried to smile. Despite the unmistakable accent he always found Parisians better disposed when he used a French rather than a German name. "Olivier Boucher."

"Very well." She didn't smile back. "What can I tell you about André Duval that hasn't already been written?"

"Isn't there somewhere we might speak in private?" He addressed her reflection in the mirror. She was good-looking, even in curlers. He could see why she'd been an actress—ivory skin, eyes that made her face dance.

"Not unless you want to wait all over again." Her brows collapsed in despair. "I must get my comb-out. I'm having a dinner party tonight for some of my husband's associates. Besides, you can say whatever you'd like in front of Veronique. She won't repeat a word, will you?"

"Me?" The stylist frowned.

Willi didn't like it but didn't feel like waiting either. The fumes around here were reminding him of the Western Front. "Somebody suggested you might be able to offer a unique perspective on Duval."

"Somebody? Oh, Jesus, not Vermette." She laughed. "Nobody pays attention to that crackpot."

"Madame must try to be still." Veronique was yanking out curlers.

"He doesn't much care for Mr. Duval," Willi pressed. "Said you might be able to shed some light on his character."

"Character! Well, it doesn't take an engineer to figure out Duval. I worked with him long enough to know how that man operates. He promises everyone plus their uncle the world and delivers what he can. Ow! Veronique!"

"I warned you."

"Do you think he's honest?"

She shrugged, parting her lips. "Let's put it this way, Monsieur Boucher: he's definitely sincere. In fact he's the most sincere man I've ever met. When André Duval believes in something, it's all the way. Of course, that's not necessarily for the best, is it?" Her wan smile soured. "He genuinely believed he could make something of our crummy little theater. Did everything first-rate. Sets. Costumes. Advertising. Treated us like royalty. Vermette most of all, yes. But the sad truth is you can't make something out of nothing, can you? As an actress I was strictly second-rate. Now I can say it. Truth hurts only when it's too near. And Vermette, well, he was popping so many pills his head was inside out. His work went from outré to insufferable.

Don't take my word; look up the reviews. André might have found another director, another star, but I think for him the magic had worn off. He had other causes. Maybe he's a dilettante. The real crime was that he didn't get out sooner. Too much confidence, that's André's fault. Blind confidence, in himself and in others."

"So you're not bitter?"

"Me? Ha! I'd never have met my darling Maurice had I continued in those rotten plays. *Mon Dieu!* I have a far better life now. Each day I count my bessings."

"I appreciate your time, Madame Crevecour. You've been most informative."

"Have I? Then I'm thrilled."

"Then who do you think *is* behind it?" Clouitier checked his watch.

"I wish I could offer such an early hypothesis, Inspector."

Vermette had motive enough to go after Duval, but it was too soon to jump to such conclusions. Others on were still Willi's list. Drag your heels, he kept telling himself. There's got to be some way through this without harming André. Or yourself.

André had mentioned a second person who might have had enough animosity to launch a smear campaign, but refused to give a name.

"How can I help if you don't tell me?"

"Because I really don't think it could be him." André had seemed upset at the idea, although Willi had a strange sense he was overdoing it. "Our quarrel's not . . . well, personal."

"Then why not tell me?"

"I just don't want to, Willi. That's all. Please. Drop the subject. Lucien had nothing to do with it."

So that was it. Family. André finally confessed. Adrienne's brother, Lucien Ruehl, trade unionist and radical leftist, had denounced his brother-in-law at every opportunity, more than once calling André an "evil genius."

"I've no idea where he is," André insisted. "We haven't had contact in years."

"What about Adrienne?"

He shook his head sadly, no. No contact at all.

"Unfortunately finding people in Paris this time of year"—Willi made excuses now to Inspector Clouitier—"isn't always feasible. I may have to wait until the end of summer holidays."

"I'm off on summer holidays too now, Inspector, so you'll have to keep plugging alone. I hope you're planning on being Duval's guest at the Grand Prix next week. His horse is top contender."

"He hasn't invited me."

"Well, make sure he does." The ferret eyes widened. "I'll want a full report Kraus, the first Monday of September."

Across from police headquarters Willi stood along the promenade looking down at the river, sweat beading on his forehead. The left branch of the Seine here ran cradled deep in stone embankments, long steps leading down to a narrow esplanade along the water's edge. Even from above you could see the reeds swaying back and forth, back and forth, in the sparkling currents, the nearby bells of Notre Dame accompanying them with melodies. September, he reminded himself, was still a month away. All that time to disentangle himself.

The wise thing would be to start off right away in search of André's brother-in-law. But the summer heat and sense of reprieve set his feet on a route all their own. The boys were in Normandy. He was in Paris by himself. The city never seemed hotter, emptier. Even the tourists appeared to have fled. Across the Right Bank he trekked to boulevard Haussmann. The halls of Galeries Lafayette were plenty crowded. Winding toward the perfume counter, he tried to dampen his expectations. When he saw her there though, his chest flamed.

That nasty black eye had apparently healed—at least externally. She was taking care of customers with an air of dignified efficiency, using an atomizer to spray wrists or inner elbows. It didn't appear she indulged in chitchat, but clearly she knew what pleased. In the short time Willi watched her Vivi made multiple sales.

Circling nearer, he could hardly help but be captivated all over again by her innate sensuality, the arms so white when she reached for bottles, her rear end so round when she bent, her breasts pressing so firmly against her blue cotton blouse. He could hardly keep from going over to talk to her. The pouty lips made her look like a child edging on thorny petulance. But she was so sweet too . . . a wild rose.

He hung around the store for several hours, and when she finished her shift, he followed her. She dressed like a lot of girls on the bus only brighter, flashier, her skirt a little tighter, her open-toed high heels showing off painted nails. The jet-black hair with its de rigueur permanent wave was parted sharply to one side, clipped with a sparkling ruby barrette. She wore a fake beauty mark on her left cheek, and a long rhinestone necklace. None of it fit in with where she disembarked.

It was a working-class neighborhood in the twelfth arrondissement. Not working-class in the sense of factory hands but "good" people, railroad engineers and skilled technicians. Rue de Madagascar, where she turned, seemed to have everything one could want: a butcher, a grocer, shoemaker. Old ladies on chairs sat watching children play. Little groups of men stood smoking pipes. It had the feel of a country village.

Vivi clutched her necklace, lowering her gaze as she walked, clearly not wanting to make eye contact, her high heels clacking the faster she went. Near the end of the block she ducked into a small dress shop, Belle Nouvelle Vous. Beautiful New You.

Approaching it, Willi slowed by the open window.

"Again nothing?" he heard a shrill woman behind the counter. "How could a store that size have nothing all week? You'd better live up to your end of the bargain, missy—or change naked on the street."

Withdrawing, Willi purchased some mints next door, perusing the newspaper headlines, hoping Vivi didn't linger. Too many people were lurking about. Luckily in a matter of minutes she darted back out to the sidewalk—dressed it seemed as someone else. Gone were the flashy barrette and tight dress, the rhinestone necklace and open-toed shoes. She was in some kind of school uniform now, blue beret pulled over her head, her feet in tasseled loafers with opaque hose, a navy blazer embossed with a crest—Richelieu Secretarial Academy.

"I'll bring something wonderful tomorrow, Marianne," she called over her shoulder. "Promise!"

As she hurried down the block, Willi saw the beauty mark was gone, the lips no longer red, her face scrubbed clean as a nun's. At the last apartment house on the block she unlocked the door and slipped in. He could hear frantic footsteps running all the way to the top.

As much as possible he trailed her all week. Her life seemed fairly circumscribed. Aside from her job the only place she went was the post office near the Polytechnique. Why there, so far out of her way? He'd seen her exit it before. This time she came out absorbed in another letter, typewritten, not even pausing to look up at the bistro where she used to meet Junot. Did she miss him? How had she learned of his murder? If only Willi could talk to her. It was getting harder to keep away.

On lunch breaks she went to a café near the Opéra, always by herself. She'd jot in a small black diary or simply people-watch. She stared intensely, as if trying to figure out something about each passing person, how the person dressed, how the person walked. Her fascination was entrancing. Willi couldn't stop watching her watch. What was she trying to gain from those she studied with such concentration? She didn't seem to want to socialize. When men came up, she brushed them off. Was she still in mourning for Junot? She worked long shifts and every evening changed into her stodgy uniform before running home. Why the double life?

Then strangely, Willi began to see her even when he wasn't following. It was as if she'd gotten burned into his retinas. Alone, waiting for a bus, he pictured her long legs stepping across the street. Returning home, he found her welcoming arms open for him. When he wasn't seeing her, he felt he was missing something. He couldn't even keep away on Sunday, when she went to church with her parents.

They were proud-looking people in their early forties, the father mild-mannered, vain perhaps, the mother handsome but worn. The couple held hands as they walked down rue de Madagascar. Several times the father tried to take Vivi's hand too, but she rebuffed him. After church they went to a park. Willi sat with his back toward them trying to eavesdrop. A flock of geese got in the way, but there was no missing the quarrel that erupted.

"Because I don't want to. I'm not a child anymore!" Vivi burst out much too loudly.

"You certainly do act like one," the mother shot back. "I don't understand your reasoning. You'll have an honorable career after school. Papa and I make every sacrifice for you. There's nothing you don't get."

"Except breathing room. I'll kill myself. I swear to God!"

People all around had turned to stare.

"Okay now." Papa took her arm. Mother packed their things. The three walked home in silence.

Directly across from their apartment house was a bar, which Willi took refuge in. He had a hunch he wouldn't have to drink much, and sure enough midway through a Pernod, their building door flew open. Vivi emerged in a tight, black skirt, spit curls stamped across her cheeks, lips bloodred. She was toting an oversize, yellow suitcase, her mother yapping at her heels: "Don't you dare come back, you little bitch. Don't you dare!"

Fourteen

Willi had a pretty good hunch where she was headed, and sure enough Vivi hauled the yellow suitcase onto a streetcar straight to Bastille, checking the thing in a public locker and walking unencumbered by all the hotels promising COMFORT MODERNE. The big-hipped women stared from doorways. The corner toughs whistled as she passed. What surprised Willi was not where she went but how on a Sunday afternoon the rue du Lappe was every bit as congested as on a Saturday night.

All the bars and *bals musettes* were packed, each with an accordion band squeezing out a sad, earthy waltz, dance floors overflowing. How clearly he recalled Junot entering these same dingy halls, one after the next, wondering what the kid was up to. How he'd seen him whispering to the bartender at the Soiled Shirt, thinking they might have exchanged something. Remembered too Tondreau of the Sûreté telling him they thought Junot was a "runner" for some big gang. Passing the Soiled Shirt again, Willi saw that tall, bald guy behind the counter. He wouldn't mind stopping in for chat. But not now.

Now he watched Vivi enter the same dance hall where she used to meet Junot. The Red Room. Why here, of all places? Was it her favorite, or did she miss the Polytechnique student so she felt compelled to return? Had she loved him as much he had her? When they danced, it had seemed so to Willi. How would she react to hear his last words had been her name—would it soothe or feel like a knife in her gut? To Willi it'd be a relief anyway, getting it off his chest. He waited a minute, then pulled the door, following her in.

The familiar punch of cheap perfume and cigarette smoke hit his nose, his ears boxed by what sounded like a hundred people talking. Allowing his eyes to adjust, he took in the imitation-leather banquettes, the ball of mirrors, the crowds of girls in their long skirts and suspenders, oiled curls swirling across faces, the guys all with cigarettes hanging from mouths, caps pulled as far back as possible. And then . . . her. The raven waves, the ruby barrette, the small, black beauty mark, and pouty, red lips. Not necessarily the prettiest girl here but by far the most attractive, he thought. The one whose energy pulsed like those cymbals and snare drums. She stood by herself, watching couples revolving on the dance floor. Was she pining for her lost love, Willi wondered, as he had done here weeks ago? Or was she already on the hunt for something new?

Eventually, turning her head, she scanned the crowd with dark-outlined eyes. When they landed on him, they widened as if she recognized him. Did she remember that day on the bus? He fell back into the shadows. He'd lingered too long; she'd caught him staring. Now she was craning her neck, curious. What to do? Keep a distance or orchestrate an encounter? Eventually he'd have to talk to her he knew, but in what capacity? As whom? His stomach felt a sudden yank when he realized she was coming his way, his hands clammy, as if he were on a roller coaster.

In the spin of the mirrored ball she was there, a sweet perfume engulfing him, anesthetizing. From up close her skin looked velvety smooth, her eyes a shimmering opal. Her voice, an inexplicable mixture of hope and irony.

"Let me guess . . . you're a talent scout and want to make a big star of me."

A strange sensation came over him that she could tie a noose around his neck and he'd be powerless against it.

"Which is it, stage, movies?"

"Neither." He shook his head. "Sorry."

"Ah, *oui*." The red lips moved, so near he could feel the tingle of her breath. "Now I can see. You couldn't be in show business. No, you have too kind a face."

"Do I?"

"Yes. Too kind and too smart."

"You look nice too."

"Big complimenter. Tell me something, monsieur—"

"Willi."

"Monsieur Willi." Her chest expanded. "Why do I feel I know you?" Her eyebrows knit, perplexed but intrigued.

"I don't know why. We never met."

"I didn't say *met*. I said *know*." The red barrette flashed every time the mirrored ball turned. "I think . . . perhaps . . . something else." She peered into his eyes. "Don't tell me you don't feel it. What made you stare at me then?"

Had Clouitier's detectives spoken with her? he wondered. Did they even know she existed? What the hell should he say to her now, tell her he was a cop? A reporter? Tell her he'd been trailing her dead boyfriend and that he'd held him as he breathed his last? Confusion threatened to turn him into a blithering idiot.

"You're not even French, are you?" She tossed him a lifeline. "A stranger from far away, yes?"

"Far enough."

She sighed, the opal eyes latching onto him in an expression of such pure, painful need it seared. "I wish you could take me there."

"I wish so too." He tried to hide the pain in his laugh.

There was a sudden lull as if the whole room had dropped silent. Then he asked her to dance, which he knew he should never have.

Le Grand Prix de Deauville was *the* event of the summer. Even a peasant such as Willi knew it, and he was more than a little embarrassed to have to try to weasel an invitation out of André. But he closed his eyes and picked up the phone, taking a deep breath as he dialed. As fate would have it, Adrienne couldn't at the last minute attend because her mother had taken ill, so it was divine providence André declared. "We'll drive up together, just the two of us."

It didn't take Willi long on this drive north to perceive how distracted his friend was. The anonymous letters that had loomed so monstrous a week ago now seemed to hardly warrant his attention; he barely listened to Willi about the meetings with Vermette and Jourdain. Willi assumed André's focus had room enough only for the race today, which he surely had a fortune riding on. But halfway to Deauville he let loose again about his Pan-Europa Bond. The further it progressed, he complained, the stiffer the resistance. There were deeply vested interests in maintaining the disunity of this continent, he told Willi, knuckles whitening on the wheel. No matter what happened though, what people did or said to try to block him—he pressed ever harder on the gas—he had to forge forward.

"Of course you do," Willi acknowledged, holding the armrest as poplar trees flew by. "Mustn't we all."

"Me, especially." André inhaled as he sped toward the Channel. The richest people on earth had flocked to Deuville for the Grand Prix. The streets were bumper-to-bumper limousines. Over the entrance to Clairefontaine Hippodrome the tricolors snapped in the coastal breeze. That it was August didn't stop women from shouldering fur stoles, or the men from wearing silk ties tight beneath their suits and hats. André took off his hat and waved it to photographers, everybody wishing him luck. Chanson d'Amour was the odds-on favorite this afternoon. But when one camera flashed with a sudden pop, the handsome face of France's most famous financier, Willi noticed, flinched as if he feared he'd been shot.

Clairefontaine was a fraction the size of Longchamp, but prettier, its Norman-style, half-timbered grandstands enveloped in a panorama of wooded hills and farms. The grass, the trees, the sculpted hedges, even the long, oval grass course itself, were all astonishingly green. Emerald.

Bright red apples hung from the trees in the VIP reception area, where André was the star of the hour. Industrialists and landed aristocracy alike clustered around him, sipping aperitifs in the minutes before the big race. Rarely did purses reach quite as large as this afternoon's national championship. "I've got a yacht staked on this," one double-chinned fellow said from the side of his mouth. "You'd better come through for me, Duval."

"I'll give it my best, I assure, Your Honor." André winked, seeming unflappable. He was shaking hands and greeting people as if he were running for office.

Meanwhile the loudspeakers were calling five minutes to post time. Willi caught a glimpse of André's face. He was grinding his jaw as if he were on speed. Willi could relate to the anxiety. On the ride up he'd nearly blown everything, all but mentioning the letters to the insurance companies he'd requested from Cloutier. He'd caught himself only in the nick of time, which was why he hated duplicity. The more you played with facts, the harder it was to get them straight. But what choice was there? He couldn't exactly tell André he was spying on him for the police.

Any more than he could tell Vivi the truth.

The moment they'd reached the dance floor that night at the Red Room, he understood he'd crossed a line, stepped into a no-man's-land laden with danger. She'd fallen altogether too magnetically into his arms. His heart beat crazily when she touched his neck, and then when her breasts pressed against his chest.

"I love looking at your face." She stared as they spun back and forth to the grinding waltz. "It's so kind and honest."

Yeah, honest. He hoped she didn't see the sweat on it. Now might be time to try a touch of that honesty because it could only get harder from here, he told himself. But the accordion was pressing out another heartbreaking melody and her perfume was so sweet, and then the cymbals crashed and she threw her head back, baring her soft, white throat. A wave of longing arose from his chest that undermined all rationality.

On the way back to his place he tried to recover some of it. "This is ridiculous, you realize that, don't you?"

She nuzzled into his arms. "Is that how it feels to you?"

He knew enough not to mix business and pleasure. Experience

had taught him that. Supposedly. And he knew enough not to see a girl who still lived at home with her parents. Whose last boyfriend was murdered on the metro. But when her soft, pouty lips had reached his own, he knew too that these were lessons not fully learned.

Sex was volcanic. They tossed beneath the covers, clutching each other, shivering, erupting. She stayed the night and then the next, and then they went to Bastille and got her suitcase. Both were at his place now. Where it could lead, he had no idea. He was just hanging on for dear life, and loving every minute between the sheets. Of one thing though, he was certain: if he ever wanted to find out who'd murdered Phillipe Junot, he was going to have to tell her the truth. Only . . . which truth was that?

"And they're off!"

A dozen horses bolted from the gate, the grandstands at Claire-fontaine swelling with cheers. "Go, go, go!" André shouted

As they'd done at Longchamp, Tempest and Chanson established themselves at the head of the pack, Chanson this time by a nose. As they thundered past the grandstands though, the crowds screaming wildly, Tempest pulled ahead, first by a neck, then a full horse length.

"Sometimes he lets the competition gain," André mumbled. "Then breaks into chase. That's what he's doing, see . . . giving chase."

At the far turn and all along the backstretch, however, Tempest dominated. Not until the final turn did Chanson seem intent on a comeback.

"It's Chanson on the outside pulling up fast."

What a perfect animal, Willi thought, watching him, straining with every fiber for victory, inching up on his rival . . . catching him!

"It's neck and neck as they enter the final two hundred. What a battle! Chanson nosing ahead now—"

Just a hundred yards out, Chanson had recaptured the lead by a length. The crowd roared and roared. Everyone but André. Willi cast a quick glance: he looked as if he'd turned to stone, completely white.

"But all at once it's Tempest picking up steam. Tempest neck and

neck. Tempest passing by a nose, crossing the finish line first. Tempest—winner of the 1933 Grand Prix de Deauville!"

A tumultuous roar surrounded them, shrieks of delight, curses of despair. Like a flock of pigeons the photographers flapped from André toward the winner's circle. André just stood there motionless, his face pale as marble. Willi's heart swelled for him. He couldn't have lost everything . . . could he? No one was that foolish. All at once though, André's face seemed to crack, and like a statue he toppled into Willi's arms.

Fifteen

A low, soft whimper fluttered from Vivi's throat. What might she be dreaming of? Willi wondered, lying next to her. The warm, safe harbor she'd found in the arms of a stranger? Or how best to exploit its resources? Through the wavering window curtain moonlight fell on her face. She looked so gentle. Helpless almost. He already knew she was not. And on this seventh night together, he'd never before felt quite so enmeshed in his conflicted feelings.

What pleasures her soft, supple body gave him, every bit as gratifying as he'd imagined, as if she'd slipped from his fantasies into his bed. How she groaned when he explored those curves and crevices. How hungrily she enfolded him as they climbed to ecstasy. Why then the inevitable miasma that filtered from somewhere deep inside and filled him with such foreboding? Was it those flashes of desperation in the fire of her eyes?

First off, he couldn't bring himself to trust her, although it was only fibs he'd caught her at. She said for instance that she was twenty-five, which was ridiculous. She couldn't have been more than twenty-one, making him fifteen years her senior. Ava of course was twenty-six, but she was a university graduate, sophisticated. Vivi acted sixteen. Something about her was terrifyingly adolescent. Her moods bounced between heights of certainty and valleys of despair. When he mentioned one morning she looked a bit tired, she acted as if he'd told her she'd turned into the Hunchback of Notre Dame. "Oh, God!" She ran to the mirror. "What am I going to do?"

"Do you think my chin's too long?" she'd ask him. "A girl at work told me my face was too wide. Do you think my eyes are funny?"

If anything, her nose was slightly off-kilter, as if it might have been broken once. But he dare not let her know he thought so. She'd probably threaten suicide. He wanted to ask her about her childhood, but the past appeared barely to exist for her, the future only of dim importance. "Maybe I'll be a model." Her world was a perpetual present of strange concerns. "Would you call me *unforgettable,* Willi?"

She told him the truth about Galeries Lafayette but gave the impression it was only a part-time job, and that she was nearing completion of the Richelieu Secretarial Academy. Why lie about that? At least she never asked for money. Not a cent. They'd gotten that out of the way the first night.

She'd looked around his apartment. "Is this where you live?"

"I'm a refugee, Vivi," he'd said straight out. "I left everything I owned in Germany. So if you're looking for a benefactor—"

"You think I'm an idiot? That I didn't notice the bus we took here? You think I thought you had money? I meet lots of rich men, Willi. Don't be a fool." She put her arms around his neck. "Can't you see it's love I need? So much of it."

When the warm lips pressed against his own, that miasma in his heart, as it did every time, steamed away in the heat of her kisses. And in bed when she turned into an animal, her uninhibited passion made Willi forget everything but her.

For a week now he'd been putting off bringing up Junot. It was completely irresponsible he knew. But he couldn't bear to puncture the sweet cloud of bliss he found himself on. After all he'd been through, it felt so wonderful. Perhaps as long as the kids were away, he told himself, a little summer fling. That's all.

The boys were having the time of their lives up in Normandy. He'd seen them last weekend after the Deauville Grand Prix. André had driven him to the Gottmans' beach house out near Cherbourg. Turned out the famous financier had not lost a dime at the races because he never bet on horses, he said. He had wept in Willi's arms after the race, he said, because of the tension and how bitter it felt to lose. And because he knew people would be angry with him, as if he'd personally done the running.

But André was calmer, far less distracted, after the race. By the end of the evening he was downright jovial. The Gottmans, whom they dined with, seemed enchanted as ever by him. Ava was spending the summer up here too, but wasn't around when Willi came to visit. Gone on a day trip with a young man, her mother informed Willi with a small, wry smile. "A journalist rather like yourself, Willi."

It was Sunday. Their "one-week" anniversary. What else did Vivi want but to go back to the rue de Lappe. "It's the only time I really feel alive." She applied her fake beauty mark carefully in the mirror. "When I'm dancing, Willi. Or making love of course." She batted her eyes at him.

He came up and kissed her. But a voice within was shouting that it had to be today. That it couldn't go on like this. One way or another he had to bring up Phillipe Junot.

As they set out by foot he started in slowly, laying the groundwork. "Look at all the people on their way to church. You ever go to church?"

She shook her head emphatically, no.

"Not even as a kid?"

"My parents didn't believe in it. They're practically Communists. On Sundays we always . . . read poetry. Or sang. That kind of stuff."

"Really."

"Yes. They're very progressive. Look at that girl, Willi. Do you think she's prettier than I am?"

"Don't be crazy."

"How can I not be?" She play slapped him.

Even early Sunday afternoon the Red Room was its usual carnival of noise and color, the floor a merry-go-round of couples dancing round and round, up and down. Willi and Vivi fell into the seductive, grinding rhythm, her body so inviting it was hard not to lose focus.

"You have brothers, sisters?" He forced himself to keep the mission in sight. If he wanted to get to the bottom of Junot's murder he had to get Vivi on his side, he knew. A delicate matter.

"Why are you asking so many questions today?"

"What do you mean why? . . . I'm curious."

"Don't be. Just dance with me." She clutched his neck. "And love me."

"If I love you, I want to know about you."

The cymbals crashed. Her chin turned up. The opal eyes clung to him. "Do you, Willi?" They seem to burn through him. "Do you love me? You haven't said it yet." She examined his face for an answer, finding it apparently. "You don't. I knew it!" She grew hysterical, trying to break away.

"I don't love when you act childishly." He held her firmly. "Aren't you supposed to be twenty-five?"

"All right." She gritted her teeth, tossing her head back. "Ask your stupid questions if you're so curious. I'll tell the truth. I've nothing to hide."

A dozen possibilities burned on his tongue. About Junot. What she knew of his death. That black eye. How had she gotten it? Who was that guy who accosted her in the street?

He started off easy, "Why the suitcase in the locker?" asking what he could have days ago, when they retrieved it from the station.

She sighed, gritting her teeth, submitting it seemed to the inevitable, but never breaking the rhythm of their dance.

"I ran away from home. I couldn't stand my parents anymore. They're not Communists, Willi. They're petit bourgeois who are trying to suffocate me. They have my whole life planned out. A secretary!" She looked at him, pleading it seemed for salvation. "Can you imagine me a secretary? I can hardly spell." Her fingers dug into him. "Go on: ask more. This is starting to feel good."

The music quickened.

"All right, tell me about"—he decided to push it—"your last boy-friend."

Her shoulders stiffened. "Why him?"

They spun around.

"I told you about Vicki. And Paula, the boot girl. I don't know anything about you. You must have had boyfriends. Tell me about your last one. Why did you break up?"

The beat drove them faster.

"We didn't."

He feigned confusion. "I don't understand." He hated doing this. Knew that she could only hate him for it too. "You're still seeing him?"

"Hardly." She gasped. They were twirling like tops. "He's dead."

Her feet stumbled. If Willi hadn't steadied her they would have hit the wall.

He pulled her to the side of the dance floor, holding her with both hands, her chest rising and falling as she panted.

"Was he sick, or was it an accident?"

She shook her head, pressing a fist between her eyes, then dropped it and looked straight at him. "He was murdered," she said matter of factly. "Two months ago."

He was silent long enough, then: "How horrible. What happened?"

"I really don't know; I wasn't there. I only read about in the papers." Her eyes latched onto his. "It was mobsters, I guess. He owed them money."

He knew that had never been in the papers.

His hand ran down her cheek. "Where did this happen?" he almost whispered to her.

"Right in the middle of a crowded metro train. Can you imagine?"

He had never been on stage, never taken an acting class. But years of detective work had taught him how to play a role without breaking character. And as much as he hated to deceive her, he could only tell her part of the truth. The rest needed to be concealed.

"What's wrong?" She saw the expression on his face. "You look as if you've seen a ghost."

"I . . . I witnessed a young man murdered in the metro. How long ago did you say your boyfriend was killed?"

"Two months."

"My God, but it couldn't be, could it? This poor fellow died in my arms on the station platform at Odéon."

She pulled away from him. "What are you saying?"

"I was leaving the train when I saw him stumble. I went to help. He was covered in blood. He only lived another minute."

Her red lips opened in astonishment. "This is too much."

She seemed about to gag, then turned and pushed her way through the crowd. He reached for her, nearly grabbing her arm, but she made it out to the street. Music from a dozen dance halls fused into one. When he caught her, her rage was explosive.

"You really do think I'm an idiot!" She turned and practically attacked him. "You knew I knew Phillipe, didn't you?" Her voice was a whispering scream. "What were you doing, following him? Following me? You goddamn bastard!"

This was it, he knew. Do or die. Turn fiction to fact. Perform.

"That's not true. I'm as stunned as you. Even more, perhaps. You're the one who suggested destiny brought us together. I don't even believe in such things. But the last word on his lips, Vivi . . . was your name."

"Stop it. Stop it you son of a bitch!"

"You think I knew you were the same person? That's insane. This is—pure coincidence. An inexplicable twist of fate."

"Then what were you doing here of all dance halls? The Red Room? Out of all the places in Paris? You're lying to me. I know you are!"

"I came to the rue de Lappe for music. It's a famous street Vivi, even in Germany. I went into several clubs before the Red Room. I'm a big fan of java. Can't you tell by the way I dance?"

She looked at the sky shaking her head, rolling her eyes like a rabbit in a snare. Finally though she hunched her shoulders and sniffed back tears.

"You do dance beautifully." Her lips were trembling.

"Vivi—" He grabbed her shoulders, going for broke. "Did the police ever question you after Phillipe was killed?"

"The police?" She snapped up. "How could they know about me?"

How could they not? The most rudimentary investigation would have turned up Junot's girlfriend. Inspector Clouitier and the Police Judiciaire clearly weren't working very hard on this case.

"And why are you so interested?" Her fury flared again. "Why, Monsieur Willi—if that's even your name. Who are you really? Tell me, goddamn son of a bitch!"

"I was behind him on the platform. I saw him fall and ran to help. That's exactly how it was."

"Then why do you still care now that he's buried?"

Willi recalled she hadn't been to his funeral. Did she not care?

"I saw a lot of men killed in the war, Vivi. None ever died in my arms the way he did. Can you understand I feel a commitment to him? I want his murderer brought to justice. Don't you?"

She threw up her hands, letting them fall back against her tight skirt. "Justice. Yes, sure. Why not."

"Then I need your help hunting him down."

"Is that what you want, to find his killer?"

"Yes."

Her fingers clutched his shirt. "Is that all you need me for?"

He took her in his arms and kissed her hard. "You know I need you for much more."

"I don't understand why you think I know anything," she whined over supper. "I told you, Willi, I met him at a bistro near his university. We almost always went dancing. That was it. He was a marvelous dancer. Like you."

Willi looked at the opal eyes pleading with him. He wanted to hear about the *bouquiniste,* the kid's gambling habits, her black eye—but he couldn't ask or it would be obvious he had been following Junot.

"Did he have any enemies? Any addictions that might have gotten him into trouble? Was he involved in anything illegal?"

She threw down her fork. "What are you, a cop?"

"Vivi—"

"Well, I don't understand why you don't just let it go. Why you want to get mixed up in something like this? Aren't you an immigrant? Can't you get in trouble?"

"Because I want to see justice done. Is that so tough to understand?"

"Oh, right, justice. I forgot."

"Sorry if I happen to believe in it. Maybe I'm a fool."

"Maybe?"

"Did Phillipe have friends we might speak to?"

"Mother of God, you don't give up. I never met any okay? When we went out, it was just the two of us. And you want to know what, Willi? I envy him. I think he's better off dead. I wish I was dead too."

"Why would you say something like that?"

"Because I want to be happy, and I can't." Her eyes began to water. Willi could see her long, red fingernails digging into her wrist. "You could make me happy. But you won't. You keep attacking me like this."

Sixteen

He was crazy too. Not just for letting a girl such as Vivi into his life, with her suitcase full of trouble. But he remained so pitifully paralyzed himself. The most obvious symptom was his persistent inability to use the metro. It was lunacy. All his attempts led to the same result: halfway down the entrance steps the wafting tunnel air weakened his knees and sent a spasm of nausea through him. It smelled to him of blood. What was fueling this reaction? He tried to analyze it as his cousin Kurt might, formerly of the Berlin Psychiatric Instutite, now at Hadassah Hospital Tel Aviv. It had to be a physicalization of his sense of helplessness . . . seeing the kid slaughtered and die in his arms, a kid he'd come to know and like and identify with. Or was it his incapacity to protect his own boys from the madness of racial hatred? He'd seen men blown up. Machinegunned down. Sawed in two. But he'd never felt as immobilized as he did now.

It was getting in the way. Costing time. Summer was drawing to an end and legwork was to be done. He managed to limp around on buses, but how he dreamed of that little silver BMW he used to race about Berlin in. Unfortunately dreams didn't get him across Paris any faster. He couldn't get a French driver's license because he wasn't a resident and he couldn't get an international one because he had no passport. He was stuck.

He still had to track down André's brother-in-law. Willi's salary from *La Vérité*, aka André, to find the origin of the disparaging letters, was embarrassingly large. Plus with his stipend from the Police Judiciaire he was practically a wealthy man. But by any means of transport, taxi, bus, or foot, Lucien Ruehl was not to be found. Willi kept getting the same intentionally vague answer from wherever the labor leader was supposed to be, at home, work, the union hall: he was off somewhere on vacation. According to what André knew of him, the man never left town.

The murder weapon remained equally elusive. Willi had spent the whole of today in search of whatever could have severed Phillipe Junot's left ventricle. Starting out with the butcher-supply stores down near the wholesale market at Les Halles, he'd gone up to the kitchen and cutlery emporiums along the Grands Boulevards, then on to two of the largest hunting shops across from the Gare Saint-Lazare. From there it was clear across town to what everyone kept telling him was best knife store in Paris, Duvier Frères, off the Place des Vosges. They carried knives from every region of France from the Basque country to the Belgian border, but nothing as long and sharp and narrow as the one Willi had sketched in his notebook based on the puncture-wound description in the police pathology report. After a full day, his feet ached and his temples pounded, but he was no closer to knowing what killed that kid.

What he *had* located yesterday at least, he recalled to encourage himself as he left the knife store, was the *bouquiniste*'s boat. Among the scores of vessels crammed side by side at the Port de l'Arsenal had been the red-hulled *Achille Baptiste*. No one was aboard. No one nearby. The only thing he'd taken note of was the small, white flag flapping from her stern. It was so unusual he'd sketched it in his notebook too: a large, black silhouette head with a white bandanna fluttering in the wind.

Now, trudging home from his fruitless weapon search, he wondered again what that flag might mean and how he could find out. Then beneath the vaulted arcades of the Place des Vosges the shafts of sunlight caused him to blink. Was he seeing right? There was no mistaking it: the brown marcel waves, the sculpted features, the sparkling, intelligent eyes. It was Ava all right, on some guy's arm.

"Willi!" He recognized the embarassed expression. For a second it hurled him back to Berlin, the Press Ball—when they got "fixed up" by Fritz. It was the night von Schleicher's government fell, the winds of political crisis whipping to a frenzy. Outside, as they'd fled for home, he'd longed to take her in his arms. But she was so furious at how he kept putting himself in harm's way, calling it selfish, childish, slamming a taxi door in his face, leaving him in the cold. They were always slightly out of sync, he and Ava.

"Paris is so ridiculously small. You remember Marc, don't you, Willi?

How could he not? Marc, whose accusations about André and Henri Beliveau had proven rather embarrassing. What a pleasure to run into him again.

"*Quel charmant!*" The fellow offered his dapper, toothy gin.

What was Ava doing back so early? Willi wondered. The kids still had another week in Normandy. Obviously she'd returned to spend a little time with Mr. Nathanson. *Quel charmant.*

"What brings you to this neighborhood, Willi?" She clearly was avoiding what *she* was doing here.

"Just finishing up some interviews." Willi did his best to smile.

"Ah, yes." Nathanson's small eyes twinkled. "You're at *La Vérité* now. Monsieur Beliveau's quite a character, eh? I'm a journalist too, so I've known him for some years. Ava and I are about to have coffee. Join us, won't you?"

If he weren't keeling over with fatigue, he'd surely have declined. As it was, Willi found himself collapsing into a wicker-backed chair at one of the arcade cafés. Across the stately old square they could see the aristocratic mansions with their steep slate roofs turning pink in the sinking sun, and the dancing fountain, so civilized.

"Perhaps it's providence we ran into you." Ava let a hand rest on her new companion's arm. "Marc here was telling me some troubling news he's just heard about your friend André."

Willi tried not to grit his teeth. Why was she so relentless about this?

"Apparently the Duvals are in arrears to the Hôtel Lutetia to the tune of several hundred thousand—"

"Nathanson"—Willi sat up, interrupting—"might I ask who this source of yours is?"

The journalist maintained his toothy grin. "Naturally I can't give his name, but I can assure you, Willi, I trust him implicitly."

"Even if it's only partially true . . ." Ava swallowed at the terrible implications.

"*If* being the key word, Ava."

If this Nathanson had gotten it right last time, Willi was thinking, there might be a reason to listen now. But how clearly he could still hear Henri Beliveau laughing at him: "Your source had it *assbackward.*"

Willi rose from the chair. "I realize I've forgotten something. Sorry. I've got to go. Perhaps we can all meet another time. I'll speak to you when the boys return, Ava."

"What is it with you?" Ava's face reddened. "You and Father both. It's like you're bewitched by that man."

Willi just smiled and crossed the Place des Vosges as quickly as his tired legs would go, the patterns of light fading on the sidewalk.

It required patience but he found André's brother-in-law all right. Lucien Ruehl kept his whereabouts under wraps because as one of the most outspoken labor leaders in France he had his share of enemies. But Willi religiously scanned half a dozen left-wing newspapers until, sure enough, he spotted Ruehl's name in tiny letters on a list of featured speakers at an emergency mass meeting.

It took an hour and a half by bus to get there, a muggy evening, the last in August. The auditorium on the far north of Paris was packed with people waiting for the opening gavel of the Confédération du Travail-Syndicaliste Révolutionnaire—the Confederation of Revolutionary Trade Unions, the atmosphere charged with tension. Outside, phalanxes of pamphleteers pushed conflicting ideologies: Pro-Moscow, Anti-Moscow, Revisionist, Neo-Socialist, even Constructive Revolutionists, who, according to the tract Willi perused in his seat, believed the state should be run not by politicans but by technocrats on the basis of rational planning.

André had told him Adrienne and her brother came from the upper-middle class; their father had made a great deal of money in trade with the African colonies. As a youth, Lucien had rebelled, refusing his father's "imperialist booty," rejecting a bourgeois lifestyle to identify with the working class. He became a machinist, always inching leftward, first as a socialist, then a Communist, finally an anarcho-syndicalist. Now, as president of the Machine Workers United of Paris, he was a major player in France's ever-more-militant trade union movement. One of its most respected and reviled leaders.

A group of dusty-looking men eventually shuffled onstage, taking chairs facing the audience, pulling out speeches and reading glasses. Willi picked out Lucien at once from an old photo André had given him. The youngest, most vibrant of the bunch, his great shock of reddish-brown hair flew in three directions, an expression of concern seemingly etched into his high, white forehead, a cigarette glued to the corner of his lips. In an otherwise placid face, hot, combative eyes.

Lucien was two years older than his sister, according to André, and had always been protective of her. They had had an unusually tight bond growing up. But Adrienne's marriage to André had severed it. Lucien refused to be in the same room with such an arch-capitalist. It was terribly sad, and strictly ideological. The two had much in common, André insisted. But brother and sister had broken all ties, which agonized Adrienne and André, yet what could they do? Unless André renounced all his wealth to the international struggle of the working classes, he was an enemy of the people, according to Lucien. The man was a fanatic.

Perhaps André and he were more akin than they were willing to admit, Willi thought, recalling Ava's accusation he was "bewitched" by André. Willi certainly doubted Max Gottman would subscribe to that description, but Willi did have to admit he found Duval a perpetually compelling figure. And why? Precisely because André *was* a fanatic, someone who believed so unshakably. *Almost childishly sincere,* Désireé Jourdain had said of him. The power of such conviction was magnetic because it was so rare in this world. Maybe André was right, Willi considered. Maybe people with that kind of personality who strove to accomplish something great in life were just asking to get shot down.

The hall was steaming up. Willi fanned himself with the pamphlets he'd received, scanning the crowd. His eyes stopped on a face he thought he recognized. Those chubby cheeks and droopy mustache, wasn't that Marsolet—Gripois—of the Sûreté Générale? Three loud bangs distracted him. A woman let loose a fearful shriek, thinking they were gunshots, and there was a moment of borderline mayhem. But when it grew clear it was only the gavel striking, laughter filled the hall, getting the proceedings off on a misleadingly lighthearted note.

There was little reason for levity, according to the Confédération chairman, Rogier Larocque. Standing at the microphone with wide, tragic eyes, he made it clear that the most momentous of choices faced the association tonight. Half a million Frenchmen had lost their jobs in the last six months. Worldwide, capitalism was teetering. The question was, would the working class allow the forces of reaction to oppress them in even more brutal forms, such as had happened in Italy and Germany, or would they seize control through direct action as they'd begun to in Spain?

"Let us start off with a report from the German Division of the International Workers of the World."

The applause was polite but hardly tumultuous for this brother from across the Rhine because, solidarity or not, blood remained blood—as illustrated by the countless leftists who fought each other during the war. Willi watched the yellow-haired fellow ascend the podium.

"I'm afraid I must correct your chairman," he began with grave solemnity. "I have no report from the German International Workers of the World—because the German Division, the largest in Europe just a year ago, no longer exists. In eight months since the Hitlerite takeover the entire German labor movement totaling in the millions has been dismembered, cowed into submission through systematic terror or vanished into labor camps from which few return. Your Nazi nextdoor neighbor, comrades," he concluded, "makes Mussolini's Italy look like a beach resort."

The audience sat in stony silence, uncertain how to take such reports. The man could after all be a paid provocateur trying to manipulate them. There were grisly enough details Willi could add. But Lucien Ruehl had taken the podium.

Not unlike André, he had an inner fire that seemed to buoy him above others. Pushing back his reddish-brown hair, the lines of anxiety were even more deeply etched on his face.

"The German catastrophe," his voice echoed from loudspeakers, "substantiates the starkness of our choice. In the past we viewed political opponents, including socialists, as our enemies. We not only refused to cooperate but we fought them . . . sometimes physically." A murmur of laughter flit through the hall. "But this strategy has led to a disaster few could have anticipated: complete class defeat. To the workers of the world Fascism has become an unprecedented threat.

"In France, we can hardly miss the now emboldened rightists taking to the streets in their uniforms and jackboots. As much as it is against our nature to compromise, the handwriting, comrades, is on the wall. The choice, though bitter, is one that we must make. We must put aside differences and join our former enemies, the socialists, the radicals, the Catholic labor unions." Boos began to rise around the hall. "Anyone who will stand shoulder to shoulder with us," Ruehl spoke even louder, "to form a united front—"

"No! No!"

"—or we will find ourselves under the same boot as our German brothers! I propose therefore we vote at once—"

"No! No!"

"—to endorse a policy promoting a Popular Front Against Fascism."

The hall broke into an uproar that even minutes of gavel banging couldn't diminish.

"Traitor! Counterrevolutionary!" people were screaming. Others came back in a rhythmical chant: "Yes! Yes! Popular Front!" A chorus sprinkled through the hall took up singing the Communist

"Internationale," until Chairman Larocque grabbed the microphone and cried with barely subdued hysteria, "Everybody must leave at once—there's been a bomb threat!"

Instantly, revolutionary fervor exploded into pandemonium. Willi got lifted off the floor as the mob stampeded for the doors. Twisted faces and flailing arms flew before his eyes, his ears ringing with determined grunts and pitiful moans for help. This can't be the way I'm going to die, he thought, squashed and gasping for air. A man next to him kept elbowing him in the gut, until Willi elbowed back. Swept into the jaws of a narrow passage he was sure he'd breathed his last, when miraculously he was disengorged into the hot, muggy night.

For a long while he just stood on the sidewalk trying to catch his breath. Then luck along with a well-trained eye provided a glimpse of Lucien Ruehl. The labor leader was being whisked away by a cluster of bodyguards all dressed in the same tan suits and black caps. Willi fought his way through the crowd and pursued them. Far down the block he could see the four, but couldn't tell which was Ruehl. They stopped on a corner, knotting in a circle until suddenly each set off a different way. It was a standard security procedure, Willi understood. Only because he knew where Ruehl lived was he able to follow the right one.

He'd visited Ruehl's building two weeks ago, a monstrous gray tenement filling a full city block. He hadn't gone in, only spoken to a gap-toothed concierge outside, one of half a dozen people that day who told him Lucien Ruehl was "off to the country." Now, from across the street he watched the union leader enter the dingy complex through an arched passage. He waited several seconds then took off after him.

Carefully pulling the door open, he slipped in. Overhead he could hear footsteps ascending the creaky stairs. What a stench! He had to force himself not to cough. The building echoed with clattering dishes, barking dogs, shouting voices. He looked up, blinking at the stairwell. A dim shaft of electric light seemed to drip down endless flights. Slowly, carefully, he started up.

Everything was covered with grime. On each floor long, narrow corridors vanished into a void. Some doors stood open in the summer heat, and you could see right inside, like one of those revolving kinescope theaters Willi used to go to as a kid that gave a close-up, three-dimensional glance then quickly moved on. A woman darning socks. A man drinking wine. A couple playing cards. On the third floor, behind closed doors, a real fight was in progress, screaming, cursing, furniture smashing. It didn't prevent the neighbors opposite from singing at the top of their lungs along with Maurice Chevalier:

Elle avait des tout petits petons—
Valentine! Valentine!

Willi found himself a little embarrassed by the intimacy of these tableaux, but no one seemed to notice him. Then he realized he'd lost the footsteps overhead, and froze. Ruehl must have turned down a corridor, maybe two flights above. Climbing to five, Willi peered around the corner just in time to spot a tan suit disappear into an apartment door.

Slowly approaching, he weighed his options. He could flash his fake police badge or his press ID from *La Vérité*. Or he could say he was a friend of Adrienne's. The odds either way weren't good, but he held his breath and knocked.

The door cracked open. A woman's face appeared. She was very black and very beautiful, her hair wrapped in a colorful cloth. *"Oui?"*

"I'd like to speak with Lucien Ruehl."

"Oh, no." Her head shook vigorously. "He hasn't been here for a very long time."

"Ma'am,"—he smiled as kindly as he could—"I just saw him enter."

Her eyes widened with fear. "Who are you?"

"I'm with . . . the *People's Weekly*." He knew he was skating on thin ice with that one, but it just came out.

"You have ID?"

"Who is it, Angelique?" Ruehl appeared behind her, holding a caramel-colored baby.

"He says he's from *People's Weekly*."

"Sorry, I've no statement just now."

"It's about your brother-in-law." Willi stuck his foot in the door. "André Duval." He noticed Ruehl wince. "We're doing a story on him. Hoped you might give us some insight. It won't take long. Just a moment or two."

"It'd take longer than that to tell you about him." Ruehl surprised Willi with a laugh. "Come in then, as long as it's for the *People's Weekly*."

"You need to be more careful." The woman looked at Ruehl crossly.

"But that's just what I am being, *chéri*," he assured her.

A tiny apartment seemed to close around Willi, stacks of books leaning in great towers. He was motioned into a kitchen almost entirely filled with a table that barely sat two. The African woman turned off what looked like a pot of mush on the stove, then took the baby from Lucien and went to another room. Ruehl sat in the chair across from Willi, running a hand through his reddish-brown hair, cigarette dangling. He was far more relaxed than he'd been at the auditorium. Genial almost. Happy, it appeared, for a chance to expound about his brother-in-law.

"But of course he's a fraud!" He laughed, blowing smoke from the side of his mouth. "The whole goddamn system's a fraud. About his company in particular I couldn't say. It's clear he's managed to foment an authentic contagion. You have to hand it to him for that."

"You think investors will lose their money?" Willi swallowed.

"On André's bonds?" Smoke shot from Ruehl's nostrils. "I doubt it. The man's an evil genius. But I can say this. Besides the big institutional buyers, look who waits in line for them each time they're issued: postmen, firemen, bakers, clerks. Everyone in this goddamn country wants to get rich. So how long can it last, eh—a civilization based on greed?"

"I understand you're related to Monsieur Duval."

Willi noticed Ruehl's cheek wince again. "Yes. My sister's married to him."

"But you despise him as an enemy of the working class?"

Ruehl shook his head emphatically, cigarette flaring. "Don't be absurd, man. It's systems I hate, not individuals. And I don't mind telling you—off the record—that André Duval is one of the finest.

He's made my sister extremely happy. It's a deep personal tragedy he's on the wrong side. I can do nothing about it."

"He happens to have some very real enemies. People who'd like to see him destroyed. More than that, people who've taken steps to do it. There've been a series of accusatory letters."

For a second Lucien looked at Willi as if he knew Willi was a cop, and that his answer, not just his words but his whole aura, was being scrutinized. He didn't seem to mind. He sat up, inhaling, smiling at Willi sadly.

"Listen, friend—André Duval may be everything I can't stand: horse racing, sports cars, pinkie rings. Short of revolution though, I'd never want to see his business hurt, and not just because he's my sister's husband. I've already sacrificed that relationship. But you see—and this is how deep the insanity runs in this country—my own union, Fédération des Industries Métallurgiques, voted last year against my objections to invest the bulk of our retirement fund with him. So I have no interest whatsoever in seeing his company go down, believe me."

Seventeen

September first, the last official day of summer, Paris was like a morgue, the only living things on the Île de la Cité a few stray tourists and the pigeons. The bells of Notre Dame chilled his neck as Willi walked toward 36 quai des Orfèvres. He could smell the Seine below flowing in silence. Inspector Clouitier would return Monday as promised, expecting a full report. Before that, Willi wanted to accomplish one thing at police headquarters.

Ever since he'd found out detectives had never interviewed Vivi, he was itching to know what they *had* done to solve Junot's murder. Today seemed his last best chance. Bullets of sweat rolled down his neck as he approached the drab gray building. It was tempting fate he knew to keep using this counterfeit badge, especially here, the most likely of all places to get caught. But the guard just nodded drowsily and let him pass, André's charm still working.

The mazes of long, bleak corridors inside were under attack by Polish washerwomen, ammonia clouds dizzying Willi as he wound his way to the Records Hall. The towering chamber was stacked floor to rafters with filing drawers. A gray matron behind the desk squinted at his badge. When she walked away without saying anything, Willi began sweating again. It was like a sword hanging over his head, this fear of discovery, that train ride back to Germany. But she returned, asking only for his signature, and handed him Junot's file.

It was awfully thin. When he sat at a reading desk and opened it, he was shocked by what was inside. Nothing. Beyond the original pathology report, which he'd already seen, there was not a single new entry. How was it possible? It had been two months since the murder. Were they covering something up, or was it just the infamous backlog here at central headquarters? He returned the file and thanked the matron, leaving the building sweatier than he'd arrived.

Vivi was waiting for him when he got home It was just past noon.

"Hello. Where have you been?" The light in her eyes flickered as she kissed him. "You didn't tell me you were going anywhere. I was a little concerned."

"Just out doing a few chores, that's all."

"On a holiday?" She took his jacket and hung it up, naked except for one of his shirts. "All work no play." Her pink lips pouted. "Wanna fuck me before lunch?"

They fell to bed kissing, her legs spreading hungrily. "You feel so goddamned great, Willi."

So did she. At moments like these, Willi thought, losing himself to her frenzied delights, Vivi was definitely worth it. She made him feel alive.

Later, they fell asleep in each other's arms. He dreamed of Berlin. Trying to get home. But the trains were on strike and he was forced to walk through a forest alone. Suddenly what felt like a tiger pounced on him and knocked the breath from his chest. His eyes popped open. To his astonishment it wasn't a dream. Vivi had landed on him in an insane rage.

"You fucking bastard—" He barely managed to hold her off. "How could you do this?" She was trying to scratch his face.

Mortified, he saw she was clutching his Police Judiciaire badge, clearly having gone through his pockets.

"Who sent you to spy on me?" Her eyes flashed. "Who?"

He pushed her off and leaped from bed, jumping back, shielding his genitals. He saw scratch marks across his chest. It was his own fault. He'd crossed the line with this girl, entered no-man's-land, and stepped on a mine, big surprise.

"You're a cop. I can't believe it!"

"Give me that back, Vivi." He held out his hand.

She taunted him, reading aloud, " 'First Inspector Olivier Boucher.' Oh, Jesus—you're not even Willi, goddamn you! Have you told me a single word of truth? Hey . . . wait." She looked at it again. "This is a joke, right?" Her nostrils flared. "There's not supposed to be a fleur-de-lis over here. The isn't real. Mother of God." She started to laugh. "You've got a fake badge."

Willi was stunned. André's forgery had worked a dozen times, and in two seconds Vivi had spotted it. Now what was he supposed to do?

"That's the funniest thing I've ever seen. What are you, a spy, Willi? A gangster? I don't even care." She threw herself at him, kissing him insanely. "As long as you're not a cop. But then—are you really Willi?"

"Of course I am. Now give me that back and I'll explain it all to you." He wondered, even as he promised, how.

Tying a robe around himself, he calmed her down, then poured them both a brandy. He was a reporter. He showed her his press card. It had his picture in it and his name, which he had other papers to verify.

"So you *were* following us." Her eyes blazed again. "That's why you were behind Phillipe the night he was—"

"No. That badge has nothing to do with either of you. You have to believe me, Vivi. It's for a story I'm working on—at the newspaper. An investigation about a very influential man. In order to inspire people to talk, I flash it at them. It's just a stupid gimmick I bought on the black market. I'm amazed anyone takes it seriously. I mean, you saw right through it."

"Yeah." She smiled. "But I'm a smart girl." She reached through his robe and clutched his balls. "Tell me how smart I am, Willi." She squeezed slightly.

"The smartest girl I ever knew."

"Just like a woman, eh?" André pointed out the carved vine motif from their table at Maxim's. "Beaux arts expresses the ideals of feminine charm, all the sensual twists and turns."

Tell me about it, Willi thought, shifting in his seat.

They'd returned to this temple of Parisan chic at the bonds man's request. Just the two of them, for lunch. "We never get to chat anymore," André had complained over the phone. Now that they were here though, he wasn't chatting but lecturing on art nouveau, studying the décor as he explained the varying styles of curliques. It was obvious what he was doing. Avoiding the unavoidable.

"I told you they were after me." He finally shot Willi a dark glance over a second martini. "And it's not finished. Oh, no. You'll see." The waves of copper hair were getting tangled in his fingers. "It's just getting started."

André had landed in a *scandale énorme*. A full two weeks after the Deauville Grand Prix, a Calais newspaper claimed his trainer, Deschevaux, confessed the race had been fixed, the jockey paid to throw the championship, that André had bet heavily against his own horse and won many tens of millions of francs. It made headlines across France. Yesterday, however, this same Deschevaux appeared before a throng of newsmen and denied ever having made such claims. At sunset he was found in the beautiful horse stalls Willi had once wandered, hanging dead—by whose hand was unclear. And the jockey who'd ridden Chanson d'Amour was nowhere to be found.

Willi saw something glowing too brightly in André's eyes.

"The further I push, the worse it will get. You'll see." André grit his teeth. "And it *is* coming, Willi. Pan-Europa's a done deal now that I can afford certain assurances. I'm so damned happy." Tears were dripping down his cheeks. "Forgive me. I'm ridiculous I know. It's just been such a long, hard fight, and now this."

"I understand. It's all right. It'll work out, you'll see." Willi tried to sound as if he meant it. His eyes flit around the jungle of stained-glass birds and butterflies. André was starting to unnerve him. And he didn't need unnerving just now.

This morning as promised, Inspector Clouitier had returned to 36 quai des Orfèvres, no more relaxed for his summer holiday. He'd wanted a full report on André's every emotion during the Grand Prix. "And don't leave anything out, Kraus. You weren't the only one observing."

"He was nervous before the race. Nervous during it. And cried after. I know for fact because he used my shoulder."

Clouitier wrote down every word as if it were military intelligence. About Lucien Ruehl he was less interested, which was why Willi spent as much time as possible telling him every detail: his quest to track the man down, the tumultuous mass meeting, how he'd managed to corner the union leader in his apartment. "Fascinating," Clouitier kept repeating. "You think he sent those letters?"

"Not at all. No motive. Which reminds me, Inspector." Willi leaned toward the desk. "Might you have procured those originals as I requested?"

With a tired sigh Cloutier reached into his drawer and drew out a slim manila folder, which he tossed over. Inside were three type-written letters, each addressed to a dfferent insurance company, each unsigned. At a first glance they appeared identical. But Willi knew first glances could lie.

"Is there a lab I might take these to have the typeface analyzed?"

The inspector sighed a second time, but jotted down the address of a company the department used. "Slow as molasses but they'll get the job done, eventually."

"Maybe you don't believe a man has a mission in life," André was loquacious by the time he'd finished his third martini at Maxim's. "But I feel infused with purpose. To undermine the foundations of war. Consider it Willi: nations mutually dependent on each other for income can't *afford* to fight each other. Their investments are pooled in *one* pot." He demonstrated with his hands. "If one knocks it over, they *all* go bankrupt." His eyes twinkled with intoxication. "Critics claim it's too far-fetched. Look at the League of Nations, falling apart already they say. But money's different. I know. Money motivates in ways ideals never can. And what if it did fail, so what?" He threw up his hands. "We can't just sit around waiting for these mani-acs to destroy Europe, which is what will happen if there's another war. I lost the only brother I had in the last one. Of course, until life brought me you." His eyes swam with affection.

Willi took a swift breath and nodded. André *was* like a brother. He'd offered a hand up when nobody else had. Stuck out his neck. Stood up for him. But there was no denying something desperate lay beneath that single-minded determination. It was more than just will-power or optimism. There was need in that glow. What generated it?

"I finally found your brother-in-law," he interjected, as if the topic of relatives had reminded him. "We had quite a chit-chat about you."

André's glass stopped in midair, a glint of discomfort in his eye.

"Lucien?" He downed the rest of his drink. "Congratulations. That's no easy man to find. But I suppose it's why I put you on it, isn't it. What did he have to say about me? Or should I say, against?"

"He had nothing but kind words. He's very fond of you. He certainly means you no harm."

"Bosh. He'd have my head if he could, though for different reasons than my right-wing opponents."

Willi shook his head, no. André couldn't see it but he was actually quite like his trade unionist brother-in-law. Both such true believers. A mortal flaw perhaps in each.

"The warmongers I call them." André was shifting back to where he wanted the conversation: that damned bond of his. "Men for whom death and destruction mean unimaginagble wealth." He sighed as he paid the bill. "They'll stop at nothing to destroy Pan-Europa because they know it means ruin for them. They won't succeed though, and you want to know why? The concepts underpinning it are based *on* human nature, not against it. Everyone wants to get rich. And everyone can! The earth is plentiful enough. But, oh, the pushing, the prodding, I have to do to make people see that." André plucked an orchid from the table and stuck it in his lapel as they rose. "The backward thinking I encounter. I feel like Sisyphus, I tell you." They headed toward the exit. "The phoning and visiting and taking people out. All the women I have to procure, big tits, little tits, hairy pussies, shaved. It never ends. I'm getting old, Willi—forty-two. I need a rest now and again. Ever been to Avignon this time of year? Absolute heaven."

Stepping from the restaurant they were surprised by the chill. The first autumnal wind had set in. André's Hispano-Suiza was at the curb. "Sure I can't drop you somewhere?" He looked genuinely depressed to have to part.

"That's okay. I need to walk off lunch."

"Well, don't be a stranger." The gray eyes seized him. "I mean it, Willi." He threw both arms around giving a bear hug. "And try to stay out of trouble, huh." He touched Willi's chin with his fist.

As the shiny limousine drove off, André waved from the back, tossing a wink the way Willi's father used to when he left on a business trip. Willi's eyes burned with a sudden surprising emotion.

"Should I hail you a cab, sir?" the doorman from Maxim's asked.

A mental alarm went off. That smell, Willi thought. The same musky, citrusy scent. When was the last time I smelled it? The metro just before Junot was murdered. He looked up, meeting the doorman's square, pugnacious face. Dark hair. Dark eyes. The guy was smiling but with his mouth only. Willi chilled when he saw the name on his uniform tag: ACHILLE BAPTISTE.

"No thanks." He hurried away.

Eighteen

"Why can't we take the metro?" Vivi pouted. "You always want to walk, Willi."

"I like walking. It's healthy for you." He'd given up trying to make it down those damned subway steps. There was no way to fight a phobia like that. It either went away or you lived with it. Some men from the war still dove at every clap of thunder. "Besides, it's only a few blocks."

"But it makes calluses. And I want my feet to be soft and lovely. Don't you?"

She nestled nearer as they walked, slipping under his arm. Autumn had arrived and Paris was alive again, the streets pulsing with people enjoying the crisp September night. It was thrilling having a beautiful girl at his side. Women nodded. Men eyed him with envy. Willi felt more masculine than he had in . . . he couldn't remember.

"Your feet are *magnifique,*" he whispered.

"Oh, Willi."

True, their relationship had lasted longer than he'd intended. It was only supposed to be a summer fling. But things had settled in for now, the scratches on his chest healed. Sex was more amazing than ever, sometimes so good he felt his eyes burn with gratitude when he held her near. He hadn't forgotten Phillipe Junot though. Fate had left it in his hands to find that kid's killer. Tonight he'd decided to probe how much his girlfriend might have known about him.

"You realize, Willi"—she pressed her cheek against him—"other than this walking crap, you're pretty perfect. About the most perfect guy I've known. The first time we met I felt a connection, didn't you?"

"I feel it now."

"But it's as if you intuit what I need. For instance, how did you know how desperately I've wanted to see a fortune-teller?"

"Just a thought." Guilt prickled him. He certainly hadn't intuited anything. He was manipulating her, wanting to see her reaction when they passed the gambling hall at 234 quai de Valmy.

"See what I mean? Ever since Phillipe died, I've wanted to have my future read. I was just imagining it the other day. Then you tell me about this lady. It's telepathy!" She squeezed his arm. "Oh, Willi, I hope she's good. I mean, if we could really know the future"—her eyes clung to him—"we wouldn't have to worry so much, would we?"

"I told you she read palms, Vivi. Not the future."

"With you in it"—she nuzzled even tighter—"I feel the future will be just . . . hey, how come we're going this way?" Her head lifted as they reached quai de Valmy. Willi noted a glint of concern in her eyes.

"Because this is where she is."

"But—"

The canal breeze enveloped them in briny air. Vivi's breath got shallow as they neared 234. When the dilapated door opened and two men walked out, he felt her shoulders tremble. She knew what was going on in there all right. She knew a lot more than she let on.

Relieved, he saw the old lady at her usual table in the café. "There she is," he reassured Vivi. "Madame Bijou. Palm reader extraordinaire."

"Her?"

"*Bon soir!*" The painted eyelids fluttered like one of those carnival mannequins at the drop of a coin. "You are seekers of spiritual guidance, I can tell."

Vivi looked at Willi, then at the woman, a swallow of consternation descending her throat. How much she wanted to believe, Willi saw. But the moth-eaten clothes, the crazy brows, the lipstick drawn more around the lips than on them, didn't fit her image. As a Catholic, though, bred to accept miracles, she pushed aside her apprehensions and supplicated as if before the Virgin.

"Madame." Vivi folded her hands in a prayerlike clasp. "Spare me not. I wish to know my destiny."

"That's a lot to ask for. It will cost fifty francs."

Willi was already digging in his wallet, figuring the investment worth it. Here he'd been feeling so guilty for manipulating her, but clearly she had secrets of her own.

"No." Vivi stopped him. "I need to pay myself or your vibrations will influence the reading. Isn't that right, madame?" She returned her gaze to Bijou, who took Vivi's bills with a shrewd nod, stuffing them into her bosom.

"Yes. Quite. Then sit mademoiselle—show me your palms."

Vivi closed her eyes.

Bijou grabbed both soft, white hands in her parched, yellow fingers, her beads and bangles jingling. Squinting, her blackened eyes gazed palm to palm, an exaggerated look of consternation, then confusion, then alarm, sequentially cracking her ancient face.

"My dear." She placed Vivi's hands back down. Even across the table Willi smelled the alcohol on her breath. "Your life line indicates great danger ahead. Even now, as we speak, it approaches here in Paris." She leaned away as if Vivi were sick. "You must do as I say! As soon as possible, leave for another part of the country. It's your only hope. I can not tell you more. Only that you must go, and never see me again, either of you." She strugged to her feet. "Your vibrations." She fumbled for her cane. "I must leave." Despite her intoxication she managed to limp off with surprising alacrity.

"Hey, you—" Vivi rose, trembling with outrage. "What kind of reading's that? Tell me more or give me back my money!"

"Don't." Willi put his arms around, wanting to protect her. "I'll reimburse you. She's obviously crazy, Vivi." He kissed her. "Forget it. We'll find someone else."

"I think maybe there was a hint of something fruity in it too, citrus."

"You are driving me nuts, Willi." Vivi's chest rose and fell. "Fruity. Rooty. Herbal. We've tried every scent in the store. I just don't know what you could be looking for, or why it's so important."

Willi hated having to constantly use her but saw no other way. There were just too many coincidences: *Achille Baptiste,* the boat, the doorman, both with the same name. And that damned scent. He was sure he'd smelled it in the train before Junot was stabbed. But he'd made Vivi take him through every men's cologne at Galeries Lafayette, and nothing came near that pungent odor. It was something wild and outdoorsy. Not boulevard Haussmann. He squeezed her hand to show his thanks.

"Oh, Willi, I'm so depressed by that woman." She slumped against the display counter. "You think it's true?" Her opal eyes swelled with tears. "Am I in danger? Should I leave?"

He pictured the man outside Junot's building confronting her that night, the *bouquiniste.* What had he said to her? It might explain so much. But he couldn't ask because he couldn't let her know he'd seen it.

"Vivi, you've got to forget that woman. You know how long she's been knocking back absinthe? Her brain's not right."

"Then why did you bring me to her?" She pouted tragically. "Sometimes I think you must hate me, Willi."

"Now look, I know you don't particularly like me." To Willi's surprise Marc Nathanson phoned later. A week after Maxim's, the scandal about André's horse had dissipated—presumably because it had no substance—and Willi didn't feel like taking any more about him from Nathanson. "But at least hear me out."

Vivi wasn't back yet when the journalist showed up with a bottle of schnapps, as if that would warm Willi up to him.

"I'm doing this because I believe in truth," Nathanson said with more than his usual pomposity. "And secondly, for Ava's sake. You can't imagine the anxiety she suffers, sleepless at night over her father's investment."

Willi tried to hide his fists. Who did this jerk think he was, saying such things to him . . . *sleepless at night*?

"Frankly I feel she has a right to her fears." Nathanson's toothy grin seemed barely to diminish. "In my opinion you need to consider this with more detachment, Willi, especially since your sons are involved. I realize Duval's a magnetic figure. He exerts a force field over half this nation. But magnets either attract or repel. And heated beyond a certain point, they lose their—"

"Get to the point, Marc, why don't you."

Nathanson frowned. He reached into his pocket and pulled out an envelope. Inside was a carbon duplicate of André's bill, allegedly, from the Hôtel Lutetia. It showed the rent on the Duval's glamorous rotunda suite in arrears of over a quarter million francs, settled two weeks ago in full. "Right after his big 'loss' at Deauville," Nathanson pointed out. "It's only logical, Willi. The guy fixed that race. And now I have it from an even more reliable source—"

"Damn your sources."

"—that the whole house of cards is about to come tumbling down. If it hasn't already."

"Get out, Marc. Really, I don't want to hear it. Talk to Max Gottman if you're so concerned. I have nothing invested with André."

"Don't you?" Nathanson slowly rose. "Think about it, Willi. Don't be so emotional." He showed himself out, but half turned before he left. "At some point did your friend happen to lay that sob story on about his brother killed in the war? Because I know for a fact, André Duval never had a brother. It's a standard marketing ploy of his."

Willi kicked the door shut behind Nathanson, then stood a long while staring out the window. The sky had turned a fiery red. His whole chest felt inflamed. He threw back a glass of schnapps, then grabbed his hat and went down to find André.

He hadn't stepped to the sidewalk when two gendarmes in blue capes took him by the elbows. "This way." They led him toward a car.

"Am I under arrest?" he managed to utter.

"No, monsieur."

"May I ask where we're going?"

"No, monsieur."

Down boulevard de Sébastopol they turned left onto rue de Rivoli, then across the river by City Hall onto the Île de la Cité. A sinking feeling rose through his chest when they parked near the Palace of Justice. Exiting the police car, he felt even worse when he spotted the newspapers being unloaded at a kiosk. The headlines turned his blood icy: AVIGNON BOND RUMORS!

It was suite 602, office of the police commissioner. The cold in his veins only thickened when he saw who else was there: half a dozen people seated like children before the big-nosed, bald-headed figure of Victoir Orsini. Among them, a number of faces he recognized from André's company, including the chief financial officer, M. Hubert, the handsome man with the dreary monotone who'd nearly bored Willi to death. And next to him, the regal figure of Adrienne Duval in a slim, blue suit edged with Persian lamb.

"Willi." Her eyes glazed when she saw him. "André's vanished—" Her voice cracked. "More than a day. Nobody knows where he is. He left for work and never arrived."

Willi's legs weakened.

"Inspektor Kraus." Orsini leaned against his giant desk, a marble sphinx weighing down his papers, the figurined clock waltzing as he spoke. The commissioner had been named Frenchman of the Year again, Willi had read, for all his charity Coeurs des Anges— Hearts of Angels—did for the homeless. "Might you have any idea where your friend André has disappeared to?"

Willi tried to breathe through all the tension in the room and the expection in the many faces fixed on him. Out the window the saints of Notre Dame seemed staring at him too. He hadn't a clue where André had gone, only that in the back of his brain he heard that old children's song crazy Vermette sang as he drove off with his bulldogs:

We all dance there . . . we all dance there.

"I have no idea, sir," he stammered. "I'm shocked as anyone."

"Why can't you tell me?" Vivi's eyes blazed. "And why won't it wait until morning? You think you're going to find a train at this hour?"

"It's only"—he checked his watch—"nine fifteen." Willi continued packing. She was right of course. Getting a train now wouldn't be easy. But fueled by a terrible mixture of rage, bewilderment, and loyalty, he felt compelled to try. André was in deep trouble. Willi couldn't just let him drown out there, however guilty he might be. Or not. "It has to do with that investigation I told you about. That very rich, powerful man."

"André Duval?"

No surprise she'd figured that out. Rumors of his disappearance were all over the radio now, along with nervous conjecture about the Confiance Royale bonds. André's face had returned to every front page in Paris.

"Are you going to look for him? I want to come."

Leaving Maxim's the other day André had mentioned what "absolute heaven" that little town in Provence was this time of year. Perhaps he'd gone down there, Willi reasoned, the origin of both his riches and his sin, to try to fix whatever mess he was in. Surely others must have surmised that possibility. But he couldn't just sit around doing nothing.

"Willi!"

"No." He snapped shut his overnight bag. "Sorry, Vivi."

"You don't trust me, damn you!" She punched his chest. "You think I'm too stupid. Christ, you make me hate myself." She clawed her own wrist. "I may not be as smart as—"

He grabbed and kissed her. "It has nothing to do with any of that. I just have to go alone." He pushed her back.

"Why?" She stamped a foot. "You asked for my help. I want to give it."

He considered, but knew again she was right. He didn't trust her, not completely. And this was far too crucial. He tightened his tie. "I should be home soon, with any luck."

"If you go"—her chest was heaving—"I won't be here when you get back."

Grabbing his bag, he stopped by the door, half wishing she had the strength to carry out her threat. "That's a chance I'll have to risk." He looked at her sadly, then backed out. "Either way, Vivi"—he blew a kiss from the hall—"take care of yourself, huh? You're a great girl."

"Screw you, Kraus." She leaned over the banister. "I don't need you!"

Book Three

LES PORTES DE LA NUIT

(The Gates of Night)

Nineteen

With its bright lights and potted palms the magnificent Gare de Lyon had the lonely air of seaside resort after season. From a sleepy clerk at the ticket counter Willi learned the only night route to Avignon was indirect and costly. The Calais-Méditerranée Express, the famous Blue Train to the Riviera, exclusively first-class, was leaving in half an hour, stopping at Dijon, Chalon, and Lyon but bypassing Avignon before heading to Marseille, Cannes, Nice, and Monte Carlo. Seats were available, but Willi would have to get off at Lyon and wait for a local train. His palms sweat as he purchased the ridiculously expensive ticket, hoping like hell his hunch was right.

Sinking into the velvet seat, he was surprised to find the car half-empty. The Depression certainly had taken its toll on luxury travel. Only a few years back he and Vicki had to all but fight for tickets on this train. Now when they pulled from the station, he was wrapped in comfortable solitude, confident at least of a few hours' sleep. How mortally exhausted he was, he realized, as if he'd been bleeding all night and didn't even know the life was ebbing from him.

As they rattled out of Paris, André's face appeared before him. The man's world was teetering, Willi knew, and he knew too how terrifying that was. Plus Adrienne and Claude, what they must be going through—separated when they needed each other most. How badly he wanted to believe these latest headlines were more baseless charges, politically motivated, anti-pan-Europists or the boulevard press trying to sell papers—that it really would all work out. What a wonderful world if instead of Hitlers and Mussolinis people like André ruled. But why had he vanished? Had he been kidnapped? Murdered? Gone into hiding? And what about this brother bullshit?

Willi drifted into a fitful sleep, dreaming of the Riviera, Vicki and the boys, the Gottmans too, all on the sunny beach chilled by a frigid wind. After a while his eyes popped open. My God. That smell. He took a deeper whiff. The same cologne again. There was no mistaking it. He snapped his head up in time to catch a figure disappearing into the next car, a man in a green fedora. His chest pounded. It couldn't be, could it? The one who'd stabbed Junot in the metro? How many green fedoras were there in France? Probably thousands. And yet . . . that cologne.

Agitation pulled him from his seat, starting him down the aisle. The next car was darker, noisier. A bar car filled with Englishmen. Willi saw no sign of a green fedora. He made his way farther, into what proved the restaurant wagon. It was awkward walking past all the candlelit tables of diners. What was he doing anyway? Countless people could be wearing that cologne, that hat.

The club car that followed was dark and crowded. A three-piece band had half a dozen couples up shuffling to a fox-trot. Willi's eyes roamed the silhouettes. Not a fedora in sight. The guy might have removed his. But whom was he even looking for? He had no idea. Another four or five cars were still ahead. What would he do if he found this guy anyway, haul him in for questioning? He stopped, clenching his fists, taking a deep breath. Feeling like an idiot, he forced himself into an about-face and headed back to his seat. He was too wound up he knew, too frazzled. He'd probably dreamed that damned cologne.

As soon as his head hit the cushion, he was asleep, and before he knew it they were screeching into Lyon. Grabbing his suitcase, he stumbled down the platform in search of the local track. It was two in the morning. Besides a few porters he seemed the only one in the station. His footsteps echoed forlornly. Just as he approached the first wagon of the Blue Train, it released a shriek of departure. He looked up, and through the window his gaze met that of the man in the green fedora, their faces just feet apart. The guy sat up. The train began to move. Dark eyes fastened on Willi as they diminished down the track. What the hell was *he* doing on the first-class night express? Willi wondered. The doorman from Maxim's.

The local pulled into Avignon shortly after dawn. It was like stepping into another world; glittering sunshine, summer heat, the sky a deep cerulean. There was no mistaking Provence, its arid hills yellow in the morning light. The trip into town filled him with unexpected delight, the first glimpse of the huge walls seeming to thumb back the chapters of history. Avignon was one of the few French cities still to have its medieval battlements and town center. As the taxi entered the ancient gates, he could see the crenellated towers of the massive, brooding palace that so dominated the city, where for nearly a century, instead of in Rome, popes and antipopes had reigned. Within the thick defensive walls the narrow streets with their shops and markets were busy with residents and tourists alike. Finding someone here would be no holiday, he realized. Especially someone who didn't want to be found. Or who might not even be here.

He checked into a small hotel off the main square, Place de l'Horloge, showered, shaved, and procured a map. The maze of winding streets was a cinch to get lost in. But his first stop proved right across the square, Avignon City Hall. The *crédits municipaux* that sponsored André's bonds had its offices inside, and while it seemed unlikely with half of France looking for him that André could really be there, perhaps, Willi thought, he might be sequestered somewhere deep in the basement, going through books, trying to figure out what went wrong. He had so much at stake now with that Pan-Europa thing. Were the "warmongers," as he called them, behind all these scandals, even the letters to the insurance companies? It was not inconceivable.

Stepping from the hotel into the hot, bright morning, Willi couldn't forget the fate of another French Jew forty years ago, Alfred Dreyfus. The conspiracy against him had been no fantasy, and the price he'd paid terrible: five years on Devil's Island, in solitary. At Maxim's André had predicted as much, that those who opposed his peacemaking bond would take ever more drastic measures to stop him. Willi really wanted to believe that.

Even from across the square, however, he could see he wasn't getting near City Hall this morning. Hundreds people, including reporters and photographers, were gathered around the white, neo-classical structure. What were they waiting for? He asked a nearby man. "Any news of Duval?"

As soon as the fellow removed his dark glasses, Willi felt certain he'd just addressed an undercover cop, probably Sûreté.

"Why do you want to know?" His eyes squinted with too much interest.

"Just wondering." Willi backed off.

The whole square, now that he noticed, was bristling with plain-clothesmen and uniformed cops, the hunt for André clearly serious. Willi knew that André could be here, but not as André. There were countless disguises he might assume. Flocking across the square for instance were a long line of nuns in great white headpieces that flapped liked bird wings. If anyone could spot someone incognito though, Willi considered, scanning their thick-soled shoes for peculiarities, his trained eyes could. They'd been honed for many years in the field. But André was not among the nuns. Willi laughed at the thought. Nor was he in the crowd. He could be anywhere in Europe by now. Or in heaven.

Despite the blazing sunshine, clouds began gathering in Willi's heart, a feeling that something bad was in the making, and that he had come here in vain. He stood in the center of the huge stone square wondering what to do. Realizing how hungry he was, he took refuge in a café that offered a view of City Hall should anything happen. But nothing did. It was as if the crowd were awaiting word of a dam break that might not occur, wanting to leave but not daring to. When he finally paid the check, he thought of the anxiety that must be building in his in-laws' apartment this morning. He ought to phone them, he knew, but didn't know what to say.

As he strolled toward the massive papal palace, its towers and turrets and eighteen-feet-thick walls made him feel about the size of a snail. He turned from its shadows and spent the morning wandering the medieval streets. In 1306, when the popes settled here for safety, Avignon became one of the most populous and wealthy cities of Europe. It was crammed with elaborately decorated churches, chapels, convents, and cloisters of every order. The cardinals built enormous palaces, turned now into museums or luxury hotels. Willi stalked the cobblestoned alleys and picturesque squares with their gurgling fountains, and the lobbies of the elegant hotels. His eyes took in everyone he passed. But André was nowhere, and everywhere, staring from beneath banner headlines screaming: *OÙ EST DUVAL?*

By midafternoon the sun had grown brutal. Sweat dripped down Willi's head. He had to take a break. At a bistro he ordered some local Côtes du Rhône and a *pot-au-feu*, recalling the time André first told him about those damned fake emeralds: *I met this man in Avignon. Ever been there? Fantastic place. An ancient walled town in Provence ... Anyway, guy had a jewelry shop ... an Italian actually, from Genoa. Brilliant. Spoke like fourteen languages.*

After lunch Willi found a phone book and wrote down the address of every jeweler listed. He spent hours tracking down each one, asking as many questions as possible. But none of the shops specialized in emeralds, and none seemed owned by any brilliant Genoese. As the afternoon began to wane, bringing welcome relief from the heat, he found it increasingly difficult to suppress the sensation that this pilgrimage had been for naught. Returning to the Place de l'Holorge, he was surprised to find the crowds even larger than before, still standing in silence. With the palace walls throwing everlonger shadows he climbed the zigzag stairs into the cathedral park to watch the sun go down.

Sculpted from a high bluff overlooking the river, to one side loomed the most imposing collection of Gothic architecture on earth, the pope's palace, the towering cathedral with its great golden Virgin, the turreted fortifications. On the other, one of Europe's most ancient trade routes, the wide-flowing Rhône, and beyond the countryside of Provence, lavender now in fading light. Arching across the silent, silver water, the famous bridge of Avignon, a monument to twelfth-century aspirations, one of the marvels of its age. For four hundred years this noble stone span connected France east to west, only gradually succumbing to the violent rampages of the mighty river it crossed. Today, just four of the original twenty-two arches remained, and it came to a jagged, precipitous halt high over the water, a sublimely haunting image. Through fire, plague, pillage, and schism though, Avignon stood breathtakingly intact. Only the audacious old bridge remained a world-class ruin.

Looking down on it from the esplanade above, watching the tourists and honeymooners having their photos taken against the backdrop of medieval splendor, that children's song skipped back through Willi's brain:

On the bridge of Avignon—
We all dance there . . . we all dance there.

Where was his friend, his confidant, his brother? Did the search for André just end here, like that bridge, dropping into nothing?

The devil seemed to be blowing through the streets the next morning. From the window in the hotel lobby Willi saw an old man chasing his hat. What those popes and cardinals must have endured . . . it was the famous mistral roaring down the valley. One needed to be cautious in weather like this, according to the desk clerk. Not merely objects but tempers flew. From this same clerk Willi learned that an eleven-thirty train would get him to Lyon in time to catch the Paris express. He intended to be on it.

At the restaurant he ordered breakfast and a newspaper. By the time he scanned the front page though, he was choking on his coffee. Marc Nathanson had gotten it all too right this time; it was worse even than that damned source had predicted.

Worse than anyone could have.

Confiance Royale had not merely collapsed, but exploded into a pillar of fire, bringing with it vast destruction. A second set of books had been turned in, exposing André's coveted Avignon bonds to be worth nothing more than paper and ink. My God, Willi's head throbbed as he read. For nearly a decade André had been pulling the wool over the eyes of all France. A hundred million francs were feared lost, tens of thousands of investors wiped out. The worst French financial scandal, according to *L'actualité d'Avignon,* of the twentieth century.

Willi sat there holding a cup, unable to lift it. Like the first time he'd gone through artillery fire his ears filled with thunder. He glanced out the window half expecting an avalanche. *How could I have been so stupid?* A wave of icy self-scorn hit. *So absolutely blind?* The big story barely breached his consciousness. All he could think was that André had deceived *him.* Him! All these months when he thought they were friends—brothers—he'd been pumped full of shit.

Forcing his eyes back to the newspaper, he read the reports on André's whereabouts. Police feared he might have fled the country or would attempt to, perhaps by ship via Marseille. A cold blade pierced him. The Blue Train had been headed directly for Marseille. Could that be why Achille Baptiste had been on it? Was he hunting for André too? Willi searched for the waiter to cancel breakfast but couldn't find him. If André was guilty, he told himself finally, just leaving money, he'd have to suffer the consequences like anyone else. But he deserved a fair trial, not a lynch mob. Or an assassin.

Willi checked his watch, seeing it was ten, wondering if he should go to Marseille. It was only another hour south. What would he do once he got there though, scour the docks? As he pushed open the door to the street, the hot wind hit him with a vengeance, drying out his eyes. From across the big square his ears picked up a strange rumble of voices. The crowd outside City Hall he saw had turned into a mob.

"Kill them!" people were screaming. "To the guillotine!"

"What's happening?" he dared ask a red-faced woman screaming along.

"They're arresting the bums; that's what. The whole damned lot."

"Duval too?"

"You can be sure that Jew's smart enough not to get caught. These are just the swine that got rich off him, running the damned *crédits municipaux*. To the guillotine!"

Willi walked away. Crawled really, inside. His thoughts groping painfully. In truth he'd never been happy about Erich and Stefan's inheriting a great deal of money. He worried what such a prospect might do to them, their motivation in life. Now he didn't have to worry, did he? It'd be tough on the Gottmans, though. Max especially, his whole life's work.

Willi took a deep breath, grasping for equilibrium. He'd been knocked down by disillusionment before, more than once in life. The first time, during the war, it had accumulated so gradually he'd hardly noticed until every pillar of faith—fatherland, king, duty— came crashing down on him. This year, the Nazi takeover brought the realization that friends and neighbors hated and wanted to expel him from his country. And now, André's betrayal, the treachery of a brother, like having the floorboards ripped out from under because his own perceptions had failed so miserably. Hadn't they?

Through shifting currents of anger and dispair he stumbled through the streets, the great glass dome of Galeries Lafayette spinning in his brain. Concave or convex? Up or down? It was impossible to tell. How much had he taken part in his own deception? He'd not been blind to André's grandiosity or that André didn't quite value truth precisely. After all, whom had André confessed to about his emeralds? Yet Willi had let it slide, accepted the assurances it was all "in the past" because he needed André to help with his own transgressions. Had it been Berlin and he hadn't had to grovel for a fake badge, he would have scented André out. He was sure of it. But here, in this topsy-turvy world where everything doubled back on itself, he was as complicit as everyone else the great confidence man had manipulated.

And what a master André was, Willi thought, winding ever deeper through the labyrinth of alleys. Every so often a cat dashed past, geraniums and bougainvillea shaking in the wind. The whole damned world had believed him. He himself believed, clearly. How else could he have convinced so many others? There was nothing vaguely cynical about André. Oh, no. *The most sincere man I've ever met,* according to Désireé, née Lulu, Jourdain, former star of the Queen Theater. He was just . . . delusional.

Only Ava had sensed it. She'd been right all along. He felt a wave of awe for her and bit of hatred too—because it was such a horrible thing to be right about. How much could Max have actually invested?

Leaning into a gust of wind, Willi swore he heard a choir of male voices echoing down the alley. A minute later he was relieved not to have been hallucinating as a small procession of men approached, all draped in black robes. They carried crosses and billowing incense and were chanting to a drumbeat. At their front a medieval banner declared them Pénitents Noirs, a fraternal order dedicated to the spiritual assistance of prisoners condemned to death. Willi's breath caught. He pressed against the wall to let them pass. *This* was where André ought to be, he thought, scanning the faces, the postures, and the shoes as they passed. Perhaps I should join them too. Maybe they were assisting André. It was preposterous. He was Jewish. But everything here was inside out. André could be anywhere, anything. Willi's stomach clenched as he swore he smelled that same damned cologne again—or was it the incense? He was going insane. The whole universe was laughing at him.

Through dizzy eyes he noticed a church across the street. Over elaborately carved doors was written LA CHAPELLE DU MIRACLE. As the last penitent passed, a two-story building next door came into view with a modern show window, merchandise inside sparkling. Was it jewelry? Why hadn't it been listed in the phone directory? Because it wasn't a jeweler's he saw as he crossed the street, but a pawnshop.

Twenty

A loud bell chimed as he entered. Two Dobermans snoring on the floor barely lifted their heads. The place looked like a Parisian boutique, filled with furs and expensive golf sets, silver cocktail shakers—a pawnshop evidently for the better set, or what had been. Willi's heart quickened when he spotted an extensive display in a locked case of what looked to be emerald jewelry. Just then an electric grinder turned off in a back room and a robust man with a bush of white hair came out removing a leather apron.

"*Ah, bonjour, monsieur.*" He smiled, dusting himself off. "How may I help you?"

"*Bonjour,*" Willi returned, pointing toward the emeralds. "Might I see some of these?"

"You've been recommended, yes? Otherwise just lucky." The fellow chuckled as he unlocked the case. "Emeralds are my specialty. People bring them from across France." He lifted out several racks on which dozens of sparkling pieces were arrayed on velvet beds: brace-lets, necklaces, earrings, pins. And several rows of rings.

"Quite a selection." Willi's eyes scanned. "How can one be certain of their quality? One hears such stories these days."

The man shrugged. "This is why a trained eye is necessary, which fortunately I have. Plus there are others in town one can feel free to consult. What is it you're interested in?"

The old fellow had a faint accent, Willi noticed. Italian perhaps?

Willi switched to English. "I'm afraid my French isn't as good as it ought to be."

"Not a problem," the gentleman responded in kind. "What exactly are you looking for?"

"I'm most comfortable in German, actually. Are you able to manage that?"

"*Natürlich.* I speak many languages."

Willi's heart was pounding now. That ring in the middle. It had to be. "May I have a look at this one?"

"Speaking of expert, your eye's most extraordinary. This"—the man lifted it from the box—"happens to be the most expensive item in the store, perhaps in all Avignon. Magnificent, isn't it?"

"Yes, quite. May I ask where it comes from?"

"A rich man short of cash naturally—as so many are these days, even the best."

"I meant the emerald."

"Ah. Ecuadorian. Finest on earth. This is an extremely valuable piece, *mein Herr.* One must be, how shall I say, quite well-to-do to afford it."

"How well-to-do?"

"One million francs."

Willi whistled. "A person could live nicely off that for a while."

"Depending on their habits, yes."

"Might you be Italian originally? I always try to guess people's accents."

"You hear it? I'm amazed. I've been here so many years."

"Not by any chance from Genoa?"

"You hear that too? Your ears are as good as your eyes."

Willi returned to French as he pulled out his police badge and held it in front of the guy. "No games, monsieur. I know that ring is Duval's. Just tell me—where is he?"

The man's jaw hung. "My God."

"I'm a friend. I want to help."

"A German refugee?"

Willi's stomach turned. Did he realize the badge was fake? "Yes."

"You're Jewish, right? Me too. Italian Jewish. So you understand . . . I can't betray him. We've known each other too long. He's like family."

"And I know all about your emerald business. So Jewish or not, if you don't tell me where he is, I'll—"

Willi saw him reach beneath the counter, wishing he hadn't. A bell upstairs rang. Hoping not to have to hurt anyone, he heard footsteps pounding down the stairs. Both dogs jumped to their feet. A side door flung open, and there was André, wide-eyed with fright.

"It's you!" He came in, flushing with relief. "But who else would find me . . . only the best in the business! What are you doing here?" He approached extending his arms.

"How about you answering first?"

André stopped, cocking his head in dismay. "Don't tell me you actually believe . . . ? But I warned you, remember at—"

"I remember." Willi couldn't help it. He half wanted to strangle the guy, half to hug him. "Just tell me—" He tried to steady his voice. "Did you ever really have a brother?"

Willi watched André's eyes darken. He turned to the older man. "Levi. Give us a little time, will you? We need to talk."

"Sure. I'll pick up some tomatoes and onions." The emerald expert put on a jacket, turning at the door. "You'll stay for lunch, Officer?"

"I don't think so."

"A pleasure to have met you."

"Come upstairs where we can sit, okay?"

A surprisingly elegant apartment opened on the second floor.

"Take a peek outside," André suggested, opening a door. "You'll appreciate the view."

Stepping onto a tiled terrace Willi squinted from the bright sunshine. Above the orange tile roofs a postcard vista opened of the

Pope's Palace and cathedral, the gold Virgin glistening in the blue sky. In the back below ran a picturesque little alley, all the stone houses covered with green vines.

"Too bad we can't sit out there. The breeze is so wonderful this time of day. But—" André shrugged. "I'm sure you understand."

He left the door wide open though, breathing in deeply as he cranked up a phonograph. Placing the needle on Brahms Second symphony rose up loud enough to muffle their conversation.

"Levi has a huge villa outside town." André motioned Willi to join on the couch. "Beautiful swimming pool. Tennis courts. Vineyards. But this place suits me for now, don't you think? Are you thirsty? You want something to drink?"

"No."

André frowned, running a hand through his copper hair. "They've gotten to you, haven't they?" He stared at Willi. "You doubt me, I can tell, brother."

Willi barely knew what to say.

"That's a word you love to use, isn't it André? Do you have any idea what it even means? Have you ever really had a brother—in truth, I mean beside *me* of course?"

"You're furious. I can understand. But what do I have to do to make you believe, Willi, that all the garbage you hear is manufactured? I told you at Maxim's they would try whatever they could to stop me. Pan-Europa threatens their—"

"*Did* you ever have a brother?"

André turned up the music.

"Yes, goddamn it!"

Willi grit his teeth, enraged at his inability to read this guy's face.

"What about that second set of books?"

"A total forgery. You think they're incapable of it? They're powerful people. The arms makers of Europe."

The dome of Galleries Lafayette was spinning again in Willi's head. Up or down. Inside or out. He'd lost all perspective.

"So what *are* you doing down here, André? Why don't you just come out and tell the world the truth if there's nothing to hide—"

"After all the lies spewed about me, how can I? People want to tear me apart!"

"Because they've been swindled. Some of them out of their whole life's savings."

"I'd be furious too. Only I haven't swindled them, Willi. The bonds are as good as ever. I just need time to make it happen."

André's eyes suddenly were ablaze with life or death struggle.

"I need to get out of France, Willi. Levi's got a friend who can ferry me to Marseille, and connections for a freighter to Istanbul. I've got to have a week. One lousy week. He's working as fast as he can but it takes time. You can't make mistakes with these things. Experts check. You need the proper saturation, hue, tone, surface fissures. If I can get to Persia, India, or even China, I could make a fortune. Bring Claude and Adrienne over. Rebuild my business. Oh Willi, one lousy week."

The mention of Adrienne and Claude hurt. Would they ever really see André again, Willi wondered?

"Are you worried about Max's money?" André seemed to be trying to guess what was going on in Willi's mind. "He'll get it back. I swear he will. Every cent, Willi—with interest. And your kids. Your beautiful boys. You think I'd do anything to hurt them? When was the last time you spoke to them, huh?" He grasped Willi's forearm. "Do you want to call? There's a phone right downstairs."

Willi's throat was so tight it hurt. André was probing to see how far he could trust him.

"That would be nice." He cleared his throat, trying not to stammer. "Just to let them know I'm all right. They must be rather concerned." He wanted to add, *as must your family be about you.* But didn't. Perhaps Adrienne knew exactly what was going on.

"Of course, of course." André frantically searched Willi's face, seeming to wonder if it was really home he was planning to call, or the police. "You'll see it down there right behind the counter."

Willi rose. André followed with his eyes.

"I'll wait here." He smiled, pretending to relax. "This is my favorite movement."

"Sure," Willi said, not looking back as he took the stairs down.

The phone was behind the cabinet of emeralds. Willi's hand trembled as he reached for it. Sweat beaded on his temples. Could he really turn André in? But how could he not? Never in his life had he abetted a criminal. Wasn't everyone equal before the law? Didn't André have to pay the piper too? Only . . . how desperately he wanted give him that week.

Upstairs the Brahms symphony lifted to a crescendo. Just as he placed the receiver to his ear, a yelp pierced the waves of violins, like a dog being kicked, followed by a distinct *woosh*. An operator came on. "What number, please?" Willi hung up. An instant later he heard feet clambering down the side of the building, a thud on the back alley. With all his might he ran upstairs. The record was circling, the needle scratching. André was still on the couch, a pistol in his hand, blood pulsing from the side of his head. Through the open terrace door Willi could just see a figure disappearing down the small back ally. He wanted to cry out, but horror paralyzed him.

Turning to André, he saw the back quarter of his skull had been blown off. His, copper hair was tangled with coils of brain. The gun had been placed in André's hand after it'd been fired, Willi saw, a silencer obviously removed. What had killed André as he sat there in symphonic rapture was a single swift knife thrust. Down his white shirt a rivulet of cherry marked its slender entry to the heart.

Willi's knees weakened as he grasped the open terrace door. In the distance the golden Virgin shone over the city. His mind grappled for clarity. Should he call the police? Perhaps they'd think he'd done it as revenge for his family's investment. What about Levi? Could he trust his "fellow Jew"? The old man had only gone for tomatoes. He didn't know Willi's name but he could describe him to police. He had to get out, Willi knew. And not by the front door either. Taking one last look at his friend, choked with grief, he opted for the killer's route, climbing the wall and using vines to repel down to the street, darting off as fast as he could.

The wind was blowing manically. At his hotel he grabbed his suitcase and had the doorman hail a cab. The next train to Lyon left in twenty minutes. With any luck he could make it out of town before anyone realized André was dead. On the station platform people were edgy, women's dresses billowing, caps flung into the tracks.

Willi prayed nobody noticed how badly the newspaper he had his face behind was shaking, and not from the mistral. He kept recalling how he'd smelled that scent again, in the street near the pawn shop, just when the penitants were passing. Might he have led the assassin to André? The possibility made him weak.

On the train he didn't dare close his eyes, just kept reading the same stories in the newspaper over and over. All three insurance companies which had invested so heavily in Avignon bonds were teetering on the abyss. At least two suicides were attributed to the crisis. Tens of thousands had been wiped out or lost retirement pensions, movie stars, politicians, working-class people, even educational endowments and charities, from one end of France to another. Meanwhile, André had been spotted in Switzerland . . . Morrocco . . . Scotland . . .

On the local train north Willi kept wondering if he was being a fool, thinking he could make it through to Paris? Should he try to lay low for a while, perhaps in Lyon? He couldn't stop picturing André slumped on that couch, half the back of his skull gone. He'd left one lunatic asylum for another, he thought. France was as crazy as Germany.

Finally the local inched into Lyon and he had to switch for the express. His knees shook as he stepped to the platform. All he wanted was to see his sons again. Have a chance to talk to them, hold them. To his great relief the few police he saw showed no interest at all in him, and an hour and a half later he was on the express safely speeding to Paris.

The nearer they got to the capital though the less he could quell the fear that his last moments of freedom were rapidly approaching. Surely by now the police had spoken to Levi, ascertained Willi was the last to see André alive, and were circulating a description of him. As they rattled into the Gare de Lyon he had to consciously slow his pounding heart. People would think he had a tropical fever the way he was sweating. But he made it from the train and all the way down the platform without running into a dreaded cordon of blue. Slowly inhaling he tried to keep calm. The palm-filled lobby brimmed with travelers, baggage, dogs, sleepy children. But no police. The main clock chimed above: ten p.m. His feet froze. Ahead, at a newskiosk the headlines screamed:

DUVAL SUICIDE!

He forced himself over and bought a copy, furiously scanning the front page. There was no room for doubt according to "eyewitnesses"—the financier had pulled the trigger on himself. Police said no other suspects were sought.

Willi clenched the paper and lowered his head, walking quickly away. Lifting his chin he stepped from the station, his tear-filled eyes suddenly blinded by the sparkling lights of Paris.

Twenty-one

A dim beam glowed under his door. Willi put the key in and turned. Vivi was at the table, back to him, one strap of her negligee hanging over her shoulder. She was writing with such concentration she didn't notice until the door closed.

"*Mon Dieu—*" She sprang up turning. "Willi, you scared me half to death." A full bottle of wine was on the table, and a half empty one. The ashtray brimmed with cigarette butts. "At least you're okay." She shoved the journal aside, yanking up her strap.

Willi fell into the chair across from her noticing her breasts, like two inviting pillows. She filled a glass and slid it his way, staring with opal eyes.

"You *are* okay? Your sister-in-law called at least three times. I didn't know what to say to her about where you were."

A shiver of guilt went through him as he gulped the whole glass at once.

She kept staring. "Tell me the truth, Willi. Why all the secrecy?

I've been trying to figure it out. What really was between you and Duval? Some kind of affair? You can tell me."

"Affair?" He put his glass down.

"Take it as you wish."

"André was a friend, Vivi." He emptied the bottle into his glass. "The best I had in France. Or so I thought. And then I saw him lying there, blood everywhere, his brains—"

He couldn't help it. Like a mine cave in, one chamber after the next collapsed until his face fell into his hands and he burst out sobbing.

Vivi got up and hugged him from behind. "It's okay. Go ahead. I like when men cry."

It took some time for him to regain himself and when he did, mopping his face, he felt like cutting through all the bullshit he'd been wallowing in since he set foot in this country.

"Vivi, I need your help."

"Whatever I can do Willi, of course."

"Let's start with Phillipe Junot. Tell me everything this time."

"Phillipe?" She sat up. "What's he got to do with it?"

"Trust me. Please, okay? No questions. Only answers."

"But you don't think there's a connec—"

"Vivi."

"What more can I say? I told you all I could about Phillipe."

"How bad was his gambling problem?"

Her face paled. "How do you know he had one?"

"I saw your reaction when we passed 234 quai de Valmy; I know what goes on there."

"Do you?" She shrugged. "Well—" She worked a screw into the new bottle. "Then, I don't need to tell you. Phillipe liked to gamble. He took me there a couple times." She blinked. "When you and I walked by that afternoon—" The cork popped. "It brought memories, that's all. Is that why you brought me to that crazy woman, to test my reaction?"

"What did Phillipe gamble on?"

"Horses." Her hand was tense as she filled them each a glass.

"Did he get into any kind of trouble because of it?"

"I don't know."

"Damn it, Vivi!" He slammed the table.

She jumped back, knocking over a glass.

"Yes! He got into trouble." She grabbed a towel to mop it up. "He worked up a debt and had to pay it off."

"To whom?"

"I don't know. He ran numbers, I think. At different bars along the rue de Lappe."

"Who was his contact?"

"I don't know." She sniveled. "Some guy along the river. One of those *bouquinistes*. Dark hair. Beard. That's all I know. Oh, God, Willi, please don't lose your temper with me."

He looked at her, shocked by the fear in her eyes.

The next day he could barely get up.

Vivi handed him coffee in bed. "Didn't you say you had things to do today?"

He lifted his head, then dropped back to the pillow. He didn't want to face any of them.

"You know," she said later over breakfast, "it's pretty obvious you're the one hiding things from me, Willi." She plunged a croissant into her coffee. "Not vice versa." Her sparkling eyes taunted him.

"How do you mean?" His reply was self-defeating.

"Look at you. I've never seen you in such a state." She chewed, staring at him. "Why are you so affected by all this? And why do you connect Phillipe Junot with André Duval?"

"Who said I did?" He felt submerged under a ton of water, eager to escape. Why had she been so terrified yesterday? She'd trembled like a puppy when he got angry. He remembered that black eye. Who had done it? "I was in a state of shock last night." He tossed aside the napkin. "Maybe I still am. I can't be held responsible for my logic." He shoved back his chair. "And though I'd love to chat all day"—he got up and kissed the top of her head—"I really do have things to get done."

"Great. So I'm the only one who has to be honest around here."

As soon as he'd stepped outside, he wished he'd checked the temperature. It hadn't even occurred to him. Half of him still thought he was back in Avignon, André alive. He shivered as he waited for the bus, dreading this visit to police headquarters, but not for the usual reasons. That single knife thrust had taken not just a friend but both his jobs. He was unemployed again. Without papers. The threat of deportation unabated. As the bus pulled up, he had to stifle the urge to let out a groan.

Gazing from the window as they lumbered down boulevard de Bonne Nouvelle, he began noticing crowds in front of banks, long lines of anxious faces waiting to get in. At Crédit Bourdeaux a veritable mob swarmed the doors. It was the first business day since Confiance Royale's collapse, and instead of universal prosperity, André, it seemed, had created a full-out bank panic. From newspapers open around the bus Willi discerned the ever-growing litany of Duval-inspired grief: business failures, suicides, institutions wiped out . . . veterans' funds . . . the orphanage run by Josephine Baker.

As they passed the offices of *La Vérité,* he sat up, staring. There was bald, little Henri Beliveau overseeing the removal of the company furnishings, shrieking when a crate of his precious plants got overturned on the sidewalk. The newspaper had evidently gone under, André its sole support. A feeling of dread rose through Willi, watching the widening scope of this disaster, recalling those last months in Berlin before the Nazis got power. It was as if the flood tide of desperation had swept across the border and chased him here.

"You're off the hook." Clouitier sat back in his squeaky chair, hands behind his head. His long, thin face looked more relaxed than Willi had ever before seen it. The rest of Paris was nervously depressed, but Clouitier acted as if Willi were an old chum dropping by. Perhaps he was just relieved to have one less case on his desk.

"Sorry it had to end this way. But now that it has, well, how shall I put it?" He shrugged. "There's nothing more we need you for." Before him piled the usual mountains of folders, files, photographs. How could he work on them all? "The good news is that since you

were budgeted for six months, I was able to get you that much pay."
He handed Willi an envelope.

"That's very generous, considering I only worked a month."

"Well, you did a dirty enough job. This should tide you over
until you find another position."

Willi tried to smile. "To find a position one needs a permit,
Inspector. Except of course if one is spying for the police."

To Willi's surprise Clouitier laughed, showing his white
incisors.

"You know, Kraus, if it were up to me, I'd make you full detective
in a second. We could use men of your caliber, willing to do whatever's necessary and keep their cards to their chests." Clouitier seemed
to know what Willi had done to protect his friend André and admire
him for it. "Unfortunately Police Judiciaire's no democracy. Or even a
meritocracy. It has an overseer that must be obeyed—not always for
the best." For half a second Clouitier's weasel face looked almost
friendly, then he sighed. "Anyway, best of luck to you."

Willi was dismissed.

He left police headquarters telling himself to be happy. He *was*
free. His odious mission as a *mouche* at an end. Hurrah. But free to
do what? To await permission to live and work, to be protected as a
citizen? And what kind of work? The only job he wanted was inside those doors, with a proper badge. Odd though, he thought,
Clouitier mentioning the "overseer." Complaining about the boss
to an underling was a breach of decorum in such an agency. Not
that it made a difference. Police Judiciaire would never hire him,
Willi knew. And they'd never find who killed André. Or Phillipe
Junot. Because they weren't looking.

But he was.

And he would.

Another three buses got him up to *Le seizième*, the sixteenth arrondissement. With its wide boulevards and grand beaux arts apartment buildings, it was one of the most beautiful areas in Paris. Willi
wondered how much longer his in-laws would be able to afford to
live here. Getting off at the rue de la Pompe, he again tried to imagine

how much Max Gottman might have lost. Ava hadn't exactly been open over the phone. *I hope you're satisfied, Willi.* As if he had anything to be satisfied about. What, their financial catastrophe? André's death? She had a right to her rage, he supposed. But what had *he* done?

As he took the last few blocks by foot, he saw the sun trying to poke through the clouds. It was still before three, the kids at school. What if they had to move in with him at that crappy place near the Saint-Denis Gate? What would he do with Vivi? The interplaying shadows made him feel as if he were on a merry-go-round. The Gottmans' had probably lost a fortune, and he had witnessed his second murder since coming to France. Everything felt dangerously in motion.

Nearing his in-laws', he noticed a black limousine pulled up at the curb, out of which a man was being bundled from the backseat into a waiting wheelchair. It was the same man he'd seen at André's on Bastille Day, the "ultranationalist," Adrienne had called him.

Willi waited to be recognized as a nurse in a blue cape wheeled him past.

"Ah, Inspector." The man's eyes lit up. "What a coincidence running into you here."

"Yes, my family lives just a few doors down."

"Really? Isn't that amazing." He offered Willi a handshake along with an amicable smile, then switched faces, frowning. "Terrible what's happened with André. Just breaks my heart." Willi noticed the pin on his lapel: FRATERNITÉ D'HONNEUR. "I really loved that guy. Knew him for years."

Willi felt like telling the general that André's death was no suicide, but he was smart enough to hold his tongue.

"André maintained he was innocent, you know," he said instead, figuring he might as well try to elicit what he could from the guy. "Claimed opponents of his Pan-Europa Bond were framing him, trying to bring him down along with the bond."

Crevecour seemed to ponder this but rejected it with a shake of his head. "André had enemies. We all do. But I think we can safely say he cooked his own goose. Don't you think?"

In a way, yes, Willi thought. But he sure hadn't killed himself.

"Time for your shot, sir," the nurse reminded.

"Well, musn't be late for that, heaven forbid!" The man laughed. "Nice running into you, Inspector. Hope we can do it again."

Two doors down, in the elevator of the Gottmans' building, Willi's sense of vertigo mounted. It was as if he were on his way to a condolence call. He ought to have brought food or something, he thought wiping his forehead. At the Gottmans' door, the maid's face appeared to signal she knew she'd lost her job and that hard times were ahead. She pointed to the dining room, where Ava and her parents were facing off across the table, grief in the air all right. It was a wonder they hadn't covered the mirrors. Instead of a funerary rite though, Willi found himself walking straight into the next act of a family drama—one of its featured players.

"Ah." Ava extended an arm. "Here he is at last." She looked radiant. More beautiful than Willi had seen her since the Press Ball in Berlin, outraged with indignation. "That other king of fools."

"Ava, don't," her mother groaned, evidently more upset by her daughter's tone than her words. Round and round Bette Gottman twisted a long pearl necklace through her fingers. She had held her own through financial crisis, political turmoil, life in exile. Today she looked as if a tidal wave had hit her. Her sagging shoulders though straightened as she pointed a shaky finger at Willi. "But if you hadn't befriended that man—"

"For God's sakes." Max stopped her. He appeared to have aged a decade since the last time Willi had seen him, thin and pale. "You're acting childish, both of you. Blaming Willi. He had nothing to do with my choice to invest in those bonds."

"We, acting childish?" Ava cinched her waist. "That's a good one, Father. The best I've heard all day. You and Willi, who are *supposed* to be wearing the pants in this family, ought to be swaddled in diapers."

"Don't be crude, Ava." Bette bunched her beads. "Willi, sit. Have some coffee."

"No thanks." Willi lowered into a chair.

Ava poured him a cup anyway, handing it to him with a defiant glare, making clear her anger was not to be contained. "It's *children* who believe in fairy tales. *Children* who confuse fantasy and reality. *Children* who can't discern credible from incredible. And who did that? Stories about handsome princes who reside in swank hotels with great schemes to make the whole world happy. My God." She started pacing. "Talk about the emperor's new clothes. And *we're* acting childish!"

"We weren't the only ones he fooled," Max said, a feeble attempt.

"Oh, no." Ava pivoted and glowered. "André Duval made history in that department, didn't he? Con man to a nation. Seducer of millions, like others we know—only he never made the trains run on time! So how did he win *your* devotion, Willi? Flattery? Adulation. Did he tell you, you were the greatest detective that ever lived? How he wished he could be as daring as you, as cunning and as skillful? Did that compensate for all the Nazis stole from you? And you, Max, who built a rag company into a million-dollar business. 'Not since Wertheim has Germany produced such an entrepreneural trailblazer.' Perfectly aimed, manipulative bullshit! And you both ate it up. What happened to all that judgment you were supposedly so famous for? Did the Nazis confiscate that too?"

"Ava." Willi reached toward her.

"No, Willi. You've got to face it. Marc repeatedly tried to warn you."

He bowed his head. What else could he do? She wanted to see him chastised.

"How bad is it?" He finally lifted his eyes.

All of them grew silent.

"Bad," Max replied at last.

Bette twisted the necklace angrily. "We won't have to move right away, if that's what you're worried about."

"We'll manage," Max seemed to incant. "We haven't lost it all."

"Just lots of it." Ava collapsed in her chair.

Bette shook her head, sighing. "It's unbelievable. We slipped through the Nazis' fingers only to be skinned alive by someone we should have been able to trust. How could a Jew do this to other Jews?"

"How can anyone do it to anyone, Mother?"

"Uch, this room." Vivi winced, squinting her eyes. "Who the hell decorated it? Those curtains. That couch."

"It came this way."

"No wonder. It can't do anything for your mood. 'Good work begins in a cheerful space.' That's what I learned at secretarial academy—the week I went. Hey, there's a Simone Simon picture at the Impérial." She turned up her profile. "I'm supposed to look like her. What do you think?"

He tried not to smile but couldn't help it. "You're a hundred times prettier."

"Oh, Willi." She threw her arms around him. "I'll never love anyone but you. Can we go then? Can we?"

Evening had fallen. The lights of the boulevards cast an amber glow, making everyone look as if they were in a romantic film. Vivi clung to him as they walked, every so often whispering something naughty. "After the movie I'm going to dip my fingers in that jar of clover honey and— What? What's wrong?" Willi had stopped walking.

Weeks ago, before he'd even gone to Avignon, he'd stopped by a public library and dug through a dozen books until he discovered that strange flag he'd seen on the yacht *Achille Baptiste*. Now, in the window of a small boutique, he saw it again, that same Moor's silhouette with the fluttering bandanna.

"Come." He tugged her into Corsica Mia.

"Oh, Willi . . . not again!"

"Men's colognes?" The man behind the counter laughed as if it were a silly question. "But isn't Corsica the Perfumed Isle, monsieur? Aren't our streets, our hills, filled with the scents of paradise? Which do you prefer: juniper and myrtle? A tinge of wild olive? A blend of honeysuckle, sage, and eucalyptus?"

The man brought out countless aftershaves, essential oils, toilet waters, and colognes, each with its own exotic label: *I'Île de Beauté*.

Monti Nord. Maison de Bonaparte. Vivi soon forgot all about the movie, sniffing bottle after bottle. After a while Willi wondered if they could even discern the differences. But the moment he got a whiff from the black bottle with the red cap, he knew that was it—the same scent he'd smelled on Achille Baptiste at Maxim's. And again on the metro before Junot was killed. And again on the Blue Train speeding south toward Avignon.

"Ah, yes. A favorite among Corsican men, especially here in Paris." The man ran it under Willi's nose, giving Willi the chills. "An unforgettable punch of lemon verbena tinged with porcupine musk. It's called Vendetta."

Willi reeled from it, trying not to see blood.

Having taken up so much time, he felt he ought to at least make a purchase, so he told Vivi to pick out something she liked for herself. She chose a long, red scarf edged with fringe and tied it around her waist, snapping her fingers like a flamenco dancer. Just as they were about to leave, a glint of silver grabbed Willi's attention.

"Beautiful, eh, monsieur?" The salesman took it out from the counter and let Willi hold it, definitely the longest, thinnest, sharpest knife he'd ever seen. Willi pricked his finger on it, instantly drawing blood. The man laughed. "It makes a wound so small you can barely see it. But it does the trick all right. Our famous Corsican stiletto."

Willi had already learned that Achille Baptiste was a common Corsican first name. And that the owner of the yacht *Achille Baptiste* had a Corsican name too. Willi had written it down that day at the motor license bureau: M. Octaviani. Whether or not the *bouquiniste* and the doorman knew each other, Willi had no idea. Only that at least two men from that rocky Mediterranean isle were up to no good in Paris.

Twenty-two

"Weekly Report."

"Monsieur Nathanson, *s'il vous plaît*." Willi had to swallow the bitterness as he clutched the receiver. He couldn't stand this guy.

"Nathanson here."

"Marc, sorry to bother you at work. It's Willi Kraus. This time I'm the one who'd like a get-together."

"I see." There was a long silence. "I could make it after work this evening."

"Great. But someplace we can't be overhead, okay?"

It was already dusk when they took a bench in the gardens of the Palais-Royal, the nearby fountain muffling their voices. Couples strolled by. A cop on a bicycle.

"It's about Duval," Willi said quietly, buttoning his jacket. He kept picturing André on that shaded lounge chair listening to Brahms, his favorite movement. If nothing else, how full of life he was. Right to the end. Willi swallowed hard, damned if he was going to let Ava's new boyfriend see a tear.

André had already been interred in private ceremony at the Division Israelite in the cemetery at Montparnasse, only his wife and son in attendance. Yesterday Willi had gone to pay his condolences at the Hôtel Lutetia, Adrienne Duval's face swollen with anguish. She kept trying to fix her hair. "I know I look awful."

"How's the boy taking it?" Willi wanted to know, shuddering to imagine someone asking the same about his own sons.

"Not well." She shook her head. "He refuses to believe his father could be guilty. Says it was all a setup; that one day the truth will come out, even if he has to dig it up himself." On the couch she pulled a handkerchief from her sleeve. "I still can't get over it. You live with someone fifteen years, share their bed, their life—and not realize half of it's a lie." She blew her nose. "How stupid can you be? But I swear to you"—she stuffed the handkerchief back—"I hadn't the vaguest idea. If I ever saw that bastard again, I'd kill him. But, oh, I miss him, Willi."

"Me too."

He didn't mention the stiletto. The idea that her husband took his own life somehow felt less cruel to live with than that he'd been killed—at least for now. Sooner or later Willi would get the bastard who murdered André. It had become apparent to him, though, he couldn't do it alone. He was a foreigner in a city he barely knew. As much as he couldn't stand Marc Nathanson, he needed him. The guy was a Parisian. A reporter.

"Duval never pulled that trigger; I know for a fact. It was only made to look like suicide."

Behind his glasses Marc Nathanson's eyes widened, not exactly surprised but astonished nonetheless. "How do you know this?"

"I was there."

"You saw the murderer?"

"Only his back."

Willi spilled his guts. For more than an hour he told Nathanson everything, from his enlistment under false pretenses by the Sûreté Générale right through André's assassination in the shadow of the Popes' Palace. It felt good finally to unload it all, plus he took comfort in having made some progress since that hellish day in Avignon.

"I'm almost positive the killer's Corsican, Marc. And that he uses a stiletto. My guess is"—Willi cast a glance over his shoulder— "A hit man for someone bigger."

"Humph." Marc shrugged. "I bet it's Orsini."

"What?" Willi was stunned. "Why would you say such a thing?

Nathanson scowled. "He may be Man of the Year—*every* year, but he's hardly Mr. Clean, you know."

"But he and Duval were allegedly friends."

"Oh yes. Like royal brothers." Marc's irony was thick. "They had plenty of reason to want to slit each other's throats. They knew far more about the other than was safe. And on top of that—" He looked at Willi with his toothy grin. "Orsini's a Corsican."

My God, Willi realized. That was where he'd gotten his first whiff of Vendetta. He'd recognized it the night of the Gottmans' anniversary dinner when Achille Baptiste let them in to Maxim's. But even then he knew he'd smelled it before, and now he understood where: that first visit to the Palace of Justice, room 602, Orsini's office.

Nathanson did the talking now, filling Willi in on the infamous police chief. Victoir Orsini might have been the shortest man since Napoléon to rule Paris like an emperor, Marc said. The rank-and-file police worshipped him. Other ministries slashed benefits, but Orsini's got generous retirement funds. The middle class was in awe of him. The violence that had plagued Berlin before Hitler could never happen here because Orsini had half the Communists locked up. Among his friends he counted politicians, newspaper editors, the whole judiciary, and much of the business elite, including, previously, André Duval.

Willi recalled how the anything-but-shy Orsini had demurred that day at the racetrack about taking photos with André. Clearly he'd already pulled back. And then he cut André off entirely. Even with all the bigwigs on hand for André's Bastille Day bash, Willi remembered, Orsini had never showed.

"Every year the press elects him Man of the Year, which shows you how deep the corruption goes in this republic. Because the truth is"—and now it was Nathanson's turn to drop his voice and look over his shoulder—"Orsini runs the biggest crime syndicate this side of the Alps."

Willi's breath caught. That was quite a charge.

"I'm not saying the whole department is in on it. The guy's built a private army, inside and out of the police. Blackmail, extortion, drug trafficking, prostitution. Orsini's got his fingers in it all."

Willi could barely believe it. Like many exiles he clung to the idea his adopted country was better, freer, more just, than the one he'd been forced to flee. Yet his boss in Berlin before the Nazis, Bernard Weiss, had been brilliant, a devoted innovator, fair to the bone. If the head of Paris police really was a major gangster, France was in trouble.

"Don't ask why no one exposes him." Nathanson pushed his glasses up. "More than one who's tried has wound up in the Seine, facedown. Last summer a cartoonist who'd made fun of Orsini's elevator shoes found himself in a car with no breaks, crashing through a storefront. And don't think I didn't aim my slingshot."

A couple strolled by humming "Parlez-Moi d'Amour." Nathanson hummed along until they passed, then continued, "Less than a year ago I took a shot at Orsini's charity. After a week the paper not only scrapped the investigation, but me. I got my nose in far enough though to smell some real stink. Made this great connection in bookkeeping who talked a blue streak—once I got her going. You think Hearts of Angels helps the homeless? Ha. It creates more—because it's a cover-up, Willi—for the biggest, hottest numbers racket in Paris. Racing, boxing, football. I never found the exact location but—"

"I know where it is."

"You?" Nathanson laughed. "That can't be true. Unless you're as good a sleuth as they say."

"How about a deal, Marc. I'll fill you in on Orsini's gambling mecca if you find out what you can about the doorman at Maxim's. Maybe"—here Willi's throat stuck—"take Ava for dinner. Don't tell her why." He hated adding a romantic evening to their itinerary, but it seemed the safest way. "It's just that, this guy most likely will recognize me and—"

"Willi"—Nathanson cut him off—"you needn't explain. It's an assignment I won't mind."

Moonlight cast dim shadows as they headed back through double rows of lime trees toward the street. The police commissioner might well have known Confiance Royale was about to implode, Willi considered. He might even have orchestrated it. Perhaps those letters to the insurance companies had been Orsini's destabilizing grenades. Or perhaps he just realized the house of cards was destined to come down. God only knew how many high officials had profited from André's schemes. Maybe they worried André would talk. Maybe Orsini decided the time had come to eliminate that worry. Still though, Willi pondered, jangling his keys as they reached the corner. It didn't explain Junot. If the student was working off a debt as Vivi claimed, why would they want him dead? Not that they'd done anything to investigate his killing. Willi recalled that empty file at 36 quai des Orfèvres.

On the sidewalk near the Bank of France Nathanson suggested Willi pursue that former bookkeeper at Hearts of Angels. "Oh, she'd love you." Marc winked. "That is of course if you don't mind old fish. You know," he added, seeing Willi's unresponsive face, "fifty-plus."

Just when Willi was starting not to hate him.

"Come on." Nathanson offered a little elbow to the shoulder. "In France we're a lot less *scientifique* than in Germany. You don't actually have to"—he gestured—"just . . ." He flicked his tongue. "She'll talk. You'll see." He pushed his glasses up, giving a toothy grin.

"Mmmmm. Like heaven." Vivi's eyes fluttered.

"Better ease up," Willi suggested. "Champagne only makes you happy at first."

Tonight was her birthday. Twenty-five, she claimed. Not that he believed that. Maybe twenty-one. He was turning thirty-seven in a week.

"Oh, Willi, this place is a dream."

He'd taken her out to the Folies Bergère. The sets, the costumes, the topless ladies parading down stairs, made her face light up like that of a kid at the circus. She was beautiful, a vibrant, sexy, unpredictable girl. But after all he'd been through, a small voice between his ears had grown a little louder, telling him that what he really needed was a woman.

After the nightclub they took a moonlight walk along the Seine. She was holding out her arms, balancing on the embankment wall, her fluttering gown draping her breasts like Nike of Samothrace— the Winged Victory—at the Louvre. She was drunk, barely able to walk. He had to hold her around the waist as one would a toddler. In the taxi home she wanted to know if he was ever going to introduce her to his boys. "Would you, Willi? Or are you ashamed of me? Oh, God, you are, aren't you?"

He put a finger on her lips. "Shhh. I warned you. You've had too much."

Finally he got her in a cab and then had to practically push her up the five flights to his apartment. As he closed the door behind them, she gave him a kiss.

"Thanks, Daddy. This was my best birthday ever!"

He wasn't sure he appreciated that. As long as she was drunk though, he figured he might as well try to get whatever he could out of her. "What about Phillipe Junot?" he probed. "Didn't he ever take you any place nice?"

"Junot?" She hiked her dress, lifting one leg on the chair, running both hands up her thigh. For a moment she appeared to be searching her memory for who he was. Then she laughed. "Oh, him! Come on. He didn't have any money." She was fumbling to get off her stocking. "Once though"—her eyes lit—"Lorilleux took us both out to—" She stopped, turning pale. "Damn these garters. They make them impossible to unhook."

"Who's Lorilleux?"

"Who?"

"Lori-lleux."

"Could you stop interrogating for once and help? I can't afford to tear these. They're silk."

When he came over though, she grabbed his necktie, twisting so violently he thought she was trying to strangle him.

"You gonna marry me, Willi?"

He had to practically snap her wrist to break the grip.

"Don't!" He threw her arm aside and stepped away, loosening his tie. "What the devil makes you do that?" He rubbed his throat.

"I don't know. You just get me all riled up."

"Well, don't try it again, Vivi, or I'll throw you out. I mean it. Now who the hell's Lorilleux?"

Her eyes drank him in, round and greedy, seeming to want to suck something from him. When she saw it wasn't forthcoming, she appeared not to be able to breathe, like a fish on land. Then she dove face-first to the bed and started pounding the pillows, screaming in her evening gown, "I'll slit my wrists. I swear I will! Why doesn't anyone love me?"

Eventually she subsided, sliding out of the gown and snoring off into drunken slumber. Willi stayed up, trying to figure out how he was going to end this. It was getting insane. He couldn't come up with any way that didn't seem to risk bloodshed though, and finally he climbed under the covers next to her, exhausted. When sunshine awoke him sometime after nine, he looked around and realized he no longer had to worry about it. Vivi had slipped from bed, taken her big yellow suitcase, and left. No note. Nothing.

Twenty-three

Dusk crept over the Place des Vosges. The mansard roofs on the grand pavilions, glistening vermilion just moments ago, darkened to deep slate. Seated alone in the arcade café, Willi looked again at his watch. Nathanson was forty minutes late.

He continued reading in the newspaper about the finance minister, discovered this morning, decapitated along a railroad track. Because of what was now referred to simply as *le Scandale,* at least ten people had committed suicide, according to *Le Journal.* Or been murdered.

His gaze wandered through the iron fence to the park. The fountain looked lonely out there. Three days had passed since Vivi had left. It was better this way of course. Detectives shouldn't get mixed up with women they were investigating. Back in Berlin he'd suffered a lot for it. Obviously he hadn't learned his lesson. Now he tried to analyze his behavior as his cousin Kurt, the psychiatrist, might. It all had to do with how powerless he'd felt—having to flee, losing everything he'd worked so hard for, not being able to provide for his family. This passionate, big-breasted French girl made him feel masculine and steady on his feet. But only because she herself was so unsteady.

He'd become dependent on her to ward off his feelings of impotency. When she left, it hurt like hell. He'd gone out looking for her. Sat in the bar across from her parents' building, scoured the rue de Lappe, waited by Les Pipos bistro—even showed up at the fragrance counter of the Galeries Lafayette. Another salesgirl told him Vivi had quit a week ago . . . was there anything *she* might help him with?

So that was it. Vivi was gone.

She'd proven the stronger of the two.

He sat up. Who on earth was that with Marc? Why had *she* come? How could they talk if she was here? The last time he'd seen Ava, she'd been pretty harsh with him. Nathanson hadn't exactly been pleasant either, with that bit about the old fish. What were they doing together?

"Hello, Willi."

"I wasn't expecting you, Ava."

"I know." She offered a hesitant smile. "I invited myself."

Marc pulled a chair out for her and they both took places at the table.

"Sorry we're late." Nathanson gave a toothy grin. "Latins have our own time, as you've no doubt ascertained."

Willi nodded meaninglessly. As if Nathanson were Latin.

Ava pulled off her gloves, fixing her eyes on Willi. She was wearing the cloisonné earrings he'd given to his wife years ago, he noticed.

"I know all about Achille Baptiste," she said up front. "It took exactly half a bottle of champagne to ply the whole thing out of Marc at Maxim's."

Willi was furious. He couldn't believe the guy. Did Nathanson imagine it was safe getting her involved, as if this were some kind of parlor game? He should have known Ava was way too smart for him. Now what? A lecture on how suicidal it was? How he'd done enough damage. Wasn't he man enough to turn it over to the police, the way any sane person would? She didn't understand: the police were probably behind it.

"I have every intention of helping you find this killer, Willi." She opened the menu, glancing it over.

"What are you talking about?"

"I know I've derided your work in the past. And I was certainly no fan of André Duval's. But this"—she let the menu drop—"has nothing to do with either of you or truth or justice, none of that crap. It's for my parents." The earrings dangled as she pleaded for his comprehension. "Oh, Willi, your sons won't miss what they never had. I'll get by. But Max and Bette—they're broken people. My father especially." Her lips trembled. "I can't just sit back and watch them like this. I've got to do something."

Her sentiments were superb, Willi thought. It was the reasoning that made no sense.

"What makes you think finding André's killer would recover any of your father's money, Ava?"

"Those millions didn't just evaporate, did they? Duval couldn't have spent it *all*. There's got to be some of it somewhere."

Now who was chasing fantasies? he wondered. He didn't want her involved.

"Don't try to stop me. I'm already in on it, Willi."

He also didn't have the energy to argue right now. "Just tell me what happened at Maxim's, okay?" He relented for the moment.

"We went Monday night." Nathanson pushed up the glasses on his nose. "Like you guys had for your parents' anniversary, right?" He waited for Ava's nod. "Anyway, Achille Baptiste wasn't on duty. So I asked the maître d'."

Willi was already uncomfortable. He didn't get the sense Marc grasped how dangerous these people were.

"The maître d' wanted to know which Achille Baptiste. There were several at Maxim's, a dishwasher, a cook. So I told him the door-man who worked Monday nights; I'd forgotten to tip him last time I was here and wanted to make it up. He was extremely polite as he informed me he *always* worked Monday nights and had no recollection of my face, which was odd because he had a *photographic* memory for faces." Marc blew air from the side of his mouth. "Can you believe it? Photographic memory! Nevertheless, I insisted I *had* been there one Monday some months ago and added—on the spur of the moment—that I'd seen André Duval across the aisle. He had dined there frequently, had he not? *Yes,* I was told. *Every Monday at eight thirty.* But I couldn't get a morsel more out of him. All he said was that if I wished to leave the tip, he'd make certain the young man got it. By the way"—Nathanson shrugged—"he's Corsican too, this maître d': Adriani."

"So was the man who took our photo," Ava said, cleaning her knife on the napkin. "Didn't you notice? What was his name? Senati, or something like that."

"Took your photo?" Willi didn't like it. "Did you get the negative?"

"Of course not." Nathanson smiled. "They have to develop it first. Then they send it in an engraved cardboard frame, first-class. It's all included."

"You gave them your address?"

"Yes, why not? At my office."

"I tried my luck with the hatcheck girl." Ava shrugged. "Discretely inquired about the beefy doorman usually there Monday evenings. 'Who, the Cervione?' she said. 'Oh, he's handsome but . . . ,' and she holds up a finger indicating his size, down you know where. Can you imagine?"

"Cervione?" Willi asked, a little embarrassed, and very disconcerted.

Ava had no idea.

Basically they'd accomplished nothing, he realized. Except to tip off Achille Baptiste that people were snooping around about him. Great.

Plus, without asking, Nathanson had gone ahead and enlisted two colleagues from his newspaper to launch an investigation into the gambling operation at 234 quai de Valmy. It freed Willi to keep working on the Corsican connection. He ought to have been thrilled. He had a little squad of musketeers on his side. But as darkness crept across the French Renaissance square, all he felt was apprehension. A police commissioner was no easy target, anywhere. A despot such as Victoir Orsini would require more than mere evidence to bring down. They'd need allies. Strong ones. Not just journalists.

To top it off, Ava now insisted she wanted to do a "job" with him Sunday. It was ridiculous. While Marc was out spying, there was a place in Belleville, she said, a well-known Corsican hangout where Willi ought to take her. They might glean something.

"Absolutely not." He shook his head.

Marc and Ava looked at him, astonished.

"It's a public restaurant, Willi. What could happen?"

Nothing probably. But what if something did? His boys couldn't take another mother figure in heaven. On the other hand a little reconnaissance could go a long way at a place like that, he couldn't deny it; the Corsican shop had been a gold mine. Now that Vivi was gone, who was there to accompany him?

"And it's your birthday." She knit her brows. "Unless you have other plans?"

That Sunday she met him at the Porte Saint-Denis after dark, dressed in a narrow suit with big shoulders, a little hat over one eye, as if they were going to Fouquet's instead of some neighborhood dive.

"I never heard of such a thing. Since when won't you take the metro?"

"Since . . . a while, Ava. Could we please not discuss it now?"

"Well, you might have informed me. I wouldn't have worn such high heels."

"I asked you if you preferred a cab."

"We can't afford one now, remember?" She hooked one of his arms and gave a tug. "Oh, come on, I'm only kidding. You know I'm always up for a good hike across Paris."

Off they marched around the stately seventeenth-century arch, up the tree-lined boulevard, past *les fromages magasins, les boucheries, les boulangeries boutiques.* Ava read aloud various advertisements that tickled her fancy: *"Brilliantine Cristallin. Pour la Beauté de la Chevelure!"* How different she was from Vivi, he thought, even in the highest heels more down-to-earth, even-keeled. Vivi was such a child, impulsive, a real seductress. Best in bed. But what foolish ideas in that brain. About palm readers. About love. And such crazy storms of emotion. He'd almost forgotten how easy it was with Ava. How much fun she could be.

"By the way." She gave him a little kiss. "Happy birthday. How does it feel?"

"Awful, thanks."

"Aw, come on. It can't be that bad. You look fantastic." She wiped his cheek.

He insisted on switching subjects. "How are your parents?"

It got her depressed. "Awful."

He felt guilty for having brought it up. Max and Bette were only in-laws, but the nearest to parents he had, and the boys' grandparents. It was infuriating to see them hurt this way. How cold-blooded could André have been, destroying those around him with a smile? Charities. Pension funds.

Still arm in arm but proceeding in silence now, Willi's mind plowed through seas of questions. Was it really the police that had killed André? Achille Baptiste had definitely been on that train to Marseille. Why would a doorman take a first-class express? Might he have come to Avignon the next day? There hadn't been any scent of Vendetta on André's terrace, but below on the street, when the penitents were passing, Willi thought he'd caught a whiff of it. The Corsican stiletto had done its job with the same efficiency as it had on Phillipe Junot. But did that make it *the same* stiletto? Or the same person using it? Just because men wore similar hats or colognes didn't make them the same person or even partners in crime, did it?

"You trying to get us run over?" Ava pulled his arm.

Traffic honked around the Place de la République, neon billboards flashing: COMPARI! DUBONNET! DR. PIERRE'S MINT-FLAVORED TOOTHPASTE!

"I'm just . . . distracted."

"I hadn't noticed."

Across the busy intersection, block by block the buildings grew more dilapidated. They had entered working-class Belleville. Not far away was the clothing factory where Willi had spent the longest weeks of his life, sewing eyeballs onto foxes.

"It's a million miles from Wilmersdorf, isn't it?" Ava said, referring to the manicured neighborhood where he and Vicki had lived with the boys in Berlin. For a second he thought if he turned, he might actually see his wife again, smiling as they strolled their old street, a trolley clanging past. But it was still her younger sister. And given the number of shady men lurking on the sidewalk, he was glad they had only a short while to go.

"Wouldn't it be nice just one more time to walk the Ku-damm?" She clung to his arm. "Or have *Baumkuchen* at Josty, or schnitzel at Lutter und Wegner?"

Yes. They'd always have that in common, wouldn't they? Home.

"Do you think we'll ever get to go back, Willi?"

He'd like to believe it. But those who'd predicted a swift Nazi downfall had been completely wrong. Der Führer had never been more popular. Jews had been barred from civil service, thrown out of the arts, forbidden to own land. No longer allowed to practice medicine except on fellow Jews. No, he couldn't imagine going back to Germany soon.

"I don't pretend to see the future, Ava," he said. Ahead were the gates of Paris's most famous cemetery, Père-Lachaise, lit up in the night. "A year ago I'd never have dreamed we'd have to run away and live as exiles."

Directly across from the final resting place of so many illustrious Frenchmen—Molière, Balzac, Proust, to name a few—nestled the cavernous Île de Beauté restaurant, BIEN MANGER CORSE—Fine Corsican Dining. It was not, as Willi had imagined, a dive, but a cozy, romantic enclave. Its low-arched ceilings, stone walls, and tiled floors conveyed a Mediterranean grotto, a sense of mountains, sky, and sea, full of smoke, laughter, and clinking glasses.

"May I suggest the wine from Porto-Vecchio, on our southeast coast?" The waiter smiled, flashing a gold tooth. "Along with a *terrine de sansonnet aux myrtes*. It's a pâté of starling and myrtle, with the most lovely woody flavor certain not to disappoint."

"Sounds marvelous," they both agreed.

The place was bustling. Not an empty table. Willi scanned the murky atmosphere taking in the faces of the customers, the waiters, the maître d'. Nothing struck him except the portraits of Victoir

Orsini and Mussolini side by side. "Just keep your eyes and ears open," he reminded Ava.

The waiter's suggestions proved infallible. Over a surprisingly superb wine and dinner they found themselves getting lost in conversation about the boys, how they were getting on in school, who their friends were. It was the most relaxed the two had been with each other in months. Since Berlin.

"Sorry I didn't get anything more useful out of that coat-check girl at Maxim's." She frowned. "I can't imagine what a *cervione* is. It wasn't listed in the Italian dictionary. You think it's some kind of slang—for 'tiny prawn' or something?"

Willi laughed. "I've no idea."

"Anyway"—she shrugged—"it's nice spending an evening with you." Her eyes grew lustrous.

"It's been a while. How are things with Marc?"

"Oh, excellent." She swallowed, nodding vehemently. "He's so incredibly attentive, really. Adores going out. We've been to the opera, ballet. A dozen little restaurants. He's the one who told me about this place."

"Really. So you're happy together?"

She wiped her lips and smiled. "Marvelously so. What about you and . . . well, I'm sorry, I don't know her name."

Willi could feel the color drain from his face. "How did you find out?"

"It's a small town." She shrugged. "Smaller than Berlin. Someone saw you at the Folies Bergère. Nothing to be ashamed of. You're a grown man. I figured you'd tell me when you were ready. I heard she's very young and beautiful."

"She is, yes. But, anyway . . . it's over. She's gone."

"Oh. I'm sorry, Willi. Truly."

By the time they were washing down the creamy ewe's cheese with chestnut liqueur, and the restaurant lights were dimming for the evening's entertainment, Willi was ready to chalk it up as a pleasant but none too profitable night out. Then came a spotlight on a small stage occupied by a large woman. "And now," she said into the microphone with breathy expectation. "*Île de Beauté* is proud to present—"

"Look," Ava nodded toward the wall lit up behind her. There was a big hand-painted map of Corsica showing its principal mountain ranges and towns.

"This evening's entertainment—"

"Up there, on the northeast coast."

"Our very own . . .

"It's a place, Willi."

"Barbari Brothers!"

"Cervione is a town."

Three earnest looking men in their early thirties crowded the stage, all stocky, dark-haired fellows with five-o'clock shadows. A fourth with a full beard and black beret sat to one side, accompanying them on a mandolin. The brothers broke into three-part harmony, holding out their hands, closing their eyes as they swayed side to side, singing the saddest tune. It was very emotional, laden with hurt pride and honor, and the audience swayed along, many in tears. Halfway through though, Willi caught a good look at the mandolin player, and what felt like cold steel pierced his heart.

My God. He stiffened. The *bouquiniste*.

His instinct was to put money down, take Ava's hand and get out. He could hardly forget that morning Junot argued with the guy, the phone call after he'd left. The murder that night. Nor could he forget the *bouquiniste* fleeing down those stairs to his boat, disappearing up the Seine. He tried to find comfort in the darkness, that there were so many people in the restaurant; how would anyone on stage pick out his face? But between songs suddenly a cake full of burning candles was borne out from the kitchen—directly to him, Ava clapping and laughing. He wanted to clobber her. The whole restaurant waited for him to blow out the candles. He froze, mortified. Especially when he noticed the mandolin player looking directly at him, so intensely even Ava noticed.

"Willi, does that guy know you?"

As soon as possible they paid and left. The first cab they saw he put Ava in, and told her he'd take the next one.

"Why Willi? What's wrong?"

"I'll tell you later. Just go."

Twenty-four

Vivi hadn't departed without leaving a little gift behind for Willi, intentionally or not. The chap whose name she'd let drop in her drunkenness was obviously a friend of Phillipe Junot. So hiking back down to the Latin Quarter Monday he broke out his counterfeit badge—the only real charm André had given him—and got a look at the student files at the École Polytechnique. There it was all right: Lorrileux, Jean-Florian. Not only had he known Phillipe, they'd been roommates.

"Finally." The kid stared when Willi flashed the badge at his door. He seemed relieved someone from Homicide had actually showed up. "I can't believe it's taken all this time. Seems pretty shoddy, if you ask me."

Tall and thin, with reddish-brown hair and a long nose, he had a far more aristocratic mien than Phillipe Junot ever had.

"What are you so anxious to talk to the police about?" Willi entered, looking around. It was a cozy enough place. Two bedrooms, one unoccupied. A living room filled with books and stacks of phonograph records in sleeves. He turned and stared at Lorilleux. "Is there something you know about the murder?"

The kid blinked. "Of course not. Or I'd have come to the police myself. But I was the victim's roommate. You'd think someone would want to talk to me, poke around here. Go through his things."

"Nobody ever did?"

"Don't you even know what goes on in your own department? What kind of disorganized, inefficient—"

"Never mind the speech. Here I am, so let's get down to business, huh?"

"Sure. What are you, Swiss?"

Willi ignored him, reaching for his notebook, wishing he didn't have his damned accent. Something always failed to blend. In Germany it'd been his face.

"Why do you think someone wanted your roommate dead?" He broke out his pen and took a look at the kid, remembering that morning on the bus when he'd accidentally come face-to-face with Junot, how bright and alive he looked. "Did Phillipe have enemies? Was he involved in anything illegal . . . politics . . . gambling . . . drugs?"

"No. I mean, yes!" The kid blushed.

It was nothing. Just the usual nerves under stress, Willi sensed.

"He got into some kind of trouble gambling. It was his weakness. Horses, I believe. Otherwise he was such a great fellow, you've no idea. Intelligent. Concerned. A finely tuned social conscience. Losing him was so painful. And then, nobody seemed to give a—"

"What kind of trouble was he in? Did he tell you?"

"Of course. Money. What else? He owed something like ten thousand francs."

"To whom?"

"I've no idea. All I can tell you, Inspector"—Willi realized he hadn't been called that in a long time—"was that Phillipe had no way of paying. He was a scholarship student here, one of the few. These hoods were making him work it off. At hourly wage, minus interest on his debt, it would have taken something like seven years."

"Did he consider fighting back?"

Lorilleux laughed.

"Running away?"

"You don't run from these guys."

"How do you know?"

The kid shook his head as if Willi were a real hick. "Come on. They get who they want. You think that scumbag André Duval really killed himself?"

Willi swallowed. "What do you know about that?"

"Just what everyone else in France does, that the only justice in this country is if you pay for it."

"What's over there?" Willi nodded toward a crate in the corner.

Lorilleux's eyes shifted uncomfortably. "Phillipe's things. I promised to send them back to his family. I've been so busy though. I feel terrible about it."

Willi took his time going through it all. Clothes. Shoes. Toiletries. Textbooks. Nothing major. Only a large, muddy-orange text he thought he might have seen before. Wasn't it the one Junot had studied so intently at Les Pipos bistro? The one he'd left on the bus and gone back for? Willi picked it up: *La Nécessité de la Planification Centrale*, The Necessity of Central Planning, by Professors Dominique and Frédéric Pasquier. Ah, yes. He wrote down their names. Junot had worked with them at the university.

A snapshot fell from the pages. His chest clenched as he recognized the face. He'd almost forgotten how sexy she was. "Who's this?" He held it up.

"Phillipe's girlfriend. Vivi."

"You knew her?"

"Casually." Lorilleux shrugged. "Phillipe brought her here a couple of times. We chatted before they went to his room."

"I see. And how long would they stay back there?"

"An hour or so. Why?"

"Was she a student at the Polytechnique?"

"No."

"What'd she do?"

"Said she was a model, but I never believed her."

"Why not?"

"Because she made things up. She was always telling stories about how she knew this or that famous person or dined here or there."

"How did you know it was made up?"

Lorilleux smiled. "Once, for Phillipe's birthday, I treated them both to dinner at the Ritz. It was so obvious she'd never been any place nice. She had no idea which fork to use. Plus she kept making little grunting noises, like a piglet."

"Was there ever any kind of rough play between them?"

"Rough?" Lorilleux looked at Willi. "Say, you're not some kind of—"

"Just answer, Lorilleux. It'd be hard not to hear in a place like this."

"I heard them all right, but it didn't sound rough to me. In fact it sounded very—hey, wait a minute." A light seemed to go off in Lorilleux's head. "You don't mean that black eye, do you?"

"What about it, Lorilleux?"

"It wasn't Phillipe who gave it to her."

"How do you know?"

"Phillipe told me."

"Then who did it?"

Lorilleux shrugged helplessly. "Phillipe figured it was the guys he owed money to, but he wasn't sure."

Nathanson yanked his collar defensively. "You've been inside. You know the scale. On a slow day they take in a million." He pushed his glasses up. "How much more on big race days or major sports events? They must remove it nightly or they'd have storerooms full of loot down there."

It was 4:00 a.m. He and Willi were in Nathanson's little Peugeot, parked in the ally behind 234 quai de Valmy, freezing. Profits from the huge gambling hall in the basement, Nathanson was convinced, were being laundered through the Hearts of Angels charity. The question was how. They'd been sitting here since midnight trying to spot a cash transfer. Informants inside reported the money went out every night, after the place closed.

Willi was not unmindful Nathanson had gotten facts wrong before. "You're certain of these sources?"

"Look, Willi, Germans might be too proud to pocket a few bills for information, but not Frenchmen. Nobody here's too proud, just too scared. If they think they can get away with it, they will. And believe me it hasn't come cheaply. I've taken a lot from my own wallet. So have my colleagues." Nathanson's expression was full of almost childlike sincerity. "If we can bring Orsini down, it'd be a great thing for this country."

France could use it, Willi was thinking. Heads of banks, ministers of state, top journalists, even judges, were being taken away in handcuffs as *le Scandale* continued rocking the republic. Mass demonstrations had been called on the right to protest "liberal" corruption. On the left, in support of workers whose pension funds had vanished with Confiance Royale. He wondered about Lucien Ruehl and his little family. Were they hiding in that apartment?

Half an hour before dawn, Nathanson clutched a pair of binoculars, scanning up and down the street. Not a vehicle had come by all night. "We'll get what we need, you'll see. Lebrun's in there with a camera in his hat. Every time he scratches his head, he's taking a picture."

Willi hoped these guys knew what they were doing. Then, where would they even take all this evidence? Clearly not to the police.

Inky-black night finally gave way to morning stars.

André must have known about Orsini's criminal empire, Willi was thinking—just as Orsini must have known about André's. It was another reason the commissioner could never allow André to face criminal charges. Why he'd rather have him dead. Willi could only hope that if they managed to expose this gambling operation, a lot of rotten things would come to light.

As the sun broke through, though, and the baker and the grocer opened their shutters, there'd been no truckloads of cash.

"There's an old canal around the corner, you know," Willi offered.

"So what?"

"So maybe that's how they take it."

"On that muddy thing?" Nathanson laughed. "I don't even think it goes anywhere."

Willi recalled seeing boats on it. He opened the car door.

"Where are you going?"

"Give me a couple of days. I'll get back to you. "

"What are you thinking? Why don't you let me in on it?"

"Sometimes I just work better alone, that's all. There is one thing though."

"What?"

"Could I borrow those?" Willi pointed at the binoculars.

Nathanson's eyes widened. "They're top-of-the-line, Willi. But . . . if you must." He handed them over reluctantly. "For God's sakes, be careful."

Thanks, Marc. I'll try, Willi thought.

Twenty-five

After midnight the Canal Saint-Martin grew eerily quiet. Workers from the nearby tanneries, founderies, and light manufacturers were long in bed. The usual habitués of the Parisian night—lovers, vagrants, *filles de joie*—carried on with discretion. Willi waited along the quai de Jemmapes, keeping his attention focused across the canal at 234 quai de Valmy. It was warm out thankfully, dark and moonless, the brackish water practically black. Only a small, gray duck broke the surface, paddling vigorously upstream. Somewhere in the distance a siren shrieked. But here, silence.

Shortly before two, his ears perked up. Finally . . . a faint *put-put*. Through the darkness a boat approached, a shallow barge maybe twenty feet long, with a wheelhouse at back. In the binoculars Willi saw three men inside. A second barge was getting towed behind, no one aboard. His heart pounded as they pulled in toward 234 and began tying up.

Two men jumped off. Nathanson's binoculars were good, all right. Even in the dark he could make out their faces down to the receding hairlines and five o'clock shadows. A chill coiled down his spine when he recognized them. It was the singers from the Corsican restaurant the other night, the Barbari brothers.

"Hurry!" One waved an arm.

Through the dilapidated doors of 234 half a dozen men paraded out lugging what looked like wine crates. Focusing the binoculars, Willi saw each was stamped on top: VIN. Nathanson's sources were right this time. It had to be the day's earnings. At least a dozen crates were loaded onto the first barge, the whole thing taking only minutes. When the Barbari brothers jumped back aboard, the barges were unmoored.

Willi returned the binoculars to their case, strapping them over his shoulder. If he hurried, he reasoned, he might be able to keep up on the footpath. But once the lead barge got under way, it became increasingly apparent that unless he was prepared to run the whole way, he'd wind up losing them. Casting about for a solution, he spotted what seemed his only chance.

Down the block an iron footbridge arched across the water. He ran for it, grabbing the handrail, leaping two steps at a time. As he reached center span, the first barge was about to go beneath. Watching the wheelhouse pass below, he waited for the second barge, then climbed over the railing, carefully lowering himself, praying he wasn't spotted. Hanging there until the last instant, he dropped with a thud to the wheelhouse roof. For a moment he just lay motionless, barely daring to lift his head, thankful for the dark night. When he risked a peek, he could see the three brothers on the boat ahead, oblivious to his having joined the passenger list. Taking a breath, he told himself to relax, enjoy the scenery. It wasn't easy.

Tree branches from both sides kept sweeping in, smacking his face. It looked as if they were going to crash into a little bridge ahead if they didn't slow down. Amazingly, by the time they got there, the span had drawn back allowing them to pass. Just minutes later, though, great iron gates blocked the canal, trapping them front and back. Violent streams of water shot in from multiple directions, pushing the whole boat up. Thunderous rumbles drummed the hull as they lifted several meters; when the water stopped, there was a sudden calm. The front gate opened and they were free once more to forge ahead.

Farther upstream another lock lifted them until they emerged into a much broader section of the canal, pulling resolutely toward what evidently was their destination. A large warehouse complex along the water bore a flashing, red neon sign leaving no doubt what it was: HEARTS OF ANGELS CHARITIES. A rusty freighter docked in front of it had MARSEILLE painted across the stern, but the flag it flew, Willi recognized, was Turkish. Through the darkness he began to make out figures along the quayside, maybe twenty. As the barges pulled in just ahead of the freighter, it occurred to him he'd better seek cover. Slipping quickly from his perch, he found a crawl space behind the wheelhouse used to store tools. It had just enough room for him.

Pulling a tarp over his head, he broke out the binoculars. Men were unloading crates of *"vin"* from the first barge and taking them to the warehouse. Meanwhile, new crates from the rusty freighter were being loaded onto the barges. Willi was shocked at the sight of the workers, gaunt and unwashed, some of them in rags. Who were they? Not union longshoremen. Orsini's "charity" cases?

Tugging the canvas entirely over him, he hid as men arrived on his barge and began piling crates just feet away. He timed his breathing, trying not to make sound, feeling the boat lower with each new crate. Eventually he heard feet stomping away. After several minutes of silence, with a slight rumbling movement they pulled from the quay. The barges were turning around, he could sense, maneuvering back in the same direction from which they'd come.

Eventually he felt safe enough to poke his head up, like from one of those gopher holes they used to use behind enemy lines. It was extremely dark, but he could see they'd reentered the locks from before. The water this time swirled in the opposite direction, lowering as it drained. Beyond this, and the second lock set, and then the little bridge, they wound up pulling in front of 234 quai de Valmy again, a round-trip of some ninety-five minutes. Willi shrank in his crawl space, jerking the tarp over his head. He didn't want to imagine what would happen if he got caught.

Luckily, only the first barge got unloaded, crate after crate directly into the gambling hall. What could they be stocking that place with? Not wine really? With his barge still full they took off again. Where did this canal even go? he wondered, wishing he had a map. The Barbari brothers seemed content enough. He watched them on the boat ahead laughing and slapping each other's back and decided to take a chance.

Among the tools in the crawl space were a hammer and a crowbar. Grabbing both, he crept to where the crates were piled, chosing one. Only two nails held the lid on. The crowbar easily opened it. Inside were neither bottles of wine nor cash, but packets wrapped in brown butcher's paper tied with cord. He picked one up, surprised by how heavy it was, quickly untying the cord. Powder. He sniffed, touching, tasting.

My God.

A loud bang sent water rushing. The barge began to sink. They were in another lock set, he realized. He used the swirling, thrashing noises to camouflage the hammer blows as he reclosed the crate, opening a second. This one did contain bottles, but not of alcohol. According to their labels they were VERONAL, SECONAL, MORPHINE. By the time they had gotten through this set of locks, Willi had a pretty good picture of the operation. Cash from gambling was used to buy narcotics smuggled in via Marseille. Barbiturates, amphetamines, cocaine, heroin. Given that the police also ran prostitution, Victoir Orsini, multiple times Frenchman of the Year, had clearly managed a horizontal monopoly over Parisian vice.

Willi resealed the final crate just as the barges plunged into a tunnel. He'd never seen such darkness. Even the sewers of Berlin had lights; this was pure black. After a few minutes of it, cold, irrational fear crept through him. The tunnel seemed to constrict around him, as if he'd been swallowed by a snake. Breathe, he told himself. Count backward from one hundred. But the air was fetid, noxious almost. He couldn't get past ninety. Sweat was pouring down his face. He had to get out. Just before he felt that he would burst though, into the night they emerged, and he greedily gulped down air, looking around, realizing he knew where they were.

They'd entered the Bassin de l'Arsenal, where the yacht *Achille Baptiste* was berthed. There she was. Even in the dark he could make out the Moor's-head flag at her mast. Sailing past her, they put out into the Seine itself, its powerful currents suddenly pulling the barges swiftly. At the Pont de Sully they veered left. Willi counted the spans they went under. Three, four, five—until there was no doubt of their destination. They'd reached Île de la Cité, pulling right up to 36 quai des Orfèvres, mooring at police headquarters.

From beneath the tarp he watched a gang of men clamber aboard and begin unloading the crates. They took them through a heavy iron gate practically along the river's edge that looked out of the Middle Ages—the entrance apparently to some kind of tunnel. It was just before 5:00 a.m. So this is how it was done in Paris, Willi thought. The police ran not only gambling and prostitution but distributed narcotics to both and probably dealt the drugs themselves. Who'd have thought the place to get heroin was your neighborhood flic?

He waited until the voices died away. Slowly he poked his head up. The barge was empty, no one in the wheelhouse ahead. Perhaps they'd gone in for a little nightcap, to celebrate a job well done.

Casting aside the tarp, he rose. The quayside was only feet away. He'd been on this block enough times to know that if he climbed the steep flight of stairs about twenty yards away and walked fast, he'd be home in an hour. Making certain the binoculars were secure, he took a breath and readied. But before he so much as got in a step, a voice on the embankment shouted, "*Merde!* Who's that?" And there was a loud *bang!* Something ricocheted off the wheelhouse much too close to Willi's ear. Either a lucky shot or a damned good one. He didn't feel like finding out.

If he made a run for it, he was dead. The whole quay was in the guy's view. When a second bullet hit even nearer, animal instinct took over. Sorry, Marc, he thought, ripping off Nathanson's binoculars and throwing them in the river. He did the same with his shoes, taking a flying dive after them.

A shock of cold embraced him, cradling him in darkness. He could hear bullets whizzing past his ears. As he frantically kicked, the current picked him up, carrying him with surprising swiftness. For a few wonderful moments the strangest sense of comfort filled him, as if everything were going to be just fine. Then his lungs began burning madly. He had no choice but to break the surface, gasping for air. Several more gun blasts reached his ears, but no bullets. He wanted to cry with relief when he realized he'd been borne out of range. Only, now what? The cold was starting to stab with what felt like Corsican stilettos, his muscles ready to spasm.

With sudden terror he perceived something massive looming ahead. Stone pillars. A bridge. Like a fish struggling against the current he tried to make it ashore. The stone pillars, though, kept looming larger; the sound of the water crashing against them filled his ears, heightening his anguish. He could feel his bones cracking into a hundred pieces. Stefan, Erich! He kept fighting. But his energy was sapping, the cold draining him. He might not make it, he understood. And just as he nearly touched the shore, he felt himself go under.

Was he at the bottom of the river? Or in hell? He lay faceup, flames kissing his toes and yet not burning. Warming. The sky, a huge vault of stone. Wasn't that . . . the Pont Neuf? He was on the pavement, a dirty blanket over him. He sat up coughing, shivering. Where were his clothes? He was naked as a baby underneath.

"There, there, everything's all right." A filthy-faced man smiled at him. The layer of dirt thick on his cheeks. "We may be bums but we're no thieves. All your clothes are right there." He pointed toward the fire. "Drying. We didn't touch anything in your pockets."

A small group of *clochard*—homeless men and women—sat around a trash-can fire, staring at him with curiosity. Talk about your fish out of water; they'd hauled him ashore they explained, stripping him so he wouldn't freeze.

"Thank you." Willi felt the warmth of gratitude. He'd been in more than his share of tight spots, but never before owed his life to a bunch of people living under a bridge.

"Take some of this, *chéri*," a gap-toothed woman offered.

He drank from a tin cup and coughed. Cheap gin.

"We saw you splashing out there," the dirty-faced man explained. "Heard the gunshots. Whatever you were doing near those barges took guts. Those swine are scum of the earth."

"You need to rest, monsieur." The woman tucked the blanket around him. "That river nearly got you."

Willi could barely keep his eyes open and quickly slipped into deep sleep.

In the morning, when he pulled on his clothes and found all the money still in his wallet, he gave it to the woman and asked her to get some *petit déjeuner* for them all. He waited and breakfasted with them.

"Dirt keeps us warm." The filthy-faced man broke a baguette and handed Willi a piece. "They drag us into their damn shelters, force us to work, and worst of all to shower!"

"Bastards," another agreed, chewing furiously. "They do far more harm than help. It's the devil's work they've got going at thirty-six."

"So it seems." Willi swallowed.

When it was time to go, he shook each of their hands.

"You're about the nicest group I've met in Paris."

"Monsieur." The dirty-faced fellow stopped him, lowering his voice. "I don't know who you are or what you do—but if you ever need any help—" He thrust his jaw. "I have many friends in this town and some skills of my own."

Twenty-six

Practically across the street from Napoléon's Tomb, the offices of the *Weekly Report* offered postcard views of the chapel of Saint-Louis des Invalides, its glistening gold dome testifying to the glories of French baroque.

"He's top dog." Nathanson pointed to the photo of a square-faced fellow in a pin-striped suit. "These two, his lieutenants."

"Everybody's from the same town." Ava showed documents she'd dug up at the library. "The Barbaris are related to the Orsinis by marriage."

A day after Willi's adventures on the waterways of Paris, she and he were behind closed doors with Nathanson's colleagues, including the editor in chief, trying to figure out a way to bring this Goliath down.

"Where are the profits going?" the editor wanted to know. "It must be a fortune."

"They're buying half of Corsica." Ava brought out more documents. "Orsini's now the single largest—"

Willi sneezed.

"You're not getting ill again." She looked at him crossly. "It wasn't even a year ago you had double—"

"I'm fine." He sneezed again, a souvenir of his swim in the Seine. As much as he appreciated Ava's investigative acumen, working with her was no joy. It was too close. Too dangerous.

"We've got more than enough to bring down this *sac de merde*." Nathanson was positive. "Question is, how?"

"If we printed it"—the editor shook his head—"we'd all be behind bars by evening."

"I know someone at the Sûreté Générale," Willi offered. "Might they be of help?"

Marc pushed his glasses up. "There's not a more incompetent agency in France, Willi. I keep trying to tell you that."

"Why not take it higher?" Ava raised the possibility. "Right to the top: Daladier. He'd be sympathetic."

"Who has contacts with him?"

"Didn't you tell me you met him at the Duval's party, Willi?" Her memory was flawless.

"Only for a second."

"Well, maybe the hostess, Mrs. Duval, could be of help."

If not a plan, they'd come up with steps to take, and for Nathanson that was cause enough for a "civilized" lunch.

"Fouquet's?" He gave Ava and Willi a hopeful look. "Oh, don't be dull. My treat," he insisted. "They have a consommé that will positively cure that cold of yours, Willi."

But the moment they stepped outside, a massive crowd engulfed them, a huge political demonstration passing in front of the building, up the boulevard des Invalides.

"I completely forgot," Nathanson shouted. "They're marching on the National Assembly today."

They were trapped in a throng of bystanders, held in place by a cordon of men in black berets and tricolor armbands. Parading past were row after row of French flags, people singing patriotic songs. Each group had a banner. LEAGUE OF YOUNG PATRIOTS. ARMY OF

HONOR. Along the sidewalk many applauded, others jeered. Nathanson looked blissfully disinterested.

"Oh, look what else I forgot." He dug in his briefcase, jostling those around him, yanking out an expensive-looking envelope from Maxim's. "It arrived while we were upstairs." He tore it open with a toothy grin. A silver cardboard folder inside contained the photograph of Ava and him taken the night they'd gone hunting for Achille Baptiste. "Isn't that lovely."

Willi was taking in the portrait when an alarm went off in his head, sending his eyes darting around. He thought he smelled Vendetta.

"I think Ava looks positively—" Nathanson stopped, his face whitening, his throat appearing to close. He gagged, reaching behind his shoulders as if to scratch an itch. But blood was suddenly squirting everywhere. Ava screamed as Marc fell. From the farthest corner of his eye Willi caught a glimpse of a green fedora vanishing into the crowd.

People were shouting, "Get help!"

Ava was hysterical. "My God, Willi, do something!"

One fast glance though and he knew there was nothing to do.

She clawed him. "Help, Willi. Help him!" But to her dismay he broke away and pushed through the crowd. He couldn't let this guy go. "Willi!" he heard. "Willi!" His eyes were already far ahead, glued on the green fedora.

At the curb, marshals stopped him. The fedora was crossing the avenue, he saw, zigzagging through the marchers. Willi broke the restraining grip, but two more marshals grabbed hold, attempting to corral him. Instead they were soon writhing on the pavement, stunned at Willi's ability to down them. They'd no idea he'd been trained in the Wehrmacht's most elite unit.

"Stop the corruption!" the marchers were chanting. "Defend our honor!"

On the far side of the road the green fedora had the lead, but Willi's gaze was locked in. Not just green, but a shade of olive, which made the hat unmistakable. Achille Baptiste had brought that photo from Maxim's, hadn't he? And waited in the throng outside to make certain the reporter inquiring about him was permanently silenced.

But now the hunter was the hunted.

Past the veterans' hospital built by the Sun King with its fifteen courtyards and miles of halls, along the tree-lined esplanade toward the river, Willi kept far enough behind but still inched nearer. At the Bourbon Palace though, where the Assemblée Nationale met, the crowds became impassable.

"Down with Daladier! Topple the government!"

Willi was only two men behind the fedora. He had the advantage of surprise he knew, and he was itching to take this guy. Like any good assassin, however, the fedora gave a sudden glance over his shoulder, and their eyes collided. It was him all right. Achille Baptiste. The moment he realized Willi was there, he pulled off the hat and elbowed through the crowd, disappearing into the metro station.

Willi reached the stairs, clutching the railing, looking down. Streams of people were pouring out. The heavy tunnel air smelled to him as it always did now, thanks to that man, like blood. He commanded his legs to move but they were insubordinate blocks of ice. He lifted a foot but his knees were melting. He was drowning, struggling against a current, about to meet a massive wall. Seized by phobic nausea, without realizing it he was inching backward, gasping for air. Trying to keep flames of shame from licking at his face.

Not sure what to feel worse about—losing Achille Baptiste, Marc, or Ava—he staggered back, feverish and sick, barely able to see straight. Nearing the corner where Nathanson had been stabbed, he realized he was again too late. Through waves of dizziness he was just able to make out Ava down the block, climbing into the back of an ambulance as it drove off, sirens howling.

He all but collapsed trying to get home. Still in his clothes he passed out in bed and slept until late in the morning. When the sun gradually opened his eyes, it all came back . . . Nathanson. The guy hadn't stood a chance. Achille Baptiste may have been a lousy doorman, but he was one hell of an assassin.

Ava though.

He rolled from the bed. After gulping down a fistful of aspirins, he showered and changed, then dragged himself downstairs, taking two buses to the sixteenth. He had to explain.

"Monsieur Boucher." A woman on the sidewalk stopped him. "Don't you recognize me?" She took off her sunglasses.

How could he forget the former star of the Queen Theater, Désireé "Lulu" Jourdain? Obviously she lived around here too. He was amazed she even recalled that fake reporter's name he'd used.

"Poor man. Quite a cold you've got."

"Yes, I caught a chill."

"Steam yourself in chamomile; it'll clear right up. Too awful about André, isn't it?" Her turbanned head shook. "According to Maurice, he'd made a huge fool of himself even before the scandal. That Pan-Europa thing." She shrugged. "Another of his scams I guess. Anyway, despite it all—I really can't bring myself to hate him, you know? He was so good-natured. But then you look at all the harm he caused. Which goes to show, I guess, looks can be deceiving. Anyway, a pleasure running into you! I'm off to the salon. Maurice is having associates for dinner. Au revoir!"

In the lobby a few doors down the elevator opened and out flew Bette Gottman, clutching a purse.

"Willi." She stopped, her face a strange cocktail of emotions. She felt close to him he knew, after all they'd been through. But a glint in her eye suggested she still blamed him too, for everything bad: Marc, André, the Nazis. Vicki getting killed by a truck. "I'm off to meet Aunt Hedda at her bank. She's tiding us over until my husband starts his job."

"Max got a job?"

"Yesterday. At Galeries Lafayette."

For a moment Willi had a horrible image of him selling lingerie on the main floor.

"They're getting him a temporary visa as a managerial consultant."

"That's wonderful."

"He thinks so. At least we'll get by."

"And . . . Ava?"

"Traumatized, as you can imagine. Hasn't left her room all day."

Willi swallowed. "I came to explain."

"Yes, I'd imagine you'd want to. By the way, your sons are fine too, Willi." She offered a slim smile.

Having long ago found it expedient only to respond to his mother-in-law's better qualities, he kissed Bette's cheek. "Thank you, for being such a wonderful grandmother."

Upstairs, it took a second to summon the nerve to knock on Ava's door.

"Come in."

She was by the window in a long, black robe, her short waves of hair uncharacteristically disheveled. When she saw who it was, she turned away. "*Now* you show up."

He stepped to her wanting to apologize, but she pivoted and slapped him hard across the face.

"Damn you!" Her eyes blazed at him.

He wanted to touch his burning cheek but stopped himself, remembering that awful moment he'd abandoned her on the sidewalk.

"How could you run away like that? Never mind Marc . . . how did you know he wasn't coming back for me?"

"Because I was chasing him, Ava."

Her face changed. "You . . . saw him?"

"Yes. There wasn't time to explain."

She wiped her eyes. "You took off after him?"

"Yes."

Her chestnut gaze drank him in, wanting to believe. "You caught him?"

"No." Shame burned at his cheeks. "But I saw him, Ava. There's no doubt about it . . . it's Achille Baptiste."

She hugged herself, turning pale. "You think it's safe here. I mean—" Her voice faltered. "I made inquiries too about him at Maxim's."

"But you didn't give them your address. Marc did."

She was silent, hanging her head. "His funeral's this afternoon. I'm afraid now to show my face."

"I understand. Don't worry. I'll go for you."

Her shoulders heaved and she started crying. He wanted to take her in his arms but she turned away, facing the window again.

"Leave me, Willi, please. You're good at it."

Hundreds gathered in the Grand Synagogue on the rue de la Victoire for Nathanson's funeral—friends, family, fellow journalists. Willi had only been in Paris half a year, and this was the third man he'd seen killed, almost certainly by the same assassin, probably working for the police. Taking a seat far in the back of the towering Byzantine sanctuary, Paris's most famous Jewish house of worship, he half expected to see Achille Baptiste show up in search of more victims. But no green fedoras appeared. No scent of Vendetta.

After the service, feeling as if he were suffocating, he walked the whole way from the ninth to the sixteenth arrondissements, surprising his sons after school and taking them to the Bois de Boulogne. Stefan chased rabbits while Willi and Erich sat on a bench and went over his arithmetic homework.

"Dad," Stefan said, kicking piles of leaves, "will we ever live together again, you know, like a real family?"

"We *are* a real family." Willi's pain returned. "And, yes, we'll live together, you'll see. Before you even know it."

It mortified him to see the look in his older boy's eyes, who understood very well that Willi still had no work permit, no way of earning a living, just charity.

That night, as exhausted as he was, he couldn't shut his eyes. He just lay there staring at the ceiling, combing over the Gottmans' anniversary dinner again. Shortly before André had introduced himself that night, the maître d' had come up and whispered something to him, Willi recalled. Marc said this same maître d' had told him André dined at Maxim's every Monday at eight thirty. Had the whole thing been a setup? By whom?

For what purpose?

A sudden knock made him sit up. The doorknob started turning.

"Willi," he heard. "Willi!"

He slid from bed and went to the door barefoot, peeking through the keyhole. In a white trench coat and black beret, looking pale, was Vivi. She bent over and waved when she saw his eye. "I hope I didn't wake you."

He opened the door. She smiled at him meekly, looking wounded. A fragile, beautiful butterfly.

"Want me to go?

"No." He shook his head, although something in him wished to God she hadn't shown up. "Come on in."

"You sure?" Her opal eyes searched his. "Because believe me, Willi, I know how hard it is to say no and really mean it."

"Come in."

She pouted. "But on one condition, okay? No questions. Not even one." He thought he saw black and blue marks on her neck but she pulled her coat collar up. "Or I will go."

"It's the middle of the night. Where would you go?"

"I told you, no questions." She sighed. "Come on, Willi, aren't you even glad to see me? I thought you were my friend."

"This isn't a hotel you can just check in and out of, no questions."

"Fuck you." She picked up the suitcase. "Like you've ever been open with me." She turned to leave but put the suitcase back down. "Just let me stay the night and I'll never bother you again."

He held the door open.

"And one more thing, if you don't mind." She bit her lip as if she knew it was a terrible thing to ask. "Is it all right if I sleep on the couch? I'm so damned exhausted, Willi."

"No questions. No sex. What the hell." He felt like an idiot. "Take the bed. I'll sleep on the couch."

"Really? You're so good to me. That's why I'll never love anyone but you."

She threw an arm around him and kissed his cheek. Which was when he saw the bruises on the whole back of her neck; the whole thing was green and purple. Definitely no love bites.

She crawled under the blanket with her trench coat still on.

"You sure you want to sleep in that?"

"You promised, Willi: no questions."

The next morning when he opened his eyes, she was already up, scribbling in her journal, still in the trench coat. How badly he wanted to pull her under the blanket with him.

"Good morning." She pushed the journal away. "Did you sleep all right? You were groaning like you were in pain."

"This couch." He sat up, trying to hide his erection. He'd had a terrible dream about a gang of kids beating a dog, and his not being able to help.

She looked away, a twitch of discomfort on her cheek. "Don't worry. I'll be out of your hair by tonight." Her chest rose and fell. "Go shower. I'll prepare breakfast."

He could just about make out the bruises behind her collar.

Steam obscured his face as he put the razor to his skin, wondering who could have hit her that way. The same guy who'd blackened her eye? It looked as if it might be belt welts. Part of him wanted to go after the son of a bitch. But he couldn't get involved in her craziness again. If only she'd let him fuck her, though. He'd be gentle.

When the doorbell rang, he nicked himself. Who the hell could that be?

"Vivi, I'll—"

She'd already answered it.

". . . be out any moment." He heard through the door, "Want some coffee?"

When he peeked from the bathroom he couldn't believe it. Ava was standing in the hallway with her arms tightly wrapped around herself. He threw on his bathrobe.

"There's a lady's to see you," Vivi curtsyed. "Doesn't seem to want to come in though."

Willi held open the door. Ava's face was the color of wax.

"I just came by to give you this." She picked up a briefcase.

His heart constricted. She was trying to mend fences, he could tell. Only she hadn't counted on Vivi.

"It was in my hands when Marc went to the morgue." Her voice was jagged with emotion. "Nobody asked for it so . . . I just hung on. Anyway, it's all there, papers, photos. I didn't want it around the house you know. So . . . I'll . . . just . . ." She bent and placed it on the threshold.

Vivi frowned, as if she knew she was being insulted. "Why you acting as if you're intruding? Willi and I are just friends."

Ava stared, saying nothing.

"Honest. He slept on the couch."

Willi appreciated the effort, even if Ava didn't seem to.

"Yes well, thanks." She nodded finally, backing away.

Willi's face felt on fire as she vanished down the stairs.

"That was kind of you, Vivi." He shut the door.

Vivi pulled the white collar tighter around herself. "Sure. What are friends for?"

Twenty-seven

The Duvals' grand suite at the Hôtel Lutetia was already half-empty. Only two chairs and a table remained in the once-sumptuous living room. The single maid left poured Willi and Adrienne tea.

"Daladier?" Adrienne inhaled, balancing the cup midair. "That's a tall order, Willi. My closest friends don't speak to me anymore."

She'd lost too much weight, he saw. Her fingers bony. Dark moons under her eyes told of sleepless nights.

"I'm pretty much of a persona non grata, especially among elected officials. But, what the heck?" She reached for the phone. ". . . Yes hello? I'd like to speak with the prime minister. This is Madame Duval." Willi could see her swallow. "That's right. Madame André Duval."

Her eyes fluttered as she waited what seemed a long time, her fingers nervously fixing her hair as if he she were expecting him to appear.

"Édouard?" Her face brightened. She offered Willi a nod. "*Bonjour.* . . . Yes. Thank you. I'm as well as can be expected. . . . I know.

That photo was awful. But how chic can one look stepping from a paddy wagon? Of course they released me. The only thing I could have been charged with was loving a swindler. *Mon cher,* I have a small favor . . ."

She smiled with grim satisfaction when she finally hung up. "I guess I still have some clout left."

Willi had an appointment for tomorrow at eleven. "I can't tell you how much this means to me."

"You were a true friend to André, as short a time as you knew each other. A real, how do you say, mensch." Her collarbones showed when she took a deep breath. "Willi"—the expression darkened on her face—"you don't think he killed himself, do you?"

He felt his heart quicken. "What makes you say that?"

"Because I knew André. Or thought I did. He'd never have shot himself. No matter how bad things got. He was terrified of guns."

"Who could have done it then, Adrienne? Might it have had to do with his Pan-Europa Bond?"

"I have no idea."

"Isn't there anything you can think of . . . anything at all you might have read or seen or overheard?"

She sighed in despair.

"Could I look at his things?"

"I'm almost certain they've all been removed. Annette," she called the maid. "Has everything from Monsieur Duval's office already been taken?"

"No, madame. In the basement, I believe, are still several boxes."

"Do you mind if I don't go with you?" Adrienne took his hand. "It still hurts."

"No, of course not. You've done so much already."

Deep in the basement the Duvals had their own caged-in storage area, all but empty now but for two large wooden crates. The maid who'd shown Willi left him alone with them. Slowly, carefully, he examined the contents. Mostly there were books, many volumes on economic theory, the history of currencies, numerous classics, Balzac, Hugo, the collected works of Conan-Doyle. Emotion yanked his heart when he found the bound volume of *Detective* magazine that André had once shown him. Flipping through, he saw the copies he'd signed with his photo on them. Probably they'd all wind up in the incinerator. A wave of sadness seized him. Suddenly though, at the bottom of the crate, something grabbed his eye. He yanked several books aside to get it, this time recognizing it at once. The same muddy orange textbook Phillipe Junot had had: *La Nécessité de la Planification Centrale,* by Professors Dominique and Frédéric Pasquier.

"We're in luck, thanks to your idea." Willi tried to placate Ava that night on the phone. "I've got an appointment with Daladier tomorrow, eleven."

She pretended to be happy but couldn't disguise the distance in her voice. "I'm so glad."

The next morning though she was waiting outside his building behind the wheel of her father's big Citroën. As Willi approached with all the evidence carefully organized in Marc Nathanson's black briefcase, she offered a small smile. "At least let me drive you . . . so you don't have to take a bus. I know you're too cheap for a taxi."

He got in next to her. "So kind of you."

Tossing a grin, she started up the engine. It was her way of reaching out.

She looked better this morning, he saw. Gotten her hair done. Her nails. But the silence between them was so heavy. By the time they were crossing the river, he couldn't take any more. "Ava . . . about the other morning . . ."

He wished he could tell her Vivi had gone. Big surprise, though, she'd begged to spend another few nights. And big surprise, he'd let her. How do you toss a girl like that out? He had the couch again while she took his bed, still in her trench coat, moody as ever. He kept waiting for the next big explosion.

"I told you, Willi"—Ava turned onto boulevard Raspail—"you owe me no explanations. Besides, I've been thinking about it. If that girl can be your friend, so can I, right? That's what we are, friends . . . who happen to be caring for your kids together. And trying to solve some murders."

"Okay. Sure." He offered his hand. "Let's be friends. It's better than enemies."

"I'm serious, Willi." She laughed.

Taking the rue de Varenne they pulled in front of the official residence of the French prime minister.

"Well." She hit the brakes. "This is it."

"Wish me luck."

She crossed her fingers. "I'll be waiting."

Inside the old palace a helmeted gendarme ushered Willi down a hallway ablaze with chandeliers. "Ten minutes," he said at the prime minister's door.

Édouard Daladier offered a meaty hand from behind his desk. "Ah, yes. Of course. The famous Berlin detective." A square-faced man with heavy eyes, he clearly possessed a politician's memory. And a politician's schedule, signing papers even as he spoke. "What is this crucial information I must have a look at?"

Willi slid him a neatly prepared folder. Daladier motioned for him to sit and took his time thumbing through each item, pausing to examine the photographs especially. Willi feared the ten minutes would end before he finished, and Willi would have to leave. But Daladier put the papers aside just on the dot.

"Sergeant." It was the marine who got the boot. "Leave us a few minutes." Daladier waited until the door had shut, then removed his glasses, turning to Willi.

"I agreed to meet you because Adrienne Duval is an old friend, Inspector. Plus, you're a man whose reputation procedes you. I confess though, I'm baffled. You've been in Paris what, six months? And in that time you claim to have uncovered a criminal syndicate of historic proportions. I'm not sure whether to congratulate you or send you back to the Germans. In any event"—he slid the evidence to Willi—"there's nothing I can do with this."

Willi took the folder back, his throat tight as a vise. Had he just made the worst mistake of his life, his last perhaps? Was Daladier in on it too?

"I'm not saying this isn't true, mind you. Everybody knows Orsini is rotten, and you've established how bad it gets. Apalling, truly. All France would benefit if he were stopped. Me included."

Willi was at least relieved to hear that.

"Unfortunately"—Daladier shrugged—"this stuff is useless. Photographs that could be doctored. Documents that could be forged. Orsini's an extremely popular man. If I ever made a move against him with such shoddy evidence, not only would my government fall, there'd be riots in the streets."

"I don't understand, sir, what more could you need?"

"Whatever it is, Kraus"—Daladier said with a little sigh and began signing papers again—"if it doesn't have the police commissioner's fingerprints all over it—don't waste my time."

"Mr. Prime Minister." Willi threw himself on the line. "If I'm to risk my life further to obtain such evidence, I would at least like some guarantees."

Both of Daladier's bushy eyebrows rose. "Oh, really?"

"Yes. Right of Domicile and work permits. Six in all."

Daladier stared at him hard.

"That's a substantial sum."

"The task is hardly insubstantial."

"Then, we'll discuss it once the task is complete."

"No. I want your word of honor. The permits for the evidence. Nothing else."

The prime minister looked at him half-scandalized, half with great admiration. "All right, damn it. It'd be worth it to get rid of that son of a bitch. Now your time is up, Inspector. *Bon chance*. I dare say you're going to need it."

"There's got to be something." Ava shifted into neutral as they slowed to a halt at Chatelet. Traffic wasn't as bad as in Berlin, but Paris was no joy to drive in either.

Amid the honking a large ad on the side of a bus proclaimed *Sérénol: Liquide & Suppositoires—États Anxieux, Émotivité, Nerveuses etc!* Willi wondered where to get some. Nathanson's briefcase sat between them. What more proof could Daladier want, a signed confession?

"Think, think," Ava chanted. "What brought André Duval down?"

Rubbing his hands together he tried to call something forth. It had started with those damned letters to the insurance companies, which he'd never found who'd sent. But those barely dented André's armor. What really brought him down was—

"The accounting books." He bunched his fists. "Ava, there's got to be a second set."

She looked at him then smiled, shaking her head.

"You've been in the sun too long, Moses. You want to get hold of the Police Commissioner's private ledgers?"

From the bottom up, the rue Foyatier had what seemed the longest set of stairs on earth. Willi would gladly have taken the cable car, but it was under a two-year renovation, so there was no choice but to climb Montmartre. Looking up, he didn't envy the heavy-hipped woman two flights above lugging bags of groceries, every step a war on gravity. How she must have cursed the city for taking away her funicular. When he couldn't bear it anymore, he jogged the two flights and caught up with her.

"Madame, may I help? Where are you going?"

"Rue . . . rue—" she gasped, handing him the sacks. "Thirty-two rue Gabrielle."

"Thirty-two? But that's where I'm going. To see a Madame Helene St-Claire."

"*Oui?*" She clutched her chest, still gasping. "You didn't know it was me? You only came to help a lady in distress? *Mon Dieu!* A saint. A handsome one at that. I only hope I can return the favor," she managed, straightening her hat.

This was the "old fish" Nathanson had told Willi about, the former bookkeeper at Hearts of Angels charity. Her address had been in a small black book Willi found in Nathanson's briefcase.

"Put those on the table, sweetheart." She kicked off her shoes when they got inside. Her apartment looked like a stage set for Marie Antoinette's boudoir, full of gilt-edged mirrors and faux-baroque furniture. Slipping into a pair of mules with pom-poms over the toes, she offered Willi a grateful smile. He felt the alveoli tighten in his lungs, his eyes swell and begin to tear. The one thing he was allergic to. Cats. This lady had a whole pride full.

"Don't say it." She immediately saw how red his eyes turned. "Shoo, shoo! Angelo. Giovanni. Luigi!" The cats scattered in a burst of energy, only to resume their lethargic interest from new positions. St-Claire threw a fresh sheet over a chair for him.

"Thank you." He got out a handkerchief, sneezing. "Let's get down to why I've come, madame."

"But of course." She broke out two glasses and a bottle. "You like caviar, no?"

"No. Not for me, thanks. Really I can't stay long."

"Pity." She put a hand on her hip, spreading her chubby fingers. "Everyone today is in such a rush."

"Yes. The fate of modernity I'm afraid. It's my understanding you used to be a bookkeeper at the Hearts of Angels charity."

"Now I know I need a drink." She poured herself a Campari and soda, squeezing herself into the love seat across from him. "What are you, a private eye? Reporter? Don't tell me Marc Nathanson sent you."

"As a matter of fact, he did."

"Mon Dieu!" Her eyes fluttered as she sipped. "What a gifted man."

"He's dead."

Her eyes grew wide. She listened, horrified, throwing back the rest of her drink and pouring herself another as he told her what had happened.

"Maybe it wasn't such a wise idea for you to come here." She reached for a cigarette. "They keep tabs on me too, you know. I'm a woman with information, which is of course why you're here." She struck a match. "I didn't think it was for my aperitif, though Marc I'm sure mentioned how delicious it is." As she inhaled she leaned toward Willi, raising one of her eyebrows. "How might I be of service?"

"You were Orsini's bookkeeper."

She leaned away from him with a slight sneer. "Yeah, so?"

"I need you to tell me where he keeps his second set of books."

Her jaw dropped. She was motionless a moment then took another quick puff of her cigarette. "Monsieur." She exhaled from the side of her mouth. "How very courageous you must be. Or very naïve." Taking a swig of her drink she seemed to search for something in

Willi's face. "But very smart too." She pondered a moment, crossing her chubby legs. Then her face flushed with a sudden red heat of excitement. "All right!" She slapped her thigh. "I'll tell you exactly where they are. And you want to know why? Not just because that bastard deserves what he gets. Seventeen years I did the man's dirty work. Treated me like a slave. But you—" She swallowed the last part of the word. "You came to my aid for no other reason than human decency. So you deserve it too." Her eyes got watery. "And something about you almost makes me believe you might succeed. Besides—" She crushed out her cigarette. "I really don't give a shit anymore if they do bump me off. When you get too old to get laid honey—*À quoi bon, eh?*"

By the time he left, Willi all but had the keys to Victoir Orsini's fate. There *was* a second set of books. He even knew where they were now, a wall safe behind a tapestry right in the commissioner's office. All he had to do was get in there, open the safe, and get out again.

Starting down the steps of the rue Foyatier, he realized a strange fog had settled over Montmartre. Neither the landing above or below was visible. Clasping the handrail, he went down cautiously, like stumbling through a cloud. He stopped. Continued. Stopped again. Was someone behind him? Or were those *his* steps echoing off the cobblestones? Every time he halted, the footsteps did too.

What was that high-pitched yell? An intense discomfort flooded him. Was it from a woman or a child? And that pounding getting louder? He turned, bracing, squinting at the darkness as a leather ball came bouncing down the steps, two teenage boys laughing as they chased it, blaming each other. One of them ran into Willi and kept going.

The fog seemed to thicken with each flight. Ghostly images flickered in the mist. A priest floating by in a long, black cassock. A couple making love in a doorway. Green feline eyes watching from a window. Someone was definitely following. He could hear footsteps one or two flights above—stopping every time he did. He looked again, but couldn't see anything. He started taking the steps two at a time. Close to three hundred, he recalled from his visit here with the boys some years ago. They never seemed to end.

At the bottom finally, relieved but no less blind, he ducked in a doorway along the rue d'Orsel and looked back up the stairs. Nothing. Just mist. But he heard them all right . . . footsteps cautiously approaching.

He thought to run to the boulevard de Rochechouart, which was always busy, only—which way was it, left, right? He had no idea. Down the block he saw an advertising column throwing a halo of light. He hurried toward it. AeroShell made the world's best motor oil, he saw. Bébé Nestlé's condensed milk was *délicieux!* Against the column, standing there in a shabby skirt and fishnet stockings, was a woman smoking a cigarette. She nodded, indicating what she was offering and how much. Getting no response, she lifted the skirt, displaying herself.

Willi moved past her, hearing the footsteps growing louder, stopping again exactly as he did. Turning rapidly, he was just in time to catch a lone silhouette in hat and coat, cautiously backing into the fog. A taxi approached. He wanted to stop it, but what good would that do? The guy could grab the one right behind and follow. He had to either shake him or bring him down.

A man with a huge belly bumped into him. "Oh, pardon me." Each time Willi moved, the belly moved the same way, laughing. "Oh, do pardon. Pardon."

Was he trying to pick Willi's pocket or, worse, was he the shadow's accomplice, delaying Willi? When they got it right though finally, the man tipped his hat and walked on, Willi's wallet safe.

The fellow had just emerged from a *vespasienne*, Willi saw—a gentlemen's pissoir. Iron sheds from the last century, fairly ubiquitous in Paris, some had room for only two, others were much larger. This one was deluxe-size, a horseshoe-shaped walk-in with marked entrance and exit. He threw himself the wrong way, into the exit, pressing against the wall in the shadows. From here he could see whoever entered. As long as he got in first jump, he calculated, trying to slow his breathing, even against a stiletto his odds were good.

He listened over his pounding heart. What was going on inside the pissoir? Slurping and grunts. The men back there weren't just peeing he realized. He made a move to leave, but suddenly a pair of pointy-toed shoes appeared, about to enter. A loud groan came from within, and the pointy shoes halted. They looked expensive. Some kind of reptile skin. Snake? Was it Achille Baptiste? Willi took a whiff. No Vendetta. Only piss. Someone's climax shook the place. The snakeskin turned and left.

Willi stood there breathing slowly taking no chances. A muscular man came out of the dark yanking up his zipper, passing through the exit, vanishing into the mist. The slurping went on. How many men were back there? Another fellow arrived from the street and disappeared into the dark. The grunts and moans were getting louder. Willi finally took a deep breath and stepped out, glancing left and right. Only too late did he spot the snakeskin. No!

From behind his arm was seized, twisted, and yanked up painfully. Something cold, hard, sharp, touched his throat.

"Ne résistez pas!"

Willi's arm was tugged almost to the breaking point. Submitting, he could feel himself dragged into a lightless doorway. Which was good, he figured. If the guy wanted him dead, he'd be playing a harp by now.

"Who you working with?" The point pressed his throat. Glancing down, even in the dark, there was no mistaking the stiletto. Just like the one he'd seen in the Corsican shop. Tears ran from Willi's eyes. He was glad the guy couldn't see.

"You going to tell me or am I going to have to—"

"Police Judiciaire," Willi whispered, his accent barely discernable beneath the strangulating pressure.

"Like hell." Even among the lowest of hoodlums killing *un flic* was not taken lightly. "Where's your badge?"

"Left breast pocket."

It was in his right, but the man was holding the stiletto in his right hand, and with his left pinning back Willi's arm. It was impossible for him to check Willi's left breast pocket without either moving the stiletto or letting go of Willi's arm. Unfortunately, he chose neither. Pressing the knife even harder, he instructed Willi to retrieve the badge, carefully.

Willi inhaled, obeying, slowly moving his right hand to his

chest, nuzzling it inside the jacket, patting around, coming out with nothing.

"It must be in the other."

"You trying to be funny?" It was an unmistakable challenge, the stiletto pressing just short of puncture point.

"I forgot I switched pockets. It's there, honest. First Inspector Olivier Bouchard, Homicide."

"It'd better be."

The guy adjusted the stiletto just enough for Willi's hand to move into the right breast pocket. Instead, his arm shot full force outward, pushing the blade back and inserting itself between the stiletto and his neck. At the same instant he threw his head backward as furiously as possible into the guy's face. With a loud cracking of nasal cartilage, the guy wobbled.

Willi spun around and kneed him hard, grabbing his wrist and making him drop the blade. It fell with a harsh clank, bouncing across the cobblestones. Now Willi really let lose, kicking, punching, beating the son of a bitch. Even when the guy was on the ground groaning, just to make certain he didn't get up and follow, he grabbed his arm and yanked the whole shoulder out of its socket. When the guy screamed, Willi got a good look at the face. It wasn't Achille Baptiste at all, but one of the Barbari brothers. What a pity, he thought wiping his hands and staring at him a moment before hurrying down the street—such a nice three-part harmony.

He punched him once in the face for good measure.

Twenty-eight

Willi's arm, his foot, his fist, all throbbed as he hobbled home, happy to be alive. Over the years he'd been shot at by machine guns, hunted by Nazis, toyed with by scapel-wielding psychopaths, but never had he had a stiletto pressed against his throat. He could feel its burning sting even now, ready to pierce the skin. How glad he was his boys still had a father! Somehow, he had to find a way for them to all live together.

The fog had lifted but he was in a daze, his thoughts oddly random. As he was halfway down the boulevard de Magenta, the cover of *La Nécessité de la Planification Centrale* flashed like neon in his brain. Why did André have the same obscure textbook as Phillipe Junot?

Reaching his building finally, dragging himself up the long flights of steps, he found himself wishing Vivi wouldn't be there when he reached the top. He needed his sleep. His bed. His sanity. But there was light beneath his apartment door.

"Ah, Willi." She was playing solitaire, halfway through a wine bottle. "Hungry?" She kept throwing cards. "There's chicken in the fridge."

At least she'd gotten out of that damned trench coat. Changed into a terry robe. His, he realized. Way too big for her.

"Vivi." He approached from behind as one might an injured animal. He understood, being injured himself, the pain one felt. He wanted to help. To get to the bottom of this. Once and for all. "Do something for me."

"What?" She held her card, looking up for the first time. "Oh, Willi, not that I don't want to, it's just—"

"Show me your bruises."

Her face froze, then she turned back and kept throwing cards. "No."

"Why not?" He came nearer. "Are you embarrassed? I don't judge you. I just want to see."

She let him step nearer. "Willi, please don't." But she let him. She wanted him to.

He reached and slipped the terry over one of her shoulders, then the other. The marks ran all the way down her back, not as violently purple as they'd been, but brutal, definitely made by a belt.

"Are you going to tell me"—he pulled the robe back over her—"who did this?"

She shook her head no, gulping down the rest of her wine.

He took a step back. His confrontation with the stiletto tonight had underscored several certainties to him. One was that he needed to reassert the boundary he'd breached with this girl. Return the relationship to what it ought to have stayed: detective and person of interest.

"Whoever did this"—he threw down some cards of his own—"is it the same one who confronted you outside Phillipe's apartment, who gave you that black eye?"

She seemed to petrify. Only slowly did her head turn, revealing her molten eyes. "You knew about those? But that means even before we met you'd been—"

"Right. Following Phillipe."

She looked at him speechless, the blood draining from her face.

"Shithead!" She threw the cards down. "I knew it. You lied straight-faced to me. Why were you following?"

"I'll tell you, if you tell me who did this and gave you the black eye. Was it the *bouquiniste*?" His first contact with a Barbari made him certain these guys were capable of anything, even beating up a girl.

"What is this, tit-for-tat?"

"If you want to call it that."

Her mouth tightened as she lifted her chin. "The bookseller had nothing to do with it. All right? Now you tell me."

"I was following Phillipe because I was being paid to."

"By whom?"

"That's a second question."

"Tell me or I won't play."

"A private detective agency." She didn't look as shocked as he would have expected. "Now tell me about the guy who stopped you on the street."

"What about him? I told you all I knew. He confronted me on the street to warn Phillipe to quit slacking off. I was supposed to tell him he could get hurt."

"Did you?"

"No."

"Why not?"

"It didn't seem important."

"Strange. And then he gets killed."

Vivi didn't say anything. Just swallowed. "You live in a dream-world, Willi."

"What's that supposed to mean?"

"Nothing."

He had a terrible urge to twist her arm and make her explain. "Did the *bouquiniste* give you that black eye?"

She laughed almost hilariously. "No. But Phillipe sure thought he had. Big idiot went and confronted the guy."

"The morning he was killed."

The laughter stopped. Her gaze turned bitter. "Seems like you know more than I do, Willi." Her eyes were suddenly cold, dead to him. "I'm not going to say I wish I could tell you any more."

Taking a breath, he stifled his frustration, knowing he couldn't force her further.

"Guess that's it then."

"Yeah," she muttered, untying his robe and letting it drop. "That's it."

Naked, she lugged her yellow suitcase out and started rummaging through it. Her smile was cruel as she hooked on a bra, hiding away her breasts.

"You can stay the night you know," he offered.

"You know, Willi"—she cast a frigid glance his way as she pulled on a sweater—"You're a handsome guy. Smart. Funny. But you never loved me. I'm glad to be free of you. You think I don't know a dozen men who are richer and more powerful than some poor, sniveling, Jewish—"

"Tell me who beat you, Vivi."

"Like you care. I could slit my wrists and you wouldn't care." She stepped into her panties, glaring. "What the hell . . . you'll never meet him. You really want to know? Who do you think did it, Willi? Gave me the black eye and these lovely welts? Dear old Dad! Yes, that's right. My papa. Beat me like a dog. And you want to know why? Because I said no to him. For the first fucking time in my life, I said no—and really meant it."

The heart of the French justice system beat in the very center of Paris on the Île de la Cité. Though it bore the stamp of numerous centuries, the Palais de Justice, an ensemble of buildings, was largely a construct of the 1860s, according to Ava—the glory days of the Second Empire.

"It's absolutely vast, Willi." She ran her finger across the diagram it had taken her several hours to render. "We're talking miles of corridors, thousands of doors."

She'd come up with a route though and marked it in red. There were half a dozen twists and turns, several stairways, different buildings. But it was a route all right—from police headquarters at 36 quai des Orfèvres right up to Orsini's office.

"I can't tell you how much this helps." He stared at the map, then at her.

They were in the main hall of the National Library on the rue de Richelieu, surrounded by millions of books. She closed her eyes as he kissed her cheek. Everything went into Nathanson's briefcase, which he carried as they walked to the street.

La Nécessité de la Planification Centrale wouldn't let go of him. Page after page he pondered the text he'd retrieved from André's basement. To him it was like reading a fairy tale. The authors were convinced that rational methodology could solve the ills of humankind. They preached a "Constructive Revolution" that would nationalize monopolies and create economic councils to scientifically plan the fulfillment of every human need. From the trenches of Flanders to the back alleys of Berlin, Willi knew only too well how much the unconscious and irrational drove human beings. But it did seem too great a coincidence that two men with such different backgrounds as Phillipe Junot and André Duval should have the same textbook on the same obscure ideology—and that each had fallen victim to a stiletto. A little more knowledge about Professors Dominique and Frédéric Pasquier, he felt, was in order.

Unfortunately they weren't so easy to find. Neither was connected any longer to the École Polytechnique nor was either listed in the Paris directory. Their publisher's office in Antwerp never seemed to answer the phone. Only one possibility occurred to Willi. At the labor meeting where Lucien Ruehl had spoken, Willi was sure he'd received a pamphlet advocating central planning. He had to have it somewhere; he tore through his desk drawers. His detective's instinct forbade him from throwing these things out. It used to drive his wife crazy.

There it was: "Technocracy—Our Future!"

Politicians and businessmen have failed, it pronounced. *The time for Constructive Revolution has come. Let those with expertise gov-*

ern! Scientists and engineers—those who have knowledge. Decisions should be based on skill, not graft.

It was signed simply Action Group X. There was no address, no telephone number. But in a tiny font Willi saw the name of the company that printed the leaflet. Group X had to be connected to the Pasquiers. How many people could be advocating central planning? Perhaps the husband and wife professors might even be behind the murders. Could Phillipe Junot, a member of their group, have somehow screwed up?

It took an hour to get to the shop out on the rue de Clingnancourt. When he arrived and flashed his badge, the printer, a gaunt-faced man with a hammer and sickle tattooed on his arm, didn't like the idea of revealing who had ordered the pamphlet.

"I can't give you that kind of stuff. It's privileged information."

The wife gave him a good, hard elbow. "Are you crazy? What do you care about those maniacs? They're ultrarightists."

"I don't think so, Antoinette. I think they're of the left."

"Bosh." She made him get the order forms.

The customers were listed simply as "Group X." The check for fifteen hundred flyers though had been signed for by Dominique Pasquier. On the back was her phone number and address. Willi thanked the concerned-looking printer and left.

He found the address easily enough and staked the place out for three nights in a row. The third night he got lucky. From a small park across the street he saw people arriving to the building and going up. There had to be a dozen who went in, all within fifteen minutes. Willi would have put down money that one of them was going to be Junot's former roommate, Florian Lorilleux. But he'd never have guessed who else he saw heading toward the building. A chill went through him. My god. He leaned from the doorway just to make sure. That was him all right, André's brother-in-law, Lucien Reuhl.

Twenty-nine

Even before dawn the next day Willi was back beneath the Ponte Neuf having a chat with the fellow who'd plucked him from the river.

"Naturally I know the best safecracker in Paris." Ledreau's filthy face erupted with delight. "You happen to be looking at him!" When he saw Willi's disappointed expression he swore up and down it was true, that Willi'd hit the jackpot this time. "Among my many talents—" He waved his dirty fingers. "These magic wands can break any lock on the continent. You think I couldn't be living at the Ritz if I wanted? I just happen to like it out here."

Willi wished like hell he could believe him. He'd no idea where else to turn and no energy to keep looking. "It's not an easy job, Ledreau," he said as much to himself as this supposed *Meister Kriminal*.

"Don't you worry about that!" Ledreau cracked his knuckles. "You can trust me! What are we after? Gold? Cash? Jewels?" His fingers twitched as if playing some imaginary instrument.

"Ledgers and files," Willi told him bluntly. "And no easy job. The safe is top-of-the-line. The location, not without certain . . . dangers."

Ledreau's eyes flamed. "What, a bank? Some company headquarters?"

"Police commissioner's office."

The flames extinguished.

"Someone's got to do it." Willi pleaded. "I can't even pay you. You'd have to do it . . . for the good of the nation."

"The nation!" Ledreau looked at him as if he were insane. "What do I care about how good she is? I'll do it for you, my friend . . . the lucky fish I pulled from the Seine! I'm as good a Frenchman as the next."

Willi hoped he was as good a safecracker as he claimed.

Quai des Orfèvres, the Goldsmiths Dock, was on the site of the old Île aux Juifs—a tiny island in the Seine where Jews and other heretics had been burned during the Inquisition. When the Pont Neuf was built at the end of the sixteenth century it was filled in and connected to the Île de la Cité. The metal door Willi had seen boxes of "*vin*" being carried through dated from the same period and was indeed, according to Ava's research, the entrance to a tunnel leading beneath the street to what was now the lowest basement of the Criminal Police building, 36 quai des Orfèvres.

The night of the job it was hard to recognize the old safecracker. Not that he looked like a new man exactly; his clothes were the same. He just smelled like one, all washed up for work.

"Nice," Willi complimented. "You have a face."

"Craggly as a crone. Plus, I'm freezing my *couilles* off."

It was nearly 3:00 a.m. The ancient stones along the quai des Orfèvres were coated by the year's first frost. Thirty or so men waiting along the river's edge huddled against the wind. Twice a week, depending on the need, ten to fifteen were chosen to unload boxes from two large barges, for which they were paid a free meal at any Hearts of Angels charity, not bad considering the work took less than fifteen minutes. Ledreau, who counted the foreman among his "oldest pals," made certain he and Willi would be among the lucky chosen.

In twenty minutes the barges arrived. Willi yanked a dusty worker's cap he'd borrowed low over his brow, hoping it made him blend in. He recognized those boats, one towing the next, and the men in the wheelhouse, reduced now from three to two—the Barbari brothers still able to walk.

Climbing onto the barge with the others, he waited his turn to hoist one of the *vin* crates. It was heavier than he expected. He had to force himself not to grunt as he followed Ledreau ashore. Through the rusted medieval gate they entered the long, dark tunnel, the air inside dank and thick, the walls of stone streaked with moss. The deeper they went, the narrower and darker it became, a single bulb in the distance vaguely beckoning. Willi began feeling like a character from a Dumas novel, forced to serve in the bowels of some monstrous prison, dreaming of justice. He couldn't help wondering how many escapes might have been pursued through here, how many assignations. Over all those years though, he was certain no one had come with quite the same intentions he had.

Eyes low, he allowed himself only a rapid glance when they passed the turnoff to the criminal courts building. Ledreau started humming the "Marseillaise." Entering the subbasement of police headquarters slightly farther on was like stepping into another century, a large, bright-lit storeroom full of metal shelves piled with cafeteria and cleaning supplies. The most ordinary place, Willi saw, where the most extraordinary transaction was taking place, the arrival of narcotics for distribution by the police.

"*Allez. Pressez!*" they were commanded. "Move it! Let's go."

When they deposited their boxes, one of the Barbari brothers checked the numbers against a manifest. Willi headed out first, Ledreau following. Rather than continuing toward the gate though, they both ducked sideways into the turnoff. One of the men still carrying a crate in noticed them.

"*Imbécile,*" he whispered. "You'll miss the vouchers after!"

"Take ours," Ledreau called back as they hurried into the darkness.

Willi led the way up a steep flight of steps into a rear corridor of the courts building, breaking out a flashlight. On the first floor he had them go right, then he quickly aimed his light beam up at a door reading PLACARD GARDIEN. Custodial Closet.

"First stop," he whispered.

Ledreau was impressed. "You've done your homework."

"It's the secret of my success."

In the past, the Berlin press had lavished adjectives on Willi such as "brilliant" or "inspired." Certain aptitudes were involved, but mostly his accomplishments were born of an insane amount of work: years of experience, compulsively driven preparation. He knew exactly the route they needed to take because he'd committed everything Ava put in Nathanson's briefcase to memory, the maps, the diagrams, even the history.

Ledreau was even further impressed by how quickly Willi jimmied the door lock open. *"Bon!"* The old-time safecracker nodded. Willi didn't want to tell him how well he'd been trained for work behind French lines, his instructors some of Berlin's best burglars.

Inside the little closet, fumes of ammonia began making them dizzy as they turned themselves into custodial workers, slipping on long, gray smocks and grabbing one of the carts filled with buckets, mops, and brooms. Closing the door quickly behind, they hurried down the hall into the Criminal Courts building.

The place was vast, as Ava had promised. Passing one austere courtroom after the next, Willi wondered how many fates had been decided here. He recognized the hall where the Countess de la Motte had been sentenced to whipping and branding in the Affair of the Diamond Necklace. She was one of the few to have escaped the claws of French justice, managing a flight disguised as a boy. Her nemisis, Marie Antoinette, was soon condemned here herself, following the execution of her husband, Louis XVI. Danton as well, sentenced by the court that he helped create. And Robespierre, corrupted by power. All to the guillotine. The French system of justice had its roots deep in the ancien régime. New courts had been installed in these old buildings, Willi knew. But did it make the justice any more—

"Ah, Jacques!" A throaty female scared the hell out of them. Willi could just make out an old *femme de ménage* leaned on a mop with an unlit cigarette in her mouth. "An answer to my prayer. Couldn't find a goddamn—hey, wait a minute, you're not Jacques. Who the hell are you two?"

"We're new," Willi said with a smile.

"Special job up in the executive offices," the safecracker had to add with a wink.

Willi could have throttled him.

"Don't look like the type that normally work here."

"You got something against my looks?" Ledreau hammed it up, pretending he was about to put away the matchbox from his pocket.

"I meant him." She threw a glance at Willi. "He looks, I dunno . . . a bit polished if you ask me."

"Just give her the light and let's go," Willi insisted.

"All right. No need to get testy." The woman looked him up and down.

When they finally reached the executive floor, they ditched the cleaning cart in another *placard gardien,* then jimmied the lock into Orsini's office. Shutting the door behind as they slipped in, Willi noticed the entrance to the service staircase he recalled going over with Ava in the diagrams. Good to know, in case they needed to make a speedy exit. Slowly he shone his flashlight around.

"*Sacré coeur—*" Ledreau stared in wonder at the commissioner's princely comforts, the Persian rugs and silk settees, the massive Louis XIV desk. "I've been living under a bridge six years and this guy's got a throne room up here."

"Real justice," Willi agreed.

The former bookkeeper had told him the wall safe was behind "one of those beautiful, old woven things with a Bible story on it." It didn't take long for Willi to spot it: a magnificent floor-to-ceiling Gobelins tapestry, probably seventeenth century, depicting the coronation of Esther. Lifting it gently away from the wall, they shone their lights behind, and sure enough, Helene St-Claire had come through. The safe's brass door reflected like gold.

Squeezing in behind the tapesty, you could smell the must of centuries. The underside was a jungle of loose threads, matted and gnarled, impossible to comprehend, a grotesque inverse of the intricately detailed Esther on the other side, sumptuous in her gowns, suffused with royal reds, not only ravishing but a valiant woman determined to save her people. Willi could only hope some of her powers seeped through.

"Ain't she lovely?" Ledreau whispered when they reached the safe. "A Cour d'Or three-wheel fireproof." Willi shone the flashlight on it as Ledreau rubbed his palms together. "Let's see, baby." He tickled the dial with his forefinger. "How do you want to open?" He leaned near, sniffing, kissing almost, then pressing an ear to it.

"There are only two basic routes to a sugar like this. You can either go four times left to the first number, three times right to the second number, two times left to the third, then one time right, slowly to stop—or the opposite: four times right to the first number, three times left to the second, two times right to the third, one time left, slowly to stop. The trick of course"—he winked at Willi—"is to know which, and then you still have to get the numbers, which is where the skill comes in. Or intuition, call it what you will. You don't mind if I chat do you? Calms my nerves for some reason."

Willi recalled sappers in the army who babbled the whole time they set explosives. "Just keep it low, will you?" Sweat was pouring down his face. Of all the things you could get in trouble for, breaking into the police commissioner's office was right up there. In the blink of an eye he could be back in Berlin, lunching with the Gestapo.

"Not to worry." Ledreau was sweating now too as he worked the dial. "These babies never resist my tender touch very—"

The room lights suddenly snapped on. Willi felt his stomach plunge as he doused his light, casting a worried glance at Ledreau.

"They're here somewhere," they heard the unmistakable voice of the *femme de ménage* they'd run into before. Willi didn't think he'd seen the last of that one. " 'Special job up in executive offices,' that's what the old one bragged."

Willi could feel Ledreau's back bristle.

"Well, if they're here, we'll find them," a gruff male voice assured. "Cabot, Dupris . . . check the custodial closet."

The Persian rug barely muffled the squeaks as the guards stomped past.

Willi prayed Queen Esther shielded them, and that Cabot and Dupris didn't notice the extra cleaning cart in that goddamned closet.

"You know, it really could be the ammonia," a second female offered sympathetically. "Remember Philomene? She saw ghosts in the Conciergerie."

Willi was shocked to discover Ledreau, still facing the wall, unable to keep his fingers off the dial, flicking it back and forth, listening to what it was whispering.

"Yeah, well, it'll be our ghosts running through the Conciergerie if anything disappears around here, mark my words. They'll have our heads."

"Nothing in the custodial closet!"

"All right, keep checking down the hall," the commander ordered. "Maybe they're trying for the Treasury."

The lights flashed out. Willi took a deep breath, wiping his forehead, shocked when exactly as the police commissioner's door slammed shut, his safe popped open.

Thirty

"If there's such a thing as heaven, you've earned your place in it," Willi thanked Ledreau as they slipped from a back door into the street behind the Palace of Justice. It was still dark, and freezing out, the cobblestones thick with frost. The job though had been a great success. At Willi's side was a canvas sack full of dirty laundry, direct from Orsini's safe.

"I've got much to atone for before I make it to heaven, *mon ami.*" Ledreau laughed. "It's you who ought to be sainted. This isn't even your country. What drives you, I don't know."

"Injustice just makes me crazy, I guess."

Ledreau's craggy face was suddenly serious. "You need to take extra care now, you know that. Once Orsini realizes what's happened—"

"You just watch your own ass, huh?" Willi patted Ledreau's shoulder. "That old bitch will remember you for sure."

"It's been a privilege." Ledreau was suddenly kissing Willi on both cheeks. "I can only hope I fish more out of the river like you.

If you ever need me again"—he tipped his cap as he departed—"you know where to find me."

A few minutes later, just as the bells of Notre Dame struck five, Ava pulled up as planned in her father's Citroën.

"Thank God you're okay. I've been a nervous wreck." She jumped out and opened the trunk. "Everything all right?"

"Perfect." He tossed the canvas sack in.

"Think it'll be enough this time?"

"Absolutely." He slammed the trunk door shut. "To the Hôtel Matignon, *s'il te plaît!*" Stashed back there were not merely years' worth of ledgers illustrating revenue from gambling, prostitution, and narcotics, but two files stuffed with bank statements showing the transfer of millions from the Hearts of Angels charity into Orsini's personal accounts, huge purchases of gold, diamonds, real estate.

"Better change out of those." Ava nodded nervously at his outfit. "I don't even want to call them clothes."

"Bring my suit?"

"Think I'd forget?"

When they reached the palace, it wasn't even 6:00 a.m. She parked along the rue de Varenne and turned off the motor. Although the sun began poking its nose across the Rive Gauche, it didn't take long for the car to chill. She started shivering. "Unfortunately what I forgot was a thermos of hot coffee."

He slid nearer, putting an arm around to embrace her inside his coat.

"Mmmm." She snuggled happily.

When their eyes met, he knew they'd come to a crossroads. Marc and Vivi both were now gone. Willi and Ava were free. He only had to lean and kiss her. But the *only* was colossal. This wasn't just some girl. This was his wife's sister, practically raising his sons since her death. He had no moral repugnance; it happened all the time, in the Bible, in life. Who cared, if it worked? Maybe they'd find real happiness, form a family. *If* . . . and here he had to be realistic . . . *if* there was sexual chemistry. Without that . . .

He'd had it in spades with Vivi, and Paula too back in Berlin. Unfortunately with them, nothing else was right. God knew he'd had it with his wife. But what if it wasn't there with her sister? Considering everyone else involved—the kids, the grandparents—a single kiss could set off an emotional chain reaction. Cracking Orsini's safe was almost preferable to the anxiety he felt about letting their lips meet, though they did look luscious in the morning light. He recalled his escape from Nazi Germany into France. And then the night he took Vivi home. He'd crossed so many frontiers this year. Too many. So he held back, embracing Ava quietly. And in a quarter of an hour both of them had fallen asleep in each other's arms.

A firm tapping on the windshield woke them, and they jumped at the sight of a gendarme.

Ava rolled down her window. "Good morning, Officer."

"May I ask what you two are doing here?"

She indicated subtly for Willi to let her reply. "My, uh, husband here has an early appointment with the prime minister."

"For what reason?"

"He has important papers to deliver."

"Let me see them?"

"In the trunk."

"Show me."

Willi had a dread sensation. The last place in the world he wanted to wind up with those documents was back in the hands of the police.

"Of course you may." Ava got out of the car and smoothed her skirt.

Willi sensed the gendarme's deference toward this bourgeois wife in her beautiful clothes and shiny car out so early chauffeuring her husband. In the sideview mirror he could see Ava speaking to him with dignified calm. What was she saying? Was she showing him the incriminating evidence against Orsini? The car trunk blocked his view of the gendarme's reaction, but her performance was flawless. When the trunk went down, the drama appeared resolved.

The gendarme came back with her and opened the driver's door. "Very well, madame." He tipped his hat. "As soon as the prime minister awakens, I shall make certain he knows you're waiting." He turned back toward the palace.

Looking at Willi, Ava didn't even try to suppress a proud little smile. "I simply told him it was evidence against a German spy ring in Paris. That always gets them."

After twenty minutes of examining the evidence, Daladier removed his glasses. "Well, there's obviously no denying it." He frowned. "The bastard's fingerprints couldn't be any clearer. He's going to have to be dealt with."

Willi felt a horizon of blue skies opening before him. When the extent of Orsini's crimes came to light, the three stiletto murders would surely be among them and its perpetrator apprehended. Until then, Achille Baptiste was still out there. And he definitely knew Willi's face.

"Unfortunately, coming so close on the heels of the Duval scandal"—Daladier gave a troubled sigh—"I don't know that the republic can stand it."

"Can it stand it to allow this to go on?"

"Of course not. But I'm afraid you'll need to have a little patience right now, Inspector." The prime minister's jaw clenched. "This will be a far from simple task, perhaps the most difficult of my career."

"Naturally, I understand. My only concern is that once the commissioner realizes his safe has been entered—"

"I said a *little*. Not a lot." Daladier raised one of his bushy eyebrows. "You may rest assured, monsieur: the only way Victoir Orsini is leaving France now will be on a prison transport. You are about to witness that French justice is not an illusion."

Willi hoped so. Should he ask for some kind of protection in the meantime for himself and his family?

"And as for our bargain"—the Prime Minister distracted Willi's attention. Willi recalled the nerve it took to make his demand—"you've done your part," Daladier acknowledged. "Now I'll do mine. Again, a little patience . . . but you'll get those papers. Six permits to work and Rights of Domicle. You've earned them, Kraus."

Two days later nothing had happened. Willi hung in suspended animation waiting for a sign that Daladier had moved, speculating about how it might play out, growing ever more agitated the longer nothing did.

It was a rainy Sunday. The kids wanted to go to the movies, so he took them to see the new adaptation of H. G. Wells's *Invisible Man,* which they adored. So did he, only a few of its themes went a bit too much under the skin: one man fighting his way back to visibility, another's insane lust for power. *"Even the moon is frightened of me!"* the mad doctor screamed. *"The whole world is frightened to death!"* How could Willi not think of *der Führer* over there, whose hatred had poisoned so much? And Willi's own struggle to reconstitute even a shred of what he'd been.

"Dad," Erich said on the way home, "I'm glad you and Aunt Ava are getting along better."

Willi drew him nearer under the umbrella, Stefan squeezing in too, the three of them walking through a downpour.

"That's in no small measure thanks to you, Erich."

"Really?"

"Yes. After your chat, I thought things over and realized you were right. You're very perceptive. Downright wise sometimes."

"You should listen to me more often!"

Willi knuckled Erich's head as they ducked into a café for hot chocolate.

After dropping the boys back home, Willi headed down the rue de la Pompe, only slightly surprised to spot the man in the wheelchair again. This time he was being carried by his chauffeur, from the town house into the waiting limousine, an umbrella-wielding nurse shielding him from the rain. Right behind, making a dash for the car as she tried to protect her hair, was none other than the former stage star Désireé Jourdain. Madame Crevecour. So *that* was her beloved Maurice? Willi had spoken to each and never realized they were married. Maurice Crevecour. He'd never learned the guy's name. Neither spotted Willi in the downpour and the limousine drove off.

The rain only worsened while he waited on the avenue Henri-Martin. What was the name of that group Crevecour headed? Fraternité d'Honneur. Largest veterans' association in France, he recalled Adrienne Duval telling him on Bastille Day.

Willi checked his watch for the third time. Buses took forever on Sundays, and this one only went as far as Saint-Lazare, where he had to switch. He'd get home in half the time if he could just surmount the terror repelling him from the metro. But he couldn't. Even thinking about it made his stomach queasy, his nostrils fill with the scent of blood. And Vendetta. It had only gotten worse since Marc and André had been killed. Perhaps he'd never ride a subway again.

When the bus arrived, he grabbed a seat and stared out the window. It was a gale out there. Streams flooded the sidewalks, turning the gutters into rivers. Perhaps it was a good omen, he considered, shaking out his umbrella—a portent of the great cleansing Paris was about to undergo. Perhaps tomorrow at this time—he took a deep breath and let himself hope—Orsini and his whole crime regime would be washed away.

At Saint-Lazare he bought a paper and scanned it hungrily, hunting for even a hint that Daladier had made a move. But nothing. In fact, the opposite: a quarter-page photo of an irritatingly smiling Victoir Orsini dancing with his fat wife at some charity dinner. Maybe that smile would never be wiped off. Maybe Daladier, as much as he might like to, realized he couldn't muster the power necessary to wield the sword of French justice.

And where would that leave me? Willi wondered.

On the second leg of the journey, uncomfortably leafing through the rest of the paper in the back of the bus, he spotted a tiny headline buried beneath an ad for radios: MARRIED FRENCH PROFESSORS MURDERED IN LONDON. My God. He sat up, heart pounding as he read the text. It was them all right. Dominique and Frédéric Pasquier, next to each other on a bench in Hyde Park. Killed by a single bullet each to the head, so the paper said.

Stunned, Willi got off at the Porte Saint-Denis, opening his umbrella against the storm, his brain pelted with questions. Why them?

Had the professors somehow run afoul of Orsini's crime ring? Why London? He suddenly felt chilled to the bone.

The rain was coming sideways now, the normally busy street practically abandoned. A block from his building the tempest of questions was drowned out by a strange foreboding mobilizing in his muscles. Somebody was following. He could feel it.

A fast look over his shoulder revealed a man in a vulcanized-rubber coat walking extremely fast. Even in the pouring rain Willi could see beneath his hat that he had on sunglasses. Was he nearing with ill intent, or just to pass? The adrenaline in Willi's veins read-ied him for the former. Certainly even if the man came from behind, Willi could take the fellow, Willi knew, but it'd be better to greet him face on. So he pivoted as if he'd remembered something and started the opposite way. He hadn't managed a complete step when from the corner of his eye a shadowy mass expanded out of a doorway. With great velocity it hit him in the shoulder, nearly knocking him down. Suddenly though, the man in the sunglasses was at his side, prevent-ing him from falling.

"Hey!" Willi shouted as he realized he was being apprehended by both arms, the umbrella torn from his hand. Before he could even ready a countermove, a black Peugeot had screeched out of nowhere, ramming on its brakes, its back door flying open. In the drenching rain a stiletto pressed firmly against Willi's neck and another in his back. There was no choice but to get shoveled into the car, knees banged, shoes and socks soaked.

As they sped into the stormy night, it didn't take long to ascertain that on either side were Barbari brothers. One just couldn't resist planting a stiletto against his throat.

"I want to so badly . . . for what you did to Julien."

"Franjo!" The other smacked his head. "Remember, untouched."

"Yeah, sure." Franjo smiled. "But once they finish with him . . ."

Willi felt a shiver when he realized where they'd come to. In the darkness the driver turned off the motor and leaned around.

"Just couldn't resist playing hero, could you?" It was the *bouquiniste*. "Now you get to find out what happens around here to heroes." He smiled.

A cloth came hard around his mouth, yanked from behind, cutting off the blood in his head. Hustled through the side door of the Palace of Justice he fought with his feet as they dragged him up a long flight of stairs. Sunday night the place was dead. He thought of his boys as he was pushed down a long marble hall straight to the commissioner's office, his eyes searching desperately for a means of escape. Orsini was sitting there behind his giant Louis XIV desk. He looked up, astonished to see Willi.

"Him?!"

"Yes, yes! Him all right!" The old *femme de ménage* was on hand to point a finger. "The moment I saw him I knew he was no janitor. And I wasn't wrong."

Orsini waved her off. "You'll be taken care of."

The gag came off of Willi's mouth. He sputtered and coughed, gasping for air, feeling like his head was about to explode. The police commissioner sat behind his desk examining him coldly.

"When they told me they'd caught the intruder, it never dawned on me it might be someone like you, Herr Inspektor." His black eyes bore into Willi like medieval torture screws. "Extraordinary, really." Orsini smiled insidiously, leaning back into his swivel throne. "A celebrated law enforcement officer such as yourself, committing a crime like this. Perhaps it's the trauma of your exile. Or perhaps"—he shrugged contemplatively, seeming to dream up his press angle—"you've had criminal tendencies all along, as the present government of your homeland contends. At any rate—did you really think you'd get away with it? That we couldn't track you down? How many men did you think there are in Paris capable of breaking into a safe like mine? And Helene St-Claire, how long did you think she'd hold out?"

Except that neither Helene St-Claire nor Ledreau knew his real name or address, Willi was well aware. So how had they found him? Had it been Vivi? he wondered miserably. Had she ratted on him? Even more likely—that night at the Corsican restaurant the *bouquiniste had* recognized him from the stage and trailed him. Thank God he'd sent Ava in a separate cab.

"Before I even bother asking why you'd do something so—well, how shall I put it, suicidal?—let me get to what concerns me most inspector—my property." The police commissioner cracked his knuckles. "Give it back quietly, all of it"—he seemed trying to constrain himself—"and we can do business, if you understand me."

Willi understood him quite clearly. Either way, he was a dead man.

"I wish I could help you, Commissioner. It's not my intention to be rude. It's just that . . . I don't have it anymore."

Orsini maintained a poker face, but his eyes flared distinctly, with more than a shade of fear. "Care to tell me where it is?"

Over the years Willi had been in enough tight spots to recognize that this was a doozy. As he formed a response, he searched for something, anything, that might help him out.

"It's all well protected."

Orsini's gaze darkened, warning Willi not to push it.

On the desktop Willi noticed the rococo clock with its porcelain figurines and a pile of papers weighed down by a black marble sphinx. There were numerous correspondences, as well as a long silver envelope opener in the unmistakable shape of a stiletto. Just behind Orsini, Willi recognized the door that led to the service stairs he'd seen the night they'd broken in.

"I don't intend to play games, Inspector." Orsini's pudgy fingers bunched. "There are rooms in this building full of devices famous for making men speak. I'm sure my friends here would be happy to demonstrate. Franjo is quite proficient at some, I understand. Is that true, Franjo?"

"Oh, yes. My specialty's Scottish thumbscrew. Unendurable agony."

Willi's head and heart were in full agreement on few occasions, but this was one. He knew he either acted now or—

The clock on Orsini's desk struck, and the little porcelain figurines began their circular dance. In a single motion, like a discus thrower, Willi snatched the black sphinx off Orsini's desk and flung it backward, hearing it land against Franjo's chest with a fracturing thud. Then, using the desk like a pommel horse, he leaped across it, grabbing the stiletto-shaped letter opener and pressing it swiftly to the police commissioner's throat. How good it felt to have the knife in his hand this time.

"Don't!" Orsini shreiked when the others moved to help him. Willi had grabbed Orsini's arm from behind and was twisting it. How tiny the big boss looked suddenly, his elevator shoes barely lifting him to Willi's chest. "Be reasonable, Kraus. You can't get out of here. Let's talk as civilized men."

On the floor, Franjo was the one now writhing in unendurable agony.

"Open the door behind you," Willi ordered the commsioner. "One wrong move, any of you, and his throat gets slit."

"Fool," Orsini bleat with a mixture of outrage and terror. "Think of your wife, your children—" He fumbled for the door.

Willi didn't have a wife. And it was for his children he was doing this. He pushed Orsini into the service stairwell and bolted the door behind, clasping his hand hard over the commissioner's mouth. Banging thundered from the other side.

"Open up, damn you! Quick, downstairs. Cut them off! On your feet Franjo!"

"Help me."

"Here—"

Willi waited until there was silence on the other side, then re-opened the door and pushed Orsini through. The marble sphinx was on the floor with its face half broken off. Past Queen Esther in her glorious robes he hustled the commissioner out to the custodial closet where Willi and Ledreau had dumped their mops. With dirty rags he gagged and bound the runt, who was struggling now like a pig. Willi shook him hard then punched him in the stomach. What joy to subdue him! Hoisting him by the suspenders, Willi tossed the mobster into the trash can.

"Enjoy your new home." He brushed his hands.

Right before he covered the bug-eyed head with the lid though, he considered the amount of misery this little caesar had caused. And smash! His fist went into the ugly nose.

Locking the door behind him, he knew he had about two seconds to figure out an escape route. The interior lights were off and the whole vast building was pitch-dark. Luckily he recalled enough of the layout to feel his way down the main stairs, hoping to find the exit he and Ledreau had used. In his haste however he failed to notice a dimly glowing lantern at the bottom of the next flight and practically ran into the bent figure of his nemesis, the *femme de ménage*, humming as she mopped.

"Ahh!" she screamed, trying to block him. "He's here! This way! Ahhhh!"

Willi shoved her hard against the wall and grabbed the lantern, then flew down the stairs.

"Which way?" he heard behind him.

"The swine took my light!"

"Which way?"

"Down, for God's sake. Down!"

Willi's heart clenched when a shot rang out. Then another. The lantern didn't help. He dumped it on the stairs and continued blindly down another flight, then through the first door he came to. In utter blackness he groped along a chilly stone hallway, his chest pounding wildly. As he passed through what looked like a massive set of iron prison gates, he realized he must have entered the Conciergerie. During the Reign of Terror these walls had been the last residence of many thousands condemned to the guillotine. Even now the empty silence held a strange foreboding. His blood tingled as his footsteps echoed hauntingly back. There was a way out of course, but *which* way? The darkness had disoriented him. He had no idea where he was even—

His feet stopped short, his breath catching. Not three feet ahead a man was staring at him. Dizziness overcame him. He could feel himself at the station in Berlin, the Gestapo awaiting—until he perceived how oddly clad the man was: a high felt hat, long red jacket, tricolor ribbon. What was this, a costume party? When the man offered not even a blink at Willi's appearance, it grew plain he was no man at all, but a painted dummy, a museum exhibit. Willi nearly laughed. According to a sign, this was the Clerk's Office, where prisoners were registered. Indeed an enormous book lay open in which the wooden man appeared ready to take Willi's name. On the wall behind were rows of huge iron keys. Willi was glad not to have been an aristocrat in 1794. A shot echoed in the distance. But he did have a Corsican gang on his tail.

Continuing into the blackness, he passed a second room with a sign explaining it as the Grooming Chamber. Here inmates were stripped of their personal possessions—jewelry, watches, snuff-boxes, etc.—and forced to have their hair cut.

Another shot rang out somewhere in the distance.

Did they know where he was or were they just aiming wildly?

Beyond the Cour du Mai, where prisoners were loaded into carts and driven past jeering throngs to the raised blades waiting at the Place de la Concorde, Willi heard someone yell. "Try in there!"

The lights flashed on.

"Look, there!"

A shot rang out.

Practically flying down the nearest staircase, he all but landed in the lap of the most famous of the guillotine's victims, Marie Antoinette. Her slender figure was deep in prayer, shrouded in a black, hooded shawl, two guards forever watching her. Maybe she was thinking of her children, Willi thought—whom she would never again see. If only he could see his again.

Down the lightless corridors, hands before him like a blind man, the amplifying echoes told him he'd likely entered the Salle des Gens d'Armes, one of few medieval sections left in the palace, a vast stone hall of vaulting arches supported by rows of columns. Willi stopped behind one of them, fearful his steps would give him away. Sweat was pouring down his forehead. As soundlessly as possible he hurried another twenty paces until he reached the next column, having no idea which way he was going, where an exit might be. He was trapped in a pitch-black maze. A moment later it got worse. The huge Gothic hall became all too visible as the lights switched on.

"There's the little shit!"

A bullet hit the ceiling just above his head, sending bits of stone crumbling on him. He crouched, and hurried blindly through the dark trying to find the next column.

"You guys, other side," he heard. "I'll close in from here."

Not good. Three armed men against one, the proverbial duck in a Gothic shooting gallery, Willi thought. Even with the lights on he couldn't see a way out, only arches and rows of columns that stood along the hall like chessmen. Behind one, the *bouquiniste* was gunning for him. And once the Barbari brothers reached the far end . . . checkmate, perhaps.

He flinched as a bullet practically nicked his ear. When another came from the opposite direction, he hit the floor with a moan.

"Out with your hands up, Kraus! We don't want to hurt you."

He inched ahead on his stomach, crawling as he once had beneath barbed wire, only here the stone was ice-cold. He heard the echo of boots getting louder. Or was that his own pounding heart? A bullet hit the stone near his hand. Another behind him. The approaching footsteps grew ever louder, echoing from what seemed a dozen directions. A bullet sent dust into his face. He coughed, closing his eyes. Something burning nicked his ankle and he could feel a warm trickle of blood.

Boots were almost upon him, pounding thundering through his ears. He waited for a flash of light, a long, dark tunnel. But nothing. He realized the pounding was passing by. He opened his eyes, daring to look up. Soldiers were running past. Was he dead already? Hallucinating?

Slowly, uncertainly, he pushed off the floor, dusting himself as he blinked in amazement. They had black berets on, he saw. Crests on the side: Second Régiment d'Infanterie.

"Hands up!" he heard from across the room, and not twenty yards away he saw the Barbari brothers comply, holding their arms overhead as they were led off with the *bouquiniste*. Daladier had made his move, Willi thought, realizing his ankle was bleeding pretty badly.

Thirty-one

"According to the papers, Daladier won't last a week." Max placed a filbert in a nutcracker and squeezed. "Half the country thinks he forged that evidence against Orsini."

Willi winced as the nut split.

A few stiches had healed his ankle but it was painful hearing how his hard work was being denied. Plus, if Daladier was removed, what would happen to those residency permits? Without them, he and his family remained under perpetual threat.

This morning a long, white envelope had been in his mailbox, and his heart raced when he tore it open. It turned out to be just the lab report analyzing those letters to insurance companies that had marked the beginning of André Duval's end. Clouitier had warned him the lab was notoriously slow, but never had Willi imagined the results would arrive long after he had any use for them. All three of the anonymous letters had been produced on the same typewriter apparently. He crumbled the report and tossed it out. It was no way to live, never knowing if each morning would bring a new lease on life or a death sentence.

"You think they'd be happy with all those terrible crooks in prison." Bette put an almond *joconde* on the table fresh from the oven. "Imagine, the police commissioner dealing drugs. It would never happen in Germany."

"That lovely country." Aunt Hedda squinted for a better look at the cake. "I was never sorry I left. Mmmm, smells divine, darling."

There was no denying it was better here than in Nazi Germany. But despite the sunshine filling the Parisian skies Willi couldn't help but see dead men floating past the window . . . Phillipe Junot . . . Marc Nathanson . . . André Duval. The boys were curled on the rug reading; a delicious dessert was in front of Willi. He should feel content, he knew. But he didn't. The tension in his stomach wouldn't dissipate.

The events of the past week were difficult for everyone to digest. Orsini's arrest and the revelations of the vast scale of his criminal empire were proving as traumatic to France as the collapse of Confiance Royale, the second "scandal of the century" in weeks. Newspapers blazed with images of handcuffed policemen being led off, over 150, big raids at gambling halls across the city, none equaling the one at quai de Valmy, where millions in francs were recovered, storerooms full of narcotics at Hearts of Angels charity facilities, and of course in the basement at police headquarters. It was one shock after another. If the Duval Scandal had thrown light on the venal, greedy side of the Third Republic, the Orsini Affair put under a microscope the extent to which even its most sacred institutions had been corrupted.

Other than Ava and the prime minister, no one, thank goodness, including his in-laws, had any idea of the role Willi'd played in the commissioner's downfall. The newspapers described Orsini as having been found "hiding in a janitor's closet" with no mention of his being bound or gagged. Willi was content to let the credit go to Daladier, whose government needed all the help it could get.

One thing troubled Willi. In all those published lists of the arrested he had yet to find the one name he'd been looking for: Achille

Baptiste. The investigative magistrates were only beginning their work, and there were sure to be many further revelations. But would those include that of the murderer he'd witnessed slay three men with a stiletto? And what about the dead professors; what had they to do with this?

"The whole French right is ready to erupt." Max cracked another filbert with foreboding. "Calling for riots to bring down the government. They think Daladier went after Orsini as revenge for Confiance Royale."

"How about that Duval, eh?" Aunt Hedda's eyes blazed with excitement. "Remember that night we saw him at Maxim's? I knew *at a glance* he was a thief. You could just see it in his—"

"Aunt Hedda," Ava interrupted. "How about some more cake?"

Willi chuckled at the woman's hindsight. Like most people Aunt Hedda had been smitten by the Duvals. But she'd just provided a convenient entrée to a topic he'd been trying to broach.

"Bette, your anniversary's the 11, isn't it?"

"Yes."

"Then, how come we celebrated it this year on the twelfth?"

"It just worked out that way. Why?"

Ava grasped what he was driving at. "Didn't you originally make a reservation with Maxim's on the eleventh, *Mutti*?"

"Yes. A month in advance. At the last minute they called to say they'd overbooked and would complimentary champagne compensate for a switch to Monday the twelfth."

The night André Duval always dined there, Willi knew. It was the one bit of information Marc Nathanson had managed to get out of the maître d'. So then . . . the whole thing *had* been a setup. Somebody wanted the famous German detective to meet the high financeer.

"You told people your plans for the eleventh before they changed, didn't you?" Ava pressed.

"I mentioned it here and there. I told you, Hedda, right?"

"Of course you told me; how else could you have invited me?"

"I might have chatted about it at the beauty parlor too, why?"

The beauty parlor. Willi had a recollection. "Bette," he asked on a hunch, "which salon do you use?"

"Around the corner on avenue Henri-Martin. Salon Sasha. Why, thinking about a permanent wave?"

"The same place Désireé Crevecour goes to."

"How did you know? I chat with her all the time."

"Don't get me started on *that* gold digger," Hedda interrupted with her mouth full of *joconde*. "Or the husband. I never believed the man was a war cripple." She swallowed. "Had to be a skiing accident. Comes from one of the richest families in France. And what a playboy, ach!" She waved her hand. "Might not be able to walk but he sure can use his—"

"Spare us, Hedda." Max pushed back from the table. "Mitzi and Fritzi need a walk."

"You'd think the wife would give a damn," Hedda continued anyway. "But not that bitch. As long as she can strut around her palace."

"Really, Hedda." Bette frowned.

"Well, it's true."

"We'll take the dogs, *Vati*," Ava volunteered. "Come, Willi. Let's walk."

On the street Willi's mind was spinning like a tornado. Might Désireé Crevecour have informed Maxim's to switch the Gottmans' dinner to when André Duval always ate there? Or might she just have told her husband? Maybe *he* was the one to have wanted Willi and André to meet. But why? Something to do with his veterans' association? It didn't make sense.

"Ava, could you do a bit more research for me?"

"What now?"

"Not what. Who. Madame and Monsieur Crevecour."

She smiled. "Sure. Should be interesting, if my aunt's to be believed. I'll get right on it." Her eyes turned to take him in. "Willi, you know how proud I am of you for bringing Orsini to justice?"

"There were others—you and Marc."

"What you accomplished was a miracle."

He looked down. "That means a lot, coming from you. You were the one who saw through Duval from the start, Ava. Not Hedda. You're a pretty perceptive lady."

"Then, what's bothering you now?"

Willi stuck his hands in his pockets. "You can see that too?"

"Clear as a billboard."

"They seemed to have gotten everyone but Achille Baptiste."

"That's what I wanted to talk to you about." She ran a finger across his coat lapel. "Remember that hatcheck girl at Maxim's who called him a Cervione and we didn't know what it meant—until we saw it was a town? Well, I went back to the library yesterday and guess what . . . Orsini, the Barbari brothers, and your friend the *bouquiniste* *all* come from the same place on the northeast coast of Corsica, called Alto. The nearest town is Cervione. The two have been rivals since practically antiquity, and for the past hundred years there's been a real vendetta between them—murder, reprisals, poisoned wells. So there's one thing you can be positive of: whichever side the men from Alto are on, the Cervione are opposite."

A lightning bolt seemed to enlighten the landscape.

"That means—"

"There isn't one, but *two* groups of Corsicans," Ava finished the thought. "Only one's on Orsini's side. The other's against him."

Willi took a deep breath.

"The question is then," he pondered aloud. "If not Orsini—for whom does Achille Baptiste wield his stiletto?"

Book Four

THE SCENT OF VENDETTA

Thirty-two

NOVEMBER 1933

Not since March 1918, when Paris shuddered under German siege guns, had the city been so tense. Beneath the double strains of scandal and economic catastrophe the national fabric, left and right, seemed to be tearing at the seams. Each side was taking to the streets, growing more confident, more fanatical, as the middle shrank. Hourly the centrist government was expected to unravel. It was beginning to feel a bit too much like Berlin, at least to Willi, who more than once found himself wondering if France really was the safest place for them to have sought refuge.

On the other hand, as he rode by bus to meet the boys for dinner, twilight casting a peaceful glow over the city, he realized that the longer they stayed in Paris, the deeper the kids sank roots here. Would it be wise to tear them up again? He could still hear the praise from their teachers the other night at parents' visitation: his boys were so bright, so diligent, so likable. Astonishingly, both claimed they wanted to be detectives when they grew up, which made Willi unsure whether to laugh or cry.

As the bus inched through the traffic around l'Étoile, the famous circular junction of twelve radiating avenues, he stared up at the monumental Arc de Triomphe. Uncertain as life might be for them here, the boys' chances were far better than at home, where it was certain there'd be no future at all. Yet . . . how many days had it been since he'd turned in the evidence to Daladier? Seven. And not a word about residency documents. The prime minister had important things to worry about, but still! He needed those papers.

At Trocadéro he transferred to the bus along avenue Henri-Martin. The streetlights were just coming on. He'd reached the part of town where uniformed nannies held children's hands and chauffeurs waited by town houses. Just blocks from the rue de la Pompe he was struck by a curvaceous female striding across the street in a long, slender overcoat and low hat, carrying a bag of groceries. Unless he'd fallen asleep and was dreaming—

Astonishment jolted him. He wasn't dreaming. It was her all right. Against all reason he rose from his seat, yanked as if by a giant magnet to the outside platform.

The conductor's arm blocked his exit. "You must wait for the bus stop, monsieur."

"But of course." Willi nodded, realizing it was two streets farther. He could see her turning a corner. Waiting several seconds with a smile, he suddenly just knocked the guy's arm aside and jumped to the pavement.

"Crazy idiot!" Willi heard from behind. Only reaching the far corner did it occur to him he could have used his police badge.

At pretty little Square Lamartine he caught sight of her silhouette slipping into a beaux arts building on the corner of avenue Victor-Hugo. Whom could she be bringing groceries to? When she disappeared, he strolled past and took a peek inside: marble floors, a fountain, chandeliers. The outside register though got him. His eyes popped when he spotted next to apartment 6A—her name.

Vivi *lived* here?

Stepping back and counting, he saw 6A had to be that corner apartment. It was massive, with a wraparound terrace. The lights went on even as he watched. How the hell had she managed this—

gotten her claws into one of those men with *more power and money than he could ever imagine,* as she once put it? Unable to stop staring, he had to force himself finally to turn away and start toward the rue de la Pompe, realizing he was strangely disconcerted. And twenty minutes late.

By the time he got to the Gottmans' the kids were starving. He took them out for spaghetti and clam sauce. All through dinner Stefan babbled on about his school trip to Château de Vincennes, the drawbridge, the moat, the prison tower, the wall where Mata Hari was shot, meanwhile getting marinara all over. Just after nine Willi brought them home. Ava was on the couch with her legs folded under her, reading. She brightened when she saw him, asking if he wanted some cake, but he declined. He told her he had a little headache and felt like getting to bed early tonight, which made her raise an eyebrow.

As soon as he left, he hurried back to the Square Lamartine. It was damp and windy, but when he saw the light still on in Vivi's apartment, he turned his collar up and waited to see if she'd come out. If he knew her, she wouldn't be content to sit home all night, if that really was her home.

Around ten the lights went off upstairs, and sure enough out she came all right, all dolled up in a fox jacket, silver heels, and that fake beauty mark on her cheek. With the hat off it was evident she'd dyed her hair platinum, like a gun moll out of some American gangster movie, harsh but sexy as hell. Leaning into the shadows, he let her pass then followed at a distance. On the avenue Henri-Martin she hailed a cab. Hoping he had enough cash, he stuck out his arm and jumped in the next one. What a cliché he felt like when he ordered the driver, *"Suivez ce taxi!"* Follow that taxi. "And step on it!"

"Oui, monsieur!"

"Police." He flashed the badge to clarify the matter. "Don't let them out of your sight, but don't let them know you're following either."

"Oui, monsieur!" The guy brightened, clearly finding this the most excitement in a while.

Willi shouldn't have been surprised where they wound up, although it didn't exactly make sense. If she was living *there,* why come *here*? Could something in her not keep away from the fleabag hotels, the hookers and the hoodlums, the pimps and the addicts, along these dark streets?

"Hope you get your man!" the driver said as Willi climbed out.

"Thanks."

He kept his distance as he trailed down the crowded, music-filled sidewalks of the rue de Lappe. Vivi made her way directly to her old haunt, the Red Room, where she'd once danced so passionately with Phillipe Junot. And him.

Now whom?

As always it was dark inside. Smoky. Loud. Once she checked her jacket, heads turned as she began to circulate. She was wearing a knit sweater that revealed the full shape of her breasts, and a long, thin skirt slit to the thigh. Numerous times he saw her decline men who asked her to dance. Was she waiting for someone special? The man, perhaps, who'd set her up in that glamour suite back off the Square Lamartine? In this dive?

When he finally saw who it was, his stomach turned. Clearly their meeting was no accident. The way they embraced, it was evident that Vivi and tall, red-haired Florian Lorilleux, Phillipe Junot's old roommate, were happy to see each other.

It turned Willi's blood cold.

He laughed at his own jealousy as he watched Vivi lead Lorilleux to the dance floor. Hadn't she held Willi just as close, looked at him with those same lustrous eyes—and Junot, and God knew how many before him? What was this girl's game?

Round and round they blended with the dancers, each couple in their own revolving galaxy. With each squeeze of the accordion the universe seemed to contract and expand, rising and falling to the beat of the snares. The universe, except him. He was the one on the outside, looking in. Wondering what was going on. Who was with whom, and why.

For what seemed hours the two clung to each other on the crowded floor, hips grinding, eyes interlocked, caressing each other's hair. But when they finally went to retrieve Vivi's fox jacket, it wasn't that late: twelve thirty on the dot. Willi watched as she and Lorilleux stepped outside, pausing for a long kiss. Would they go home together? Back to that crummy student apartment she used to go to with Junot? Or would she take him to her swank new digs, a lover behind her lover's back?

He took a deep breath as he peered from the door and saw them under a streetlamp, leaning into each other, whispering. When had this started? Had they plotted all along against Junot? But why? Waiting by the door, he prepared to follow, then realized they were going separate ways. For a moment he didn't know whom to pursue. Stepping to the street, he saw Vivi hail a cab. Lorilleux had turned down rue de la Roquette in the direction of Bastille.

Suddenly, Willi didn't feel like following either. He was sick of the whole damn game. He wanted to go home. Not that dump he lived in. To a real home, with a real family. But he set off down rue de la Roquette, telling himself that all the buses started from Bastille anyway, and there was only a short time to catch the last one. Just as he saw the kid hurry down into the metro, a slight scent in the air made the hairs on his neck stand. My God. Not again. Vendetta.

Quickly he scanned left and right, but he didn't see anyone. There had to be people other than Corsican gangsters who wore the stuff, he reasoned. A moment later though, there it was: a green fedora. And the former doorman from Maxim's, Achille Baptiste, hand in pocket, went strolling down the metro steps.

Willi staggered. An artillery shell seemed to explode in his head. Vivi and Lorilleux were no coconspiritors. She must have set the kid up! Just as she must have done to Junot. That damned bitch! She was leading victims to Achille Baptiste. Who were they working for?

Running to the metro entrance, he gripped the rail and stared into the abyss. The smell of the air from below made his stomach turn. Another poor soul was about feel the bite of a Corsican stiletto, he knew, unless he forced himself down.

He took two steps, then his legs went gummy. The stench of blood filled his nostrils. He felt Phillipe Junot in his arms again and heard his final, choking words: "Vivi. Her—"

What a fool he'd been! All this time he'd taken it as a testament of love but now he understood: it wasn't love; it was an accusation.

Only too late did Phillipe Junot realize Vivi had led him like a sheep to slaughter. Now it was his roommate's turn.

Step by step Willi forced himself down, clinging to the rail. The advertisements around him were spinning. *Campari . . . Dubonnet . . . Docteur Pierre . . . Savon . . . Pâté . . . Eau.* He could hear a train rumbling nearer. He wasn't going to make it.

"Vicki—" he mumbled when saw his dead wife at the bottom of the stairs. She was holding her arms out, urging him to come.

One more step and then another, he felt the platform beneath his feet, not even knowing how. Then suddenly the train had arrived and he was on it.

As soon as the doors closed, his anxiety, like a storm tide, receded with gratifying swiftness. His breathing slowed. His vision cleared. None of the bloody associations in his brain had to do with the train he realized; it was only the platform. So he wiped the sweat from his face with his handkerchief and took a look around. The car was full of people but where were Lorilleux and Achille Baptiste? Had he even gotten on the right train?

A bunch of Italian tourists surrounded him, talking a mile a minute. Past them, several sleepy clerks, a grumpy-faced waitress. A snoring man. Two boyish women sat side by side slapping each other in some childish game. But no Lorilleux. Nor a Corsican assassin. Willi's eyes fluttered as he took a deep breath. There was only one stop before the Gare d'Orléans, he calculated. When they got there, he'd have to move up one more car and keep looking.

The opening doors at quai de la Rapée straightaway brought back his queasiness. On the platform the concrete floor turned gelatinous, walls, ceiling, everything. What was mere yards away appeared many miles. He wanted to shout, *Someone help me, please!* But he prodded himself . . . *You're halfway there; just keep going.* One step. Two. Only one more. And right before the doors on the car ahead closed, he threw himself inside.

The nausea again mercifully dissipated. But a slow scan around revealed neither killer nor victim on this car either. Which meant he was going to have to get off at the next stop, Gare d'Orléans and pray he reached Florian Lorilleux before Achille Baptiste did.

When they pulled into the big station, practically everybody got off at once, wanting to transfer to Line 10 for the last westbound train. Willi joined the stampede, hoping by some miracle to transcend his symptoms. But as soon as he stepped to the platform, the dizziness seized with a vengeance. Scores of people were trampling through the tunnel, every footstep like an explosion in his brain. Through the nausea and swimming vision, however, a dozen or so people ahead, he spotted it . . . the goddamned green fedora. A shot of adrenaline settled his stomach and instantly focused his attention.

He maneuvered sideways, bumping into the grumpy waitress from the first car, passing the snoring man, the chattery tourists, gaining until he was practically behind the murderer when all at once his blood ran cold. There it was in Achille Baptiste's fist, poised to plunge, the long, slim, deadly stiletto. Just one person ahead, in ignorant bliss, strode the ginger-haired figure of Florian Lorilleux.

Achille Baptiste and the stiletto both would not be hard to get to the ground, Willi knew. But then what? With all these people around the police would inevitably show up and they'd find his fake ID badge, which he couldn't allow. He'd have to settle on just disarming the bastard and saving Lorilleux.

Taking a deep breath he moved into position, tensed his muscles, then with one swift kick to Baptiste's wrist he sent the weapon flying.

Stunned, Achille Baptiste spun around. For a second their gazes locked. A murderous rage filled the Corsican's eyes when he recognized his assailant. It grew even worse as Willi grabbed the stiletto from the floor. When a woman screamed at the top of her lungs, the would-be assassin appeared to concur that this was no place to settle their score. Diving into the crowd he vanished, and Willi rushed to young Lorilleux, who had already spotted Willi and was standing frozen in shock.

"Just walk quickly," Willi whispered to him. "You almost got knifed."

Upstairs, the student hung his head, trying to get ahold of himself. "I've been pretending it couldn't happen to me. But it's obvious they're knocking us off one by one."

"Who is? Who's doing it?"

The boy looked up terrified. "I've no idea!" His voice broke. "Someone powerful." He tried to control it but his chest heaved and he burst out crying. "I read about the professors in London They got them too."

Yeah, and André in Provence too, Willi was thinking, feeling the sharp stiletto in his pocket. He tried to comfort the lad, squeezing his shoulder, but told him it wouldn't be safe to go home. So they went back to Willi's place and he gave Lorilleux the couch.

"Florian," Willi said just before he turned the lights out. "One of the members of your group was André Duval, wasn't he?"

The kid turned whiter than his undershirt. "I . . . I can't talk about that." He withdrew beneath the cover.

So it was true, Willi knew. Labor leader Lucien Ruehl and his now infamous brother-in-law had only staged the years-long estrangement to cover up their mutual membership in an underground movement.

More than likely too, Lucien Ruehl would be next on the hit list.

Thirty-three

Ruehl's sister, Adrienne Duval, looked a little embarrassed the next evening when Willi showed up at her father's house in Reims. "My goodness. How did you find me?"

It had taken a fifty-franc note in the palm of the concierge at the Hôtel Lutetia.

"I should have phoned first, I know, but I just happened to be in the neighborhood and—"

"In the neighborhood, eighty miles from Paris?"

"I need to speak with you, Adrienne. Might I come in?"

"Of course." She kissed him on each cheek, even thinner and paler than before. "May I offer you something?" She nervously fixed her hair, smoothing her skirt as they sat.

"I'm afraid I need your help again." He got right to the point. Achille Baptiste was onto him now, so there was no time to lose. This morning he'd sent Lorilleux packing to Bordeaux, where the kid had a second cousin. Hopefully they wouldn't find him there. "You've got to tell me—where is your brother?"

"My—"

Willi's eyes made it clear there was no point trying to maintain the façade she had no contact with him. He'd spent most of the day trying to find Ruehl: his apartment, the union office, the leftist newspapers. But neither the labor leader nor his wife nor baby was to be found, so he'd taken the train out here.

"He's in very grave danger."

"That's not new." Her mouth pinched.

"They're killing off members of his group one by one."

She stiffened, swallowing, but stared at him as if she had no idea what he was talking about.

"I know all about André and Lucien belonging to the same—"

Her hand came quickly over his mouth. "Forgive me, Willi." She smiled tragically, letting it drop. "Have some tea, please. You must tell me about the boys, how are they?"

He stared at her incredulous, her loyalty awe-inspiring. To what end though?

Someone powerful, Lorilleux had described whoever was hunting them. Willi was beginning to think that was an understatement. He stared out the window into the darkness as the train headed back to Paris. How had they managed to find André so expediently in Avignon? That night he was packing to go look for him, Vivi had guessed whom, but not *where*. Yet, after heading to Marseille, Achille Baptiste had shown up precisely where he needed to be. Had she somehow found out? Willi felt like going to her apartment and beating the truth out of her. Only he knew he'd never be able to do it.

The maître d' at Maxim's knew. But there was no approaching him. Willi dare not show his face anywhere near that restaurant. And the police were still of no use. An interim commissioner had been named, but by all accounts 36 quai des Orfèvres remained in shambles. If Adrienne Duval wouldn't help save her brother and capture her husband's killer, there was only one place he could think of to turn, because he couldn't do it alone.

By the time he got back he was exhausted. And starving. Across the street from his apartment building was a restaurant he never went to because it was obviously pricey. Tonight he didn't care. He needed a decent meal.

Inside, a dazzling vision of peacocks and nymphs greeted him, a world of mirrors and moldings and glass mosaics in art nouveau. He wound up having a sublime if contemplative three-course feast, accompanied by wine and finished off by a crème brûlée *avec* vanilla flambé. Wiping his mouth as he finished, down the center aisle came a man in a wheelchair pushed by his wife. Willi couldn't believe it. Désireé Crevecour and her beloved Maurice.

They spotted him instantly. "Ah, well, look who it is!"

"Bonsoir." He rose to greet them, reminding himself to keep smiling. Beads of sweat were forming on the back of his neck.

Ava had done her research on these two. The paralyzed Crevecour had fought in the war, all right. Been a general, highly decorated. Try as she might though, she couldn't find out if he'd been injured by a German bullet as he had told Willi, or in a skiing accident as Aunt Hedda claimed.

"I should have found *something*," she insisted. "What I can confirm is that he was at Verdun, and that now he heads a huge veterans' association called Fraternité d'Honneur. Apparently he still wields considerable influence in the military, one of the chief proponents of the Maginot Line."

An ultranationalist with outspoken contempt for anything left of the center, she added, he had a vehement hatred of communism but, interestingly enough, was not, like the majority of his ilk, an anti-Semite.

"In fact he's a rare philo-Semite," she said. "Apparently he was genuinely fond of André Duval. And married former stage star Désireé Jourdain, who's also Jewish by the way—no wonder Hedda hates her. A rival!"

"Imagine running into you here." The general shook Willi's hand from his wheelchair with a crushing grip. "Julien is one of our favorite restaurants. I trust you had a fine meal."

"Just superb. Thank you."

"I didn't know you knew Monsieur Boucher." His wife looked surprised.

"Boucher?" The general exceeded her in puzzlement. "I thought he had a German name. Klaus, or something."

"Kraus," Willi corrected, swallowing miserably. "Boucher was a nom de plume I used while I was working as a reporter. But that newspaper closed, so I no longer have the job."

Both the ex–stage star and ex-general stared at him.

Willi smiled awkwardly, hoping they didn't notice the slight twitching of his left cheek. There was no way of knowing whether this guy's *Fraternité d'Honneur* had anything to do with the assasination of Group X members, but according to Ava's research Crevecour had the means and possibly the political motive to undertake such a campaign of murder.

"Well, I hope you enjoy your meal as much as I did. I have an early appointment tomorrow," Willi said. "So I've got to get running. *Bon appétit!*"

When the alarm went off, it roused him from a deathlike sleep. He shook his head and banged the button down, reaching for the phone. Using the card he still kept with the private number, he managed to book an appointment—but not until four. On the edge of the bed he sat there bleary-eyed, looking around. His apartment was a mess. He didn't have the energy to clean it though. So he fell back into bed, astonished when he didn't wake up until two.

Still cloudy-headed, he dragged himself downstairs and ordered *petit déjeuner* at the café next door. Daladier was on the radio making a speech.

"Our will is fast and firm! Justice has been set in motion!"

"Too bad it's going in circles," the waiter quipped as he put down coffee.

The prime minister was proposing to fix the justice system, a series of laws that would usher in a new era of accountability. To achieve this he promised to sacrifice even his own career. He then asked the Chamber of Deputies for a vote of confidence tomorrow.

How about my Right of Domicile papers? Willi kept thinking. A bargain's a bargain, monsieur.

After finishing the last of his coffee he walked to Château d'Eau and stood atop the metro stairs looking down. He'd be damned if he was going to let this idiotic fear cripple him any longer. Step by step he felt the queasiness rising through his stomach. But it was with less intensity now. He made it to the platform and then onto the train with relatively minor discomfort. As he took a seat and breathed in slowly, a sense of triumph filled him. Perhaps confronting Achille Baptiste and helping out Lorilleux had enabled him to break the cycle of fear and response. He would be glad to be able to get around again with some expediency.

Unfortunately, other signs of trouble were on board. Instead of the usual passengers he noticed everyone seemed to be carrying placards and banners.

For a week now Paris had seethed with demonstrations. Along the Grands Boulevards, in front of the stock exchange, down by the Chamber of Deputies, massive crowds had gathered. On the left they demonstrated against the ruling classes. *Defend the workers! Away with oppression!* On the right they decried national decay. *Save our country! Viva la France! Down with liberalism and its incoherencies!* The factionalism looked too chillingly familiar to Willi, growing meaner by the day. Windows smashed. Tram lines short-circuited.

Exiting at Jeu de Paume, intending to walk the rest of the way, he emerged from the metro in a tidal wave of humanity, stunned by the spectacle he found himself witness to. Thousands of people were pouring from every direction into the giant Place de la Concorde, the air echoing with furious cries for the overthrow of the government. Restoration of national honor. The dropping of all charges against Victoir Orsini and his return as police commissioner.

Could they really want that?

According to their banners, the demonstrators intended to seize the Assemblée Nationale tonight, and "throw the scoundrels into the Seine!" Helmeted police units however were guarding the bridge they'd have to cross to reach the Palais Bourbon.

Paris was no stranger to uprisings. One of the reasons the city was given its famous long, straight boulevards was so that the army could fire from farther ranges at revolutionary barricades. Now, where the guillotine once filled baskets a new revolt of far-right nationalists appeared to have reached ignition point.

Fixed by the spectacle, Willi stood with his back to a lamppost watching the explosion form. There were repeated calls from the police via loudspeaker for the crowd to disburse. When these had no effect from behind a row of police buses a squadron of mounted gendarmes, thirty, maybe forty, strong, trotted out in capes and silver helmets. Formed into a V, at the sound of a bugle they began to canter forward, slowly at first, then picking up speed, until they broke into a full-out gallop, capes flying, clubs pummeling. There was pushing, screaming. People started going down, holding bloody heads. It looked as if the marchers' ranks would shatter, until it was police themselves being yanked off their mounts. Horses toppling. One of the buses exploding in flame. The crowd cheered as the mounted cops beat a hasty retreat.

The emboldened demonstrators pressed forward, vowing to take the bridge and beyond. Willi realized it was time to get out. The critical mass had been reached. Pushing his way across the street, he rounded the corner onto the rue Royale just as a terrible roar reached his ears. There was no mistaking it: the army had arrived and opened fire. Screams of agony filled the air. From much too near, along the rue de Rivoli, a terrifying clatter of automatic fire arose, and people were running by trying to flee an armored truck spraying them with bullets. If Willi didn't have the reflexes he had from years in the field, he could easily have wound up like scores of others that day, washing the cobblestones with blood.

Bruised and more than a little shaken, he made it to the rue de Saussaires. Across the street a small mob was trying to tear down the gates of the presidential palace. The afternoon was filled with tear gas, smashing glass, and gunshots.

At number 11 he was glad not to have to sneak in. Last time he'd been here, Director Tondreau had given him his private number. "It's extremely urgent, sir," Willi had assured him this morning when he used it. He was certain the head of Sureté Générale would want to know about the murderous plot he'd uncovered. Tondreau agreed to meet him, but that was before all hell had broken out.

The nervous marines at the main gate had to call upstairs three times to confirm Willi's appointment. He was finally admitted but kept waiting outside the director's office as people hurried to and from in the hall, all with what seemed urgent business. An hour went by, then a second. Still, he was convinced the Sûreté Générale was his best bet. Once Achille Baptiste finished off Action Group X, there was no doubt whom his stiletto would be aiming for next. If someone as powerful as Crevecour and his Fraternité d'Honneur was behind it, Willi needed all the help he could get.

"Kraus? That you?" It was Marsolet, the former Gripois, fatter than ever now, dour-faced. "Can you believe it? They're attacking government buildings all over Paris! Dozens of people are dead. The hospitals are overflowing with injured. What are you doing here?"

"I have an appointment with Tondreau."

"Does he know?"

"I should think so. He made it this morning."

"Hold on, let me check." After several minutes he lumbered back out of the director's office. "He's really sorry, Kraus. It's been so crazy today. Come on in."

"Inspector." Tondreau put down the phone as Willi entered, the salt-and-pepper hair immaculately parted to one side.

"I'm so sorry to intrude at such an hour." Willi shook his hand.

"Yes, well, no one exactly expected this. Sit, sit." He motioned Willi. "There's nothing we can do now anyway. The army's moved in, as you probably know. So tell me, Inspector, what is it you wished to speak to me about?"

Willi suddenly felt like an idiot. Paris was on the edge of revolution, and here he was bothering the head of national security with a criminal investigation.

Nevertheless.

"There's been a series of murders I fear are very much related. Phillipe Junot you know about. But then there was a reporter named Nathanson, and two professors in London, plus André Duval."

"Duval?"

"He didn't kill himself, Monsieur Director. I can prove it with the autopsy reports. He and Phillipe Junot and the professors were all part of the same political group."

"This is beginning to sound interesting." Tondreau leaned back in his chair, closing his eyes slightly as if listening to a campfire story. "Go on, Inspector."

"They call themselves Action Group X, centered on some sort of economic ideology called *planisme,* central planning. Obviously somebody is trying to—"

Willi's throat stuck as if he'd just swallowed glue. On Tondreau's desk suddenly he noticed: the typewriter.

Before he'd thrown out that report from the lab that finally showed up the other day . . . he'd read it. Technicians identified documents by tiny variants in letter alignment, and this technician was quite certain all three unsigned letters to France's largest insurance companies had been produced by a single machine: an Olivetti MPI, introduced last year as the world's first "portable" typewriter. Not many people in Paris owned these rather expensive machines, Willi understood. But one was on Tondreau's desk. A bright, shiny, new green one.

He swallowed painfully. What a fool he'd been.

"Please, go on." Tondreau sat up, offering a slender smile, his hands folded on the desk. Willi recalled how he'd swallowed the crumbs from it last time and couldn't open his mouth.

"You've managed to paint yourself into an untidy corner, hey, Inspector?" Tondreau cocked his head the way a teacher might at a smart-aleck kid. "Pity, really. You've been doing such outstanding work."

Willi had to brace himself on the chair.

He knew very well he'd been up against something every bit as devious and deadly as Orsini's crime ring. And he'd had his suspicions, often acute. But maybe because he was a foreigner, a refugee in a new land, he hadn't trusted his intuition and been led astray. Now that the picture grew suddenly clear before him, it was too late.

As if a fog had lifted, he finally perceived the landscape he'd been wandering through. The stage on which he'd been made to perform since he'd first arrived in France. The backdrop of mirrored sets and double entendres, dramatis personae all smiles and stabs in the back. Pulling the strings from the start—as if he'd been little wooden Pinocchio—had been the Sûreté Générale. And for the dance they'd made him do, they'd gotten their money's worth.

They'd hooked him first to follow Junot. After the kid's murder, when Willi confronted them, Tondreau claimed they "regretted" having to deceive him but that it was "for his own good." They were on the trail of a crime network they feared might penetrate into the Police Judiciaire itself. It was all part of their strategy.

Willi was Germany's most famous detective. With his reputation as a bloodhound they counted on him to help bring down their archnemesis, who ruled an even larger law-enforcement agency, a rival with whom they had to cooperate but loathed, and whose power made him untouchable. They wanted Willi to discover Junot's gambling habit, to uncover his connection with the Corsican henchmen and keep sniffing his way right to Orsini. Tondreau's little Jewish David had brought down Goliath.

But that was only part of it.

A ringmaster of surveillance and death, Sûreté Générale wielded its whip not by any set of laws but as it saw fit, doing away with those they deemed dangerous and employing whoever was expedient to help do the dirty work. Willi. Vivi. Achille Baptiste.

"You've been of great service to us, Kraus. And by that I do mean France. You're a brilliant detective, but I'm afraid you know, well . . . a little too much now."

Sûreté had orchestrated Willi's meeting André Duval that night at Maxim's, using their connections to make sure the men's paths crossed. Willi recalled the maître d' there pointing Willi out to André. The agency wanted an association between the two and got it. Police Judiciaire had used him for its own purposes; Willi could hardly forget Inspector Clouitier. But at least he'd been aware of what they were doing. Sûreté Générale had played him like a chess master. And to think people called them incompetent.

Tondreau shrugged. "Our job's to protect this nation against all who wish her harm."

"Like the maniacs out there tearing up the city?"

"They have no idea what they want, only that they don't like what they have. Action Group X was different, believe me."

"How?"

Tondreau looked up at Willi coolly. "For all your obvious intelligence you can be quite naïve in some ways, Inspector. I'm surprised you can't put the pieces together. A cadre of brilliant professionals and their disciples. The cover of legitimacy. A vague socioeconomic agenda. Highly secretive. Aggressive. Militant."

When Willi's face still showed no recognition, Tondreau grew irritated. "Don't tell me you've never heard of Comintern? The Third International? The worldwide movement sworn by all means to fight for the overthrow of the international bourgeoisie? Yes, that's right, Inspector. Direct from Moscow. Action Group X. Don't look so dumbfounded. These people are carefully recruited. Trained to blend in. They're convinced the capitalist system is in its period of final collapse and their time has come. Action Group X was developing very real plans to seize control of the major means of production here by the end of the decade and create Soviet France—which by the way André Duval's brilliant Pan-Europa Bond was meant to finance."

Willi just sat there. He wanted to go to bed. He didn't like France. Didn't like Germany. Didn't know where he liked.

André, a Communist?

"So instead of bringing charges against them you just . . . exterminate them?"

"Yes. Like bedbugs. Even the smallest, even the eggs. In France, Kraus, we don't wait for revolutionaries to start revolutions."

"That's almost funny, Director Tond—"

A loud crash cut him off, followed by a swift, ominous scent of smoke.

"My God." Tondreau rose. "What the—"

Marsolet stampeded in. "They're storming the building, sir."

"Who is?"

"Demonstrators. The army turned them back from the Élysée Palace and now they're here. They got through the outer gate. I expect they'll be inside momentarily. I highly suggest the rear exit, your car—"

"Very well. Call an armed guard."

"What are you going to do with me?"

"Bind his hands." Tondreau pointed when the marine arrived. There was another, even louder crash. Willi turned to throw a punch, having no intention of letting anyone tie him. But a moment later, when he heard Marsolet's pistol cock at the back of his head, he miserably relented as his arms were yanked from behind and bound.

With Marsolet bringing up the rear and Willi's hands bound behind him, they rushed for the service stairwell, the smell of smoke worsening. They reached a small garage and piled into a black Renault limousine, and the marine guard started the engine. Tondreau, visibly relieved, returned his attention to Willi with a little, regretful smile.

"To address your previous question, Kraus . . . ever hear of Cayenne? It's one of our equatorial colonies. Charming, I'm assured."

They turned several corners reaching the rue du Faubourg Saint-Honoré, where to everyone's shock they wound up driving directly into a raging mob. It didn't help that the Renault limo flew French flags and had official license plates. The crowd, in its mutinous fervor, took any government symbol as fair game and immediately engulfed them, pounding the windows, rocking them back and forth, trying to open the doors.

"For God's sakes lock the—"

Too late. The window next to Willi shattered, and the door yanked open. He was pulled to the street, a dozen fists pounding him. He wailed, unable to defend himself, but the beating ceased as soon as they saw his wrists.

"Hey, this one's a prisoner!" someone shouted.

"Untie him, untie him," people started calling.

The car meanwhile was rocking ever more furiously with the rest of the occupants still inside. Tondreau, holding on for dear life, shouted abuses, swearing to have the whole lot of them shot. Suddenly the vehicle flipped. "Stand back!" people were crying. Someone threw a bottle stinking of gasoline, and in one terrible instant the whole Renault burst into a ball of orange and black flame, the screaming inside lasting an eternity.

Thirty-four

Willi walked in a daze, stepping over shards of glass and blood-stained pavement, his wrists still stinging from where they'd been bound. The center of Paris was deserted. Smoke and tear gas hung in the air. How tired he was of all this, the blinding passions and self-righteousness of men, their cruel manipulations. It made him want to flee someplace where people didn't plot murder or burn each other alive. But even as he fantasized, he pressed through the dark, empty streets because, if one thing was certain in this topsy-turvy town tonight, Achille Baptiste was still out there. And he was just the kind of maniac who wouldn't leave a job undone. A sanctioned assassin was the worst type.

Even if Lucien Ruehl was under direct orders from Stalin, Willi told himself as he turned a collar against the cold, the guy was still a father, a husband, a brother. He had a right to justice—as all men did. As André had. And Phillipe Junot. And the Pasquiers. One last time Willi was going to look for the union leader to warn him.

Not knowing where else to go, he decided to try Ruehl's apartment; people on the run sometimes returned to places no one expected them anymore. All public transport though had shut because of the unrest, and sleet had started falling, slush on the sidewalk soaking through his shoes. How to get to the far north of the city? Not a taxi passed. He trudged along the boulevard Haussmann hoping for a miracle but came across only a smelly fish truck completing a delivery: FESCHETTI & SONS SEAFOOD.

He knocked on the window. It rolled down. Willi considered flashing his fake police badge but thought the better of it, tonight.

"Any chance of a lift? It's getting nasty out here."

"Sure, sure!" The fellow seemed happy. "I could use a little company." He sounded Italian. "Not many people around tonight." He motioned Willi to come around the other side.

Willi climbed in. "Must be a lonely job."

"I'd like to say you get used to it, but I never do. Which way you going?"

"Porte Clignancourt."

"Ah, sure, no problem. What a night, eh?" The man drove around a burned-out bus down the block. "This city's gone crazy. Where I come from, they never allow it. Il Duce. But I prefer self-expression, you understand? Even if it gets a little out of hand sometimes. That's why I'm here—ten years, a refugee from the Fascisti."

"Small world," Willi said.

"*Comunisto?*" The man raised his fist, checking Willi hopefully.

As he climbed the gloomy staircase to the Ruehls' apartment, Willi could understand why people turned to ideologies that promised better worlds. The air was so fetid he had to breathe through his mouth not to gag. Each long corridor seemed to vanish into nothing. How could people live this way, like rabbits in a putrid warren?

Landing by landing he climbed, oppressed as much by the wretched conditions as the night he'd just lived through. He couldn't stop hearing Tondreau and Marsolet screaming as the flames consumed them. Then suddenly, between floors, he froze. That smell, again! He had to be imagining it for sure this time, he told himself, losing it to a stronger odor of fresh vomit. The brain's expecting it so much it was creating an olfactory illusion. One flight up, however there was no mistaking it. His nose wasn't lying. The assassin must have information Willi didn't because Achille Baptiste had definitely been here.

The Ruehls lived at the end of the hallway, the last apartment. With sweaty palms he tiptoed toward the door, seeing no light from underneath. Putting an ear to it, he heard nothing. He looked both ways, then bent to one knee, peering through the keyhole. Darkness. He checked his wristwatch. Eleven o'clock. Putting his nose to the keyhole he inhaled, feeling a chill in his arms. The Corsican had either been in there or was still in there now. It was Vendetta all right. But only slightly.

As gently as possible, he turned the knob, finding it locked. Taking out his pocketknife he jimmied the lock open with two little clicks, slipping into the pitch-dark apartment, trying to remember what it looked like. To his right, a tiny kitchen with a table that barely sat two. He pictured Lucien Ruehl across from him, running a hand through his reddish-brown hair, cigarette in mouth. Happy for a chance to expound about his brother-in-law. "It's systems I hate, not people, comrade. And in this case I don't mind telling you—André Duval is one of the finest."

Even in the absence of light Willi began making out books along walls, stacked in towers, the scent of Vendetta only vaguely perceivable. Perhaps the killer had already been here and done his dirty work. It didn't take that bastard long. He recalled the day in Avignon going downstairs to make a phone call, a minute later finding André on the couch, his head a fountain of blood. Perhaps the bodies of Lucien Ruehl and his—

Something squeaked, electrifying Willi's muscles. A drop of sweat slid down his brow, hanging from his lashes. He blinked. The bedroom door was swinging from what looked like a breeze. The living-room windows were shut tight, he saw. He moved to his right, back to the wall, toward the little bedroom.

During the war he'd honed his vision in minefields and behind enemy lines and could still make out things other men couldn't. The Ruehls bed took shape. No one in it. The bedspread was smooth. The crib in the corner also unslept in. From the reflection in the mirror he could see no one was lurking either side of the door, or on the floor. He took a step nearer, entering. The bedroom hadn't been used in a week, he estimated from the layer of dust. The Vendetta scent however magnified.

A sudden *snap* hit like a leather whip. The curtain flapped. The window was wide-open. Why would anyone leave a room that way? They wouldn't, Willi knew. Achille Baptiste was out there in the cold, wet night, waiting. Perhaps he had information the Ruehls would soon be home. Perhaps they were climbing the stairs even now. From outside Baptiste would be able see the living-room lights turn on and step back in here, ready to greet them with a nice, warm welcome.

Willi backed out, all the way, leaving the apartment and closing the door behind him. The logical thing would be to wait in the hall, to warn the Ruehls before they ever stepped foot inside. But he had no intention of letting that son of a bitch get away. Not this time.

Willi never carried a gun or a knife. His weapons were his hands. But that living room had only two windows, and if he tried to open either, he knew, Baptiste would gain critical seconds to use his stiletto before Willi could gain a footing. No thanks. There had to be another way. This was the top floor. Surely there was roof access. Near his shoes he noticed patterns of shadows seeming to drip across the floor. A window at the end of the hall. Only feet away. As gently as he could, he slid it open and stuck his head out.

A thin, freezing drizzle hit his face. He looked down. It was a dormer, jutting from the roof a yard above the bottom ledge lined by gutters. Beyond that, a sheer drop, seven stories to a courtyard.

It was easy to climb out. The hard part was the ledge. It was icy, and nothing to hold on to. A typical French mansard roof, tin shingles, rising at a steep angle from the ledge to a peak of chimneys and ventilation shafts another ten or so feet up. Willi had to hold his arms out like a high-wire gymnast, carefully placing one foot in front of the other, and keep his eyes riveted on the corner. Around it, he was certain he'd be able to assess the exact position of the assassin-in-waiting.

Even through the icy mist as he neared his goal, he began to smell Vendetta. Clutching the roof panels, slowly, carefully, he peered around the edge, his mind flashing back to a black night outside Soissons in 1917, when he knew enemy soldiers were in the same set of trenches, and each side was gunning for the other.

He'd barely survived that one.

On the other side, about the same distance he'd just come, he could make out the dormer windows from the Ruehls' apartment. Right beyond the first, between the bedroom and the living room, a shadowy figure leaned on the outcropping, smoking a cigarette.

Willi swallowed. He'd vowed to bring André's killer to justice. Phillipe Junot's too. Well, there he was. For whatever reason Baptiste had done it—money, politics, vendetta—it made no difference. His time had come to pay.

Directly along the ledge there was no way to approach without being seen. The only possible route was up top, chimney level, get around the son of a bitch from behind. He made his way back to the dormer window and scrambled up its side, balancing his feet on its narrow peak. Above him, a small clay chimney pipe rose exactly out of reach. He tried several times, nearly killing himself when his foot slipped, until it occurred to him to use his necktie. Pulling it off and knotting it, he cast it like a lasso. On the second attempt he couldn't help smiling when it made a perfect noose around the pipe, and he was able to pull himself up.

As soon as he reached the top, he could stand, but barely breathe. Black coal soot engulfed his face from the chimney vents. He squinted, tyring to see ahead, desperate not to cough. Unlike Willi, so rigorously trained, the Corsican probably operated by instinct, with the hearing of a wolf.

There was barely an inch on which to balance. Every few feet another chimney belching soot broke through the shingles. He made his way foward, sleet blowing against his face, going into his eyes along with the smoke, blurring everything, freezing underfoot, every step perilous. Something loud banged against the brick. Casting a fearful glance down, he saw laundry lines flapping across the courtyard. A pulley with buckets slamming against the wall.

Then it happened. He slipped, lost his footing, threw up his arms to regain it, and just as he did, something sharp pinched his shoulder. He turned and, as if in a nightmare, found himself face-to-face with

Achille Baptiste. Those homicidal eyes. Blood-thirsty. Vengeful. Willi had recognized them that very first encounter at Maxim's, at the Gottmans' dinner. Now they were centimeters away.

The slip had saved him, he realized—that scratch on the shoulder the point of stiletto aimed for his heart. Because he'd moved, it only grazed him. But now, rising again in the Corsican's hand, it was readying for a second try.

Beneath that accursed green fedora Baptiste's eyes flared with black fury. His breath burned like a blowtorch. Trained always to gain the first blow, a split second before the stiletto reached him, Willi shot a hammer fist hard into the approaching elbow, knocking Baptiste's palm open and sending the stiletto flying. It hit the roof and slid down with a scratching sound, catching in the gutter. Baptiste lunged for Willi's throat, grabbing it with both hands. Willi let loose a swift strike to the solar plexus, which knocked the wind out of the Corsican but didn't release his hands. Instead, they both started slipping down the the side of the roof, Baptiste's fingers still around Willi's throat.

The slick tin roofing sent them sliding irrevocably down toward the edge. To avoid certain death they united long enough to fall together, and lock their shoes into the gutters. Willi used the moment to return the stranglehold on Baptiste—and they fell into a mutual death clasp, rolling about on top of each other.

Baptiste was shorter but his muscles were like iron. On the slippery slope the two spun like a top, until both men's heads were over the edge. Baptiste's green fedora fell, rising in the wind like a ghostly apparition before dropping to the dark. The Corisican reacted as if losing a brother, intensifying his assault in a tantrum. Underneath him Willi felt he'd rolled atop a band of wiring. It was digging into his back. Baptiste's fingers on his windpipe were sending waves of dizziness through his brain. With his head hanging upside down now, he saw himself not on an icy roof but beneath the giant glass dome of the Galleries Lafayette, its swirls of colors shifting like a kaleidoscope. He had only a second or two left he knew.

With all his might he lifted his head. Just a foot away, in the gutter, he made out the stiletto still lying there. Releasing Baptiste's throat he grabbed for it. Baptiste got there first. Willi knocked Baptiste's other hand from his throat and gulped down air. Looking up though, he saw the stiletto aiming at his heart.

As hard as he could, he threw himself left. The blade plunged into the bundle of wiring, piercing its protective skin as easily as it would have Willi's. A loud hiss was followed by a burning, acrid smell then an eruption of sparks like a Roman candle. The Corsican's eyes bulged. His body shimmied. His arms flapped as if in a war dance, then tottering, tilting, he let out a scream, plunging backward over the edge. Willi saw him fall away still clutching his stiletto before crashing onto the concrete below with a crushing thud.

For the longest while, Willi couldn't move, his body turned to stone. Peering over the edge of the roof he saw the killer lying face up, seeming to be smiling. Finally, brushing off, Willi used his handkerchief to mop up his face, and made his way back.

In the hallway, breathless from lugging suitcases up the stairs, appeared the Ruehls. "My goodness, what are you doing here?" The union leader, cigarette hanging from his mouth, looked at Willi astonished.

"It's . . . a bit of a story."

"Come inside." The African wife in her dashiki smiled, baby in arms. "Join us for tea. Tell us about it."

Thirty-five

The case was closed. The conspiracy revealed. The bloody spree put to an end. So where was Willi's payoff? he wondered angrily, stripping sheets from his bed the next day. Over the radio, the vote from the House of Deputies was running three to one against. The prime minister clearly was on his way out. Son of a bitch. Willi smashed two pillows together. Without those Rights of Domicile his family could only stay for one year. And without a country, they could only survive, not live. Sinking to the edge of the bed, he watched dust fly out the window as surely as Daladier's promises. Typical French. Breaking their word.

An oddly pointed object scratched the back of his leg. Between the bed frame and mattress, he saw, a book was sticking out. Retrieving it, he stared at the cover filled with a strange, dark longing. Why on earth would she have she left it? he wondered, his fingers running across the soft binding. By accident or on purpose? Why hadn't she retrieved it? Flicking off the radio, he leaned back into the mattress. Obviously she wanted me to find it, he thought, fluffing up the pillows. He pulled the cover gently open, peering into Vivi's diary.

It began two years ago when she was nineteen. So she was twenty-one now as he'd suspected. The first entries described her parents' efforts to enroll her in secretarial academy, which she'd dropped after a week without telling them. "So boring I'd rather commit suicide." After securing a part-time job at the Galeries La-fayette she concocted a plan to deceive them. "That bitch at the dress shop says I can change into my school uniform there, in exchange for stealing from the Galeries as weekly payment. I'll get away with giving the cunt as little as possible."

Her relationships with men seemed barely better.

"Charles and I are so close," she wrote the week she turned twenty. "If only he weren't such a liar." A month later she had a "burning hunch" Louis was the one for her, but he was sailing away so soon with the navy.

Most of it was rather trite. She complained of toothaches, her skin, her parents.

In October 1932 she began referring to a much older gentleman she'd met while "waiting for a bus" one night in Montmartre. His "giant black limousine stopped for me, its great door swinging open."

"I asked this guy for 400 francs just to see if he'd give it to me," she continued. "He's not handsome but I said I'd do anything for it. I'm such a good liar. Ha!"

The man, who referred to himself only as C, fell "desperately" in love with her. Of course he was married. A man of vast wealth and power.

If she could just live in one of those grand apartments in the six-teenth arrondissement she told him the second night they met. She'd do anything for a kind, generous man.

He could be generous C told her, as long as she was generous too. He had friends with certain jobs suited for an attractive female such as herself.

"Really? I'm clever too. You'll see."

If she proved valuable, he had assured, she could find herself in far better circumstances indeed.

"The sixteenth?" she'd asked directly.

"Why not? It's where I live. That would make things convenient."

Willi put the book down a moment and stared into space.

According to the diary she'd done things she "shouldn't have" but never meant to hurt anyone. It worked this way: C gave her keys to a post office box. Every day she was supposed to check for instructions and drop off reports—to whom she had no idea. Athough she found this curious, as long as she got new shoes, scarves, handbags, etc., she didn't seem to care. In her diary at least she never speculated. What she did put down was that she found the whole thing "as exciting as lovemaking." And to her delight her first assignment combined the joys of both: sex and espionage. She was to get as close as possible to a student at the École Polytechnique, find out all she could about the secret organization he belonged to.

Unfortunately, she got a little too close.

Willi felt strangely relieved when he read that Vivi had fallen for Junot. Her face, her body language back then had been too genuine. And the kid was crazy for her. According to an entry in June, Junot was so convinced she'd gotten a black eye from the gambling thugs he was involved with that even though she told him it had been her father who'd done it, he didn't believe her. At the Red Room that night he was so upset he would hardly look at her.

Willi read the next entries carefully, seeing everything again as he had witnessed it from the shadows. Apparently, after reporting via postbox the next day, Vivi was surprised to receive a telegram instructing her to get Junot to the metro entrance near the Polytechnique at seven thirty that night, and to make certain to give him a good night kiss atop the steps. She had no idea why, but did as told even though it was mayhem because of the Bal des Quat'z' Arts.

In the same florid penmanship she always used, she wrote how "horror-stricken" she was the next day to read of Junot's murder. Immediately she penned a note to C, who assured her everything was for her country, and that it had nothing to do with murder. She surmised Junot had been killed by the mobsters, Corsicans. But she didn't ponder much because a week after his death she wrote "Phillipe was such a lovely person. What can I do now except try to find someone as wonderful?"

Her next assignment was Willi.

He nearly choked to learn that their meeting too had been carefully staged. That she'd gone to the bus stop near his house for days trying to get him to spot her and follow. What a fool he'd been to think he'd been spying on her! How stupid to let her move in. Her handlers at Sûreté Générale must have loved that. He'd told Tondreau how beautiful she was, so they'd sent her after him. And he'd snatched the bait twelve different ways.

What a gifted little actress she turned out to be, he thought, recalling her many performances. According to what she wrote, "the Refugee" was strictly business. She liked him well enough. He was actually quite sexy in bed. But she couldn't stand that "dump" he lived in. It was almost worse than her parents'. She wanted some place with style, her own. Finally she got a chance to earn it. When the whole world was hunting for André Duval, she sent definitive word that Willi had gone to look for him—in Avignon. How she'd learned this, she'd failed to note. But she gushed in triumph that C was "thrilled" by the information and that, as a reward, a set of keys had been promised to a certain pied-à-terre at 32 Parc Lamartine.

"I fucking did it," she wrote.

When he showed up that night at her door, her luscious smile twisted sardonically. "Look who it is." She motioned him to enter. "Just in time for cocktails. You must not clean that room of yours often."

"Not enough," he admitted, trying not to stare. She certainly filled out the black crepe-de-chine dress whose plunging neckline revealed half her cleavage. He could have swept her in his arms. Or strangled her.

Rouged lips parted as she held out her hand, inviting him to look around. "I've done pretty well for myself, don't you think?" The foyer was bigger than his room.

"Let me guess: it comes with a staff."

"Don't you think I deserve one?"

"Anyone does, if they've earned it."

"Oh, I've earned it all right. You better than anyone should grant me that." A subtle smile curled her lips. She led him into a well-appointed parlor and began pouring Dubonnet into a cocktail glass. "I followed you by taxi," she said, mixing in some gin.

"What?"

"After you bought your ticket at Gare de Lyon, the night you went looking for Duval. I got the counter clerk to tell me where it was to."

"How?"

She laughed, clenching her hip, looking at him without apology. "How do you think?"

He simply handed her the diary. "I believe you forgot this."

She took it, keeping her eyes on him, slowly assuming a look of amused contempt. "You don't really suppose it was accidental, do you? I thought you were smart, but you haven't gotten this game at all." They stood for a moment facing off. She looked cruel and beautiful. "Come on, Willi. This was planted days ago by C's people. He wants to have a chat with you." She put the diary down and mixed another drink. "And he happens to be here right now. So close your mouth. It makes you look like a dullard."

It had been six months since he'd crossed the border, and never for a moment had he felt at ease here, only deceived and manipulated. More and more these days he found himself dreaming of leaving Europe altogether, pulling up stakes and starting anew in Australia or America. But how?

"All this seems a rather roundabout way to arrange a meeting."

She frowned, shrugging. "That's how we French are, *mon amour*. The diary was my way of letting you know the facts." Her face screwed into an expression resembling pity, as if to say: *I never meant you any harm.*

He cracked her hard across the cheek, causing red Dubonnet to splash across the counter. She may not have meant it, but she'd harmed him all right. Way too much.

Her eyes fluttered as she held herself, stunned a moment. Then she reached for an ice cube to hold against her skin. "If I had a franc for every man who ever did that"—she glared at him, trembling—"I could buy an apartment twice this size." She threw away the ice and dried her cheek angrily, then pressed the button on an intercom.

"The cat's in the bag," she said into the speaker. "I told you it'd be easy." Releasing the button she picked up a tray with the drinks. "Come on. C's dying to meet you."

Her heels clacked as she led him down a black- and white-tiled hallway. Anger roiled within him. "You think this guy couldn't throw you out as fast as he put you in here?" he said with as much disdain as he could muster. "This place isn't *yours*, Vivi. All he has to do is change the goddamn—"

"Fuck you," she cut him off, bursting into tears.

Still bawling, she led them through a set of double doors. Willi swallowed when he saw the paralyzed general, Crevecour, deep in the cushions of an armchair.

"What now, my dear?" he frowned, holding out an arm to Vivi. "Come sit." He pat the chair, offering his handkerchief. "I never saw a girl cry so much." He smiled to Willi. "She could go on all day, heh Inspector? Funny how you and I keep running into each other, isn't it? And that we both know Vivi. In my mind she's one of France's great natural resources."

Above the handkerchief Willi saw Vivi's eyes fill with sadistic pleasure.

"How pleased I am to see you unharmed." Crevecour looked Willi up and down. "What happened to Director Tondreau was awful." His eyes narrowed. "You're a lucky man."

The room seemed to spin around then stop. That the general had been privy to Willi's whereabouts the other night said it all. Willi recalled the man's connections not merely to millions of veterans, but to the current leaders of the French military. Crevecour clearly was liaison to the General Staff. Sûreté Générale reported to him.

"We French may not be as efficient as you Germans. But we can be quite ingenious in our own way." The paralyzed general chuckled. "You should never have let Orsini get your face in the newpapers."

Willi felt his stomach sour.

"The police commissioner was a cancer, Kraus, festering in the heart of Paris. He had to be eliminated. As did Group X, the whole nest. You assisted us with both superbly. We expected nothing less. Your exploits in Germany, as well as those behind our lines during the war, well . . ." the general trailed off, greatly impressed.

The old patrician had a look of assurance Willi had seen before only in the barons of Germany, weaned since birth on entitlement and power. The Corsican police commissioner had never had that look. Nor did André Duval. They were men who, beneath the all the savoir faire, were fueled by fear, and driven by a desperate ambition to overcome it. What about Willi? Did the same fear drive him? Wasn't his need to pursue justice only a weak palliative against the horrors of the world?

"Look," the general continued when Willi failed to say anything, "I liked Duval very much. There was no denying his charm. But he was using you, Inspector."

"Weren't you?"

The general grinned. "I'm on the right side. He was not. It's that simple. Duval would have slit your throat if Moscow ordered it. I realize that's painful to hear, especially since you're both fellow Jews."

It was back to that, naturally.

"And just whose side are *you* on, General?"

"France's. Whoever threatens her, left or right, is my enemy."

"Then perhaps you ought to focus a bit more on the dictators tearing up treaties across your border." They both knew Willi referred to Hitler's recent withdrawal of Germany from the League of Nations.

"Our frontiers will soon be impregnable," the general assured.

Willi's jaw tightened. "What will happen to Lucien Ruehl and his family?" He felt the back of his head ache.

"Apparently they've already slipped the border to Spain, along with their comrade Lorilleux."

Willi inhaled. "And me?"

The general's eyes lit. "I'm afraid I can't see you as a threat, Inspector."

"I killed that fellow in your employ, that Corsican knifeman."

"He fell for his country. You were defending yourself. I hardly find that objectionable. In fact, I applaud you wholeheartedly. In the few short months you've been in this country you've done tremendous service. You've earned your right to stay."

"I'm afraid I don't understand." Willi looked at him.

"Put down your roots. Make this your home."

"That requires certain documents, sir. In case you weren't aware."

"Vivi." He snapped his fingers. She rose and fetched a dark brown folder tied with red ribbons and handed it to Willi without a smile. Inside were six certificates, Rights of Domicile, one for Willi and each of the kids, plus Ava and her parents.

"You've done your work, Inspector." The general stretched out his hand. "France welcomes you."